I0588317

DEEP MAGIC

VOLUME 2

JEFF WHEELER   JEANNA MASON STAY

PATRICK HURLEY   ERIC JAMES STONE   K. D. JULICHER

KEN LIU   CHARLIE N. HOLMBERG   ANTHONY RYAN

STEVE DUBOIS   CHARITY WEST   CHRISTOPH WEBER

WULF MOON   BRENDON TAYLOR

BRITTANY RAINSDON   ALYSSA ECKLES

MICHAEL J. SULLIVAN   KM DAILEY

OLIVERHEBERBOOKS

"Deep Magic: Volume II" © 2021 *Jeff Wheeler*, Editor

"Forged in Iron and Blood" by *Jeanna Mason Stay* © 2021 by *Jeanna Mason Stay*

"The Poisoner's Revenge—A Kingfountain Tale" by *Jeff Wheeler* © 2021 by *Jeff Wheeler*

"The Red Walls of Ishri" by *Patrick Hurley* © 2021 by *Patrick Hurley*

"The Devil Went Down to the Daniel Webster Charter School Pta's Annual Halloween Chili Cook-Off Fundraiser" by *Eric James Stone* © 2021 by *Eric James Stone*

"His Lady's Favor" by *K. D. Julicher* © 2021 by *K. D. Julicher*

"The Ten Suns" by *Ken Liu* © 2021 by *Ken Liu*

"Grave Secrets" by *Charlie N. Holmberg* © 2021 by *Charlie N. Holmberg*

"The Hall Of The Diamond Queen" by *Anthony Ryan* © 2021 by *Anthony Ryan*

"The Lady of Pain" by *Steve Dubois* © 2021 by *Steve Dubois*

"Love in the Time of Holodecks" by *Charity West* © 2021 by *Charity West*

"Hanging Trees" by *Christoph Weber* © 2021 by *Christoph Weber*

"Muzik Man" by *Wulf Moon* © 2021 by *Wulf Moon*

"Darned Socks" by *Brendon Taylor* © 2021 by *Brendon Taylor*

"Perfectly Painted Lies" by *Brittany Rainsdon* © 2021 by *Brittany Rainsdon*

"The Job Prospects of History Majors" by *Alyssa Eckles* © 2021 by *Alyssa Eckles*

"Pile Of Bones" by *Michael J. Sullivan* © 2021 by *Michael J. Sullivan*

"Don't Wake the Dreamer" by *KM Dailey* © 2021 by *KM Dailey*

Cover design by Covers by JV Arts

Published by Oliver-Heber Books

0 9 8 7 6 5 4 3 2 1

I

FORGED IN IRON AND BLOOD
BY JEANNA MASON STAY

LINA HAD LEFT the war long behind her. That's what she told herself, anyway. Especially on nights like this when dusk fell through the open doors of the smithy and the fire blazed in the forge and in her blood. But the crash of her hammer against the metal was too like the clamor of battle, and the memories kept flooding back.

The pulse of the fight, the tang of blood in the air. Friends bleeding and dying, both fae and human, their lifeless bodies strewn across the field. Such pointless, wretched loss. She swung the hammer again, hoping to drive out the pain and forget herself in the work. To forget their naivety— *her* naivety—in believing that peace could come so easily. The oathbinding magic was certainly rare and powerful. But no promise made to one foolish half-blood fairy could end the simmering tension between the two countries as quickly as it ended the actual battles. If only she'd—

"Lina-smith," a bright voice called from the doorway.

Lina shook herself from the memories and turned around, a practiced smile covering her thoughts. "Seelah," she greeted with false cheer. "How are you this evening? How's the newest grandchild?"

"Delightful, of course," Seelah said, beaming as she bustled in. She dropped her basket on a table and eased herself onto a stool. "Oh, but don't let me stop you"—she gestured for Lina to keep working—"I'm just here to have a little rest."

Lina chuckled to herself and stoked the fire again, enjoying the distraction; a "little rest" meant Seelah had gossip to share.

"You'll never guess what I heard today," Seelah began, pausing to speak between the clangs of Lina's hammer. "Jinnel was arguing with her husband—well, you know that's nothing new—but she brought up her great-aunt, and she threatened to head off there and stay with her for good. And then he…"

Lina let the stream of words wash over her, Seelah's voice a soothing reminder of the peace that Lina had fought and killed and sacrificed to protect.

"…So I thought I would drop by some soup tomorrow and just check in on her. Would you care to join me?"

Lina snapped out of her thoughts again. "Oh, um, yes. Always glad to lend a hand," she replied. "Come by tomorrow at dusk?"

Seelah agreed but lingered, waiting.

In answer to the unspoken question, Lina smiled wanly. "I'd invite you over tonight for tea, but I'm exhausted. It's straight to bed for me." She looked toward the open doors. "Must be the cold weather coming, always makes me sleepy."

Seelah picked up her basket to go. "Another time, then. I do enjoy our chats by the fire."

"I do too," Lina said, and she meant it.

Maybe it was time to move on, though. She'd been living in Solime for years, getting too comfortable in her role, playing the friendly grandmother maybe a little too well. She was bound to accidentally reveal something true about herself, make a mistake she couldn't afford.

Or maybe she was just getting old; her hair was more gray than black now, and though smithing had kept her strong, it was getting harder to creak out of bed in the mornings. Maybe it was just natural that she was restless and thought more about the war these days, as she was drawing near to leaving everything behind for good. She'd played her part for as long as she could, but she couldn't avoid the end forever.

Lina stepped back from the forge and surveyed her smithy—a few small worktables, stacks and buckets of scrap metal, projects and tools hanging from the ceiling and lining the walls. A good place. A place to forget and be forgotten.

She stripped the heavy leather gloves from her fingers and stretched her hands, easing their tired muscles and massaging the scars that crossed her palms. She'd amassed more burns and cuts than she could count. She rolled her shoulders to release the strain of hours bent over her work. A cold breeze blew in through the doors, and she welcomed the chill. She was right—the weather was cooling. There would be snow soon.

She raked the coals from the fire, set them to cooling, and made sure her tools were put away for the night. With everything in its place, Lina closed the shutters over her window and took one of her smaller hammers down from the wall; being a blacksmith meant that no one thought it odd for her to walk around with weaponry. She latched the door shut, dropping a small nail in the dirt so it leaned carelessly against the door. The actions had become automatic, almost meaning-less, but there was comfort in the familiar.

The path home was short, her little cottage nestled in the space just behind the smithy. As she approached, she slowed and eyed her surroundings. Nothing disturbed. A particular pebble lying on her porch was in the same spot as usual. She stepped over it, slipped inside, and set her hammer by the front door.

She twitched her rug to the side, checking that the entrance to her hidden room was undisturbed, and glanced toward the brick in the hearth that covered a store of coins. Everything was in its place. She could rest, banish the clash of weapons still echoing in her mind. For now at least. She closed her eyes and listened to the stillness with a smile. Tomorrow, maybe, she'd think about moving on.

Lina startled awake, her eyes wide and staring, her heart pounding. She'd been dreaming, of course—of Mollen. Her dearest friend, her brother-in-arms, her once-upon-a-time hope for the future. In her dream, she watched him fight, just as she had so many times in life. He was grace and beauty, the swing of the sword, all dance and brilliance. Watching him, it was easy to forget, for the moment, the devastation of war.

Then the sunlight had flashed against the torque around his neck, and the dream became a nightmare, a memory.

But that wasn't what woke her now, in the gray hours before dawn. There had been a noise. She listened, her body tense.

Then she heard it again. Outside and very near. A grunt of pain. A sound almost as familiar as ringing iron.

She pulled on her overdress, picked up her hammer, and crept out to investigate, every sense alive to danger. Though dawn was near, the space behind her smithy was swallowed in darkness. Lina listened again, raising the hammer, as her eyes darted from shadow to shadow.

In one of the deeper shadows, Lina saw it. Something, anyway. A huddled form, large enough to be a grown adult, curled up against the wall where the heat from the forge warmed the bricks. It didn't move. It didn't belong.

Maybe this would be the moment when danger finally caught up with her. Maybe she would find out if she could still fight. Her blood pumped with vigor, her heart answering the possibility for battle. She stole forward.

A whimper and a few muttered words emerged from under what she could now see was a torn, stained cloak. "Hurts...stop...can't..." The voice was deep enough to be male, though human or fae she didn't know.

Lina breathed deeply once for calm. "Hello?"

He writhed and moaned but didn't respond. Lina peered more closely, almost feeling the waves of panic rolling off him. She adjusted her grip on the hammer's wooden handle. His face was hidden, and he wrapped his arms protectively around himself under the cloak. She studied him, warrior and grandmother battling inside her. She could help him. It could be a trick. She should protect him. She should watch her back.

After a moment of indecision, the grandmother took over. She crouched and set her hammer beside her. If anything was amiss, there was always the dagger concealed in her skirts.

"I'm going to help you," she whispered soothingly, the way she would talk to a terrified child. She got a hand under his arm, pulling him to his feet. He was frail, lighter than she'd expected, even as he leaned heavily on her, one hand now reaching up to rub against his neck. She shuffled him forward, bearing most of his weight and still scanning for danger, until they reached her cottage.

With a bit of maneuvering—and a brief, regretful glance at her clean blanket—Lina settled the man in a heap on her bed. She locked the door and checked that her window shutters were tightly closed, then started a hearth fire going. She kept one eye on the stranger.

Now that he was stretched out in the glow of her fire, she had her first clear view of his clothing and cloak, both of fine wool but ragged beyond hope of repair. His hair, a dirty brown, hung lank and tangled, and he had maybe a week's growth of beard. Whatever he was running from, he'd been running awhile.

He started to mumble again, tears slowly streaking his face. "Need help…Can't think…Hide." He reached his arms toward her, then yanked them back and tugged his tattered cloak more tightly around his neck. "No." He convulsed. "Yes." He shook his head.

The pain tugged at her, and she forced herself to ignore the tightness in her throat at his suffering. *Focus on what you can do, focus on solvable problems,* she thought. So she fetched a cup of water and dipped a cool cloth into it. She brushed the cloth across his forehead and his bright red cheeks as she looked him over. No obvious external wounds, but by the way he alternately rubbed at his neck, then tugged his cloak more tightly around him, something must be wrong with his neck. He groaned when she moved his head and batted at her hands when she reached for the clasp of his cloak. She stifled a sigh at his resistance, then pushed his hands away and yanked at the two sides of the cloak.

It tore apart, revealing the man's neck. And around the man's neck, a familiar metal torque—an echo of her nightmares—caught the glow of the firelight.

She leaped to her feet and drew her hidden dagger, her joints protesting at the speed of her movement.

The war *had* come back to her, in a way she'd tried to never think of again.

Her muscles tensed, and her heart raced as she crouched in a fighting stance, waiting for him to pounce. He didn't look like a warrior —in fact, he looked more than half dead. But she had no idea the extent of the torque's powers. For all she knew, it could make even the half dead fight like dragons.

"Please," he muttered. "Help me." He opened glassy eyes and looked up at her, pleading, clawing at his neck like an animal caught in a trap. "Don't"—he shook his head slowly—"don't let them have me."

"Who? Why are you here?" A thought suddenly struck her with a wave of horror. "Do you know who I am? Were you here for me?"

But he had lapsed into unconsciousness, and no matter how she nudged at him—dagger at the ready—he only tossed feverishly.

She fetched some cord from a cupboard and bound him quickly to the bed, then backed away to a safer distance, where she could observe the man and think. She *had* to think, ignore emotion, ignore the queasy wash of sadness and anger and fear that lapped through her.

If someone was making these torques, something dangerous was on the horizon. Of course, it couldn't be war again, not with the oath-bound pact still in place. The rulers of both lands had sworn in carefully worded oaths that there would be no war between their countries, and that pact would have to be honored as long as the oathbinder lived. But even without causing outright war, the torque could make plenty of mischief.

Or maybe it had nothing to do with the tension between the two lands, but whatever it was, it had to be stopped.

As she settled onto the edge of her kitchen chair, her eyes were drawn to the torque again. It caught the firelight and flickered almost like a living thing. Where an opening should be, allowing the wearer to remove the torque from around the neck, there was only smooth metal. She couldn't look away, and she couldn't stop the memories that she'd tried to hide from for so many years.

The only other time she'd seen an object like this had been during the war, when Mollen had disappeared for two weeks, then suddenly come back, changed. They'd thought he was captured by the enemy while on a secret mission, so when he returned, she'd rejoiced and rushed to greet him. He didn't even glance her way. She'd taken him to report to the commanding officers, hiding her pain at his treatment. Other soldiers had gathered to hear where he'd been. He'd stood in front of them all, and then, without any warning beyond one short cry of pain, he'd thrust his sword through the commander and started cutting down his fellow soldiers. His movements were jerky, not his usual perfect grace—almost like a separate battle raged within him. A strange metal torque around his neck shone in the sunlight as he moved.

The torque the stranger wore was the same. She examined it carefully. The skin around his neck was red and raw, and when she touched it, he moaned. She swallowed and closed her eyes against the man's suffering, but that only took her back to Mollen. She had watched in shock for a moment; then she and several other soldiers had flown into action, striking at him with shocked rage. A part of her detached itself then, unwilling to feel the agony of that battle. Within minutes, he was dead, and Lina was numbly thankful that someone else had struck the fatal blow. She didn't know if she could have survived killing him.

After Mollen's death, several fae spellworkers—only the fae had magic, of course, and only a few truly understood how it worked—had studied the torque. It had been imbued with mindturning, a magic forbidden, and largely forgotten, for centuries. Mollen's treachery was not his fault. Someone had broken his will, turned his mind, and sent him back as an assassin.

Now someone was using this magic again. The knowledge seared through her. Mollen. She'd tried so hard to forget him and the pain of his death. She'd turned that pain to good, to helping stop the war once and for all. Or at least for a long while, hopefully long enough for real peace to settle in. She'd sought—and found—her own measure of that peace.

But seeing that torque again...Rage burned within her, brilliant yellow and malleable like iron in the forge, waiting to be shaped to her purpose. Someone had dared to experiment with such brutal magic again, and it could not be tolerated. *She* could not tolerate it.

Lina crept back to the smithy to gather her tools and returned to her still-unconscious visitor.

She examined his neck and the torque again, then placed clamps on its edges and began to tighten them. Tricky work to remove the cursed item without killing the man beneath; she might have given up if she hadn't known what it was. She gritted her teeth and continued applying pressure.

Finally, with a satisfying snap, the torque broke and fell to the dirt floor. The man breathed in sharply, then rolled to his side. He opened his eyes, glassy and unfocused. "Thank you," he whispered, then he closed his eyes and took a deep breath.

"Who did this?" Lina asked, desperate now for answers. He didn't respond. She nudged him, gently at first, but with increasing strength. "Where are they?" she asked, shaking him now.

Still no response. It was as if removing the torque had released him from life and pain. She watched helplessly as his breathing slowed, becoming gentler, softer, until it dwindled to nothing.

She leaned back, sighing. The yellow burning inside her dulled under the weight of death, and she swiped at her eyes.

She straightened his hands to his sides, swallowing to relax the shaking of her own hands. "From dust to dust," she murmured over the body, speaking the human last rites. "From breath to tears." She'd said these words over so many others, she hardly had to think about it. She paused, then added the fae blessing for good measure—more words she knew by heart. "Full circle, like the moon. Full season, like the earth. Rest now, beneath them both." He didn't look fae, but she knew very well there were plenty of mixed-bloods who could pass for human. The burning of iron on fae skin was the only foolproof way to tell, and since she hadn't tried it on the poor tormented man, she'd never know if he was mixed-blood. The iron test didn't work on the dead.

She closed her eyes for a moment of stillness. Fae or human, she wished him peace.

But the moment couldn't last. What if he *had* been there for her? Did they know where and who she was?

Probably not. Solime was a busy town despite its size, with people coming through all the time. It was likely just the wildest of luck that he had happened upon Lina.

Still, she'd be careful. It was definitely time to leave, one way or another. Just as soon as she'd dealt with things here.

She couldn't ask anyone to come to her aid. The local watch weren't equipped to deal with powerful magic, and the only other help was too far away. When the war had finally ended with the oathbound pact, Lina had disappeared. All but one of her old contacts thought her dead, and she meant to keep it that way. As soon as she could, though, she'd write to that one contact, her "sister" in Hillfar. Her sister would inform those who still watched for such dangers, they would hunt down whoever had created this torque…and Lina would disappear again.

But that was a job for later in the day. No one would arrive in time to help her with her more immediate problems: a body in her house, the torque on her hands, and no idea who was coming or how long it would take them to get here.

She peeked out her shutters. Muddy light was brightening by the minute, and soon the whole town would wake. She picked up the torque and stared at it with loathing. It was beautiful, if you didn't know what it was for. The carvings were delicate, in an old fae script. Lina knew little of the metal used to make it—she'd not been a smith that first time long ago, and the gleaming silvery material was far too rich, too rare, too difficult to work for a lowly blacksmith. The magic too.

Who had made this new torque? None of the fae she'd known during the war could have done it, and anyone who'd been able to had been executed.

She'd thought.

She wrapped the torque in a tea towel and placed it in the pocket of her dress. All her thoughts turned to one purpose: to destroy it. Heat it to the upper limits of her forge's ability so it would melt down to liquid, then mix the metal with so much iron and impurity that it would be unrecognizable. Cool it back into a lump of scrap and bury it where it would never be found.

She left her house, noting the pebble's location with more care than usual, and scurried to her smithy, formulating a plan. She'd destroy the torque as quickly as possible, and if they came looking before she had a chance to disappear, she'd play the innocent, ever-so-helpful grandmother. She smiled grimly as she lit and stoked the fire, imagining her part.

She drew the torque from her pocket and stared at it again, revulsion and fascination intertwined. Some people said that mindturning was a bit like oathbinding. Both were magical interference with a person's will, after all. With a simple promise, a person was absolutely bound to carry out their words. With a powerful and careful enough promise, like the pact that ended the war, the course of history could change. Two sovereigns of two lands had sworn to cease fighting and do all they could to ensure peace—and for years they had. Some believed a mindturn could do just as much good.

She shuddered as she thought of Mollen. Those people were wrong. Some oathbinding, it was true, involved a bit of trickery, but it could never take from someone more than they were willing to speak. The monarchs who had promised to stop fighting had done so of their own accord. Their people were tired and hurting. They hadn't been forced into magical enslavement. An object of mindturning destroyed a person's will and deserved, in turn, to be destroyed.

The fire was almost hot enough now—a little longer and then she could do it.

A knock at the door interrupted her. Startled, she shoved the wrapped torque into a bucket of scrap iron beside her and kicked the bucket to the side as Seelah pushed her way into the room.

"Good morning, Lina!" she cried, dropping that ever-present basket on Lina's counter as usual and launching into a story about a neighbor down the road who had lost a goat and wasn't that a shame and what could have happened to it and that reminded her of the new strangers in town who had arrived just recently and how they looked rich and—

Lina often thought that as a source of information, Seelah would have been infinitely useful in the war. As a keeper of secrets, though, she would have ruined everything.

Suddenly one detail of Seelah's words stood out. "Did you say strangers?" Lina interrupted.

"Oh yes. I mean, of course there are always strangers, but these men seemed...you know...somehow different." She leaned forward. "Powerful. Rich." She smiled. "Maybe they'll need a new sword, or one of their horses will throw a shoe. You might get some business."

But Lina wasn't listening—now was not the time to start a long round of gossip. She picked up Seelah's basket, pushed it into her arms, and started nudging her toward the door.

Just as three men stepped into the doorway.

The first was richly dressed and short—she'd imagined whoever came would be tall—and had the fine features that often betrayed a bit of fae blood. Interesting. The others followed behind him like servants as he strode casually into the room. Lina wasn't fooled. They strolled, but their muscles were tense. The one to the right kept his hand near his sword, and the short one prowled like a cat preparing to pounce. There would be no new sword or thrown shoe to deal with, just the torque and the dead man.

Lina kept her eyes from wandering to where she'd hidden the torque, but her mind began to spin. This was going to make things much more difficult. She cursed herself for her stupidity. She'd been so slow, too slow.

"Greetings," she said, her voice friendly. "I'll be with you in a moment." For now she just needed to get Seelah out of danger. She continued to push her friend toward the door. "Thank you so much for stopping by," she said. "It was nice to see you, and I'll come visit you later, *just like we planned*." She wanted to establish, in front of these men, that she'd be missed if she disappeared.

Seelah gave her a hard look, glancing quickly between Lina and the men. "Yes," she said slowly. "Yes, just like we planned. I'll expect to see you in...an hour or two."

Lina nodded. "Have a lovely day!" she chirped, pushing Seelah out the door and shutting it behind her.

She'd known Seelah would remember their plan to meet and deliver soup today, but that was later in the evening. Why did Seelah say they'd meet so soon? Whatever the reason, Lina shrugged and set it aside. It worked better this way—now the men knew that if she disappeared, she'd be missed very, very soon.

She turned back to face them. "Good day to you."

The short one nodded in return. "And to you." He'd been looking around the smithy, and while his glance suggested a casual appraisal, the sharpness of his eyes missed little.

"What may I do for you this fine day?" she asked.

He moved away from the wall of tools he'd been scrutinizing, his appraising stare on her now.

She continued to smile. How could she salvage her plan? In her imagination, the torque was safely destroyed before they came for it, not sitting in a bucket of scrap metal a few feet away.

"My name is Tyblith," the man said. "I'm looking for a friend. I've been taking care of him, but he ran away. He's terribly sick, you see. He gets confused. Ends up thinking I'm his enemy and runs off." He shook his head, all sorrow and worry and honest innocence, but he watched her closely. "Have you seen him?"

Lina's thoughts flitted. Part of her said to trust him, he was so honest and thoughtful and—she mentally shook herself. What was she thinking?

No, she couldn't trust him, and she had to come up with a plan. Now. "Oh! I'm so glad you've come," she said breathlessly. "I've been wondering what to do. He's sleeping in my house, but he was afraid to let anyone know where he was. He's been so very distraught and feverish—well, you know that, of course. I just didn't know what to do! But now that you're here, I'm sure he'll be happy to see a friend." She finished and drew a breath, ready to start babbling again if necessary.

"You found him, then?" the man asked sharply.

"He's in my home, just behind the smithy. You can all go see him and—"

"Maresk, Toren, look for him. I'll stay here and talk with this"—he turned a charming smile on Lina, his voice softening—"this lovely lady here."

"Oh, I don't mind if you all go check on him. He's probably resting anyway."

"No, my men will be able to take care of him. I'd much rather you tell me how he appeared at your home."

Tyblith nodded at the other men, and they swiftly left.

Blood of the nix, he was staying with her. She'd hoped they might all go together so she could still throw the torque on the fire in the minutes they were gone. Time for a different plan. Again.

"Oh, the poor man! He just showed up last night and collapsed!" She clutched at her chest. "I took him in, of course. Nothing else I could do, poor creature. He reminded me of my dear aunt Milla, when she came down with the—"

Tyblith interrupted, already bored by her narrative. "Did he...say anything?"

"Well, not—"

The other men burst back into the shop. "It wasn't there," one of them said abruptly. "And he's dead."

"Dead?" She gasped. "No, he couldn't be! I just left him less than an hour ago, and he was only sleeping." She wrung her hands. "Oh, so cruel. Fever sickness is terrible."

Tyblith glared at Lina. "Did he say anything to you? Give you anything? Tell me!"

She cringed, looking back and forth between the three men. She reached over and took a large iron chisel down from her wall, holding it out in front of her awkwardly, as if she hoped to use it to protect herself but had no idea how. Hopefully, it made her look afraid and also reminded them that she couldn't be fae. "I don't know what you mean...I was just trying to help him. Don't hurt me." She made her voice tremble in fear, even as her blood pumped with anticipation.

He sighed and rubbed his hand across his forehead, his whole demeanor softening back into his original charm. "I'm sorry," he said, the note in his voice turning pleading. "I didn't mean to alarm you. I'm just so stricken by his death. He was my good friend, you know."

The shift in his emotion was so abrupt, Lina almost swayed toward him, longing to comfort him in his grief. So he was a charmspeaker, then. Her earlier desire to trust him made sense now.

"Yes, I can see that," she replied, and she, too, softened her voice. She lowered the chisel. "I'm so sorry for your loss. You must have been close."

He frowned. "Yes. I'll miss him. And he was in my care, so I feel responsible for him. His mother will be devastated."

Lina nodded. "Poor woman."

"He had a gift from her. He wore it all the time, even though it chafed awfully." He stared at her as he spoke his next words. "It was a torque."

Lina widened her eyes. "A gift from his mother, you say? Someone he *loved*?"

Maresk and Toren seemed to shift uneasily, but Tyblith only hesitated for a moment. "Yes." She could almost see his thoughts flying. "But...they'd been fighting. Yes, they'd been fighting, and he was very angry at her. So you can see even more why she'll be so upset. I was just hoping to comfort her, let her know he had it with him to the end."

Lina visibly relaxed the tension from her shoulders—they noticed it, of course—and smiled. "Oh, that explains it!" She tittered. "He was babbling on and on about how I needed to destroy it right then and not let anyone have it or do anything bad with it." She shook her head. "He was probably just being spiteful, hmmm? Didn't want her to know that he'd forgiven her and was still wearing it. People do silly things when they're fighting, don't they?" She tsked, shaking her head.

"So you have it, then?" he asked, leaning toward her in his eagerness.

"Of course I have it. Honestly, I'm a little relieved to give it to someone else to take care of." She paused—this was the most dangerous moment—and looked into Tyblith's eyes. "Can I trust you?"

He exuded honesty, almost like a scent. "Of course you can."

Lina leaned in and whispered, "Look, I just don't know what to do. This poor sick young man showed up at my home, and of course I took him in. But then he started ranting and wailing, and he made me swear I would help him and that I had to keep the torque away from the wrong people. Now, I'm not the kind of person who breaks promises." She paused, looking at him with concern.

"No, of course you wouldn't do that," he said, but his eyes darted around the room, looking hungrily for where the torque might be.

She shook her head. "No, I wouldn't." Her voice took on a desperate edge. "You're telling me it was a gift from his mother, but how can I know? I promised him the torque wouldn't be used for ill. That's all he seemed to care about." She forced a quiver into her lip, then bit it to stop the tremble. "And now he's dead, and that makes it his dying wish, and of course I have to do what I can to help him, and here I am just a tired old woman." She tugged his sleeve with the hand not holding the chisel. "You understand, don't you? Why I don't know what to do with it or who to trust?"

He patted her hand and spoke soothingly. "Of course I understand. Such things are so difficult. But I can assure you I was his friend." He looked into her eyes, sincerity in his every feature. "You can give me the torque," he said. "You don't have to worry anymore." She felt his charm fall over her like a warm blanket, soothing, telling her to believe.

She blinked, breathing deeply. *Focus on your purpose,* she thought. *Focus on Mollen and the torque.* Her mind stayed clear. "But are you the right person? He was so worried something bad would be done with it." *Come,* she thought, *say what I need you to say.*

"If you give it to me, nothing bad will be done with it." His voice was so smooth, his charmspeaking so very easy to believe.

She blinked again, straining against the magic. "You promise?" she wheedled. "No one will use this torque for anything bad?" She nearly held her breath.

He opened his mouth to speak, then paused.

Maybe she'd gone too far.

His eyes flicked to the chisel and her bare hand wrapped around it. She could almost see his thoughts. *This old woman is a simple blacksmith. A promise to her is meaningless.* "Of course I promise," he assured her, all friendliness and honesty.

Lina blew out a breath and smiled her first real smile since they'd come. "Oh, I feel so much better. I know it's crazy, but thank you for humoring a poor old woman."

He shrugged. "Of course, dear lady. Nothing to it. The only thing that torque is good for is comforting another woman like yourself, after all." He held out his hand.

She stepped to the bucket and fished out the torque. "I'm just glad to be rid of it."

He snatched the metal from her and examined it.

"I'm sorry it's broken." Then, as if she'd just thought of it: "I could fix it for you if you'd like!" It might give her a chance to come up with a better plan than this; she still hated seeing that object in his hands.

He shook his head, not looking up from the metal. "No matter, I have a friend who can fix it."

She nodded. This would have to be good enough, then.

They should be going now, but Tyblith didn't move. He just placed the torque in a pouch at his side and turned his eyes on Lina. Maresk and Toren glanced at him, waiting, muscles tensing beneath their tunics. A nearly imperceptible difference in the air had Lina tensing too. Moments passed, and she shifted her weight to prepare for an attack. Part of her hoped they would try something, despite how fool-hardy it would be to attack the town blacksmith in her shop in daylight. The idea of letting them leave with that torque—no matter what she'd done to keep them from using it—stoked the anger again. Maybe it was good she still held the chisel.

Tyblith turned to the side, gesturing to his men. Lina took a steadying breath.

"Lina!" a familiar voice cried as the smithy doors swung open. All four bodies swiveled toward the noise. Seelah burst through the doors, an even larger basket in her arms this time. That woman had so many baskets. She looked back and forth between the men and Lina. "I'm so sorry to interrupt. I forgot you were in the middle of something. I'm just so overcome!" She blinked rapidly. "I've just received a messenger from Innalue in Hillfar. You know, the one who's friends with *your sister*. There's been a terrible accident, and she's asked for us at once."

Lina could only blink and stare, yanked out of her preparation for battle. She didn't *have* a sister in Hillfar—how could this Innalue woman be friends with her? What, by the nix, was Seelah doing?

Seelah leaned toward the men, explaining in an undertone, "I'm her best friend, and I must have Lina's help, so you see we simply must go. Immediately." She paused and looked piercingly at Lina. "You're needed there, Lina. Everyone will be expecting you."

Lina blinked again, then shook herself from her stupor. She had no idea what Seelah was playing at, but she would go along with it. "Well, good sirs, I'm so sorry, but it looks like I'm needed at once. I'm sorry about your friend too. Do give my best to his mother for me."

A moment passed, then the men sprang back to life. "Yes, thank you, Lina-smith; we will," Tyblith said. "May we retrieve his body from your home?"

"Of course. I'll come with you." After they left, she could get to her hidden bags and leave Solime. Seelah had given her the perfect excuse.

The men left the smithy ahead of her, and when Seelah stepped out, Lina dropped the chisel into her pocket with a quiet hiss. She'd have to examine the damage to her palm later, when she was alone. For now, she curled her fingers softly around the bright, angry burn marks.

The entire group headed to Lina's house, and the men quickly picked up the body and hauled it out to the cart they'd left in front of her smithy. Tyblith turned back once to stare at Lina standing in her doorway for a moment—then at Seelah—before nodding and disappearing down the road.

Would she ever hear of them again or know what became of the torque? She hoped not. Better that they, and their plans, fade quietly into obscurity.

When the sound of horse hooves had faded, Lina breathed a sigh of relief and focused her gaze on Seelah.

"Do be quick with your bags," Seelah chided. "I'd rather be gone from here in case they decide to come back." She shivered. "I'll get the one in the hearth, but you'd better get that one." She pointed toward the underground room. "I don't think I can get up and down any ladder you've got down there."

Lina's mind reeled. "How did you—?"

"Come now, I've known about your hidey holes for ages. You really need to stop glancing at them during tea." She shook her head in mock reproach.

Lina's mouth dropped open for an instant, then she began to laugh. "All these years—I've underestimated you, Seelah."

Seelah shrugged. "Just because I like the town gossip doesn't mean I don't know when to keep my mouth shut."

Lina shook her head in wonder. Apparently, Lina was not the only woman in town who was not what she seemed.

The two of them worked swiftly to gather what little Lina wanted to take with her—and of course her hidden stores. They put most in her pack and the rest in Seelah's basket.

"Now, I don't know exactly what's going on here, but I'm going with you to Hillfar, or at least far enough to be sure you're safe. You can tell me all about it, or not, as you please."

Lina nodded. It would be good to have someone else with her in case Tyblith and his men decided to follow her. Or in case they found a way around the hurried oathbinding she'd set him to. If they were smart, they might realize that the irresistible desire to be done with that torque had come directly after Lina had convinced Tyblith to make that promise.

And if they realized she was responsible for that, they might wonder if Lina was the one who'd bound the pact to end the war. And then she'd be running, hard and fast. There were people who would like to exact revenge on the one who'd helped create the peace. A few, most of all, who would like to kill the oathbinder to release the magic of the pact.

She glanced down at her hand again, at the red blisters seared across older, faded lines. All the times she'd held iron and pretended that it didn't burn. All the ways she'd hidden in plain sight—who would suspect a blacksmith of having fae blood? She looked at Seelah. She'd done it alone for so long, but she really was getting older. It might be good to have a friend who knew the truth, who could help her if the war followed her again.

As it always did. It was always in her heart, burning in her blood like iron. But she would create all the peace she could, as long as she lived.

She turned to Seelah as they left the house. "What do you know about the end of the war?" she asked. She didn't reset the pebble.

ABOUT JEANNA MASON STAY

Jeanna Mason Stay loves a good fantasy yarn, particularly if it comes with a happy ending. She especially loves fairy tales—the romantic, the gruesome, the utterly bizarre—and many of her stories echo the magic of these old tales. Her favorite fairy tale of all, though, is a bit more modern: it's the one she lives with her handsome husband and their four charming children. They are currently adventuring, battling thorny devils, and happily-ever-aftering in Alice Springs, Australia.

Jeanna also loves fireflies, serial commas, birds of paradise, and the latest addition to her bird craze: the loud-yet-lovely galah. She dreams of one day sculpting a clay Medusa head and owning a herd of Chia sheep.

Website: calloohcallaycallay.blogspot.com/
Facebook: JeannaMasonStay
Twitter: @JeannaMStay
Email: jeanna.mason.stay@gmail.com

2

THE POISONER'S REVENGE —A KINGFOUNTAIN TALE

BY JEFF WHEELER

ANKARETTE'S WRISTS WERE bound, as were her legs, and a little splash of water came over the edge of the canoe as it hurtled along the river. She heard the roar of the falls coming as she gritted her teeth and fought against her bonds. The ropes on her wrists were beginning to give, loosening under the strain and pressure of her movements. She'd been trained at the poisoner school to escape bonds. But never had she needed to do so against the urgent rush of dwindling time. The canoe was heading toward the falls. The king's brother wanted her dead and had arranged a midnight arrest, a false trial, and now had taken on the role of executioner himself as well. The image of his face leering at her helplessness was scalded into her mind.

"My wife is dead because of you," he'd rasped with vengeance in his voice. "You failed, Ankarette. Now embrace my revenge." She could still remember the sour smell of wine on his breath. It had made her want to vomit.

Jerking hard one last time, she freed her wrists and quickly unraveled the ropes. The confinement of the canoe hedged her in, but she managed to sit up, just enough to see the stunning sanctuary of Our Lady, its tall spires lit by torches in the night. It sat on an island in the midst of a churning river, at the head of the falls. The palace was on her left—dark, foreboding. The king was visiting the fortress of

Dundrennan in the North. He was days away, too far away to learn about her plight. Too far to save her.

The river was ink black, the sky devoid of moon but straddled with stars. There were no cheering crowds lining the bridge, watching in macabre fascination as another victim of justice was thrown into the waters, a life paid in tribute to the Fountain.

She started working on her legs, realizing the futility of escaping. She had a minute left, at the most. Even if she had oars and paddles, it would be an impossible labor to steer toward the sanctuary in time. Her heart was pounding in her chest with the dread anticipation of coming death. The plunge was just beyond the sound of the roar.

Still she fought to untie her legs. The need to survive, at any cost, drove her. Soon the bonds were loose. But it was too late. The boat began to shake as the violent surge of waters nearly upended her. A childhood memory of jumping off a massive boulder into a river came spurting into her mind. And then the void opened up before her, the waves acting as a catapult as they shoved the canoe into open air.

Falling, falling, falling.

She awoke with a gasp, as she always did at that part of the dream. It was too terrible even for sleep. The room was predominantly dark, save for the fat stub of a candle she'd left burning on the table. The curtains on the bed blocked most of the light, and she sat up, damp with sweat, her heart still pounding at the memory. She'd dreamed it a dozen times since it had happened. And yet, each time, she felt the terror anew.

The night King Eredur's brother had tried to murder her.

Then she heard the footsteps marching up the stairs to the tower where her room lay. The person made no attempt to hide the sound of their approach. The poisoner's tower in the palace of Kingfountain was her private lair, her peaceful domain. There were no servants who came to light the brazier for warmth or to clean her linens. All the ways leading up to it had been secured long ago, and only the Espion tunnels led there now.

The person approaching was making noise deliberately. They were probably afraid she might kill them.

Ankarette parted the curtain and slid her legs off the bed. Her stomach cramped painfully, and it took a moment for it to subside. At the top of the bedstead were some small shelves that held some of her little treasures of memory. From one she removed a vial with a screwed-on cap and quickly twisted it. She took a little swallow of the ichor, cringing at its awful flavor before it slithered down her throat. It would ease the pain in her stomach. She rested a moment, clutching the bottle to her middle, and then put the cap back on and returned it to its place.

The newcomer arrived at the door. She saw the light from his lantern at the base and saw the marks of shadow. There was a hesitation. She rose, fetching the dagger she kept near her pillow, and waited.

A timid knock sounded.

Ankarette rose from the bed and came forward, her bare feet silent on the rug. She waited to respond, drawing closer.

Another knock sounded.

Ankarette reached it, watching the handle to see if it would move. It didn't.

"Yes?" she asked, whispering just loud enough to be heard.

"The…uh…the king," said the muffled voice. "Wishes to see you."

Eredur never summoned her during the night. Not anymore. The news must be dire. She shifted her grip on the dagger. "Very well," she answered. She said no more. Whoever the messenger was, probably some Espion lackey, he waited a moment longer and then started back down the tower steps. She rested her forehead on the door, feeling the grain of wood against her brow. A knot of dread entered her heart.

Who would the king want her to kill next?

Coming down from the tower was an agony. Ankarette's insides were still ravaged by the poison she'd been given years before by the Occitanian poisoner, Lord Hux. He'd also provided the vial, and several others, with her name engraved in beautiful letters, containing not the antidote, but a serum that would forestall its effects. She'd spent years trying to unmask a cure and had failed. Whatever plant his poison came from remained a secret to the best apothecaries in Ceredigion, Brugia, and even, on her secret trips, in Occitania. But she had a suspicion that the poison came from farther afield. The East Kingdoms, perhaps? After so many journeys, Eredur had finally forbidden her to leave court in search of the cure. Perhaps her absence was just what

Lord Hux wanted before he struck at Eredur. The treaty between Ceredigion and Occitania that had been signed years before was still in force, but Ankarette felt the Occitanian king was only biding his time, waiting for Eredur's power to wane.

She reached the royal bedchamber through the Espion tunnels and opened the secret latch to the room. There was plenty of light beyond, and she found the king standing before the remains of the nightly fire. He wore his breeches and a comfortable robe, which was open, revealing his massive chest and unwanted girth. He was no longer the soldier of his youth, the young man who had fought in brutal wars to become the wearer of the hollow crown. He did not look ready for war.

Queen Elyse sat at the edge of the bed, also wearing a night robe. Her flaxen hair had some silver in it now, but she was a stately woman, and her eyes were full of concern as she stared at her husband. She was the first to notice Ankarette's arrival.

"She's here," Elyse said and rose from the bed to come and embrace her. The two were friends, having shared many adventures as well as many tragedies together. Ankarette's nickname among the Espion was the Queen's Poisoner. The two embraced, and Elyse pressed a kiss to Ankarette's cheek. "You look pained."

Ankarette smiled sadly. "It will pass soon."

The king turned away from the hearth and faced her, his eyes containing the secret. Some of his chest hairs were silver now. He looked weary, weighed down, depressed.

"You summoned me?" Ankarette asked, tilting her head. After the king's brother Dunsdworth had sent her over the falls, her survival had been a closely guarded secret. She did not walk the corridors of the palace now, keeping to the shadows where she could advise the king and queen in secret. Sometimes her recommendation went counter to the king's privy council. And more often than not, he heeded her advice over theirs.

"A messenger from the North just arrived," Eredur said. "From Tom." Ankarette's eyes narrowed. Even after so many years, hearing his name made her flinch inside, made the ache flare anew. They had loved one another. But that had ended when he'd married Duke Horwath's daughter. They had a little girl, Ankarette knew. Lord Thomas Mortimer believed Ankarette was dead, that she'd been killed at the falls in an act of treason by Dunsdworth. She wanted to keep it that way. His marriage had not been an overtly happy one. But there was no doubt he doted on his daughter.

"What did it say?" Ankarette asked. She gave an air of unconcern, which she knew didn't deceive Elyse. Their hearts were knit too close for such deceptions.

It was Elyse who answered the question. "Morvared is dead."

Ankarette turned, gazing sharply at the queen. That was unexpected news. "When did this happen?"

"King Lewis has kept it a secret for the most part," Eredur said, his look turning darker. "The Espion didn't know. But Tom has friends in many distant ports. Someone who thought he would want to know that Morvared hated him as well. He sent me word right away."

"Ankarette," Elyse said warily, shaking her head. "We don't know for certain if it is true. The old queen's health may have been failing. Or perhaps she was...poisoned."

A feeling of dizziness had come over Ankarette. She felt like she needed to sit down. Lord Hux had told her that as long as Eredur spared Queen Morvared's life, that Ankarette's own would be spared. He had provided, in ways mysterious, replenishment vials to replace hers. Ankarette had used them sparingly, trying to keep extra in reserve. At least twice a year the replacement would arrive. She had an entire vial that had not been opened yet.

Eredur folded his arms. "Why the Occitanian king has kept it secret, I don't know. But I don't trust Lewis. He may have replaced Hux as his herald, but I don't believe he means to keep the terms of the treaty. We've been collecting the tributes he's paid. But I knew they might come to an end eventually. He wants his daughter to marry our eldest son. To keep the peace between our realms. To unite Occitania and Ceredigion once again. Or is that a pretext as well? They're both children."

Elyse nodded in agreement. "Has he been intending to call it off all along? We don't know. But Morvared's death comes at a suspicious time. And we couldn't help but remember the warning Lord Hux gave you, in particular, Ankarette."

She mastered her feelings and gripped the queen's hand in return. "You didn't summon me in the dead of night simply to share the news with me. You want me to go to Occitania and find out if she's truly dead."

Eredur smirked and let out a low chuckle. "Yes, that was our exact intent, Ankarette. Tom's message said she died at the castle in Dompier."

Ankarette nodded. "Then that is where I will go. Do you know where Lord Hux is? Has there been any word from him?"

Eredur shook his head. "Unfortunately no. Lewis chose a new herald years ago, and so Hux's movements are a mystery. He's probably still at Shynom." The king looked at her pointedly. "Are you going to seek him out, Ankarette?"

The queen also looked at her worriedly.

Ankarette and Hux's rivalry had lasted for years. He was the master poisoner. The most powerful one serving any kingdom. Yes, she'd managed to outsmart him on occasion. But it seemed like conflict between them was inevitable now. It was impossible to guess his actions or his reasons.

"It may be best if I did," Ankarette said. "If I could get him to breathe a little nightshade, I could force him to tell me the secret of the cure."

The king's lips were pressed together worriedly, and he stepped forward. "I can't afford to lose you, Ankarette Tryneowy. Not when my children are so young. I'm feeling my age more every day. In ten years, my sons will be ready to rule in my stead, and I can relinquish more power to them. For now, I have to rely on my brother, Severn."

The queen's look darkened at that statement. Yes, there was bad blood between the Duke of Glosstyr and the queen. Severn was Eredur's right hand, the leader of his armies and keeper of peace of the realm. Eredur relied on him, but Severn's biting sarcasm and inability to forgive had earned him many enemies, including members of Elyse's family. It was strange, but Eredur and Elyse's oldest child, the queen's namesake, had a great fondness for her uncle. The boys, on the other hand, preferred their mother's family.

"You don't think I should seek out Lord Hux, then," Ankarette said.

"I won't forbid you to," he replied. "I trust you too much. I know you won't act out of spite or without reason. Go where the trail leads you. If it leads you to Hux..." He paused, shrugging. Then his eyes turned deadly earnest. "Then ensure he cannot interfere in our realm any more than he already has in the past."

"I will," Ankarette said, nodding. "I will take a ship at first light. Dompier is west of Averanche in the heart of Occitania."

"If you need anything, send word to Duke Kiskaddon in Tatton Hall," Eredur said. "I have Bennett stationed there. He'll help you if you need it."

Ankarette tilted her head and thought a moment. Bennett was a solid Espion and had been her friend many years. But she trusted her own instincts best and her Fountain magic. Going alone would be easier. "Does the duke know I'm still alive?" She had fond feelings for the duke and his family. She'd helped their youngest son at his birth. It was the first and only time she'd used her Fountain magic to bring a stillborn back to life. As a young woman, she'd been trained as a midwife. That was how she saw herself—a bringer of life, not of death.

Eredur shook his head. "None of them know, Ankarette. That is how you wanted it."

She wondered how the duke's little boy was doing. But saw no reason to break free of her self-imposed concealment. She especially didn't trust the king's other brother not to attempt to continue what Dunsdworth had begun. Killing Dunsdworth still caused her pain. But Eredur had ordered it. She hoped he would never order her to kill his other brother too.

She was about to leave when the door handle turned and the door to the hall opened. All three turned, trying to see who was entering their room in the middle of the night without knocking. Ankarette had reached for her dagger, but it turned out to be their eldest daughter, named after her mother. Another child Ankarette had helped save during childbirth.

"What is it darling?" the queen asked, coming to meet her.

"I heard voices...one I didn't know," said the young woman who was sixteen and looked so much like her mother. "Who is she?"

"I will tell you later, Daughter. Go back to bed," Elyse said to the girl, who eyed Ankarette with interest and curiosity.

The fortress of Averanche was illuminated by torchlight as the ship approached from the north with the tide. The ramparts were set in rows of jagged teeth, and it was clear there were sentries patrolling them by the glow of the flames that moved along the upper walls. Ankarette had purchased passage on a Genevese trading ship with a cargo of green olives and mackerels. The pain in her stomach had subsided with the dose she'd taken the day before. She stared at the walls of the fortress, which was built on a cliff above the harbor. This fortress was part of the Occitanian lands, and she knew that once she stepped foot on the docks, she was in enemy territory. No doubt King Lewis had spies in all the major port cities. Her cloak concealed much of her features, but she would take no chances. She'd prepared the implements of her trade—poisoned rings, daggers, hairpins, along with small cylinders containing other devices that would disable or kill. Occitania was the land of Lord Hux, her nemesis, who could smile with charm while stabbing someone in the back. It had been years since they'd faced each other. Years since he'd defeated her and forced her to drink the poison that was slowly killing her.

She had trained more rigorously since then. She was older, more experienced. He'd be approaching fifty now, so she had some natural advantages this time. When she next brought out her dagger against him, she did not expect to lose.

Within the hour, the ship had reached the docks, and the captain began shouting orders to prepare the vessel to be inspected. He gave her a curt nod as the gangway was lowered, and she swiftly descended and entered the town. She was fluent in Occitanian and knew how to disguise her voice to change her age just by the inflection she used.

The first thing she did was determine if she was being followed. She went to a nearby tavern, which was loud and rowdy, and ducked inside. Immediately she went to the kitchen, walked past a bewildered cook, and then exited out the back. In the shadows of the alley, she made her way past a chicken coop, through a short gate with squeaky hinges, and then walked a little distance to the next street and turned the corner. There, she waited, listening, opening the hood of her cloak to hear better.

After several minutes, where all she heard was the scrape of leaves being dragged by the breeze and the nearby bluster of the tavern, she heard the squeak of the gate. She carefully looked around the corner, spying two men. They looked confused, unsure of which way she had gone. They obviously decided to split up, because one went the other way while one came in her direction. She twisted her poisoner's ring, exposing the needle. Divide your opponents' forces. Remove the lesser pieces one by one. Just like the game Wizr.

Ankarette pressed her back against the wall, listening for the sound of advancing footsteps. The man was being especially careful, but she did make out the subtle scuffing sounds that increased in volume as he approached the corner. He was walking quickly, which meant he was trying to catch up, believing her to be much farther ahead than she was.

His shadow suddenly appeared around the corner. He had a knife in his hand, the blade pointed forward.

He saw her.

Too late.

Ankarette gripped his wrist to control the dagger and jabbed her hand against the side of his neck, where the needle pricked his skin and caused a little rivulet of blood when he jerked in surprise. Suddenly his elbow jutted at her face, but she dodged it, keeping his wrist gripped firmly. He grunted at the pain and tried to call out in warning. She twisted and covered his mouth with her hand, the ring slashing part of his lip in the process. He was strong, vigorous, and terrified, which added to his strength. He tried to twist the dagger around to stab her in the stomach, and it took all her effort to keep the blade pointed away.

Then the poison finally worked, and he slumped in a heap on the cobblestones, but she still held his wrist and neck and gently laid him down. Although her heart was racing at the sudden violence, she listened keenly for the sound of his partner pursuing her. Nothing.

She quickly disarmed him, taking his weapons for herself, as well as his pouch of coins. Then touching his throat, she ensured he was still living. The poison would last for hours, and he'd have no knowledge of where she'd gone. She dragged his body deeper into the shadows to make it more difficult to find in the dark. They might not discover him until morning, by which time she'd be well away. Twisting her ring again, she concealed the tip. Then she left the alley.

Each kingdom had a network of courier horses. Messages were dispatched and returned at all hours of the day and night, depending on the severity. The king had his own royal couriers to use, but messengers could be dispatched for the right amount of coin. She had no intention of waiting until day to buy a horse, which would be conspicuous. Her goal was to steal a horse and ride to Dompier directly, in the disguise of a courier. She had perused the Espion maps of Averanche in the Star Chamber of the palace before leaving and knew where the porter doors were. These doors were locked during the night, but guards were stationed there in case riders appeared. A watchword was required to gain access.

'When she reached the porter door, she saw two men sitting on chairs and dicing, chuckling at one another in the cool evening. They shared a wineskin between them, no doubt adding to the humor

Waiting in the shadows, she watched the two dice and steal each other's coins. Patience was one of her specialties. She watched them, listening to their banter, studying the wineskin they continued to pass to each other. It was still full, which meant they intended it to last through the night. Soon enough, one of them rose from his chair and went to relieve himself in the garderobe inside the small gatehouse. There was a brazier by the chairs to keep them both warm, and the other rose and stood over it, rubbing his hands above the coals. Ankarette approached from behind swiftly. The light of the fire kept her shadow behind her. She took the flagon dangling from the back of the chair and then pulled the chair back slightly. Twisting open the cap, she dumped a small packet of powder into the wineskin. The man sniffed, rubbing his hands continually over the brazier, unaware that she was standing just behind him. She set down the leather bladder and stepped back into the shadows again. The man came back to sit down, but the chair had been moved, so he fell on his rump and let out a bark of confusion and pain. She pressed her back to the wall, her dark cloak absorbing light. The other fellow returned, tying up his pants, and started to laugh at his friend who was still sitting confused on the ground.

They shared more wine. Within the hour, both men were sound asleep, one of them snoring obnoxiously loud.

Ankarette borrowed the key from one of their belts and unlocked the porter door. She returned the key to his belt and went out into the darkness, shutting the heavy door behind her. She'd left no trace of leaving Averanche. It would take days before news of her arrival reached King Lewis or Lord Hux.

That was all the time she needed.

The courier thundered down the road well past midnight, and she heard him coming from a distance. She'd chosen the spot of ambush along the road from Averanche to Pree, choosing a small area with dry scrub and some thick yew trees. It was a great place to conceal herself, and the yew had provided branches and leaves to help in her plot. She'd broken off several large branches and dragged them into the

30

middle of the road, making it seem like they'd fallen naturally. A horse would sense the obstruction and halt. That would give her time to subdue the rider.

The sound of the galloping hooves grew louder, and she waited behind the trunk of the largest yew where she could watch the approach and attack from behind the rider. Although she was weary, she kept her senses alert and focused. It was just a single rider, a courier. She didn't know if was a royal one or not but would find out soon enough.

The pounding hooves came up the road swiftly, and she waited, eyeing the road until she saw the smudge of black silhouetted in the moonlight. The rider reached the road in front of her hiding place, and the horse suddenly snorted and banked in.

"What is this?" growled the rider, trying to see in the darkness. The branches and leaves appeared a much more formidable barrier than they really were. Ankarette slipped out from behind the yew and stabbed a needle into the rider's leg with a quick-acting paralytic. He would remain conscious, but wouldn't be able to move his body.

"Ouch!" he gasped, turning in shock at the source of the pain. He tottered off the saddle, and she caught him, grunting herself at his weight. The horse became even more agitated, but she knew how to handle animals and had grown up riding with the Duke of Warrewik's daughter. She tethered the reins to one of the branches of the yew she'd hidden behind, and then dragged the man to the scrub. He was blinking rapidly, his face worried. He wore the uniform of King Lewis and the royal badge of the fleur-de-lis.

Even better.

"Who are you?" he said, his voice quavering. His whole body trembled under the effects of the poison.

Ankarette withdrew a small packet of nightshade and judged his weight by having dragged him over. She dumped a dose into her gloved palm and then approached him.

"Who are you!" he said, panicking.

She didn't answer and blew the dust into his face. Almost immediately, his body relaxed as the toxin took effect. Too much would have killed him. The right amount made a victim particularly pliable to answering questions.

"What is the watchword for the gates?" she asked him, leaning closer. She touched his throat and felt his heartbeat racing.

"Alys. The king's mistress," he said in a slightly giddy voice.

"What does she look like? Is she pretty?"

"I don't know," he babbled. "I've never seen her. The king has seen no one in weeks."

Ankarette knitted her brow. "Is the king at the palace in Pree?"

"No, he's hidden himself at his estate in Plessis."

"What do you mean?" Ankarette pressed. "Hidden himself?"

"He's made a prison for himself. No one can see him. He's fearful."

"What is he afraid of?" Ankarette asked, growing even more concerned.

"He's afraid of being poisoned," said the man, laughing. "There is a fence around the chateau. An iron fence. Four hundred archers patrol it. And sixty crossbowmen. No one comes in unless summoned. Or they are killed."

Ankarette blinked in surprise. The Espion had not been told of this. Then again, it was difficult keeping able people in Lewis's court. This was troubling news. Why was Lewis so afraid? Or had he had a falling out with Lord Hux? Was he afraid for his life from his one-time poisoner?

"Where is Lord Hux?" she asked.

"Who?"

"Lord Hux."

"I don't know that name. Lord Hux? I don't know Lord Hux."

She jostled his to keep him coherent. "Where is the king?"

"I told you that," he said. "He's at his chateau in Plessis."

"Where is Plessis? What city is it near?"

"It is by Vierzon. But you cannot go there. If you are not invited, the archers will slay you."

She did know the name of that city. It was deep in Occitania, far from the machinations of the court of Pree. What was going on? Had Lord Hux turned renegade against his master? Had another king managed to win Lord Hux's loyalty?

The man started to snore.

"Wake up," Ankarette said, jostling him again.

"Wha—what?" he groaned.

"Queen Morvared. Where is she?"

"The Queen of Ceredigion…is dead," the man said, mumbling.

A spasm of dread went through Ankarette's heart. Yes, Morvared had once been the Queen of Ceredigion. She probably considered herself the queen still, even though she'd lost the crown years before. Thanks to Ankarette's help, Eredur's queen wore the crown. But the thought of something happening to Elyse made Ankarette dread the words.

"What is your name?" she asked him.

"Marion, but they call me La Fleche. I ride like an arrow." He sniffed, and Ankarette could sense the change in his voice, the sound of someone rousing from the thrall of nightshade. It was like someone realizing they were talking in their sleep. Another dose, so soon, would kill him. There was much she still wanted to know. But she'd learned much so far.

King Lewis was afraid. Morvared was indeed dead.

But could Ankarette be sure? Could she trust the report of a courier?

No. She needed to know for herself. Because if Morvared was dead, it meant Lord Hux would stop providing the cure.

And then Ankarette would die.

The town of Dompier was on the Orle River, which had acted as a natural moat against the invading armies of prior decades. The castle was on a hillside above the town, behind a vast fortified wall interspersed with small guard towers. The fortress itself was beautiful, constructed in the Occitanian style that was different from the palaces of Ceredigion. Dompier was a square chateau with four large towers at each corner with tall angled roofs made of adjoining panels that rose to a central peak. The shingles were made of dark slate, all uniform in color, while the blanched gray walls were a similar, lighter patina. The towers weren't rounded but hard edged. At the top of each tower was a spike of bronze. The front façade, which faced Ankarette from across the river, had a beautifully constructed gatehouse behind massive stone walls. It was the kind of castle that could withstand a siege for years. While the townsfolk below might be compromised, the keep itself was highly defensible.

It was late afternoon by the time Ankarette had arrived. She wore the uniform she'd stolen off La Fleche and had practiced all day speaking in his tone of voice and accent. She'd bound up her hair in twisting braids and concealed it against the broad hat he'd been wearing. No one had bothered her along the journey, nor asked where she was going.

She rested on the horse, gazing up at the fortress, wondering whether she should keep her disguise or trade it for another. Yet, it was probably the best way to enter the castle without being questioned. No one knew she was coming. Messengers were not always the best informed of people either, although they relished gossip. She hoped to confirm the rider's news, but she'd need to be careful. The castle looked truly formidable. There was no ivy growing on its walls, no trees to use to climb to one of the upper windows. Even the chimneys, which the structure abounded in, seemed too narrow to squeeze through. She continued to study it, watching it for signs of activity. It was quiet and still. No bustling servants. What was happening on the inside, it was impossible to know.

Darkness was a friend, so she waited until near sunset to approach the river. A ferryman was loitering below, and when he saw her approach and noticed the badge, he directed her to bring the horse on the ferry, where she dismounted.

"Good news, sir?" the ferryman asked her inquisitively.

She frowned at him and turned away, adopting a haughty pose.

The man, chagrined, continued about his work, and soon they were launched in the river. There was a guide rope that helped the barge against the current, and in a half hour they'd crossed and darkness had settled over the town. It was smaller than Averanche, and she bought some food from the sole street vendor before riding up the slope to the walls.

The outer gate didn't even ask for a watchword. They just let her in, and she wondered at the lax standards in the realm. Though it was not a time of war. Or was trouble on the horizon?

She'd already read the courier's message, which he'd been taking to Averanche. It was orders to the mayor to prepare for an inspection of the city defenses by one of the dukes. She'd then forged another document, using the same handwriting style, requesting in similar language an inspection of the fortress of Dompier, and she'd pried loose the seal and reaffixed it to her note. She rode with the bearing of a man, giving the illusion that she was La Fleche. The real man she'd tied up and left back in the yew trees. She'd chosen not to gag him so that he could, eventually, be discovered and freed. But he'd not remember her or know where she was going. By the time Lord Hux discovered she'd been in Occitania, she'd be back at the palace of Kingfountain.

The horse's hooves clopped up the ramp heading to the fortress. The torches were not lit yet, and the walls looked like bleached bones in the sunset. Looking back, she saw the glimmer of the waters of the Orle River. She was tempted to use her Fountain magic to discern danger, but if she did and Lord Hux was there, he would know it—just as she could sense his power when he used it.

As she neared the doors, they opened, and two guards came out holding pikes.

"Welcome to Dompier," one of them said. "We didn't know you were coming."

"You weren't supposed to know," Ankarette replied, making her voice more husky. She handed the message to the guard. "But it will be clear soon enough."

The guard looked at the seal and then up at her. "What's the watchword?"

"Alys," she answered, sounding bored.

The other guard nodded, and the first handed the note back to her. "Bring your horse inside the courtyard. The castellan is eating dinner. We'll take you straightaway."

Ankarette nodded and urged the horse forward. Once inside, they shut the doors as she dismounted. There were two other guards inside. Four total watching the front doors. Hardly a strong defense. She imagined the entire castle had fifty men assigned to it. Formidable—but not impossible. Not that she'd try to fight them all at once, but she felt confident she could escape if she needed to.

After they took her horse, she was brought into the castle of Dompier. The inner corridors were lit by burning torches. Tapestries with colorful Occitanian fashions adorned the walls. The interior had been decorated with the subtle touches of a woman's hand. It was not a military garrison. No, it was more like a castle had been transformed into a manor house fit for a queen.

What if Morvared was still alive? Would she recognize Ankarette after all these years? The last time they'd met, Ankarette had thrown a dagger and impaled the old queen's wrist. But people saw what they expected to see. A rider, a courier. Someone of no importance. If Morvared were dead, Ankarette would inspect the corpse for the scar.

That would be the evidence she'd trust. And why she had needed to come quickly before more decay happened.

But Ankarette did not suspect the old queen was alive. The news would not have traveled so quickly to Eredur otherwise. No, this was just a confirmation.

The castellan did not have a family or even a wife. He was a thickset man with wavy hair combed forward in the Occitanian style. His doublet was fine, his fingers greasy from the dinner, and he chewed rapidly before mopping his lips with the napkin. He glanced at Ankarette and then held out his hand for the note.

She delivered it and stood back again, hands clasped behind her back, studying the chamber, looking for the various doors.

He broke the seal and quickly scanned the note.

"An inspection? What for?" he said, sounding angered. "This makes no sense."

Ankarette shrugged mildly, continuing to gaze around the chamber.

"Why would Duke Brabant be coming again so soon after the funeral? The king isn't coming here. He's not going anywhere."

Ankarette sniffed. "I don't know, my lord."

"Of course you don't know. You don't know anything." He threw down the message. "Go to the servants' quarters and get a meal. The duke is paranoid, that's all."

Ankarette bowed and then slipped out. She was led to the kitchen where the cook pulled together some food for her and where she quickly learned that a funeral for Queen Morvared had been held recently. Not many dignitaries had attended, but the Duke of Brabant was one of them, and so it did seem odd that he'd be coming again so soon. Ankarette listened and applied some subtle questioning to learn that the queen had been interred in the crypt below the castle. A stone sarcophagus had been carved for her, depicting the queen in tranquil repose. Some visitors had already come to pay respects to it, some leaving flowers for the dead queen that needed to be cleaned up later.

That was all she needed to know.

Ankarette found out how to get to the crypt to pay her respects, and since the castle was so quiet and the guards had already eaten, she was able to visit it alone without anyone accompanying her.

The crypt was at the bottom of some stairs, and torches had been set in wall sconces to illuminate the way. The steps were made of stone, and it would be easy to hear if anyone followed her. Still, she waited after going down, listening for the sound of pursuers. No one bothered with her.

So Ankarette followed the pathway, past stone columns into a vault-like room. The ceiling was low, but not enough to make her duck. The sarcophagus was plain to see, set in the middle of the room. There was a stone lip around it, with kneeling cushions for those wanting to come pay their respects. Ankarette saw some dried flowers as well and a small stone decorative fountain, which had two dozen coins shimmering in the bottom of it. The final respect paid to the dead.

Yes, all appeared to confirm the news that Sir Thomas bore. Everything, except seeing the corpse for herself. Ankarette could not turn back now, not after coming this far. She felt a sense of dread staring at the carving of the queen. It resembled the woman, and the visage brought back memories from Shynom palace and a command pavilion that she'd sooner forget. Memories of a voice that sounded almost childlike but was full of vengeance and pride. The woman had lost her only son in that final battle against Eredur. And Ankarette had helped in that defeat.

She stood for several moments, trying to quell the memories of the past that haunted her. Sir Thomas, she'd thought, had declared himself to her...only to forsake her for Duke Horwath's daughter. Pain clenched in her heart.

Now was not the time to be maudlin. She cocked her head, listening again for the sound of anyone coming. The little decorative fountain was still, causing no interference in her ability to hear. If she tried dragging the stone lid away, it would make a sound. She bit her lip.

She had to do this. She had to know for certain.

If Morvared were laid out in the same manner as her effigy, then the wounded wrist would be on one side. Ankarette let out her breath and then pressed her hands against the stone. It should be able to slide off. If it was set in, then she'd have to lift it up. Ankarette tried pushing against it. It didn't budge.

Why would it be easy?

She sighed and then stood at the head of the lid, bending her knees, and then hefted against it. She felt it giving, scraping softly stone to stone. She held her breath, prepared for the odor of decay. Surely they'd have embalmed her. But no one relished the smell of death.

Ankarette's muscles strained, but the lid moved up. There was a torch nearby, offering light on the shadowed crevice. Higher it went, higher. Then she saw the bleached face of the dead woman, the sunken cheeks, the grayish skin. The dark cushion of hair. It was horrible and mesmerizing to look at.

Then she heard the sound of a strand breaking.

And an iron gate crashed down against the stone at the bottom of the stairs. There were locking noises, the click and snap of machinery. The torches wavered as the realization struck her in the pit of her stomach.

She was trapped in the crypt with a corpse.

⸻

The sound of boots came down the steps hours later. The castellan carried a lantern in his hand and approached the bars warily. Ankarette had realized the trap had been set, and she was caught in it. Gears had locked the gate from above, and she'd tried everything she knew in order to budge the iron bars, but they were immovable.

The castellan approached and looked at her suspiciously, then shook his head. "I'll admit, you surprised me," he said, cocking his head. "I really thought you were a royal courier and that your message was real. Thankfully, Lord Hux isn't such a fool." He shone the light on her face, but she didn't flinch from it.

The gnawing feeling of desperation wriggled inside her. She had to escape. She had to find a way out.

"If you release me, you will be a very wealthy man," Ankarette said. "The King of Ceredigion—"

He laughed at her face. "Now you're mocking my intelligence. Hux designed this trap himself, and only he has the key. Even if I wanted to help you—and I don't—I couldn't. Besides, your king will not be king for much longer." His eyes flashed malevolently, his tone revealing the depth of his hatred. "The queen gets her revenge on you at last. She's been here for years, Poisoner. Plotting it. Planning it. Waiting for your guard to go down to strike. I'll say no more, my dear. You can remove your disguise whenever you wish. I'll have a chamber pot and food brought to you. Hux said he'd come for you himself. Eventually."

Her feelings roiled with intensity. She had to get free! She stared at the castellan, wanting to hurl a poisoned dagger into his belly. But what good would that do? One man with a crossbow could end her life just as easily. Maybe death would be preferred.

Ankarette came to the bars, clenching them with her hands. The castellan flinched and backed away. He might be angry, but he was still afraid.

"You could batter down these bars," she said. "If you wanted to. But I swear to you, if you do not release me, you will suffer. I won't kill you, sir. I'll make you wish you were dead. You have no idea what I'm capable of."

He smirked, staying well out of reach. "Oh, I think I do. I've a friend named Vauclair who was tricked by you years ago, when you were a young thing." He gave her a nasty smile. "I know who you are. You're good at betraying your friends as well as your enemies. I have one more thing to tell you. A message from Lord Hux. 'Threat. And mate.'"

The only time Ankarette had been imprisoned was when Lord Dunsdworth had arrested her and then sentenced her to death for the murder of his wife. She'd hated the helpless feeling then, but this was much worse. There was no sun to reveal the passage of time. New torches were brought daily, along with a meager set of rations, brought twice a day. They'd gone through the saddle bag from the courier's horse and brought her gown down to her, which she'd changed into. But her poisoner bag, which she always kept at hand, held nothing that would solve her problem in time.

And time was something she had now in abundance. Time to pace. Time to think. She wished she had her needles and thread, and although she'd ask for a set, she'd been denied. She'd used her Fountain magic to try to find a way to escape. But she may as well have been buried with the corpse of Queen Morvared. She'd examined the remains and found the tell-tale scar on her wrist. At least Morvared had escaped her exile at last. There was no way out of the confinement for Ankarette, however. She'd also examined the gears and locking mechanism. The keyhole was on the other side of the bars, higher than she could reach. Her cage had been designed by someone who knew the poisoner's arts.

Days passed. Each one making her agony grow. After a week, the effects of the vial she'd drunk before leaving Kingfountain began to ebb, and the pain started again. It was an acute form of torture, trapping her in her agony, with no way to find relief. After the second week, her frantic feelings had grown worse. Eredur knew where she was. Had he sent Espion to try to find her? Surely King Lewis and Lord Hux were expecting it. And by doing so, her king had deprived himself of those who could best protect him.

There was no doubt in Ankarette's mind that Lord Hux was going to try to kill Eredur. He would have to get past the Espion, of course. But without Ankarette there to warn him, he would be vulnerable. She ate her rations, feeling the oppression of her confinement.

After a month, while her insides chafed with pain, the temperature began to cool. Winter was coming soon. Guards brought two braziers to the bottom of the steps, leaving her some degree of warmth. And then another month passed. She took small sips from her near-empty vial, to prolong her life. She'd bent her hairpin into a needle and had used the courier's uniform as her canvas. Sewing had been her passion, a skill she'd adopted from her mother. Needlework strengthened her Fountain magic, gave her insights. She came to realize how trapped she truly was. But the worst part was the torture of suspense. Not knowing what was happening in Ceredigion. Being helpless.

The Espion tried to rescue her on midwinter's eve. She only knew it was that day because one of her jailors had mentioned it.

She heard the noises of alarm coming from the castle above. There were shouts, even the clash of arms. She was so sick and weak, but still she rose and went to the bars, listening to the sounds, trying to understand what was happening. Her mind quickened with hope. She'd been a prisoner for several months, her vial almost empty of the syrupy ichor that sustained her life. Hux hadn't provided anything new.

There was a crashing noise above, which startled her. The noises of conflict made her pulse race. Eredur had sent people to rescue her. She was certain of it. A battering ram would open the gate. Even metal would give to the use of force.

The door at the top of the steps opened, and a figure came rushing down. He was bleeding from a wound on his scalp, but she recognized his face. Bennet—one of the Espion who was her friend.

"Ankarette!" he said, seeing her at the bars.

Her heart swelled with gratitude. "Bennet," she said, reaching for him through the bars.

He was smiling, overjoyed to see her. "We found you at last. The king ordered this rescue a month ago, but it's taken time to slip into the country unawares."

"Bennet," Ankarette said, shaking her head. "The king lives?"

"Yes," he said, nodding vigorously. "We need to get you out of there."

"Lord Hux has the key," Ankarette said. "But the bars can be broken with enough strength."

"You look so weak," Bennet said. "Here...the king said to give you—"

The twang of a crossbow sounded, and the bolt struck Bennet in the back. Pain contorted his face, and he slumped against the bars. He gasped, trying to breathe. His legs crumpled as his broken spine lost its ability to support him. She cried out in anguish, trying to clutch him through the bars. He had something in his hand, something he was about to give her.

Another vial of the serum. The one she'd kept in reserve at the palace in her tower.

"Ankarette," Bennet wheezed, then his eyes rolled back in his head.

Two guards, each holding a crossbow, came down the steps. She managed to slip the vial into her pocket, but the tears she shed were very real.

Within the hour, the noises had faded. The castellan came down, mopping the sweat from his brow. "Well, my dear," he said grimly. "Your king fancies you for certain. I lost twelve men tonight. But we killed them all, I think. Some fled into the snow. They'll be easy to hunt. I've sent the dogs to go after them. One by one, they'll be slain. Like this one." He nudged Bennet's body with the toe of his boot. Then he spat on him.

Ankarette lunged against the bars, trying to grab the castellan. But he'd wisely stayed out of her reach.

"Still some fire left in you," he said with a smile. "Good. Hux said you had spirit. And he wanted to see it crushed."

Although she could not see the sun, she kept track of days by carving into the stone sarcophagus. Meals were brought twice a day, so she had

41

a way to measure it. By her estimation, she had been confined for four more months since the attempted break-out.

There was no way to escape the prison. She'd examined it from every angle. She'd used her magic on it again and again, then replenished her stores by stitching with the courier's uniform. She'd worked over the cloak, the tunic, using threads from other parts to stitch with. In the cell, she'd even made friends with a little gray spider who spun a web in the corner to catch moths that were attracted to the lights. Ankarette liked watching the spider at work, and studied its elegant legs as it spun and wove its silk-threaded net.

The day Eredur died, she felt it. A ripple within her Fountain magic announced it to her. Maybe it was his ghost whispering to her before departing to the Deep Fathoms. She had the nightmare about the falls again that night. The speeding canoe as it rushed to the edge of the waters. Only, she didn't awaken on the fall. The canoe smashed on the churning water. Ankarette had survived the attempt to kill her, but it had broken her body. It had taken months to heal, and the injuries added pain to her life daily.

The death of her king was a new pain. It was a deep sadness that evoked her darkest thoughts, one that drained her spirit. The king's brother, Severn, would be chosen as the protector of the realm. And while she did not like the duke, she knew he was loyal to his brother. Queen Elyse didn't like him either, nor did she trust him as much as Eredur did. Ankarette wished she was back at the palace to advise the queen. But it wasn't possible. Morvared would have her revenge from beyond the Deep Fathoms. To make Ankarette suffer in confinement.

The castellan brought the news the next day, a smug look on his face. But she'd already known.

"King Eredur has died," he said. His smile broadened. "I received the message from Lord Hux just now. He's enjoying his stay in your city. It's a beautiful spring day. He may return soon. Or he may not. He wanted you to know."

Ankarette gave him a listless look and then turned away. She'd known it would happen eventually. There was nothing she could have done to prevent it.

"I'm having a lamprey pie for supper," said the castellan. "I'll have one made for you. I think that was the dish, if I'm not mistaken, which killed your king. We can both celebrate…in our own way. No Eredur… no threat of war."

Ankarette sighed. "You don't know the king's brother like I do," she said.

The castellan snorted. "Oh, I'm convinced Lord Hux has plans for him as well."

That night, or what she thought was night, Ankarette poured her ration of water into the small dry fountain at the head of the sepulcher. And she tossed a coin into the waters, listening to the sound of it splash. And then she wept.

In all, she had six months in which to plan her revenge. She knew Lord Hux would come to gloat when his mischief was over. Would he try to woo her into his service? She doubted that. There could be no trust between them after this. He would know without doubt that she would get revenge on his king. Which was why, she had come to realize, King Lewis was hiding at his estate in Plessis. He'd hidden there to prevent being abducted by the Espion. Or killed, in case Ankarette escaped. Yes, Hux had thought of everything. Including how he would face her at the end. Was this his final act as poisoner before he retired? His grand drama? She imagined so. He would protect his king's interests and provide years of security for himself by causing instability—and probably civil war—within Ceredigion.

So Ankarette had made her plan, woven together night after night, day after day, in the solemn drudgery of her prison. Little snips of hair. Food rations withheld and preserved. Same with her water rations. She was biding her time. Preparing for the confrontation she knew was coming. Hux didn't want to fight her. He wanted to prove he didn't need to.

Ankarette was determined that it wouldn't happen on his terms. She would make him come to Dompier the only way she knew how.

By making him think she was dead.

She set her trap with care. Refusing to eat the food brought to her. Sitting listless and sullen, wrapped in her cloak. Moaning when the servants came with her meals. Then she lay still, exposed to the light of the torches, letting her shoulders rise and fall slowly. Her actions unsettled the guards. The castellan came to speak to her, asking if she needed anything, and she refused to respond to him, only moaning.

Then, on the third day of not eating or drinking, she set the trap.

She knew the castellan was in communication with Lord Hux. Her strange behavior would be reported. And he would respond.

When he arrived at Dompier, she sensed his Fountain magic as just a faint ripple. He had no reason to disguise it. She waited patiently, like the little gray spider that spun its web in the corner. Sounds came, the door opened, and Hux and the castellan came down the steps. She felt his magic probing, reaching, trying to find her. She'd used up her reserves already, giving herself nothing left for him to find.

"How long has she been dead?" Lord Hux asked. She recognized his voice. She'd heard it many times. He didn't sound confident now. He sounded worried. From her concealment, she saw his face. His goatee, which was new, was well streaked with gray.

"Four days, Lord Hux," said the castellan. "She stopped eating and drinking. Look, she's not even moving. Not breathing."

"I can see that," Hux said. He sounded disappointed. He hadn't gotten the full dose of revenge he'd wanted. Or that Morvared had wanted.

"She's not moved in days. She was moaning in pain. And the smell. She smells like she's dead."

"She had more serum," Hux said with suspicion. "One of the Espion smuggled it to her. It can't be gone yet."

"What if she drank it all at once?" the castellan said. "I think she killed herself in despair. That's blood on the floor."

"There is only one way to find out," Hux answered. "Fetch a guard with a crossbow. I want to make sure she's dead."

"At once, my lord," said the castellan.

Ankarette watched Lord Hux's face. He was gazing intently at the floor, not at her. He could see the blond hair coming out of her cloak.

Soon a guard appeared, holding a dreaded crossbow.

"Aim at the corpse's back," said Hux dispassionately. "Even if she's feigning death, she couldn't help but flinch in pain." He changed his voice. "If this is a trick, my dear, you'd best reveal yourself now. I have no hesitation killing you."

Ankarette smiled and waited.

The guard hefted the crossbow and brought the front to the bars. He wouldn't miss, not at that range. The crossbow twanged, and the bolt went true. The sickening crunch of bone sounded. The corpse was rigid.

She waited, breathing slowly.

"She's dead," Hux said, frowning. "I thought she would have lasted longer. Years even. But when hope is stolen away…it breaks the spirit."

"What do we do, my lord?" the castellan asked.

"Throw the body in the moat. She can feed the trout. I'm going back to Kingfountain."

"Very well. Where's the key? You have it?"

Hux produced it from his belt and handed it over. Then he departed up the stairs.

The castellan ordered the man to fetch a ladder, which he did, but it took a quarter hour for him to return, and then the castellan, grumbling in impatience, climbed up to the keyhole that was well beyond Ankarette's reach. He inserted the key, and the locking mechanism clicked once, then twice. On the third time, the castellan climbed back down.

"Grab the bars. It will take two of us to lift it," he said to the guard.

The two men grunted and heaved at the bars, and the gate lifted up. It was heavy for two men, but they were strong enough now that the locking mechanism had been disabled. When it reached the height, another clicking noise sounded, fixing the gate to where it had been concealed before.

"There," the castellan said, rubbing his hands together. "Now, you grab her legs, and I'll grab her arms."

The two men started toward the body.

And that was when Ankarette sprung her trap.

From her concealment inside the sarcophagus, which she'd wedged open just enough to see out of, she shoved the lid up. The trigger inside had already been reset, and the gate came slamming down on both men, pinning them to the floor. As she had known, they were both larger than her, providing enough room to wriggle out.

Ankarette shoved the lid off completely, letting it crash to the floor, and then vaulted out of the tomb. The corpse on the floor, which had been facing her all the time, showed Morvared's grinning skull, the head cushioned by Ankarette's own hair.

The castellan was groaning, blood streaming from a gash in his head. The gate had landed on him first. The other guard, in a panic, was squirming to get free of the bars. He was a smaller man and desperate to get away, and he was one of the ones who had frequently tormented her. Ankarette struck him in the neck hard enough to break it. He went rigid and then still.

The castellan, blood streaming into his head, looked up and saw her looming over him, wearing the dead queen's gown. By the expression of fear on his face, he knew he was a dead man.

She didn't disappoint him.

The village of Aynan in Occitania was a humble one, but it had a comfortable inn called the Speery, and it was there that Lord Hux had chosen to spend the night after leaving Dompier. Ankarette hadn't followed his horse. No, that would have revealed her. But after poisoning one of the guards, she'd learned what Hux's stallion looked like and had asked those she'd passed on the way about it until arriving at Aynan.

The Speery had a warm fire and many guests. Lord Hux was clearly well known throughout the realm, and she saw the delight in the faces of the patrons as he regaled them with stories of Ceredigion. She'd joined the crowd, concealing herself, and listened to him speak.

"How King Eredur died, I'll never know," Hux said disingenuously. "He was rather fat at the end. Apoplexy, I should think."

"You knew the king, though," said the innkeeper. "You were once the herald, Lord Hux!"

"Yes, I knew him," Hux said. "A handsome man. A valiant warrior, to be sure. But too greedy, as all those from Ceredigion are. And foolish to sign that peace treaty. But he's gone to the Deep Fathoms now. And the kingdom is roiling because of it. They will not seek to fight us again. Not for many, many years."

"Not while the boar rules Ceredigion!" someone said with a sneer.

"Indeed not," said Hux slyly. "He murdered his own nephews to seize the throne. I'm shocked, truly. Eredur trusted him so much."

Ankarette listened in silence as the patrons laughed. There was a stab of pain in her heart. A small ember still lived on apparently. Now it was truly dead. Eredur and Elyse's sons were murdered as well. She regretted that she hadn't been there to stop it. Grief wrenched at her heart. Poor Elyse. Poor devastated Elyse.

"Here's another round to peace with our enemies!" said the innkeeper. A cheer went up among the group. Ankarette had already noticed which young woman had been serving Lord Hux. She'd followed the girl with her eyes as she went to go get another bottle of wine.

Ankarette rose from the table and crossed over behind the girl, brushing against her, and dropped a coin on the floor by her foot. The girl, hearing the sound, bent down and retrieved this.

"Is this yours, madame?" the girl asked, seeing Ankarette.

"Yes, I dropped it," she replied. "Thank you. But you keep it. I needed to pay for my meal anyway. You can save the rest for your honesty."

"Why thank you, madame!" The girl pocketed it with a smile, and then carried the wine bottle and the goblet over to the table.

Ankarette chose another table, one closer to Lord Hux, who was busying himself with the wine cork and popped the lid off. Of course he'd open the bottle himself. He still couldn't trust people. Nor should he.

"Let us have another drink, then!" said Lord Hux. "To the future king of Ceredigion!"

"And who is that?" chuckled the innkeeper. "You don't think the boar will live long, Lord Hux? Are you a Wizr to make such a prediction?"

"I am not a Wizr," said Lord Hux. "I'm just a retired herald who will live the remainder of his days in peace and solitude." He poured himself some wine and took a sip and smiled broadly. "Excellent! No, I think the boar will not rule long. A rival has been seeking an army from His Majesty, King Lewis. A rival who will invade Ceredigion and claim the throne himself. Then, my friends, we shall all live in peace. Let's drink to it!"

"To peace!" everyone shouted, raising their cups.

Lord Hux drank his down and leaned back in his chair, a wistful look on his face. He rubbed his mouth thoughtfully, watching the patrons. He had such a kindly face, an agreeable air. It was what made him so deadly, Ankarette realized.

She watched and waited, arms folded, studying him.

He smelled something off. His nostrils flared. His eyes darted around the room. Then he pulled his hand away from his face. His brow wrinkled in concern. Holding his fingertips near his nose, he smelled them.

The serving girl was walking toward the kitchen, clutching her stomach. She disappeared behind the doors. The coin dusted in poison was doing its work.

Hux's brow began to dot with sweat. Ankarette kept watching his face, realizing the symptoms he was now feeling had alerted him to the poison running through his system. Poison that hadn't been in the drink. Poison he'd touched on the goblet.

"Are you well, Lord Hux?" asked the innkeeper. His smile was fading, becoming worried.

Tremors began to seize Lord Hux's muscles. He tried to reach for something across the table, but he couldn't coordinate himself, and his arm jostled the plate and overturned the wine goblet, spilling the red liquid on the table. It looked like blood.

Ankarette had just a little Fountain magic now. It was seeping into her pores now that she was free. Just a hint of it. She'd need to find some needlework to recuperate the rest. But she invoked it, letting the power exude from her.

Lord Hux turned his head in astonishment, seeing her at a nearby table. Ankarette inclined her head to him, as if asking a silent question. What's wrong, Lord Hux? Do you not feel well?

The tremors began to convulse through him. It was a powerful dose. Enough to kill him. More than enough.

"Someone fetch the apothecary!" the innkeeper shouted in concern. "He's sick!"

Ankarette rose from the table and approached. "I'm a midwife," she told him.

"Help him! Help him!" the innkeeper said, looking relieved.

"Carry him to a room," Ankarette said.

While Hux trembled and shook, several of the men lifted him and carried him to one of the nearby rooms in the inn. They laid him on the bed.

"I need a basin of water. Go!" she told the innkeeper, and he hurriedly left.

Hux was choking. He stared at her in terror, especially after they were alone. She removed the packet of nightshade and poured plenty into her palm. She blew the powder into his face, and he was unable to stop her. She waited until his tremors began to subside. A dizzy look came into his eyes. It was a powerful dose.

A fatal dose.

"What is the cure for the poison you gave me?" she asked him in a whisper, bending near his ear. "Do you have it with you?"

He blinked several times, his body relaxing despite the poison raging inside his body. "There is none," he said. "Only the serum to halt its progress. But not forever. Even it lessens with time. Surely you've felt it. You were always going to die."

His answer didn't surprise her. He'd controlled her life for years, ruining any chance of having children, having a life outside her deadly trade.

"I thought that might be the case," she answered. "I did look hard for one."

"Are you killing me, Ankarette Tryneowy?" he asked her calmly. His face had become pale. The poison worked quickly.

"Yes, dear Lord Hux," she answered. "And then I will kill your king. We both lose this game. I will leave a note with your body. To warn him I'm coming."

Coming back to the city of Kingfountain felt like a dream—or more appropriately, a nightmare. Ankarette had purchased fare on an Atabyrion trading vessel, which delivered her to Kingfountain just after noon at high tide at the end of summer. It was less than a year since she'd left, but felt more like a lifetime. She had been to the city so many times, but it felt otherworldly to her now. The roaring of the falls gave her a premonition of dread, but what was even worse was not seeing Eredur's banner anywhere. It had been replaced with the black banner of the White Boar, the standard of King Severn Argentine. She'd loved to embroider things with Eredur's banner, the Sun and Rose. She didn't have a fancy for dark thread, though.

She walked the streets of Kingfountain, picking up clues of the events she'd missed out on during her imprisonment. News used to invigorate her, stimulate her mind, even replenish her Fountain magic. But she was a woman with a death sentence, one that had been secured by Lord Hux years before. There was no cure for the poison he'd given her. Only a delay. She'd come to terms with her possible death years ago. She would never become an old woman. Instead, she would stay alive until the last sips of the vial were gone. She'd last another year perhaps, if she used it sparingly. Not enough time. But then, life was full of vagaries anyway.

It did not take long to reach the bridge that straddled the river over the falls and connected to the island of the sanctuary of Our Lady. All the reports suggested that Queen Elyse had sought sanctuary there—one last time. Memories from the past flittered through her mind. The Duke of Warrewik. Eredur, when he was younger. Sir Thomas arresting her from the inn across the street. A sad smile came to her. She'd lived an interesting life, even if it would be short.

She watched the gates of the sanctuary, observing the sanctuary men—the rogues of the city—going in and out, passing news and stolen goods amongst themselves. Although she wanted to see Elyse again, she dreaded the interview. But, not one to flinch from duty, Ankarette rose after finishing her meal and raised her hood, crossing the road and entering the sanctuary grounds.

There were many families there, people coming to toss in coins. There was no shortage of prayers to the Fountain these days. Ankarette stopped at one of the pools, pausing to gaze up at the monumental structure. Her faith in the Fountain felt diminished. She'd been shattered by her experiences. For so much of her life, she'd had success. Until now. She'd fallen for Hux's trap and been unable to prevent her king's demise. Failure was a bitter thing. No one enjoyed its flavor.

There was a man sitting against the rail of the fountain, a very fat man whom she noticed because he stomped and frightened away the pigeons. Then he chuckled and started sending out crumbs again to lure them back. He had a foreign look to him—Genevese perhaps. Something about him felt off, and so she reached out with her Fountain magic, trying to discern something about him. He didn't turn his head at her intrusion of magic. But it was revealed to her that he was part of the Espion, trying to infiltrate the sanctuary men.

Knowing this, she remained out of his view and approached the sanctuary steps and mounted them. When she reached the doors, she was about to lower her hood, but she felt a premonition not to. Walking inside, she felt the solemnity of the place. The windows in the upper walls let in the streaming sun, but it still was darker than the courtyard outside, and it took time for eyes to adjust.

She was about to lower her cowl again, to show respect for the Fountain and those assembled to honor it, when she saw a little girl, probably six years old, with a braid in her dark hair, gripping her father's hand. The little girl talked in a gush.

"But why can't we take the coins from the fountain, Papa? It's not like anyone uses them. Don't they just get rusty?"

The man who held the little girl's hand was Sir Thomas, and it made Ankarette stop dead in her tracks. They were heading right for her. She turned, ducking around a nearby column, her heart panging in alarm of being recognized.

Sir Thomas's voice was full of humor. It made her ache to hear it again. "What? You don't think the coins disappear in answer to the prayers?"

"Don't be ridiculous, Papa," the little girl said. "That doesn't happen."

From her secret vantage point, she watched the two of them banter as they left the sanctuary. Sir Thomas had some gray in his hair, but not much. He was still hale, strong, a warrior born for the saddle and the battlefield. Ankarette brought news of the pretender's intention of invading Ceredigion. A challenger to Severn's newly won throne. Sir Thomas would be called on again for his experience and loyalty to the Argentines. She watched him and his daughter descend the steps, hand in hand. She remembered the little girl's name suddenly. Elizabeth Victoria Mortimer. She smiled at them in secret, then continued deeper into the sanctuary.

When she reached the deconeus's chamber, she didn't pause to knock. After twisting the door handle, she cracked it open and found an aging man sitting there, alone, reading from a book. She pushed the door open and then shut it.

When he looked up, he stiffened. "Who are you? Why are you here?"

"Where is John Tunmore?" Ankarette asked in surprise.

The man snorted. "The Deconeus of Ely? He's in Brakenbury Dungeon in Westmarch. Who are you? Why are you here?"

"I'm a servant of Queen Elyse," Ankarette said. "I have news she must hear. Can you bring me to her? I need to see her alone."

He gazed at her, his expression dumbfounded. He leaned back in his chair, looking perturbed. "She doesn't get many visitors these days. But you knew my predecessor?"

"I did. The queen knows me. She will vouch for me."

The man sniffed. "She's with her daughter right now. I'll ask the princess to come and see me. I have another letter for her anyway, which arrived this morning. The queen has some visitors, on occasion. Well, those that do come want her daughter's hand. The sanctuary has been busy of late."

"Thank you, Deconeus."

Elyse's private chamber in the sanctuary paled in comparison to her regal apartments at the palace of Kingfountain. The official queen of Ceredigion was Severn's wife, Nanette. But in Ankarette's eyes, it would always be her friend, her confidante.

"Blessed be the Fountain, you're alive!" Elyse said in wonder, rising from her writing table and hurrying across the room.

The two women embraced, the tears flowing freely. Their friendship had been born of years, had survived childbirth and wars, and now even death.

"You cut your hair," the queen finally said after wiping her nose and lowering Ankarette's cowl.

"I didn't want to, but it was necessary," Ankarette said, smiling. "I am glad to see you again. But my heart aches that I was not here to stop Eredur's death."

The queen sighed, nodding firmly. "You were imprisoned," she said. "I think my husband would have invaded Occitania to rescue you. If it weren't for the winter storms, he might have."

"That was part of Lord Hux's plan," Ankarette said. "There is much we must speak of."

"Come, sit with me," the queen said, bringing her over to a humble couch.

Ankarette did, and they held each other's hands. "News should be arriving soon. I wanted you to be the first to hear it. King Lewis is dead."

Elyse's eyes widened. "That is news. I've heard he's spent much of the last year hidden at his estate in Plessis under heavy guard. He wouldn't see our heralds, refused to outright. He wouldn't even see most of his own nobles. Some feared he died during the winter, but he would summon some of them, randomly, and disinherit them. Just to prove that he was alive…and still the king."

Ankarette nodded. "He died in Plessis."

The queen couldn't help but smile. "How did you...how did you do it?"

Ankarette stroked the queen's hand. "I'll share this one secret with you, but I ask you to keep it to yourself. Some secrets should remain so. One thing I learned in Pisan is the power of believing. If someone believes they are sick, they can become sick. When I finally broke free of my prison, after hearing about the death of your husband...your sons"—Ankarette's throat caught, but she persisted—"I wanted to be sure that our enemies who planned this were brought to justice. After I killed Lord Hux, I put a message on his body, one that I knew would be found and brought to Lewis. It was a warning that I was coming for him."

Elyse nodded eagerly. "I'm sure he was racked with worry, then."

Ankarette smiled. "I never tried to break in to his manor. Instead, I broke in to his mind. I made him worry that every meal might be his last. I injured his guards. I made him doubt everyone he trusted. He was already agitated enough, with enemies to spare, that he quickly went mad. The last message I sent him was that he'd already been poisoned. He died yesterday morning after being awake all night jumping at shadows. I watched from outside the bars. The prince came to take his body back to Pree for internment. He wasn't killed by poison. He only believed he'd been."

Elyse stared at her somberly. "And Morvared is truly dead as well?"

Ankarette nodded and then quickly told her about her imprisonment and how she'd finally escaped. She also told her the news she'd learned from Lord Hux, that there wasn't a cure. There had never been one. Once her vial was empty, Ankarette would die.

The queen embraced her, and the two friends held one another, mourning for the losses they'd endured.

"But you are not dead yet," Elyse said, sniffling. "There is one more thing you can do for me."

"I cannot bring your sons back," Ankarette said, grieving.

"No, you cannot. Severn has asked to see me, here in the sanctuary. He even sent his young son to try to convince me. The poor dear is so upset that his cousins...are not here. Not that Severn would trust the truth to his child. It pains me so much. The anguish of losing a child. I wouldn't wish that on anyone. Not even Severn. So I have continually refused. He says he wishes to tell me what he knows of my sons' deaths. But I...I just cannot bring myself...to trust myself to believe him. My mother's heart wants to believe he didn't murder my sons. But I feel too vulnerable to deceit. He has a way when speaking," she said, shaking her head. "He's powerful. And persuasive. If I see him, I would like you to be there, in secret, of course. That way, I may know whether he speaks the truth or not. I don't believe you, with your Fountain magic, would be deceived."

"I can do that," Ankarette agreed. "Have the deconeus invite him to the sanctuary."

"I will," Elyse said, squeezing her hands firmly. "I want you to stay with me...here at the sanctuary. Let us spend your time together. I will take care of you."

Ankarette shook her head. "I can't," she said, staring at the walls, at the prison they were. "I couldn't bear to live here, listening to the roar of the falls day and night." She pursed her lips. "I think it would drive me mad."

"Where will you go? I need your near me, Ankarette."

"I will always be near you," she said. "I was going to return to my tower. Who is running the Espion now? Whom did Severn choose?"

Elyse frowned. "Dickon Ratcliffe. Utterly ambitious. Utterly incompetent. But not like Bletchley. That man...he was a knave. Eredur never trusted him. But Severn did. To his downfall."

"Bletchley was in league with Lord Hux, I think," Ankarette said, nodding. "It wouldn't surprise me. But he's dead now, isn't he?"

Elyse nodded. "Be careful, Ankarette. Severn knows about you. Not your name. Many times I heard him plead with Eredur to reveal your identity to him. He doesn't know all that you've done for us. He would try to kill you. He's...changed so much since Eredur died."

"We all have," Ankarette said.

It was the same nightmare again. Ankarette thrashed against her bonds, trying to escape the canoe as it hurtled toward the falls. She felt the rushing river beneath her, the splashes of water that kicked up over the rim of the boat. Could smell the river. The power of it, churning, carrying her relentlessly toward death.

But this time, she awoke before plummeting over the edge. The feeling of the river had roused her. The tingling of power, the ripple of magic coursing through her. Ankarette sat up in bed, looking at the stubby candle that was still halfway down, the flame strong and bright. She was in her room again, at the poisoner's tower. The smells of dried herbs were familiar, friendly. She saw her works, the needlecraft she'd done since returning to the palace.

The magic was racing inside her, filling her with alarm. She blinked, summoning the power that was already there. People were coming up the tower steps to do her harm. Ratcliffe's men. Liona, the cook, had warned her the day before that the Espion had discovered Ankarette's presence in the palace. And the king had ordered them to hunt her down.

Ankarette rose from the bed, grabbing the knife under her pillow. The men on the stairs didn't make any noise. But she knew they were coming all the same. The magic of the Fountain had warned her.

Why?

She didn't understand, but she accepted its help. They would try to murder her as she slept. Perhaps she'd need to start sleeping during the day instead.

Three men.

Ratcliffe had no idea what he was up against. She'd defeated an entire garrison at Dompier.

Ankarette leaned over and blew out the candle.

About Jeff Wheeler

Wall Street Journal bestselling author Jeff Wheeler took an early retirement from his career at Intel in 2014 to write full-time. He is a husband, father of five, and a devout member of The Church of Jesus Christ of Latter-day Saints. Jeff lives in the Rocky Mountains.

Facebook: muirwoodwheeler
Twitter: @muirwoodwheeler

3
THE RED WALLS OF ISHRI
BY PATRICK HURLEY

THERE IS ONE unbroken tradition in the city-state of Ishri. Every year, for a single day, the immortal Zaltin steps down from power and a citizen is chosen by lottery to act in his place. For that day, the chosen Ishrian is given all the privilege of the Zaltin. They are known as the Zaltin-ari. It matters not whether they are merchant, maid, or thief, if their lot is drawn, they will rule for a day. They may partake in the revels in the Harem of Shades, sip the Wine of the Ancients, declare war on neighboring cities, or hang all prisoners. They may give half the treasury to the poor, throw all weapons into the sea, or command a day without clothing. The word and power of the Zaltin-ari is absolute.

For a single day.

At the end of that day, no matter the havoc the Zaltin-ari might have wrought, the Zaltin would step in to fix what was broken, and his citizens reflect on the wisdom and power of their benevolent ruler. After all, their sorcerer-king had conquered death itself.

Veila Jyn almost missed the lottery for Zaltin-ari that year. She'd celebrated the success of her latest job long into the night and woke with a mouth dryer than the Mojanna Desert and a head that rang like the gongs in the Temple of Gii. Those who hired Veila Jyn thought of her as merely a thief. Those she stole from believed her to be a ghost. And those who pursued her bounty considered her in terms of dead or alive.

Veila Jyn thought herself an acquirer of objects of great value.

However, today, with months of leisure ahead, the only thing Veila wished to acquire was a cure for her hangover. She took to the streets with a thirst on her lips and silver jangling in her pocket. Only when the bells of Ishri rang three times did she remember the annual lottery. Witnessing this year's Zaltin-ari sounded as interesting as anything else, so Veila made her way toward the marketplace at the center of Ishri.

The sun reflected brightly off the buildings surrounding the city square, exposing the cracks in the red clay walls the way morning sobriety shows the true appearance of last night's lover. The marketplace smelled of sweat and spices, of wool and oil and cooked meat. Veila found a table at a small café facing the fountain and placed a coin into a waiter's hand, bidding him to bring her bread and wine.

A voice called out to her from across the street. "How far have we fallen, when devious rogues now frequent cafes as if they're law-abiding citizens of Ishri?"

Veila turned to see Mahj Garustar grinning at her from behind his baker's stall. While certain circles of Ishri knew Veila's name, if not her face, everyone knew Mahj and his wife, Dyan. They were the most sought-after bakers in the city. Everyone from poor urchin to high-born noble loved their sweet rolls for breakfast, their meat pies for lunch, and their pastries for dessert. Their bread tasted moist and hearty, perfect for soaking up a sauce or stew. Their cakes were never too sweet, the perfect balance of icing and sponge.

Every year, the day after the Zaltin-ari's rule, the Crimson Tower hosted a tremendous Feast Day banquet, culminating in the presentation of a magnificent seven-layer cake. And every year, the Crimson Tower called upon Mahj and Dyan to bake the Ishri Feast Day cake.

"Come join me, you fat flour-monger!" Veila shouted back. Mahj left one of his assistants to tend his stall and ambled over to Veila's table. If ever two people looked like exact opposites, it was Veila Jyn and Mahj Garustar. Where Veila was lithe and wiry, Mahj was plump and stolid. Where Veila was devious and quick-witted, Mahj was plodding and meticulous. To look at Mahj, one would never know that at one time he'd been the second greatest thief in all Ishri. In fact, Veila and Mahj had been the greatest pair of rogues to run the city's rooftops. In their youth, both could scale a wall and pick a lock faster than a hungry child could eat a pie.

"Some wine?" Veila offered.

"It's not even noon, Veila."

"It'll keep you cool; unless you want the sun to sweat your fat away?"

Mahj laughed and Veila snapped a finger at the waiter for a cup.

"Usually it is I who supplies the bread and wine when we meet, sister."

"I've been doing well, Mahj."

"Ah-ah-ah, tell me nothing! I fear the day when I'll see you dragged along the Thief's Way. I dread even more when the Crimson Warders kick down my door to put me to the question."

Veila's face grew serious. "That would never happen."

Mahj's smile vanished. "I know," he said soberly.

"For one thing," Veila continued, allowing herself a small grin, "if I were ever taken along the Gallowstreet, it would only be after I'd eliminated you as a witness."

Mahj looked at Veila for a moment, then they both burst into laughter.

"How is your family?" Veila asked. Mahj had fallen in love back in the days of their roguish youth and given up the thieving life to turn his hand toward baking and becoming respectable; he'd excelled at both.

"Well indeed. Every time I turn around, it seems another child has been added to the mix. Where Dyan keeps pulling them out of, I don't know."

"I believe your neighbor Kahim pays her a call while you are up late in the night, preparing the dough for next morning's rolls."

"This explains why some of the brats are so thin and ugly."

Veila guffawed. Mahj gestured toward the bread and wine. "So you do well then?"

"Quite well, Mahj. But next month, who can say?"

"Indeed, fortunes change fast in Ishri."

"Speaking of which," said Veila, pointing at plaza center where the lottery would take place, "how go the preparations for Feast Day?"

"Ah, the cake is nearly done. The bottom layers have been set. The only thing left is the frosting. I'm having trouble getting it the right shade of red. I've tried cherries but—" Before Mahj could finish, trumpets sounded throughout the square. A large column of masked, crimson-clad soldiers bearing glittering scimitars spread out along the barriers of the square. From the column's center emerged four men carrying an ornate box of gilded cherry wood, which they laid in the center of the square.

The crowd grew silent; even the wind stilled itself in anticipation. The palace herald addressed the crowd. "Citizens of Ishri, today one amongst you shall be called forth to serve the city as the Zaltin-ari.

"For one day, your fortune will burn brief and hot. You shall know the power, the awesome responsibility of the Zaltin. Thus it has been, and thus it shall always be." The herald reached into the box's opening and pulled out a small strip of paper. He appeared to read the name to himself, then turned and faced the crowd.

"Mahj Garustar, the gods have chosen you to be Zaltin-ari of Ishri."

Veila stared at her friend in shock. Mahj looked as if he could barely believe the news. The official at the fountain called out, "Is Mahj Garustar in the square or shall the Crimson Warders be sent to fetch him?"

Veila leaned forward, "Go with them. I'll let Dyan and the children know the good news."

Mahj nodded with a grin, then stood up and cried, "I am Mahj Garustar."

Like a wave of blood, the Crimson Warders surged forward to escort Mahj to the waiting platform. Veila watched the crowd cheer as the baker was led to the palace. Hangover forgotten, she ran all the way to the baker's shop to tell Dyan the good news. Out front, a long line of customers waited.

Veila slipped around the side of the bakery and through the back door, catching Mahj's wife kneading dough in the back while her older children took orders up front.

"Blessings upon all in this house," Veila announced. The normal hustle and bustle of the Garustar home came to a halt.

"Aunt Veila!" The younger children ignored the customers, ran to her, and tugged on her sleeve, To the Garustar children, Veila Jyn was a source of amazing stories and wondrous presents.

"Veila," Dyan said, after kissing her cheek, "how good to see you!"

"You as well," Veila said, shutting the curtain between the customers and the backroom. Once they were separate from the noise of the main bakery, she turned to Dyan. "Your husband has been chosen as Zaltin-ari."

"What?" Dyan cried. She lightly swatted Veila's arm. "How dare you joke with me. We've already enough to do with putting the finishing touches on the Feast Day cake."

"It's no jest, Dyan. I sat next to him as he was chosen."

"You're serious?"

"I am," Veila said with a smile. "The Crimson Warders are on their way to escort you and the children to the palace. I wanted to give you all enough time to make yourselves presentable."

Not minutes after Dyan had finished scrubbing her youngest, there came a loud knocking on the door. Dyan opened it to find a contingent of the red-clad palace guards waiting for her. They confirmed Veila's news, but when Dyan looked over to thank her friend, Veila had already vanished.

From the rooftop, Veila Jyn watched in satisfaction as the Crimson Warders escorted the Garustars through the streets. With dark chalk, she refreshed the proper symbols on the Garustars' roof, letting any would-be thieves know the baker's shop was under her protection.

If anyone deserved to be king for a day, it was Mahj. Of course, Veila couldn't help but speculate how she might use such a fortuitous turn of events to her advantage. Veila produced a small dagger, one of many she kept hidden on her person, and juggled it in complex patterns as she considered the possibilities. She had several outstanding warrants she wouldn't mind seeing expunged.

To celebrate her friend's good fortune, Veila chose a path along the rooftops to her favorite tavern, The Restful Shade. As watering holes went, the Shade lived up to its name by having no windows and as few lamps as possible. It was a tavern made up of tucked-away alcoves and private booths, perfect for clientele to discuss business. Veila raised a finger at the bartender, who nodded and slid her favorite red over in a clay cup. On a small stage to one side, a man danced while a woman played a flute behind him.

"Another," Veila said, finishing the wine in three large gulps. "And some food. The good stuff—lamb, glazed with honey."

The bartender nodded. "You're in a spending mood today, Veila Jyn."

"I'm celebrating my friend Mahj Garustar's good fortune," said Veila, "which I'm confident will trickle down unto well-loved friends."

"The baker?" the bartender said. "Come into some money, has he?"

"Even better," said Veila, taking a pull from the second cup. "He has been chosen to be Zaltin-ari."

A silent astonishment fell over the bar. Several patrons began a similar calculus to Veila's, factoring their relationship with the baker and how they could turn his newfound prestige to their advantage.

"To Mahj Garustar," Veila said, raising her wine. "Friend, baker, and Zaltin-ari. May his reign be short and prosperous."

Nearly everyone in the Restful Shade raised their glasses to Mahj. All save one. As the patrons downed their drinks, an old woman in the corner of the bar spat on the floor and grumbled, "Better the poor fool had never been born."

Veila felt a prickle of unease as she recognized the speaker. The old woman was known around the less savory parts of Ishri as Mother Spider. Some said she was a witch, some said she was a seer. All agreed she offered services savory and unsavory, provided one could meet her exorbitant prices. One did not cross Mother Spider; one did not contradict her, not if they wished to live a long and prosperous life. Still, Mahj was closer than a brother, so after the tumult died down, Veila walked over to where the old woman brooded.

"You heard me then, Veila Jyn?" said Mother Spider before Veila could take a seat next to her.

"I did," replied Veila carefully. "Might I ask why you said that?"

Mother Spider beckoned her to come closer. Veila did, watching to make sure the old woman's hands stayed tucked within her black robes. In the darkness of the Shade, Mother Spider's wrinkles were deep crevasses; her dark eyes glittered from black pits. Only her thin white hair, like a silken web, shimmered against the candlelight.

"Do you ever wonder what happens to the Zaltin-ari, once their day is done?" asked Mother Spider.

"All know this," answered Veila. "We're not one of those barbaric countries to the north who sacrifice their kings. After their day of rule, the former Zaltin-ari live in the palace, if they so choose, and sit on the Zaltin's council."

Mother Spider cackled. "Do they now, Veila Jyn? Do they? Most interesting. Then no doubt you can tell me the last few Zaltin-ari who've joined the council, yes?"

The question made Veila's head hurt. She tried to recall who'd been chosen last year, and the year prior, but no names came to mind. She began to wonder why she'd even tried to recall this when everyone knew—

Veila gasped as Mother Spider pinched her arm. "You fought it longer than most," the old woman said, "but you were starting to forget. I could see the enchantment gaining hold."

"What enchantment?" Veila asked.

Mother Spider glanced about to make sure none spied on their conversation, but the Shade's other patrons were all entrenched in their own stories. "The enchantment laid over all Ishri. The enchantment that causes us to forget the Zaltin-ari after their day is done, to never question what happens to them after their reign. The enchantment that keeps us from remembering the city's terrible truth."

Veila shivered. The old woman's words terrified her, but she could not have said why. "What is this truth?"

Mother Spider's crooked yellow teeth gleamed in the soft darkness. "At the end of their day, the Zaltin-ari is sacrificed so the Zaltin stays alive and in power."

Veila almost dropped her wine. "That can't be right!"

"Oh no?" Mother Spider asked. "Why not? Does your doubt come from within you, or is there another voice inside your mind?"

"We would know!" Veila said, seizing upon this. "There would be rumors."

"Not if the enchantment is strong enough," said Mother Spider. "I've never met a single person, not a friend, relative, or neighbor of a Zaltin-ari. And I know many folk in Ishri." The old woman took a long sip from her tea.

"Even if such a spell were possible," said Veila, "people can't just vanish. There'd be children wondering why they have just one parent, business partners asking why the desk across from them sits empty."

"Ah, that's the marvel of the Zaltin's spell," said Mother Spider, her tone filled with grudging respect. "Not only do we forget the Zaltin-ari, but the magic also provides an alternate story in the minds of the Ishrians—they remember how a husband went away on business and never returned or how loose masonry fell and crushed their colleague's skull. They don't remember them as Zaltin-ari, just a tragedy. In all Ishri, I'm the only one who remembers a Zaltin-ari."

"What makes you so special?" Veila asked, forgetting for a moment that she spoke to Mother Spider.

"The Zaltin's spell affects the memory of the heart and mind," said the old woman, her voice almost a whisper. "We spiders store our memory where we store our prey: in our webs."

Veila shivered. If Mother Spider was right, Mahj was in grave danger. Yet even as she considered the idea, doubts crept in. How could he be in danger? The whole idea seemed foolish. Even Mother Spider could be wrong sometimes…

Something soft slid around her wrist. Veila looked down to see a thin, shimmering band of what looked like Mother Spider's hair. The old woman tightened the knot, and those persistent doubts vanished.

"This should give you some immunity to the Zaltin's spell," Mother Spider said.

Veila nodded in thanks. She now found she could remember the last few Zaltin-ari if she tried. Worse, she found she couldn't remember hearing of them after their day of rule.

"What would you have of me?" Veila asked, for she knew Mother Spider's gifts never came without cost.

"When you rescue your baker friend," said Mother Spider, "see if you can find anything about this name." The old woman slid a thin parchment across the table. Veila committed the name to memory. When she looked up again, Mother Spider had vanished.

Minutes later, Veila Jyn ran along the city rooftops as effortlessly as if strolling through a market. Ahead, dominating the skyline, waited the Crimson Tower, the palace of the Zaltin. Despite its singular name, it was in reality a vast collection of towers built from the same deep-red stone, sprouting from a colossal keep hundreds of feet tall.

It was said there were many ways into the Crimson Tower, but few ways out. Its walls were high, the Crimson Warders plentiful. Veila could probably gain a personal invitation from Mahj once he became Zaltin-ari, but then she'd be closely watched.

Without an official invitation, only with great skill and luck could one hope to breach the Crimson Tower. Veila knew she possessed these prerequisites, but she also possessed one thing more, which guided her past the front gates without so much as a grapnel thrown or wall scaled: an expansive wardrobe.

Any good thief kept a supply of disguises to help them move freely through their city, and Veila Jyn was a very good thief. She'd long ago acquired the full Crimson Warder regalia and made a close study of their patterns and practices. Just in case she might one day need to acquire some rare object of value within the Crimson Tower.

It wasn't too difficult to shadow a large patrol and slip into their ranks as they returned to the Crimson Tower for Mahj's coronation. From there, Veila's red uniform gave her freedom of the palace, which allowed her to join the patrol assigned to escort the new Zaltin-ari.

Veila found Mahj pacing in an opulent red and gold chamber, surrounded by his favorite foods. From the ranks of the red-clad guard, she watched him pluck a square of purple cheese, sip sweet butter-cream, and savor a lush green olive.

With a loud clanking, the chamber's great doors opened and in walked a tall man with a close-cropped white beard and long crimson robe.

"I am the Zaltin of Ishri," the man said. "I trust all is to your liking, Master Garustar?"

The Zaltin resembled a kindly grandfather, with a warm smile and laugh lines around his mouth. When Veila studied his eyes, though, she saw more. The Zaltin reminded her of the cruel men who bred dogs for fighting pits. The sparkle in his eyes might have been amusement—so long as the animal performed as trained.

Mahj bowed. "It's an honor to meet you, sire."

"Once you step through this doorway," the Zaltin said, "you will be in my—excuse me—*your* throne room. After your coronation, those attending will do anything you command."

The Zaltin proclaimed Mahj Zaltin-ari before a host of cheering Ishrians while Veila watched for signs of trouble. After the coronation, she continued to watch as neighbor, friend, and relative petitioned Mahj for favors in the throne room—including several petitioners from the Restful Shade. Mahj's family joined him for lunch in the Jade Gardens, and his children played among emerald statues of winged elephants, three-headed giraffes, and crystal unicorns.

She watched as Mahj, after a pointed look from Dyan, declined to visit the Harem of Shades, which contained the ghosts of the most famous courtesans of Ishri. She watched him sip the Wine of the Ancients, though from his expression, Veila could tell he found the vintage disappointing. She waited for an opportunity to warn her friend, but as his day drew to a close, none came.

The Zaltin promised Mahj he would meet the rest of the ruling council at the end of his reign. When the bells tolled at sunset, Mahj kissed his children goodnight and told them to relish their one and only night at the castle. Then the Zaltin's retinue of Crimson Warders, with Veila in tow, escorted Mahj down a long stone passage leading deep beneath the earth. With every step, Veila felt the jaws of the trap closing around them.

Their path ended at a gargantuan blood-red marble wall displaying a bizarre tableau of crimson sculptures. Each sculpture seemed to be a man or woman in various states of drowning into the red marble. At the far end of the massive scene, fingertips and hands stuck out from the wall, and at the closer end, a red-stone man was sunk to his waist, desperately reaching outward. The craftsmanship was as superb as it was disturbing. All the sculptures looked terrified; all seemed to be attempting to flee

"Welcome, Zaltin-ari of Ishri, to your council room," said the Zaltin as he emerged from the shadows.

"What is this?" said Mahj as the Crimson Wardens seized him.

"I've grown bored with monologues over the centuries," the Zaltin replied. "They give would-be heroes a chance to make their move. Wouldn't you agree, Mistress Jyn?"

Before she could draw her dagger, the Crimson Warders grabbed Veila's arms and tore off her red veil.

"Hello, Zaltin," said Veila, feigning a bravado she did not feel.

"Hello, little thief."

"How did you know?" Veila asked.

"You are skilled, Mistress Jyn, but I can sense when my spell is threatened," the Zaltin answered. He turned to his guard. "Place the Zaltin-ari within."

"Wait!" Veila cried as the Crimson Warders dragged Mahj forward.

"Yes?" the Zaltin said, stopping the soldiers with an upraised finger.

"Take me instead. He has a family."

The sorcerer-king threw his head back and laughed. "You think you can just substitute yourself, thief? The Heart of Ishri must feed on one who *has ruled*."

"Please. I would do anything to save my friend."

"Your sentiment is noble," the Zaltin said, his eyes flashing. "To reward it, I will feed you both to the Heart of Ishri. Who knows? Perhaps the city has a taste for thieves."

The Crimson Warders shoved both Veila and Mahj against the red marble wall. Veila screamed as the red stone immediately clung to her, creeping over her arms and up her torso. She looked over at Mahj, an expression of stunned horror on his face as the red wall crawled up his struggling body. Instead of solid stone, the scarlet surface felt fluid and alive. She could feel it moving up her neck toward her face, feel the Heart of Ishri pulling her into itself.

"My one regret, Master Garustar, is that we cannot enjoy your Feast Day cake next year. My appreciation for the sweeter things in life has grown over the centuries, and yours are the best cakes I've tasted in several generations. Ah well, I'll simply have to savor this one." As the Zaltin finished speaking, the red marble at the tower's base encased Veila and Mahj in a glowing layer of red glaze. With a satisfied smile, the sorcerer-king marched from the chamber with his Crimson Warders.

Slowly, the red stone grew thicker over Veila and Mahj. Veila could neither hear nor see. She wondered if this was how babes felt before birth, cocooned in warm, sticky wetness—though they probably didn't feel her horror.

Then something tickled the edge of Veila's perception.

What's this? Two meals?

It wasn't a voice one could hear; the words made themselves known in her head, like icicles in her mind. *Yet one is flavorless. You have not ruled, have not decided anyone's fate save your own.*

Veila floated in the nothingness, unsure what to say.

Yet this...

Something tugged Mother Spider's bracelet.

Part of us recognizes this, has felt its magic before. We feed on the king's blood. You are not a ruler and you carry magic part of us knew.

. . .

Who or what are you?

The chorus of voices came together as one. She even sensed Mahj in there, struggling to keep from being absorbed into the Heart of Ishri.

I'm no ruler, Veila answered with her mind. Just an acquirer of objects of great value.

The voices buzzed. How do you come to wear the spider-woman's ward? She was married to one of us.

She gave it to me, Veila replied, to find out what happened to her husband.

She heard a sadness run through the collective voices.

Why were you fed to us? the Heart of Ishri whined. We require the blood of kings and you are no king, not even a paltry day-long ruler like those we've subsisted on.

What answer could she give that would keep the Heart from destroying her or Mahj? Veila didn't know, but she did recall an old trick from her youth: when captured, answer a question with a question. *Why don't you tell me your story?* Veila asked back. *I imagine the history of such an august entity as yourself is far more interesting than my little life.*

For a long time, there was no answer. Then the voice in the dark told Veila a story.

A thousand years ago, a powerful Zaltin ruled Ishri. To honor his many years of rule, a djinn flew into the Zaltin's court and proffered a cherry wood chest. Inside was a single block of pure white marble.

The Zaltin didn't know what to say. Yes, the marble was beautiful, but it seemed a poor tribute from one as powerful as the djinn.

"This is no mere marble block," the djinn explained. "What you see is the heart of a castle, of a whole city itself, if you let it grow."

The Zaltin seemed fascinated. "What must one do, to grow a whole city?"

"There is but one thing a city needs for it to grow, oh great Zaltin."

"And that is?"

"The blood of kings," said the djinn.

The Zaltin grew still. "Explain."

The djinn bowed. "If you water this marble block with a few drops of your blood, it will grow, so in ten years you'll have a castle, and after a hundred, a whole new city."

The Zaltin thanked the djinn for the gift, but he ordered the cherry wood chest locked away. For the Zaltin, powerful though he was, had one great fear. He could not abide pain; shedding blood—even a drop

—terrified him. The thought of his own death filled his sleep with nightmares.

Shortly after, a great fire broke out and consumed most of the city and the palace. The people cried out for help and the Zaltin remembered the marble block.

How much blood, the Zaltin wondered, would such a thing need to grow to a new city quickly? Must he sacrifice himself? How would Ishri survive the loss of their king? Without his guidance, even with a new city, they would be lost. Sheep with no shepherd. Perhaps these thoughts only justified the truth within—that though the Zaltin had been good to his people, he was not willing to sacrifice even a drop of his own blood for them.

The Zaltin fell asleep in the chamber where the marble block was kept and had a strange dream that night. The next morning, he emerged and called his counselors. He told them he had been building a new city in secret, a refuge in case of emergency.

To celebrate this new fortress and commence his peoples' exodus, the Zaltin would enact a new tradition.

The Heart of Ishri fell silent.

To grow you faster and keep you fed, the Zaltin created the Zaltin-ari? asked Veila.

To keep me fed and keep himself from death, said the Heart of Ishri. I can feed on the king's blood at any time, but by the nature of the forgetting spell the Zaltin cast, he may only gain immortality from a Zaltin-ari but once a year.

Veila thought hard about how to phrase her proposal.

What if you fed on the Zaltin himself, who has ruled for a millennium?

From within Veila's stone cocoon it sounded as though the Heart of Ishri giggled.

A millennium of tyrannical cruelty, ruling with an iron fist and god-like power? Oh, what a delectable delight the true Zaltin would be! We could sustain ourselves on him alone for a thousand years or more.

What if I delivered him to you? asked Veila.

Silence. Then, after an endless moment—

Can you do so?

I am an acquirer of objects of great value. If you release me, I promise it will be done.

The Heart fell silent for a time. It had no face, no body language

71

for Veila to read, but she could feel its desire to devour the immortal Zaltin.

Very well, the Heart of Ishri said. *Done.*

I require one thing more, Veila said.

Is your freedom not enough?

My friend, the baker. Release him as well.

The Heart of Ishri rumbled. Releasing him would weaken me. Why should I not keep him as hostage to ensure you fulfill your task?

He is necessary to my plan.

The Heart of Ishri paused. Veila heard a susurration of whispers and wondered if it consulted with its various captives.

Done and done.

A deafening crack sounded, but Veila couldn't cover her ears. A blazing light smote Veila through the darkness.

Another snap followed by more beams of light.

The cracks grew louder, the light blinding, and Veila was thrown back into the world of mortals. She looked up and saw a familiar face.

"Mahj," she croaked. It took Veila a moment to gather her bearings. As her friend helped her to her feet, Veila noticed they were both covered in crimson dust.

"Are you all right?" Mahj asked.

"I've been better," Veila said, "We should leave, before the Zaltin realizes we're free."

Veila took Mahj by the arm and began to run, tracing their steps back to the surface. Many Warders still patrolled the Crimson Tower and it took all Veila's skill to avoid them. As they neared the exit, the baker tried to speak, but Veila covered his mouth and dragged him behind a stack of crates as a red squadron marched past. Outside, the moon glowed full and bright. Veila gave it a baleful glance—it would be far too easy for a Crimson Warder to find them on the streets.

"We have to get up high," she said.

Mahj didn't move. "Then what?" he asked bitterly. "I don't suppose you have a spare army we might use?"

"We're going to see Mother Spider," Veila said.

Mahj hadn't worked the streets in years, but he still recognized that name.

"You know Mother Spider?" he asked.

"We met yesterday," said Veila. "It was she who gave me this." She held up the silver hair bound around her wrist. It glittered in the moonlight. "She warned me of your peril. Perhaps she can help us now, though it will not come cheap."

"My family is in the Crimson Tower." Mahj curled his hands into fists. "I'd give my heart twice over to keep them safe."

"The rooftops are our best chance. Can you manage?" Veila asked.

"For my family? Yes," Mahj said with a determined look.

Veila's muscles were stiff from their recent imprisonment, and she worried Mahj would cramp or fail, but her friend still retained a remnant of his old skill. The two met with no trouble on their path across the rooftops, for these late in-between hours are the province of bakers and thieves.

The shadows of Ishri seemed deeper around Mother Spider's building; the moon above shone less brightly. It was said Mother Spider lived alone, though many strange voices could be heard inside the house throughout the day. The only time her front door opened was for customers.

Veila tried not to shiver as the front door creaked open before she could knock. Small lamps flickered to life, one after the other, leading to another door at the end of a dimly lit hallway. The thief and the baker stepped into the house and the front door gently closed behind them.

Like a moth to the flame, Veila thought. *Or a fly to a web.* She tried not to notice the cobwebs brush against her face as they followed the lamps to Mother Spider's parlor. The old woman sat waiting for them. She did not speak when the two friends came inside, merely gestured for them to sit down. The old woman had wrapped herself in blankets and shadows, sitting in a rocking chair, creaking back and forth. For some time, she studied them both, her long, bent fingers steepled beneath her sharp chin.

"How was it done?" Mother Spider finally whispered.

Mahj described how the red marble wall within the Crimson Tower absorbed all the Zaltin-ari. Veila told of her conversation with the Heart of Ishri. When she described how part of the entity recognized Mother Spider's bracelet, the old woman's eyes blazed. Veila then told how she'd bargained with the Heart of Ishri, promising it the Zaltin in exchange for their release.

"Did you find it strange the Heart of Ishri required no assurance you would keep your bargain?" Mother Spider asked.

"I did," Veila admitted. "We've had no time to contemplate the matter. Staying ahead of the Crimson Warders has been our priority."

The old woman reached out and plucked something off Mahj's shoulder. In the faint light, Veila could see a few grains of red dust on the old woman's fingers.

"Ah," the old woman said softly. "Here is the Heart's insurance."

"It is but red dust," said Mahj. "Crumblings from the Heart. We both were covered in such after our release."

A grim smile flitted across Mother Spider's face. "It is much more, Mahj Garustar. Every part of that red wall is filled with Ishri's magic." She took a small vial from her robe and brushed the red dust therein. "Should you attempt to flee the city or cry off your bargain with the Heart of Ishri, this red dust would serve a far more nefarious purpose."

"Is it poison?" Mahj asked.

"It would render you a statue," said Mother Spider, "just like it did when you were at the Heart. After which, you would be collected by the Crimson Warders and rejoin the Heart of Ishri."

The old woman stoppered the vial and tucked it away in her robes as both Veila and Mahj began to brush all the red dust off themselves.

Veila looked thoughtful. "What if we used the red dust on the Zaltin himself?"

"Yes…that could work," said Mother Spider slowly. "And your bargain with the city's heart could be fulfilled."

"Then our way forward is clear," Veila said.

The door to Mother Spider's parlor slammed shut and all the lamps went out, plunging the parlor into darkness. Veila reached for her daggers, but before she could move, thick webs bound her wrists and ankles. Mahj was similarly immobilized.

"I care nothing for your bargain," said Mother Spider, her voice low and guttural, seeming to come from everywhere in the room. "The Heart of Ishri deprived me of a husband. I wish to kill it *and* the Zaltin. You have given me the means to do both. If I keep you here, the Heart will go hungry and the magic preserving the Zaltin will fail."

The webbing began to grow thicker and thicker, crawling up Veila's wrists and torso. In its own way, it was more horrible than any crimson wall. Hot breath brushed her hair as many pattering footsteps drew closer to her. It was all Veila could do to keep from screaming. Before the webs could cover her mouth, she shouted, "There's a better way!"

The creeping webs grew still.

"A better way?" said the old woman in the dark. "What do you mean, Veila Jyn?"

"The Heart of Ishri is a magical device the Zaltin has perverted to foul purpose," said Veila. "The Heart is desperate for the life of the Zaltin. Perhaps desperate enough to trade him for the Zaltin-ari who still live."

"How would you convince the Heart to release the others?" asked Mother Spider.

"From what the Heart claimed," Veila said, "since the Zaltin has ruled for a thousand years, it could subsist on him for just as long. It wouldn't need the Zaltin-ari."

Veila felt the silk coils release her and gasped with relief. The lamps lit once more. Veila and Mahj found themselves standing before Mother Spider, who sat in her rocking chair as though she'd never left it.

She felt weighed and judged by Mother Spider's gaze. "How do you propose we subdue the Zaltin, then? For his magic is more powerful than mine."

Now that her hands were free, Veila slipped her favorite dagger from its spot and began to juggle the blade back and forth in complicated patterns, conjuring up a plan.

"We will stop the Zaltin with trickery, guile,"—Veila stopped and studied Mahj a moment before grinning wildly—"and delicious baked goods."

Great and sumptuous was the Ishri Feast Day celebration in the banquet hall of the Crimson Tower. The most important Ishrians lounged on couches, in booths, or around long tables, talking, laughing, listening to musicians play ballads extolling the virtues of Ishri and their immortal Zaltin. They munched on honey-glazed almonds, they grazed on curried lamb, they feasted on pheasant stuffed with plum figs. Wine was drunk by the tun, coffee and beer by the gallon.

The Zaltin sat at the high table above them all, sampling every dish, giving nods of approval when necessary. To his side sat the Garustar family; they alone didn't seem to appreciate the feast's gaiety.

As the guests finished the final dinner course, two veiled servants wheeled in the great Feast Day cake of Ishri. The attendees of the feast sighed in wonder. Seven layers high, each layer coated in the same glistening cherry frosting, it was a masterwork of sugar and glaze.

Fireworks exploded in the sky as the great cake's procession halted before the Zaltin's throne. The city's ruler stood, and the banquet hall grew silent, waiting for the Zaltin's traditional celebratory speech before he ate the first slice of Feast Day cake. He stood and gazed over his citizens, but just as he was about to step down from the dais, the Zaltin halted and stared hard at the cake.

"There is rot in Ishri," the Zaltin finally announced, to the crowd's shock. "A foul conspiracy seeks to change the way we've lived for a thousand years. Luckily for you all, our city has a ruler who knows how to deal with such threats."

A snap of the Zaltin's fingers summoned a squadron of Crimson Warders.

"There," said the Zaltin, pointing at the towering confection that stood before him. The guards looked confused, so he added, "Someone's hiding in the cake, fools!"

The Crimson Warders found it best never to question the Zaltin if they wished to retain their employment and their life. As they approached the dessert with drawn swords, the lowest level of the cake exploded as Veila Jyn leapt out, a scarlet-coated dagger in hand. She tripped the first Crimson Warder who charged her, elbowed the second who tried to grab her from behind, and flowed like water around the sword stroke of the third attacker before hurling her dagger at the Zaltin. Her blade flew true, but just before it could pierce the Zaltin's skin, it rebounded off the air as if striking hidden glass.

"Must I do everything myself?" growled the Zaltin. Dark nimbuses of power briefly emanated around the sorcerer-king's palms. He curled his fingers, and Veila was lifted upward as if by invisible hands.

The Zaltin released his grip, and the aura of magic vanished. Veila fell to the ground, knocking the breath from her lungs, and was immediately tackled by Crimson Warders. Other Warders surrounded the servants who'd wheeled the cake in, tearing away their veils to reveal Mahj Garustar and Mother Spider. Upon seeing her husband, Dyan and her children gave a loud cry, but with a gesture from the Zaltin, the Warders seized them, too.

The sorcerer-king strode down from his elevated throne and examined Mahj closely. "I wondered how your family still remembered you,

Mahj Garustar. Have no fear, Zaltin-ari, you will be fed to the Heart once again."

With a growl, Veila lunged at the Zaltin, but the Crimson Guard held her fast.

The Zaltin next walked over to Mother Spider. "So, you finally crept out of your web to challenge me, little weaver. Indeed, I'd hoped to draw you out after choosing your husband to feed the Heart all those years ago, but you hid then, like a coward."

With her arms pinned to her sides by Crimson Warders, Mother Spider looked surprisingly frail. She tried to spit on the Zaltin, but the sorcerer-king stepped out of the way with a smirk.

"Finally, the little thief. I mean really, Mistress Jyn, hiding in a cake?" said the Zaltin. "That was your master plan, to stab me like a common assassin? Most disappointing."

The guests of the feast stared at the floor uncomfortably. The benevolent mask of their ruler had been pulled askew. They found themselves wondering why they let such a creature rule their city.

"And to waste this magnificent Feast Day cake!" cried the Zaltin. He circled the remnants of the enormous confection with greedy eyes. "Especially the final cake of Mahj Garustar." Even half-ruined, the great pastry looked delectable, its yellow cake moist and soft, its cherry frosting shining bright. The Zaltin swiped a finger across the frosting.

The moment it touched his skin, Veila Jyn smiled.

The Zaltin's eyes widened as a thin layer of red burst from the frosting onto his fingers and began to cocoon him. He tried to run, but as he turned, his legs were encased in crimson clay. He tried to cast a devastating spell, but as he gestured with his fingers, they became trapped in scarlet stone. He tried to command his guards, but as he opened his mouth, crimson flooded over his lips, freezing them in a blood-red shout.

For a moment, the whole hall stood as frozen as the Zaltin. When the Crimson Warders reached for weapons, Mother Spider struck. Gray hair shot out from her robes, thick as jungle vines, wrapping the guards nearest to her in layers of webbing, hoisting them up high until they hung from the ceiling. Those guards who weren't immediately subdued fled as if ten thousand demons chased them.

"I hid within as insurance," Veila said to the Zaltin's statue as she began brushing cake off her vest. Her original plan had simply been to serve the sorcerer-king the treated cake. But they knew the Zaltin's magic could warn him of danger, so they placed Veila inside the pastry with a dust-coated blade should the Zaltin try to skip his just dessert. "Mostly, we hoped you'd just eat the damn cake."

It hadn't been easy for Mahj to reconstruct his original cake around Veila, nor to mix the red dust into a frosting so tempting even a nigh-immortal Zaltin couldn't resist its allure, but he was an even better baker than he'd been a thief. He'd told Veila the Heart's crumble actually gave the frosting the deep red color he'd been hoping to achieve.

"The job's not yet done," said Veila, turning to Mother Spider. "I believe we still need to accomplish the final part of our bargain?"

Mother Spider nodded. Several thick strands of webbing coiled around the shocked statue of the Zaltin. "Time to serve the Heart of Ishri the meal it craves."

With the help of Veila and the Garustars, Mother Spider dragged the Zaltin's statue before the Heart of Ishri. For a moment, all Dyan and Mother Spider could do was stare in horror at the macabre statues still embedded in the walls. As they drew closer, a space in the red marble opened, just large enough to fit the encased Zaltin.

But Veila made no move to sate the Heart of Ishri's hunger.

"Heart of Ishri, before we feed you this feast of a thousand years," said Veila, "we ask you to release all the Zaltin-ari who still live."

For a moment, Veila worried the Heart would refuse her request and she would be left to face an angry Mother Spider. Then, dozens of statues erupted from the crimson wall and landed sprawling on the floor, coated in red dust.

The Crimson Tower began to shudder. Cracks formed along its walls.

"The palace. It's collapsing!" Dyan shouted.

"Quickly, before the Heart fails," Mother Spider commanded, her thin hands grasping an arm of the immobile statue. Together, they shoved the Zaltin into the red wall. As the marble merged with the Zaltin, Veila fancied she could hear the trapped ruler begging for mercy. The Heart of Ishri absorbed him with a gurgling cry, and the palace grew still and whole.

Veila heard another cry and saw Mother Spider embrace an old man sitting up from the floor. It was, she decided, time to leave. Best to be gone before awkward questions were asked. Besides, during her time as a Crimson Warder, Veila had noticed several treasures in the palace she felt sure no one would miss. With a nod to Mahj, she slipped away.

He seemed to have anticipated Veila's plan, for when she finally left the Crimson Tower, she found him and his family waiting for her just outside the main gate.

"Thank you, sister," Mahj said, as all the Garustars enveloped her in a hug. Here at last was a trap from which Veila Jyn could not escape. Not that she'd ever wish to.

"It was nothing," said Veila as she disentangled herself.

"Nonsense," Dyan said. "We can never repay all you have done for us."

Veila stared at the floor, embarrassed. How to answer such a compliment? While many riches had passed through her hands over the years, none were so great as the trust of Mahj and his family. She knew how precious such a gift was, how rare.

She was, after all, an acquirer of objects of great value.

ABOUT PATRICK HURLEY

Patrick Hurley is a writer and editor living Seattle. He's had fiction published in dozens of markets, including Abyss & Apex, Cosmic Roots & Eldritch Shores, Flame Tree Press, and Paizo's Pathfinder universe. In 2017, he participated in the Taos Toolbox Writer's Workshop taught by Nancy Kress and Walter Jon Williams. In 2018, he was a finalist for the Baen Fantasy Award. Patrick works as an editor for Paizo and is a proud member of SFWA and the Dreamcrashers.

Website: https://patrickhurleywrites.com
Facebook: hurlepat
Twitter: @hurlepat
Email: hurlepat7@gmail.com

4

THE DEVIL WENT DOWN TO THE DANIEL WEBSTER CHARTER SCHOOL PTA'S ANNUAL HALLOWEEN CHILI COOK-OFF FUNDRAISER

BY ERIC JAMES STONE

OK, OK, IT wasn't really that the Devil went down to the chili cook-off. He was summoned, with "up" being the most likely direction. The title's just worded that way because of the Charlie Daniels song. (If you don't know which song, Google it.) But the rest of it's true. Here's how it happened.

Every year, the judges gave out enough awards so that each contestant got one. You might think that meant they were all happy to get an award, but everybody knew only two prizes really mattered: Best-Tasting Chili and Hottest Chili.

And as far as Margie Simmons was concerned, only one mattered. She had been the undisputed champion of Hottest Chili for six years before Hugo Casares won an upset victory using ghost peppers in his chili, and she'd had to settle for Reddest Chili. Since then, she had only won Hottest Chili once, and now she and Hugo were tied at seven wins apiece.

Over the past four years, Margie and Hugo had both tried their hands at growing their own ultra-hot chili peppers. (Neither of them would even think of just pouring in some pure capsaicin—that would be cheating.)

Margie was determined to beat Hugo this year.

At this point, seeing as how the title of this story promised a visit from the Devil, you might suspect that Margie was so determined to win that she would sell her soul to be able to grow the hottest chili peppers in the world. Or perhaps that Hugo had already done so, or maybe he even was the Devil himself.

But if you actually knew Margie and Hugo, such suspicions would be ridiculous. They were both God-fearing folk—Margie a Methodist, Hugo a Catholic—and this annual competition was nothing more than a friendly rivalry between them. The most important thing for both of them was raising funds for the Daniel Webster Charter School PTA in order to support the students.

No, the Devil didn't show up on account of anything done by Margie or Hugo, at least not directly. It was Margie's grandson, Layton, and Hugo's daughter, Alejandra, who helped summon Old Scratch himself to the school gym.

Not on purpose, mind you. The chili cook-off was traditionally held on the Friday before Halloween (unless, as on this particular year, Halloween was on a Friday, in which case it was held the day of), in conjunction with the trunk-or-treat in the school parking lot and before the school dance. As members of the student council, Layton and Alejandra were in the gym the Thursday before the big event, helping to put up decorations, and someone—nobody ever remembered who, exactly—suggested making a giant pentagram on the floor.

While others were putting up fake tombstones and black crepe paper, Layton and Alejandra used measuring tape, twine, and chalk to sketch out a mathematically precise pentagram within a circle that was almost as wide as the basketball court. The circle turned out to be a little over 13.31 meters in diameter—a detail that would be utterly insignificant if not for the fact that this meant the circle had an area of 666 square cubits.

The Devil, as they say, is in the details. And he doesn't use the metric system.

Still, a pentagram and a little numerology wouldn't usually have been sufficient to summon the Devil.

But Jamaal Washington, standing by one point of the star, lit a candle to check out how spooky a jack-o-lantern with a devil's face carved into it looked, even though he knew they were only supposed to use fake candles because of the fire code. At the exact same time, Scott Hwang, kneeling by another point of the star, accidentally cut his finger with a box cutter he was using to carve tombstone shapes out of cardboard, causing a drop of blood to land within the pentagram. And also at the exact same time, Madison Morris, sitting by a third point of the star, painting cardboard tombstones gray, just happened to be preparing for tomorrow's Latin test by conjugating the verb *vocare* (to summon).

Add all that to the Devil's two-centuries-old grudge against Daniel Webster, and it was close enough.

It started as a whirlwind in the central pentagon of the pentagram. Layton and Alejandra, who had been standing near the center admiring their handiwork, were flung across the gym floor, each of them finally sliding to a halt on the two empty points of the star.

Sparks spun up from the vortex and out into the gym. Several strands of crepe paper caught fire and had to be stomped out by students nearby.

The pentagon in the middle of the pentagram filled with inky smoke, and the smell of sulfur pervaded the atmosphere. The smoke gradually cleared, revealing the Devil in the center of the pentagram. In his tailored shark-gray suit, he looked like the CEO of a Fortune 500 company, except for the horns and the glowing red eyes. His face was the spitting image of what was carved onto the pumpkin Jamaal had lit up.

You might think that, it being the night before Halloween, the people in the gym would mistake the Devil for someone in a devil costume. But everyone there had no doubt who he was, for they could feel his sheer malevolent presence.

"Well, you summoned me, so I'm here," said the Devil, his quiet voice carrying quite clearly to everyone in the gym. "How can I be of service?"

Alejandra crossed herself.

Nobody said anything.

The Devil looked at Jamaal, Scott, Madison, Alejandra, and Layton at each point of the pentagram. "I don't have all day. What do you desire in exchange for your souls?"

Layton managed to find his voice. "It was an accident. We didn't mean to summon you."

"An 'accident'? You summoned me—Lucifer, Satan, Beelzebub, the Beast, the Father of Lies, the Prince of Darkness—to a school gym by 'accident'?"

Layton's mouth went dry.

Alejandra managed to whisper, "Yes."

"It's supposed to be pretty straightforward," the Devil said. "I get summoned, I make a deal, I get a soul." He sighed and looked around the room, taking in the Halloween decorations. His gaze stopped at the west end of the gym, where a hand-painted banner declared "Halloween Chili Cook-Off."

"A chili cook-off?" He took a long, deep sniff. "I don't smell it."

"It's not till tomorrow night," Layton managed to say.

"Ah, excellent. I'll come back then to enter my chili."

"You…You're going to make chili?" Alejandra asked.

"Make it? Child, who do you think *invented* chili? I'll make you a deal: If my chili tomorrow is not the hottest chili anyone here's ever tasted, I'll give your PTA enough to fund it for the next ten years."

Jamaal said, "So, you're not going to take our souls?"

The Devil chuckled, revealing very white, too-sharp teeth. "Not tonight. You're lucky I like a good chili. But if I win Hottest Chili tomorrow, the souls of you five are mine."

His body began to spin, faster and faster, while his head remained still. (Later, each of the five students at the points of the pentagram would swear he was looking straight at them the whole time.) Smoke and sparks rose around him, then faded away, leaving the central pentagon empty.

Between the student council, volunteers, and faculty advisors, there were twenty-five people in that gym during the Devil's apparition. None of the adults thought to pull out their smartphones and record what was happening, but four of the teenagers did.

Of course, they immediately wanted to post the video online. Unfortunately, when viewed, all four videos consisted of nothing but random red-and-black static on the screen, with an audio track of distorted, unintelligible noise. Someone had the bright idea that maybe the noise would make sense if played backward, and downloaded an app to reverse-play the video. But it sounded exactly the same whether played forward or backward.

Meanwhile, the rest of the teenagers used texts and social media to spread word about what had happened. The following is typical of how those conversations went:

OMG the device just showed up in the gym 4 realz!!!

???

Stupid autocorrect! The DEVELOPER!!!!!

STAN!!!

Who's Stan?

Stan!!! The father of Liza!!!!!

I thought Liza's dad was named Ryan.

The Princess of Disney!!

Lucy!!

Beers of Bud!!

R u drunk?

Probably!!

I DID NOT SEND THAT LAST MESSAGE!!!!!

Still, despite the communication glitches, enough word-of-mouth got around for people to decide that something weird was going on, and a number of people who had been planning to go to the chili cook-off decided to stay home. About the same number of people who had not been planning to go decided to see what all the fuss was about, so it was pretty much a wash.

Layton and Alejandra decided not to tell their families that the Devil would claim their souls if he won the Hottest Chili contest. Keeping a secret from their families was not a new thing for them: they were dating, and part of the thrill of their relationship was the Romeo-and-Juliet forbiddenness of their love due to the Hottest Chili rivalry. They would have been both relieved and disappointed to learn that neither family would have had any objection to their dating.

"Grandma," said Layton after he got home, where he'd lived with her ever since his parents had died in a car wreck, "what can I do to help you make the hottest chili ever for the cook-off?"

Meanwhile, Alejandra told her dad, "I want to help you make tomorrow's chili the hottest in the world."

So it was that those two teens, feeling dread mixed with hope, spent precious time with their families in preparation for the Halloween chili cook-off that would decide their fate.

The next night was Friday. Halloween. Over two hundred people showed up for the fundraiser, at ten dollars a head. That was about average, but the gym felt more crowded than normal because everyone avoided stepping inside the circle around the pentagram.

As the entry deadline of five o'clock approached, the buzz of conversation died down, and more and more people began staring at the center of the pentagram.

"Last call for entries in the chili cook-off," said Mayor Vestry, using the microphone at the podium.

He had been the emcee for the cook-off the last six years. He was also one of the chili judges. And he just happened to be Madison Morris's stepdad. Madison had told him everything, and despite being a politician, he was a good enough man that he tried his best to believe her, even though he didn't believe in Satan. So he was hoping to close off entries before the Devil put in an appearance.

"Last call," he said as the red second hand on the wall clock swept up toward the twelve. "And...entries are closed. Let the tasting begin!"

Five very relieved teenagers, plus a mostly confused crowd of people unsure whether to be disappointed or relieved, gathered near the tables with the chili pots to watch the judging.

Now, you might think that was somewhat anticlimactic, and you'd be right, except for the fact that five minutes earlier, nobody had paid much attention to a man in a dark suit filling out a chili cook-off entry form at a table under the "Halloween Chili Cook-Off" sign. He had written Nick Morningstar as his name and handed the form, along with a giant black pot, to one of the volunteers. Then he had joined the crowd in staring at the center of the pentagram.

That man now slipped his way to the front of the crowd, somehow managing to do so without touching anybody. As Mayor Vestry ladled a couple of spoonfuls of chili from the first pot into a small, numbered bowl on a tray, the man said, "Hold on a minute. There are name cards in front of these pots. Isn't the judging anonymous?"

Mayor Vestry stopped. "I'm sorry, Mister..."

"Morningstar. Nick Morningstar."

On hearing the man's voice, five teenagers felt chills run up their spines.

"Mr. Morningstar," said Mayor Vestry. "A pleasure to meet you. Anyways, members of the panel are all upright, honest folk, who will judge the chili based on its merits, not who made it."

"Well, OK," said the man. "I'll take your word for it. Carry on." He slipped back into the crowd.

Madison walked up to Mayor Vestry and quietly said, "Dad, that was him."

Mayor Vestry blinked rapidly. "Him? But he didn't have horns or anything."

"It's the same voice," Madison said. "Please, no matter what, don't let him win Hottest Chili."

"I'll take care of it," he whispered, then proceeded with ladling chili samples into the bowls on his tray.

Ten minutes later, the judges had turned in their scorecards, and Mayor Vestry stepped up to the podium to read the results. His forehead sweated profusely as he gave out awards for Best-Looking Chili, Chunkiest Chili, Smoothest Chili, Mildest Chili, Meatiest Chili, and a dozen more. Finally, there were only four chilis without an award: Margie's, Hugo's, Rita Washington's, and Nick Morningstar's.

Now, if you were paying close attention during the scene in the gym, you might remember that Jamaal's last name is Washington, and put two and two together to conclude that this Rita Washington was related to Jamaal, and maybe speculate further that he had told her she needed to make the hottest chili ever in order to save his soul.

Of course they were related—you go far enough back on the family tree, and every human is related. But they weren't related closely enough that they had ever spoken even one word between them.

No, the reason she was one of the last four was simple: Rita Washington usually made a very tasty chili, and no one would be surprised in the least at her winning the Best-Tasting Chili award, which was traditionally presented last.

But it was quite a shock when Mayor Vestry announced her as the winner of the Most Creative Chili award.

Only three chilis remained.

"We have an unprecedented situation this evening," said Mayor Vestry. "We have a tie for Hottest Chili: Margie Simmons and Hugo Casares. And the winner of the Best-Tasting Chili award is Nick Morningstar. Let's give them all a hand."

The crowd's applause was cut short by a quiet voice that carried around the gym. "You're lying."

"What?" said Mayor Vestry. "Uh, no, these are the results." He held up a paper.

The man calling himself Nick Morningstar approached the

podium. Horns sprouted from his forehead, and his eyes lit up with a red glow.

The crowd backed away from him.

"I'm the Father of Lies," the Devil said. "Don't think you can lie to me. You obviously doctored the results to give me the Best-Tasting Chili award instead of the Hottest Chili award. Deny it at your peril."

Mayor Vestry wiped the sweat from his brow. "OK, you got me. But what was I supposed to do, let you take these poor, innocent kids? They didn't mean to summon you. It's not right."

The Devil shrugged. "Five people summoned me. I figure I'm owed five souls."

"Then"—Mayor Vestry swallowed hard—"then take my soul instead of Madison's."

Hugo said, "Take mine instead of Alejandra's."

Scott's mother and Jamaal's father both volunteered themselves to take their sons' places.

All eyes turned to Margie.

"Grandma?" Layton said.

"I'm thinking," she said. "Give me a moment."

"Grandma!" Layton stared at her with wide eyes.

"I don't believe it," Margie said. "There's no way Hugo and I tied for Hottest Chili."

Mayor Vestry held up his hands. "Fine, you're right. After tasting the Devil's chili, our mouths were so fried we didn't even bother to taste yours and Hugo's. We just gave you the tie."

Margie smiled grimly. "I knew it. So nobody actually knows which chili is really the hottest." She turned to the Devil and said, "You can't claim any of these souls unless your chili really is the hottest. And we can't rely on anyone else to judge it, so there's only one way to settle the question between us."

The Devil cocked an eyebrow. "And that is?"

"A chili-eating contest. If you can eat more of my chili than I can of yours, you win five souls. If I can eat more of yours than you can of mine, you get no souls."

"And if we tie?"

"No souls."

"Well, that puts me at a disadvantage."

"Fine. If we tie, you get my soul, no one else's."

"One soul for one summoning. I can live with that. We've got a deal."

It only took a few minutes to set up a table and chairs with both their pots of chili, a bowl and spoon for each of them, and two measuring cups.

"Mind if I go first?" the Devil asked.

"Be my guest," Margie replied.

He scooped a cup of Margie's chili into his bowl. But instead of using a spoon, he picked up the bowl and drank down the chili in one long slurp. He plopped the bowl down on the table and opened his mouth as if to speak.

But then his eyes bulged, and he raised his head up, opened his jaws wider than any human possibly could, and belched forth a cloud of smoke like a coal-burning-factory smokestack. Lightning crackled in the smoke.

After about forty seconds of this, the smoke and lightning tailed off, and he closed his mouth. He shook himself all over, and finally said, "Well, that is one hot chili. I may need to take it a little slower than I thought."

Margie scooped a cup of the Devil's chili into her bowl. Using her spoon, she took one bite, then another and another. By the fifth spoonful, beads of perspiration began to appear on her forehead. As she finished off the cup with her sixteenth spoonful, rivulets flowed down her wrinkled face.

She coughed, then said, "Time for round two."

The devil scooped another cup into his bowl. This time, he used his spoon to take bite after bite. When he was halfway through, he winced as a black scorpion crawled out of his right ear and scurried up into his hair. He flicked it off with a finger, and it landed near some onlookers who immediately backed away.

By the time he finished the bowl, he'd had three scorpions escape from the right ear and two from the left.

Margie worked her way methodically through her second cup. By the end, her shoulders and chest were sopping wet, and her hands were trembling.

"Ready for round three?" she asked, voice hoarse.

The Devil took a long look at her pot, then sighed. "You willing to call it a draw?"

She scooped another cup into her bowl and ate one spoonful. "Can you match it?" she wheezed.

The Devil pulled another scorpion out of his left ear and squashed it. "I could do this all night, but, frankly, it's not worth it for five souls, or even just one. I have places to be and things to do. So I'll concede this silly little contest."

And with that, he disappeared in a puff of smoke.

Someone gave Margie a glass of cold milk, and she gulped it down, followed by three refills, without responding to people's clamorous questions.

Finally, Mayor Vestry got everyone to quiet down, and he said, "Look, Margie, I've tasted the Devil's chili, and there's no way yours was hotter than his. How on earth did you manage to beat him?"

Someone of a more philosophical mind might have said something like "Good is more powerful than evil" or "I figured love was stronger than pride," but Margie was a more practical sort, so she just shrugged and said, "Sheer stubbornness, I suppose."

She reached out her hand to Layton. "Take me home, please. I need to rest."

The crowd applauded as Layton helped her out of the gym.

Now, you'll need to be the judge on whether this last bit was just a coincidence, but later that night the convenience store closest to the school reported that all the milk in its refrigerators had been stolen. When police reviewed the security camera recordings, all they found was red-and-black static.

Oh, and one more thing. Remember how the Devil promised to fund the PTA for ten years if his wasn't the hottest chili anyone had ever tasted? Well, you might think he lied about that, him being the Father of Lies and all, but the truth of the matter is that the PTA treasurer, Hans White, noticed there was something left behind on the Devil's chair: a chili pepper about eight inches long and two-and-a-half inches across. It was made of solid gold, and it sold for about a half-million dollars.

That money would have funded the PTA for the next ten years, if Hans hadn't kept it for himself and run off to Mexico. So the Devil did get himself one soul out of the deal.

ABOUT ERIC JAMES STONE

Eric James Stone is a past Nebula Award winner, Hugo Award nominee, and Writers of the Future Contest winner. Over fifty of his stories have been published in venues such as Year's Best SF, Analog Science Fiction & Fact, and Nature. His debut novel, a science fiction thriller titled Unforgettable, published by Baen Books, has been optioned by Hollywood multiple times.

Eric's life has been filled with a variety of experiences. As the son of an immigrant from Argentina, he grew up bilingual and spent most of his childhood living in Latin America. He also lived for five years in England and became trilingual while serving a two-year mission for his church in Italy. He majored in political science at BYU (where he sang in the Russian Choir for two years) and then got a law degree from Baylor. He did political work in Washington, D.C., for several years before shifting career tracks. He now works as a systems administrator and programmer.

Eric lives in Utah with his wife, Darci, who is an award-winning author herself, in addition to being a high school science teacher and programmer.

Website: www.ericjamesstone.com
Facebook: Eric-James-Stone
Twitter: @EricJamesStone

5

HIS LADY'S FAVOR
BY K. D. JULICHER

THE FIGHTING-PIT CROWD erupted with cheers for the pair of wrestlers down on the sands. Rina fought her way through the screaming crowd, watching her footing and not the match. She clutched the cloth-wrapped gauntlet to her chest with both hands like a protective amulet. If she turned back, she'd never find the courage to beg Edrick to be her champion. Rina threaded her way between two large packs of raucous drunkards, the shadowed floor sticky under her thin-soled boots. How could he have ended up in a place like this?

Edrick was her last hope. Two years ago he'd abandoned everything. Tournaments, armor, and her. Since she'd been cast out of Master Mourial's rune forge, she had nowhere else to turn. Edrick was a slim hope but her only chance to land a new position as a runesmith.

Rina reached the far side of the crowded platform. Below, in a sectioned-off corner, the upcoming fighters and the pit team waited for the end of the match. She ducked right under the ropes and leaned over the edge. Some of the pit men were dashing water over an unconscious man. His mouth hung open. He drooled blood from the place where he'd lost two teeth. Rina cleared her throat.

Six pit men and four fighters looked up at her, all blinking back surprise.

"Get back," one of the crew snarled up at her. "No spectators allowed past the ropes."

"I'm looking for your bouncer," she said.

"Keep this up, and you'll find him, chit," the man said.

Rina hadn't come all this way to be turned aside by pit men. The pit floor was eight feet down. Tucking her gauntlet under one arm, Rina crouched, then let herself drop. She hit the ground, knees bent, and straightened up. "Your bouncer," Rina said, in her best imitation of Lord Norill's manner. "Now."

The pit boss stared at her. Rina's cloak had slipped from her shoulders. He eyed her dark hair, pulled back neatly in a tight braid and pinned behind her head, glanced at her sturdy leather-and-wool work clothes, then down at her hands. His brow furrowed. "What are you, girl?" he asked. No doubt they didn't get many women down there, and no journeyman runesmiths at all.

Rina smiled tightly. "Not your problem once you've called your bouncer," she said, and marveled at the calmness of her voice. Nothing about this afternoon had felt real, not since Owen's injury and her dismissal.

"Better fetch him, boss," one of the pit men whispered. "Look at her. Chance she's some nob's stray daughter, the way she talks."

"Looks more like a merchant girl to me," another of the crew said.

"I can hear you, you know," Rina pointed out.

"Get him," the pit boss said, and one of the men ran. "Send Huber and his man out there before the crowd start eating each other!" he added as a chant went up from the crowd—*"Blood! Blood! Blood!"*

"In here, girl," said the nearest pit man, a balding man past his prime. He opened the wooden door beside him. Rina stared into a long, white-washed stone room. Long wooden benches ran down the length of the room, while tall wooden cabinets, some locked, lined one wall. Her heart raced as she crossed the threshold. The thought of seeing Edrick again, after all this time, made her as nervous as an apprentice on her first day of runing.

"He'll be along." The pit man closed the door behind her.

Rina unwrapped the gauntlet she'd been carrying all this time. She let the linen fall away.

The gauntlet itself had been crafted by one of Lord Norill's armorsmiths. Steel, lined with wool to protect the wearer's hand, and with a leather strap and buckle to secure it, it shone even in the flickering light. She knew every inch of this gauntlet, from the tiny dent on the index finger to a thickening of the metal in the wrist. She had spent weeks working it, etching runes into every surface. This piece had convinced Master Mourial to allow her ambitious project, the suit of armor that could have won the Crucible of Armor.

"You."

She hadn't heard the far door open. Rina started at the chill in that once dear voice. Her heart felt like a runaway horse galloping in her chest. Her mouth dry, Rina turned.

Edrick stood in the doorway, looking at her, face closed off from her. More than a head taller than Rina, clothed in black close-weave fabrics, his sleeves were rolled up to his shoulders. Well-fitted boots came halfway up his calves. He wore an unfamiliar beard, lighter brown than his hair. He seemed fit, at least, so maybe he had kept up his training. His hands flexed as he stared at her. "Why are you here?" he demanded.

Words poured out of Rina, rushing forth in a surge of anger. How could he have just…moved on, made a new life for himself, without her? What sort of a life was this, anyway? "Why are you?" she asked. "A bouncer, in a pit club? When you could beat any of these…these fighting dogs, with one arm in a sling?"

"I only have to break the heads of the deserving this way," he said, his tone flat. "Besides, like you said, it wouldn't be fair sport."

"You walked away from"—*from me*—"from the tournament ring for this?" she demanded. "You were the greatest, Edrick! Nobody could stand before you in armor. You would have earned your knighthood by the end of the season! Lord Norill would have given you a place in his household. Position, and armor, and the keeping for a family," she said, tears leaping to her eyes.

Edrick hesitated. She thought there was regret in his face. "The cost was too high," he said at last.

"Instead you just walked away without even a word? Even to me?" she said.

"You know why I did," he said.

"Nobody blamed you for the accident," she said. "You tried to save him after you knocked him from the saddle. He didn't know how to use the armor, Edrick. It was his fault, not yours."

"That's what everyone said." Edrick's voice echoed hollowly around the room. "I killed a half-trained squire who had stolen his brother's armor and entered the lists because I couldn't tell a stripling from a knight. And no one blamed me. Not one damned soul in the whole place. That's when I knew I was done, Rina." He hooked a thumb toward the fighting pits, where the crowd shouted their lust for blood. "The pits are honest. We pay men for their blood and, aye, for their lives. The crowds at the tournament ground dress it up with pageantry and manners and nobility, and they're just as vicious, just as bloodthirsty. He wasn't the first boy to have his lifeblood drain onto the tournament grounds, and he won't be the last."

Rina looked away. "That's no reason to throw yourself away on this," she said.

"If you're just here to tell me my failings, I'm done," Edrick said, turning toward the door.

"No!" Rina ran to him, her soft boots nearly silent on the rush-strewn floor. She grabbed his sleeve with her free hand and tugged. Edrick turned back toward her. They were inches apart, Edrick looming over, his dark eyes intent, peering into her.

Rina caught her breath, staring up, her plea forgotten. Edrick licked his lips. "Rina," he said huskily, "you shouldn't...you belong in that world, not down here."

"Not anymore," she said fiercely. "I've known where you were for a year, Edrick, and I left you alone because I...I had no claim on you." He started to protest, and she raised a hand. "No, belov—that is, plans made in the darkness may never see dawn. They aren't...aren't promises," she said hurriedly. "You were free to leave." She inhaled sharply. "But the Crucible is starting in two days. Lord Norill sponsored a suit of armor, and my master, all of us, have been working for months now. We have a revolutionary design. I had the breakthrough—never mind. Owen was our runewielder. You remember him."

"He's the best you could get?" Edrick asked, his eyebrows furrowing. "With Lord Norill's backing?"

"The thing is, Master Mourial is old, and he let me do most of the design, and well, Owen was the only one willing to try. I know what I'm doing!" she added quickly. "Imagine, Edrick, if the wielder could fight twice as long before the runesense leaves him? How that would change tournaments! Or battles? And we were there...nearly. I just needed to tweak it a little."

Edrick smiled, and Rina caught her breath. His whole face changed. For a moment he was the man she'd known since girlhood, the one she'd worked alongside to reach their dreams—landless squire and girl from a merchant family together against peers from wealthy or noble backgrounds. A hundred fragmented memories swirled around her. He was going to be the greatest tournament knight of all time, and she would design his armor, and together they would rise above their humble origins. Their names would become legend. So many whispered hopes, so many stolen moments together. All burned to ash in a single summer afternoon when Edrick's lance had found too soft a target.

And this day had been almost as bad. She remembered suddenly where she was, was aware of Edrick's eyes on her. "Owen was badly injured today in practice. The rest of Norill's men said it's my armor. Norill cast me out." Her eyes blurred with hot tears of shame. "But it's not, I swear. Owen smoked haze. I caught him a week ago, and he swore he'd never touch it again if I didn't tell. So I didn't. But his eyes today were red, and his breath stank of tar."

Edrick swore. "Idiot!" he said. "With that stuff in his lungs, he'd have gotten hurt with training splints, let alone whatever madness you've come up with this time." But his tone was fond, and he reached out toward her cheek with one hand before catching himself and letting his hand drop.

The door behind them opened. A wall of sound, the crowd cheering, hit them, and Rina turned to see two of the pit men helping a limping, shirtless man off the field. "Last fight!" one of the men called. "It's the new fellow, the one with the scars, up next. Boss said to have you standing near, Thumper."

"I will," Edrick said. He made to move past Rina, but she tugged his sleeve once more.

"I need you," she said. "I've been turned off. Norill is going to blackball me. I'll never find another post. Best I can hope is to sell splints and hope the duke's inquisitors don't catch me working magic without sponsorship. But if I can just show off my armor at the Crucible, it won't matter what Lord Norill says. The duke himself would be my patron! Or anyone rich enough to have me."

"I can't," Edrick said, pulling free.

"I need *you*," she insisted. "By now the story's all over town. No runewielder would have me, even assuming there's one who isn't already engaged this close to the Crucible."

The pit men left the loser moaning on a bench and went out again. Edrick glanced after them, as though looking for escape. "I swore I wouldn't set foot in the tournament ring again," he said softly, but Rina thought she heard reluctance in his tone.

"You swore you'd make me the greatest runesmith in the world too," Rina said, raising her chin and trying for a glare but fearing she fell short. Then her bravado crumpled. "Please, Edrick. I need you. If ever…if you once—"

Edrick enveloped her hand in his. "Rina, don't."

"I brought this," she said. She held up the gauntlet. "Take it, Edrick. It's useless without a runewielder. But look at it, feel it, wear it. You'll see what I mean. I've found a whole new way to scribe the runes. Most of them are too stupid to see it, but you're the most gifted runewielder I've ever known."

Edrick stared down at it. "I can't," he said again, but his eyes were hungry as he followed the runes engraved in its surface.

The door banged open, and the old pit man ran in. Blood poured from a cut over his eye. Rina started. The crowd was screaming again, but in fear and dismay, not appreciation. "New man!" he shouted. "He's something—don't know what—battle magic! Took Goldilocks apart, and he's ripping the place asunder!"

Edrick didn't hesitate. He sprinted toward the door, shouting over his shoulder, "Rina! Get out of here!"

Her heart pounding, Rina followed. The pit man intercepted her, pulling her away from the door to the pit. "No, girl!" he said. "Not that way!"

"I have to see him," Rina said, shaking free of his hands, still clutching her gauntlet.

Edrick burst through the door into the fighting pit, sizing the scene up as fast as he could. His boots kicked up a spray of sand as he hurtled past the pit men. Two were down, with the others standing over them holding staffs. Across the sand, a snarling fighter was trying to climb the wall, scrabbling for a handhold on the lip at the edge of the pit.

Goldilocks was down too. The man had been king of the pits for months, staining the sand with his opponents' blood in half a dozen different pits across the city. But he lay ominously still, his arm twisted in an unnatural angle, long blond hair limp against the sand.

The crowd was in chaos. Men jostled and fought their way toward the narrow steps leading out of the spectator ring, pushing each other down. A couple of women, faces white under their scarlet paint, huddled near the railing where they'd been forced by the scrum. The upper crew would handle the patrons. Edrick's job was the madman.

The new man was half a head shorter than him, and probably forty pounds less. He was wiry, with short dark hair and scars on his back, scrabbling at the wooden walls of the fighting pit. He wore the standard skimpy fighting wrap, too small and tight to hide even the most basic runed splint. But the way he was hanging by one hand off the wide ledge that overhung the pit, eight feet up, said he was more than a mere man. Which could be bad, very bad. Few battle magics could be safely used even by a trained man. Runed splints or mail from an expert mage. Methlan skinwards. The Aradori bear spirits, and one or two other magics Edrick had heard about, but none of those left a man howling in anger, blood rage leaving him blind to his surroundings.

The man looked down at him, still hanging from the ledge. Oh, hells. His eyes were wide and staring, yellow with long pupils like a cat's, and small horns protruded from his head. Demon-touched. Edrick had feared as much. Some poor fool who'd gotten hold of a hedge witch or a cheap potion to make him invulnerable in the ring, and suddenly he had demon hooks in his soul. What made a man risk his life and sanity for an edge in a fight?

"Send for the duke's inquisitors!" Edrick shouted over his shoulder to the pit men, knowing it would be long over before the inquisitors could arrive. They stayed out of the lower levels.

"Edrick!"

Rina's heart-piercing cry jerked him around. She'd disobeyed him. Unfamiliar fear plucked at him. He started to shout at her, to tell her to get out where she would be safe.

She'd cast off her cloak, and her eyes shone. For one moment everything was just right. He was about to fight his heart out, and Rina was there to watch him. No—that was long ago, in another life.

Orran pulled at Rina, whose eyes were wide with fear. She held up the shining metal gauntlet. "Here!"

She tossed the gauntlet toward Edrick. He leaped for it, grabbing it from the air. One gauntlet wasn't much, but it was better than facing a madman in the throes of possession completely unaided. Edrick thrust his right hand into the gauntlet. "Hey!" he shouted at the crazed man. "You want me, not them!"

The demon-tainted man smiled. His lips curled back, back, back, and long pointed teeth gleamed ice blue in his too-large mouth. His shoulder flexed—Edrick's only warning—and he leaped.

Edrick darted back. He had a short truncheon at his belt, the only tool he usually needed to serve as bouncer for the fighting pit. The demon-tainted man was unarmed, but that didn't make a fair fight.

He opened his runesense as the man circled him, feeling out the bracer Rina had given him. It had been two years since he'd used runes at all, eschewing even splints since he'd left the ring, but as he opened himself, it came rushing back like a flood. The runes on the bracer leaped up to surround him. He caught his breath under the torrent. How had Rina fit so many intricate runes into a single piece of armor? Strength, speed, stamina, they were all there, worked together in a pattern he'd never seen before. Almost too many. He needed to—

The demon-infested man threw himself at Edrick, his whirlwind rush catching Edrick off guard. His shoulder drove into Edrick's stomach and pushed him back. Edrick slammed his gauntleted fist into the exposed neck, but the man didn't flinch. Snarling, he bore Edrick back, into the wooden wall of the fighting pit. They crashed together against the boards, which flexed under Edrick's back.

Edrick dropped to one knee. His enemy's weight shifted off balance. Edrick threw him aside, then scrambled up. He hadn't felt this alive in two years. His blood sang in his ears. Keeping his back against the wall, he caught his breath, watched his foe, and returned to his runesense.

The shimmering runes surrounded him again, too thick a forest for him to embrace them. Ordinarily he would have put on a whole suit of armor and, with help from one or more mages and a couple of squires, assimilated the magic into his consciousness, making it part of him. Using a single gauntlet, during a fight, with no instruction...he didn't even have the breastplate, where the heartrune would be writ large, offering the key to tuning the whole symphony to himself.

Edrick shifted farther from the demon man, still writhing on the sand, as he struggled with his long-dormant runesense.

No, wait. The shapes swam more into focus. There was a heartrune there after all. Edrick turned the gauntlet over and looked down into the palm. The unmistakable lines of a heartrune shimmered in both sights. Graceful curves marked the metal of the gauntlet; shining golden magic traced a heartrune through the whole spiderweb of spells.

He couldn't help grinning despite himself, even as his opponent shook himself and got to his feet. Rina had always been a genius with runesmithing. What was she up to?

But having a heartrune was only part of the puzzle. He had to tune it to himself, and that could take time. Edrick reached out with his runesense and absorbed the heartrune.

Like a sudden gust of wind, the runes rushed toward him. He blinked, and there was almost a popping sensation. His skin tingled. The hairs on his bare arms stood up. He blinked again as his senses sharpened. The roar of the crowd was in his ears like an ocean. Sweat and blood assaulted his nostrils, and underneath was the sweet-sick scent of demon. He didn't need to tune this at all; it was perfect already.

The demon man rushed him, and Edrick ran, still grinning, to greet him. He smashed his gauntleted fist against the man's midsection and sent him tumbling to the sand with a shower of dust. The magic sang in his ears, his stomach, his heart. The screams and cries of the crowd were transformed, almost, to the old cheers. For an instant, he was on a sunny tournament ground once more, facing a worthy opponent.

The demon-man's skin had changed to gray-and-green scales. His long-clawed hands scraped the ground, sending a wave of sand at Edrick. Instinctively he threw up his left arm to shield his face, and as he did, he heard the demon's scream and the sound of him throwing himself forward. Edrick grabbed blindly and caught one arm. With the strength granted by Rina's gauntlet, he planted his feet and swung, letting the demon-man's motion carry him farther. He released, and the creature flew toward the wall, crashing against the boards and collapsing in a heap.

Edrick called the speed runes surging in his veins and dashed after the demon. He reached the huddled figure, lifted him by the scruff of his neck, and slammed the gauntlet against the demon-man's face. Blood and yellow ichor poured down his cheek and jaw. Edrick steeled himself. A man this lost, where the demon spirit had begun to transform his body, could not be saved. He'd seen it only a few times, but the priests and the duke's inquisitors made it clear. The poor fool had to be put down.

Even as he pounded and pounded, the man opened one snakelike eye and hissed up at him. "My teeth in your throat," he spat, "before the end."

How long could his strength last? Rina said her changes doubled the usual length, but he was using a single piece of armor like an entire suit. He didn't have time for this. He needed to end it.

"Thumper!" Orran shouted, and four of the pit men emerged, clutching short spears. Where had they—no, they'd lashed knives to their staffs. Good, they'd remembered the drills he'd put them through, despite their grumblings at the time. Hopefully, they held the discipline he'd tried to instill.

"Do it!" he shouted, pinning the demon to the wall with his forearm and leaving his thrashing torso clear. He raked Edrick with clawed feet. Edrick grit his teeth against the pain.

Orran and the others drove their spears into the demon, again and again. He thrashed and spit and struggled, growing weaker. At last he hung limp. Edrick lowered him to the dirt.

"Is he dead?" Orran asked.

"I don't know," Edrick said wearily. "The inquisitors will know. Nobody move until they get here."

Orran shot a quick look at him. "You're wounded," he said. "That's gonna fester if you don't get it looked at. I've seen demon wounds."

Edrick glanced aside. Rina was still watching from the edge of the room off the pit. "I know how to handle it," he said.

Orran jerked his head toward the preparation room, where Rina stood clinging to the doorframe. "Get the girl out of here. She don't belong anywhere near this place." He looked Edrick up and down. "And maybe you don't neither. That sort of fighting…you coulda beat Goldilocks anytime you wanted."

"I didn't want," Edrick said quietly, holding Orran's eyes. At last the old pit man nodded, and Edrick turned away, going to Rina.

Her face was pale, but her eyes glowed. She reached toward him, then let her hand fall. "You—that was magnificent," she said.

His stomach twisted at the look in her eyes. He needed to get her out of there. This wasn't her place. She was a runesmith, a gentle girl. Seeing her there brought the shabby reality of this place crashing down on him.

He handed her the gauntlet. "In there," he said, gesturing toward the cleanup room. He followed her and shut the door.

Rina paced as he went to the cabinet of supplies. He bathed the wound with bad brandy, taking a pull of the soured stuff for himself in good measure, then bound the wound with clean linen bandages.

"How...how was it?" Rina asked.

"Haven't fought a demon in years," Edrick said. "Comes back easy, though."

"I meant the gauntlet."

He started to give a glib answer, but the urgency in her eyes reached him. Edrick arranged the shreds of his tunic back over his chest as best he could. "Like nothing I've used before," he said. "This was all you?"

She flushed. "This piece. Yes. Some of the other parts of Owen's armor weren't, and I think that's what went wrong."

"Or maybe having a dozen heartrunes to manage at once is harder than you think," he suggested.

"No, you don't understand. You have to feel it, you'll get it then." Her face shone as she looked from the gauntlet to him. "But I saw, Edrick, the way the runes attuned to you. It was perfect. Just the way I'd imagined."

"Yes," he said. He hesitated. He wanted this so much, and that meant he should say no. The roar of the crowd...the thrill of combat...the way he felt whole when the runes tuned to him. He wanted it as much as fools like Owen wanted haze. "I'll do it," he said. His words came out harsher than he'd expected.

Rina's face lit. "You will!"

"Just this once," he said. "I...I did promise, once, to help you become the greatest runesmith in the world. I can't go back to that life, Rina, but I can help in the Crucible."

"That's all I'm asking," she whispered.

Rina stopped dead on the threshold of her workshop. Dust motes floated in the morning sun, filtering in from the deep shafts in the red stone walls, bringing a bit of fresh air and light into the guild hall.

A rack of tools stood as she'd left it along one wall. Her tables were cluttered with sketches, models, leather replicas, and old books. Her graving stand, its magnifier glinting in the light, waited in the center of the room. But the armor rack was empty.

"I didn't expect to see you back here, girl."

Rina whirled, her cheeks heating with rage at that voice, and found herself face-to-face with Jaelin, first assistant to Master Mourial. His blue-and-white runesmiths' guild ribbon gleamed at her from his shoulder, and she stared at the golden hammer.

"Yes, that's right," Jaelin said, smirking at her. "Master Mourial has announced his intention to retire, and Lord Norill's patronage devolves to me. The guild's already elevated me to master rank." He folded his arms across his chest. "So I really must thank you, for all that you've wasted our time these last three months and we're going to have to scramble to have anything to present to the Crucible in time."

All her carefully prepared speeches had been for Master Mourial, not Jaelin. He'd always hated her...well, not always. When she'd first come to the workshop as an apprentice, fifteen years old and barely able to hold a graver, he'd paid her flattering attention, even offering her private lessons. Then she'd learned what tools he meant her to use, and refused. He'd pursued anyway until Edrick interceded.

She had to try anyway. Rina raised her chin. "I found us another wielder," she said. "We can still enter."

"I have all the wielders I need," Jaelin said. "Plenty of hungry squires looking to appear as Lord Norill's champion, just not in that abomination you've been crafting."

She grasped at the offering. "Then let me have the armor," she said. "You don't need it; no one wants it. Give me my chance."

"You've been dismissed with prejudice, Rina," he said. "Your name has been given to the guild. I find it most unlikely you'll find another patron, but you will most certainly not use Lord Norill's property to win a place." He took a step toward her, and she shrank back. His smile grew. "Now, shall I have you thrown out, or will you walk?"

Her heart pounded in her chest. *What now?* Without armor, it was useless. She didn't have time or resources or coin to make a new suit. "Well?" Jaelin demanded. He reached toward her, grasping for her shoulder.

And a huge hand wrapped around his wrist and spun him around. "I thought I told you what would happen if you touched her again," Edrick growled.

Rina gasped in surprise. "Edrick!"

He had a bag slung from his shoulder. "Told you I'd meet you this morning," he said, shoving Jaelin aside.

"You!" Jaelin almost howled. "So this is your wielder, Rina? A washed-up squire who ran off when he was confronted with a little blood? I almost wish I could give you the armor, I'd make a fortune taking wagers against you."

Edrick ignored him. "Get what you need," he said. There was no warmth in his voice. Rina wondered if she'd been imagining last night that any trace of his old affection remained.

That was a damned fool thing to be worrying about right then. She stepped farther into the workshop, spinning around, trying to think.

"I told you; you're out," Jaelin shouted after her. "Now leave!"

"Not without my belongings." She turned her back on him, her words more defiance than a real plan. "Apprentice pieces belong to the prentice," she said. She listened to her own words tumbling out and started to feel a flicker of hope. They'd work better than the armor she'd tuned to Owen anyway. "So that we can go in front of the guild on our own, should the master turn us off, which you have. Yes. My prenticework is mine!"

"Take it and go, then," Jaelin snarled.

Rina snatched up a large sack. She dug through the litter on her benches, finding the gauntlet she'd made ages ago, when the inspiration first hit. It went into the bag, followed by a mismatched pair of greaves, then a helmet she'd finished three months back. Piece by piece, she reclaimed her work. The bag filled, she found another and continued.

"I want you gone!" Jaelin called. Edrick said something in a low voice, and he shut up.

Rina cast a wishful glance at the graver stand, but that was workshop property. Her leather roll of tools was hers, though. She couldn't help looking at Edrick as she put it into the sack, wondering if he remembered when he'd given it to her, but his face was as cold as the stone walls.

Second bag full, she let it drop to the flagged floor with a crash and turned in place, looking for anything else worth claiming.

Edrick stepped into her shop space. He stooped and lifted both sacks. "Ready?" he asked, and there was a gentleness under his gruff tone.

"You'll present those sacks to me for inspection," Jaelin began.

"Oh, shove it," Edrick said. "You stood here and watched her pack."

"Fine!" Jaelin snarled. "I don't know what you're up to, but I intend to give your name to every prospective patron in the city and have you blacklisted!"

Fire leaped up inside Rina. She marched over and stabbed a finger into Jaelin's chest. "Try," she said. "You've been jealous of me ever since Master Mourial said he was thinking of recommending me to Lord Norill to take his place in a few years. You can try to stop me, but I will create the greatest rune armor any of us has ever seen. And I will *win* the Crucible of Armor!"

Jaelin stepped back under her wrath. "I'm ready, Edrick," she said, and stomped past, crossing the threshold of her workshop with hardly a flinch.

They had to march all the way through the hall, past dozens of wide-open doorways into spaces like the one that had been Rina's. They skirted the great forge room, where the armorsmiths labored under the direction of journeymen to craft the pieces, past apprentices carrying worked gauntlets and helmets out for testing and blank ones to be engraved and enchanted. For seven years, this had been home. Suddenly she had just two sacks of mismatched armor and her pride.

Edrick walked a pace behind her and didn't speak. Rina couldn't have replied anyway. Her mind whirled. *What now?* She had a runewielder and most of a suit of armor. Her purse still had the majority of her six months' allotment from Master Mourial, but that would go fast.

The door wardens opened the great brass-bound oak entryway. Rina nodded to them on her way through. If she returned, they would refuse to let her pass; Jaelin would see to that. The doors rumbled shut behind her, and she found herself standing on the step, lost.

Edrick set the sacks down at her feet. He stepped down the wide stairs to the street beyond. Master Mourial's establishment was high up the Street of Artificers, where all the best artisans lived, so the street was full of chair bearers and porters balancing baskets on their heads. Edrick waded out across the stone street. The passersby flowed around him like water around a tall stone. Rina tried to marshal her thoughts.

The street meandered upward, the walls on both sides rising dozens of feet. Like most of Astran City, this district was hewn out of the red-orange rock. Windows and doors opened from the stone that was all one piece with the street. Sunlight fell in from the high canyon over-head. It was near noonday, and the street was brightly lit. In two hours the afternoon shadows would begin to gather, and long before nightfall,

Astran's lights would kindle. She needed to be firmly planted before then.

Edrick returned, leading a man pushing a wheelbarrow. Without asking, he scooped Rina's sacks up and dumped them into the barrow. "Where to?" the porter asked.

They exchanged a look. Rina bit her lip. "To the Skyfield," she said at last, and the barrowman wheeled his cart out onto the street.

"What's your plan?" Edrick asked.

If she lost him, she had nothing. She had to present confidence. "I'm going to rent a preparation chamber, if there's any left, at the field." The chambers were carved below the field itself, a labyrinth of passages and small rooms. The chambers allowed runewielders to dress and get ready before their fights. With the Crucible of Armor so close, they might not have any available.

But the gate warden at the Skyfield passed them along to a lean woman who said she was the chamberlain on duty. She showed them a narrow room, maybe ten paces by four, with a high shelf lining the ceiling, a low table filling the back wall, and nothing more.

Rina asked the price of the room and bit her lip to keep from screaming. She counted coins into the woman's hand, bright silver Astran eagles and a single gold sovereign with the seal of Therador on its raised face, and her light pouch barely jangled as she stowed it away.

The woman shut the door behind them, and Rina was suddenly alone with Edrick. Panic bubbled up inside her.

Edrick sidled past her with the sacks. He dumped them onto the table, spreading the armor out. "Well, Rina?" he asked.

Panic gave way to despair as she surveyed the armor. None of the pieces matched, and they had no breastplate at all. Her shoulders slumped. "I guess it's hopeless," she said. "There's no need for you to waste your time, Edrick."

"Hmm?" He had picked up the helmet and was turning it over and over, a distant look in his eye. "They all have heartrunes. Is that what Jaelin disliked?"

"It's more work," Rina said. She watched him closely, to see if he noticed anything else about the heartrune. "You have to have the same mage scribe each heartrune, there's no chance of them matching otherwise. And you know how Jaelin hates taking direction from others. How do you think he liked me handing him a helmet that I'd put a heartrune on and saying, 'Now add a dozen sense runes and maybe some stamina'?"

"Not well," Edrick said, a rueful smile on his lips.

"If we'd had more time!" Rina turned away. "If I could have done all the work myself...As it was, we were short on time, and Jaelin insisted on making the breastplate himself. The heartrunes weren't compatible, and I said so. I said maybe a better runewielder could make it work, but Owen wasn't the man."

"So you're going to give up?" Edrick said. "The idea's sound. Jaelin is a fool but not that big a fool. You know that's why he took the armor. He'll make his own, and in six months he'll be the genius who revolutionized how we make rune armor."

"I know." Rina slid down against the wall till she was crouching, her face in her hands. "But I can't send you out into the ring like this!"

"Why not?" Edrick put the helmet on. He drew one gauntlet over his hand and flexed. "I don't know what you did, Rina, but these heartrunes feel like putting on a worn pair of boots. I barely have to touch them with my runesense, and they're mine to command."

She looked up. Edrick wasn't looking at her; he had one hand raised and was staring through the visor. For a moment he looked like the man she'd known before. Maybe he still was, deep down, if the heartrunes spoke to him like that.

"I don't have a sponsor, and you're not a squire anymore," she said. "We can't enter the ring. Maybe we can put enough of a suit together to demonstrate to some of the other lords. Or at least their men-at-arms. We could sell...the idea of it, perhaps. If I got a patron..."

Edrick crouched in front of her. He raised the lid of his visor. His dark eyes blazed. "Come! You'll never find the patron you deserve that way."

"Then what?" she cried. "I've got nothing."

"You have most of a suit," he said. "It's six days till the Grand Melee. Anyone can take his chances there. Make me a breastplate, and I'll enter the melee."

She stared at him. "Six days? It took me a month to do the gauntlet!"

"You don't have a month," he said roughly.

"A decent breastplate, even unruned, costs too much."

"I'll find you one." He stood up and stared down at the pile. "I—we talked about our futures once, Rina."

Her heart stopped beating while he spoke.

"It's not my future anymore, but it could be yours," he continued, and Rina sighed. She didn't know Edrick anymore, this man who faced demons in a pit barehanded and cowed Jaelin with a look. Once he'd looked at her with tenderness, but she felt almost afraid to meet his gaze.

"You said you wanted to make the greatest armor in the world," Edrick prompted. "This isn't it, but...it could be."

She nodded, not trusting her voice.

"What else do you need?"

Decent light. A graving stand. Truesilver, to strengthen the runes. She shook her head. "I'll make do. Food, water. A blanket or two. I'll sleep here, what sleep I can get."

Edrick stood. He offered his bare hand, and she accepted it. His touch was cool on her skin, and her stomach barely fluttered. "Six days," he said. "Six days, and we'll show the city what you're made of."

"Yes," she said, as her stomach roiled.

Edrick went out, and she stared after him for too long. Shaking herself, she took herself over to the table and began looking over her armor scraps.

The marshal paused as he reached Edrick standing in line with the other entrants to the melee. His eyes traveled from Edrick's winged helmet to his mismatched pauldrons—one rounded, the other a swept-back point—down the battered breastplate bright with new runes. That was far enough, apparently. His gaze snapped back to meet Edrick's. "You," he said. "Name? Where did you train?"

"Edrick of Thad's Mill," Edrick said promptly. "Trained in Lord Norill's yards, six years. Been out two."

"No lord? No allegiance?"

Edrick shook his head. "I'm wielding for Mage Rina Telassi," he said. "Our entry fee's paid."

"And this...suit." The marshal's eyes slid downward again, and he gave a little shudder. Edrick's neighbors snickered. "Mage Telassi's work? Does this...style...have a name?"

Rina might have a word for her new work, but Edrick didn't know it, and he didn't like the way this marshal sneered. Fool, not looking past the surface to see the masterwork beneath. "Piebald," he snapped. "Put down 'piebald.'"

"Very well." The marshal made a note on his slate. "Wielder Edrick, for Mage Telassi, in the piebald suit." He moved on down the line.

Two duke's inquisitors and a bondmage followed, securing weapons. Edrick presented his short sword, and the mage applied a spell to dull the edge, surrounding the blade with a cushion of air. The melee would be a mad, crashing throng of armored men, but nobody was supposed to die. The mage had a bored expression on his face as he worked the spell, but as he handed back the sword, his eyes narrowed. Edrick stirred. "Is there a problem?"

"Your armor," he said, frowning. "Is there...more than one heartrune?"

Edrick's fellows craned their necks around. A low muttering went up. Edrick grinned. "Know something about armorsmithing?"

The bondmage shook his head. "I washed out two months in," he admitted. "But I know a heartrune when I see one, and I think..." His eyes widened. "By Alabik...every piece?"

"What's the slowing?" the marshal called, several men farther along. The bondmage shook himself and moved to the next man, his attention darting back to Edrick several times before he'd gotten too far along.

One of the duke's inquisitors lingered. Dressed in well-matched black armor with darkened leather fittings, a short sword similar to Edrick's hanging from his belt, he wore a silver amulet on his neck as the sign of his office. "Mage Telassi is in good standing with the rune-smiths' guild?" he inquired.

"Of course," Edrick said.

"Who is her patron?"

"We don't have one," Edrick said shortly. "Why else would she hire a wielder who hasn't entered the ring in two years?"

The inquisitor nodded, but fingered his sword hilt as he moved along.

Edrick let out a sigh of relief and leaned back against the wall, closing his eyes and feeling out the runes. This was the first time he'd worn the whole suit together. Rina had only finished the last runes on the breastplate this morning. He'd picked the battered piece up used, in a junk market, and beaten the bigger dents out himself. Rina hadn't complained, but he'd seen how her brow furrowed as she bent over it, working by flickering candlelight long into the night. The shadows had made her look old before her time. He'd gone to sleep like that the previous night, sitting against the wall as she worked.

Her work would pay off. He'd make a good showing in the ring, and Rina would have a dozen offers of patronage by nightfall. Then he could…do what? Go back to the pit? As long as Rina was settled, it didn't matter what happened to him. She should have a workshop and a dozen assistants and every tool she needed. Not a tiny cell and scrap armor.

"Fighters!"

A man emerged from the tunnel they would take to reach the field. Edrick recognized him from his own squiring days. Sir Rolan, the duke's own master-of-arms, who had charge of the duke's sworn men, his squires, his arms, and his person. Sir Rolan was wearing a sky-blue tunic with a silver-tasseled sash over scarlet trousers. He carried a long wooden baton tipped with silver.

The fighters straightened up. Edrick had the urge to run his fingers through his hair, which was ridiculous since he wore both gauntlets and a helmet.

"In a moment, I will have the honor of introducing Astran City to the men who intend to fight for her amusement today," Sir Rolan announced. "I know you need no reminder what a privilege it is to be here, participating in the Crucible of Armor. In the past four days we have seen some of the greatest knights in the land compete to display their own prowess and the skill of the runesmiths who outfitted them. Today, you have your chance for glory. Some of you are lordless, here to impress men like me who might well offer you a place." His eyes ran down the line of men. Men nodded or murmured agreement. "Others are wielding on behalf of mages seeking fame and position. Whatever your purpose, remember: fight with courage, with honor, and with all your heart. Fortune favors the brave!"

The men cheered, Edrick adding his own voice to the throng, the old thrill warming him. For just this day, he could pretend this was still his place. Just one day, he'd let himself enjoy the melee without guilt.

"And, as though any of you needed more encouragement, in addition to the winner's purse of fifty sovereigns, the winner will tomorrow participate in a show match against the duke's own heir, who won the jousting matches yesterday. I *guarantee* that man will have the eyes of every master-of-arms in Astran on him, so keep that prize in mind as you fight today!"

The men cheered again, and Sir Rolan began to instruct them in how to enter the field. Edrick's thoughts were elsewhere. A single-combat match against the duke's heir—that would show off Rina's armor in ways the Grand Melee couldn't offer. He hadn't intended to win the melee, just to have a good enough showing to attract a little attention. But…this was Rina's chance. An image of her sprang to mind, bent over his breastplate, a wisp of dark hair escaping from her tightly coiled braid, weariness and worry painted on her face. Some of those worry lines were his fault. He couldn't make amends, but maybe he could erase just a few of them.

"When the trumpet sounds, emerge!" Sir Rolan concluded, and disappeared back up the tunnel. The marshals herded the fighters toward the entrance, and Edrick took a moment to size up his opponents.

There were about thirty men, all in armor and bearing various weapons. His suit was by far the oddest, but several men wore mismatched pieces. On the other hand, at least a dozen men wore polished suits with runes picked out in truesilver. Even without his runesense he could tell those would be formidable opponents.

His advantage was the sheer number of heartrunes on his armor. Assuming he could tune them to himself once he reached the field, they would give him the ability to fight longer than a single heartrune would permit. He needed to outlast the field, not beat them down.

The men trudged up the tunnel, the clank of armor echoing off the red stone walls. Ahead hung a brilliant blue patch of sky. Sir Rolan was addressing the crowd. Edrick could hear his tones but not his words. The crowd cheered and roared at intervals. Edrick held his sword, grinning under his helmet, as the throb of feet pounding on stone and the roar of the crowd flamed his blood into fire.

A trumpet blast sounded, and the melee fighters charged up the tunnel. Edrick burst out into daylight, breaking right as he'd been instructed. The men fanned out around the field to thunderous applause.

He hadn't set foot on the Skyfield for two years, but it was as though he'd never left. On three sides, the stone stands rose, carved into open boxes and terraces. The fourth side opened out into the air. An eight-foot-tall wall was all that separated the field from the yawning drop-off. The Skyfield took up a wide ledge on the outside of the great spire of rock that Astran City was built on and into, three hundred feet above the river. Only the duke's palace was any higher.

Sir Rolan concluded his introductions and strode over to the duke's pavilion, which was built right down on the field and covered with cloth-of-gold canopies to protect it from the sun. He bowed to the duke, who lifted a thin age-spotted hand and nodded. Sir Rolan turned back to the field. "Runewielders!" he shouted. "Prepare!"

Edrick opened his runesense, and the familiar rush of runes surrounded him, whirling around him, glowing, and calling to him. He had practiced with three pieces of the armor at once, but ten heartrunes were blossoming blue around him.

"Present!" Sir Rolan shouted, and the fighters raised their weapons. Most of them would already have their runes fully incorporated. A trained wielder took only seconds to embrace a normal suit of runes. Edrick was out of practice and trying to do something he'd never done before.

"Fight!"

The crowds in the stand echoed Sir Rolan's command, and the runewielders fell on each other. Edrick didn't have time to waste. He plunged himself into the runes.

They soaked into him like someone had dumped a pail of cold water over him. He shuddered and shook himself, and the runes were there, running through him. The heartrunes blended into a seamless whole. Edrick caught the blade of the man racing at him and threw him back, then whirled to block an attack from his other side. He didn't need to tune any of the heartunes, didn't even have to think about them.

The fighters clashed in a great roiling mass, cheered on by the crowd. Rina was there somewhere watching. He didn't have time to try to pick her out in the stands, but he knew she was there, and it warmed him. He'd always fought better knowing Rina watched him.

The marshals, wearing bright yellow tabards over their tunics, ran up and down the field. They called fouls and judged men out when they'd taken too many blows. Once a fighter stumbled and fell under too vigorous a blow from his opponent. At a trumpet blast, the whole field lowered their swords and stepped back, letting the marshals call in squires to carry off the fallen man. Sir Rolan spoke to the man who'd dealt the blow, but he was permitted to remain.

The field was down to fewer than half the men who had started, and most were flagging. Edrick felt nearly as fresh as when he'd started. Most of the remaining men were those he'd picked out as wearing the best suits. Their truesilver runes gleamed golden in the sunlight.

Two of them broke away from the pack and approached him. Edrick met their attack. "Two on one?" he grunted. "Hardly fair."

"It's in the rules. And we can't have some junk-cart squire making us look bad," one of his attackers said, closing in on him.

Edrick's fine mood sizzled and vanished. He caught the attack, then smashed an elbow into the man's visor. Insult Rina's armor? Hells if he was going to take that.

The other attacker took a step back, perhaps sensing his mood change. Edrick drove the attack, swinging furiously. The attacker gave ground. His fellow hovered near but couldn't find an opening.

Their armor was better, and they were practiced. Edrick had spent two years as a bouncer, not a squire. His muscles were strong but not tuned. His instincts were off. Wearing armor again was awkward, but he was not going to lose to these fools. Not when he had something real to fight for.

His next blow knocked the sword from his opponent's hand. The man cried out and fell back, throwing up his arms. A yellow-tabard ran over and shouted him off the nearly empty field, and Edrick turned back to the other.

The runewielder had a longer sword than he did, giving him reach, and he was good. He parried Edrick's blows furiously. Edrick slowed his attacks. He had the advantage. All he had to do was outlast.

His opponent apparently sensed weakness, because he threw himself forward. Edrick parried and countered, using as little strength as he could, husbanding his armor.

Then, suddenly, the bright heartrune across his opponent's chest winked out. The man cried aloud, and Edrick drove in. He caught the man with a blow to the midriff, denting his chest piece. The man fell to one knee, holding up a hand, and Edrick stepped back.

A whole flurry of yellow-tabards surrounded them. Edrick raised his visor, confused. Had he broken some rule?

Then Sir Rolan was beside him, raising his sword arm skyward. "Astran!" he thundered. "Your melee champion—the Piebald!"

The stands roared. The crowd were on their feet, cheering. "Piebald! Piebald!"

Edrick ripped his helmet off, letting the breeze cool the sweat plastering his hair to his head. His face ached from the width of his grin. Where was Rina? This was her moment too.

If she'd been on the field the moment Edrick was proclaimed the champion, Rina would have thrown her arms around his neck. Instead she found herself jumping up and down in the stands, hugging herself, screaming into the ears of those standing near, tears streaming down her face. "He did it! He did it!"

The woman beside her said, "Just shows you can't tell from appearances. A piebald champion! Now that's like something from a story!"

Rina hugged herself even tighter, feeling like bursting. She'd watched the fight with her runesense, and at the start, as Edrick woke his runes, she'd been unable to breathe. Then the heartrunes merged, as she'd known they would and feared they wouldn't, and her heart unfroze.

She forced her way through the cheering crowd. No chance of getting anywhere near the field. She'd better meet Edrick back at the preparation room. They'd hired a pair of squires to help him dress this morning, but she could manage to take the armor off herself. And she'd have to look it over and repair any damage. He had another match on the morrow, and that was beyond all expectation.

He wasn't at the chamber. Rina paced back and forth, her strides too big for the cramped room. Of course, he'd be taking congratulations from a thousand well-wishers.

At last the door opened, and she whirled, but her bright greeting died on her lips. Edrick was escorted by a man in somber black clothes, well cut and trimmed with green-dyed lace.

"Rina," Edrick said, "This is Sir Lindron. The duke's man of business."

Rina's eyes widened. She essayed a bow. The man nodded to her.

"Sir, Mage Telassi is the one who made my armor."

"I see." Sir Lindron looked around the room with faint distaste. "This won't take long, but I would like privacy. May I?"

"Of course," Rina said. She scooted back into a corner, letting Edrick slide in beside her, and Sir Lindron stepped in and shut the door.

He didn't speak at once, instead looking them both over. Rina was too aware of the smudge on her cheek, the crumpled clothes she'd been wearing for days.

"Well," he said. "An upset! That will certainly have the town talking." He laughed but didn't seem amused. Rina felt no impulse to match him.

"Mage Telassi. I am fortunate that I was watching the fight in company with an acquaintance of you both, so I am well informed about the circumstances that led you...here." He glanced around the tiny preparation room. "A turned-off runesmith and a walked-away squire, now our melee champions." His cold smile didn't touch his eyes.

Rina reached out toward Edrick, but he was all armored, no comfort there. She raised her chin. "I can guess your informant," she said. "Journeyman Jaelin is—"

"Master Jaelin," Sir Lindron corrected. "Yes. Well." He sniffed, nostrils flaring. "The Piebald here is to face the duke's grandson and heir tomorrow in a show match. I never liked the idea, but now it is intolerable. My lord's dignity...I am the duke's man of business, as you said, and I am here with a business offer."

Rina's hackles raised, but Edrick said mildly, "Yes?"

"You will appear on the field tomorrow, of course. Arrayed like... this." Sir Lindron's lips curled. "You will face my lord, and you will fight, and you will lose. Not too fast, but don't drag the farce out forever. His Grace has outfitted my lord in the best rune armor money can buy, and there's no chance your piebald atrocity will stand up to him, but if it takes too long, he'll be a laughingstock."

Rina's blood froze. She tried to speak, but nothing came out. Sir Lindron held up a hand. "You will be compensated, of course. Your achievements are...noteworthy. The duke's purse will open for...shall we say two hundred sovereigns? Four times what you won today. And Mage Telassi, several high masters of the runesmithing art are to be His Grace's guests at the fight tomorrow. You will also be invited. I have no doubt your achievements will interest them."

All she could think to say under his cold stare was "I can't possibly accept...I have nothing to wear—"

"That will be remedied as well," Sir Lindron said. "As I said, this is a minor matter." He bowed. "Thank you for your time, Mage Telassi, Master Edrick." A moment later he was gone, the door swinging shut behind him.

Rina turned to Edrick, indignation rising, but Edrick was grinning like a boy with a new whistle. He whooped. "Rina! We've done it!" He threw an armored arm around her, then drew back. "Sorry, I forgot," he said. He shook his head, still grinning. "Two hundred sovereigns. I can go anywhere, start over. And you, if you don't have six masters fighting over you by noon tomorrow, I miss my guess!"

Rina said through numb lips, "But to throw a fight?"

He shook his head. "I'm not going to throw it. This armor is marvelous, Rina, but I'm not up to it. A trained man, in the best armor his grandfather the duke can buy, will wipe the floor with me. All I have to do is not draw it out too long."

"Don't you see, that's what they're really worried about," Rina said. "Jaelin will have told him that's the strength, that my armor can go longer than a regular suit. There's a chance you could outlast His Lordship and...and win!" Blood pounded in her ears.

"Help me off with this; my back itches," Edrick said, and stooped so Rina could get at the straps.

She removed one piece of armor at a time, while Edrick rambled on about how he'd been thinking about leaving the city for a while, but hadn't had the funds.

"I thought——" Rina blurted out.

"What?" he asked, turning to her. She caught her breath as his eyes caught her face. Didn't Edrick understand how magnificent he had been? Didn't he know how she longed to see him in the ring again, for good this time?

"I thought perhaps...you'd find your way back to the ring," she said lamely. "The crowd loved you, Edrick."

Edrick's face closed off. His eyes went cold. "They don't care if it's me or some other fool," he said. "They just want a good fight."

She bent and picked up the strewn bits of armor. Straightening up, she set them on the worktable.

Edrick pulled his breastplate over his head. He examined the leather straps. "One of the shoulder straps is marred partway through," he noted, no emotion in his voice. "I took a blow there earlier. I'll see if I can fix it."

She nodded, not trusting her voice, as she looked over the pieces, assessing the damage. The gauntlets were fine, but both pauldrons needed repairs made to their runes, and one of the greaves had a huge dent she should try to work out.

Edrick put a hand on her shoulder, and she looked up, trying to swallow past the lump in her throat. "I'm grateful to you for pulling me out of the fighting pit, Rina," he said. "I'd lost my way down there. Standing on the field brings it all back. My head's clearer now. I need a new start. The gold buys me that, and you'll be where you're supposed to be. Making the greatest armor anyone's ever seen." He smiled down at her, and her heart felt as if he'd just stepped on it.

"I could go too," she said, the words rushing out of her. "Away from here, with you."

"I couldn't take you," he said softly. He stroked her cheek with one finger. "Any more than I could when I walked away last time. Making rune armor, that's where you belong. Someday I'm going to come to a tournament and see the champions all wearing your armor. I know it."

But she didn't want him there watching, she wanted him beside her all the way. Rina swallowed, cursing herself for a coward. Edrick wanted no part of this life. Better to let him walk away, again, than to have him reject her to her face. On the morrow, Edrick would walk onto the field wearing her armor, to a cheering crowd one last time. That would have to be enough.

"Thank you, Edrick," she managed. "Will you...hand me that helmet, please?"

Edrick had been waiting in a sideline pen all morning, dressed for combat. It couldn't have been much past dawn when a trio of boys—two squires and a page—had arrived at the preparation room "Compliments of Sir Lindron." The page whisked Rina off to be dressed for the duke's box, and the squires had buckled Edrick into his armor. Irritating, when he and Rina had planned to use the morning to finish going over every scratch and dent they could in the armor. He would have liked to polish the dingy breastplate a bit more.

Instead he waited in the pen. Pages brought him food and drink. The canopy kept the sun off, and he had a grand view of the morning events. Jugglers, a pair of dancing dogs, tumblers, and a band of troupers took turns amusing the crowds as the stands filled up. Finally a flurry of fanfare announced the duke's arrival. Edrick craned his neck, but he couldn't see the duke's pavilion from there. He wondered how Rina was faring.

Sir Rolan stopped outside his box. "You're next, Sir Piebald," he said, smiling.

"Just Piebald, remember?" Edrick said, standing up. "My opponent is here?"

"His Lordship, Aelfred Constans, has arrived and is waiting across from you," Sir Rolan said. "He sends his compliments. Now, the niceties—"

"I trained under Lord Norill. I know the etiquette," Edrick interrupted.

Sir Rolan nodded. "Just so, then." His smile slipped. "Lord Norill's squires find places easily, yet you…"

"I walked away," Edrick said quietly. "There was an accident, you see."

Sir Rolan's eyes widened. "Of course. I do remember you. That was in no way your fault."

"So they assured me, but the boy was dead," Edrick said briefly.

"Well. At any rate, I look forward to seeing a most enjoyable fight today."

Edrick peered at Sir Rolan. Was he taunting him? No, he looked sincere. He must not know what Sir Lindron had done. It spoke well of Sir Rolan, at least. Good to know some knights, at least, might believe the values they espoused.

"In a moment, then, Master Piebald," Sir Rolan said, his easy smile back in place. He strode away, baton in hand, and Edrick lowered his visor.

The trumpets sounded, and Edrick strode out onto the field to cheers of "Piebald!" It warmed him, despite his determination to stay hardened to the call of the arena.

He took his place in the center, just in front of the duke's box. There was Rina, off to one side, her face grave.

The duke's heir approached, the crowd cheering "Constans!" His armor was immaculate. It gleamed silver, and the truesilver runes were like lines of starlight caught on the surfaces. His helmet was thrown back, and an open, honest smile showed on his face. Lord Aelfred was younger than Edrick had expected, not yet twenty, and Edrick knew at a glance that he had no idea the fight was fixed. Something knotted in his chest.

Sir Rolan approached and began the introductions. An impulse struck Edrick, to make this last tournament appearance everything he'd once imagined. "Sir Rolan," he said, "may I approach my lady and beg her favor?"

Rolan's eyes twinkled. "Of course," he said, and Edrick made straight for the duke's pavilion.

Rina realized what he was doing. She blushed red and stood up. She was in some strange purple silk dress that must be the height of fashion and didn't suit her at all. She was beautiful, of course, but he liked her better with leather work aprons and smudges of polish on her cheek.

Edrick bent over her, his visor open. "I beg your favor, my lady runesmith," he said loudly.

Rina stared up at him. Her eyes were wide. "Oh," she said. "Oh, I…of course." She bent and fumbled with her handbag—someone must have given her that—and fished out a scrap of pink linen. She held it out, then a shiver crossed her whole body, and she crumpled the handkerchief into her hand.

"Edrick," she said. She glanced around her, then swallowed and looked back up into his face, leaned closer, and whispered, "Edrick, I… I lied. When I said I wanted to make the greatest armor the world's ever seen. I don't give a damn about that. I wanted to make armor for *you*. That's why, why the heartrunes are so easy for you to tune. I made them for you. Every single one of them." Her eyes shone with tears. "*That's* my favor, Edrick. Surrounding you, right now. All of it."

He couldn't speak. Rina took his gauntlet in her hands and slipped the handkerchief inside the wrist. He touched her hand with his other glove.

Sir Rolan called him back to his place, and on numb legs he returned.

"Are you all right, sir?" Lord Aelfred asked.

"I…will be," Edrick said, closing his visor. His mind roiled. He should have seen it the moment he first put Rina's gauntlet on, except he'd been so distracted with everything else going on he'd just accepted how easily the heartrune tuned to him, without the usual moment of adjustment. That was how great runesmiths made custom armor for a wealthy patron, by designing the heartrune specifically for that one man. All the other armor he'd ever used had been made for general use and took work to get the most from the heartrune.

All the hours, weeks, maybe years that Rina had spent working on armor on her own, practicing her rune art, she'd been graving it for him. Every stroke of her heartrune spoke to him, telling him that she still loved him, and he hadn't noticed it.

And he was going to take gold to throw a fight, in her priceless gift.

Edrick lowered the visor. "Ready?" Sir Rolan asked.

Lord Aelfred said, "Ready," and Edrick echoed.

"Then, my lords, prepare!"

Edrick opened his runesight. The ten heartrunes whirled around him, all perfectly tuned to him. His height, his balance, the way he liked to lead with his left when an opening presented itself, it was all in there.

"Present!"

Edrick raised his sword skyward. The shining golden runes were so close he could almost taste them. They hummed and whirred, playing the same perfect note.

"Fight!"

The heartrunes melted into him, like a piece of his soul returning to its place.

Lord Aelfred charged him, glowing like the sun in his runesense. Damn, the lordling was strong! It almost hurt to look at him. Edrick blocked his swing. Their swords clashed, sending shivers up Edrick's arms. He took a step backward and turned. Lord Aelfred rushed past him. Edrick swung, and Lord Aelfred, pivoting on the spot, caught him.

Back and forth around the field they went, like a dance, Edrick now leading, now following. Every moment on the field made him feel more himself, more alive. Block and parry, watch his opponent, feel the runes encircle him. Oh, how he'd missed this.

He mustn't lose himself in the seductive call of the ring. This wasn't his place anymore. The crowd screaming for him and his opponent didn't care. They'd cheer someone else later and forget he'd ever been born.

But...there was such honesty in this. Lord Aelfred didn't know the fight was fixed, that was obvious from the way he strove every moment to overcome.

Lord Aelfred attacked. Edrick parried, too slow. The blade smashed against one pauldron, driving him to one knee. The crowd roared Aelfred's name.

This was the chance to surrender. Edrick stole a glance at the duke's box. Rina sat on the edge of her seat, twisting her hands in her lap, tension on her face. Her gift…he had hardly shown any of its strength yet. Just a bit longer, then.

Edrick rose. He touched his helmet, signaling appreciation and readiness to his opponent, and they crossed swords again, the crowd roaring approval as they fought.

Edrick swung and hit Lord Aelfred a blow against the helmet. The crowd cheered "Piebald!" as Lord Aelfred staggered back. Edrick waited as Aelfred recovered.

The afternoon wore on, hot sun baking him in his armor. A trumpet blast signaled them to fall apart. Lord Aelfred raised his visor, Edrick following suit, as squires ran out onto the field with water. Sir Rolan followed in their wake. "You fight well!" Lord Aelfred said, accepting a waterskin from his squire. "Why haven't we crossed swords before, man?"

Edrick drained the offered water in two long swigs. "I've been away," he said in reply.

Sir Rolan asked each of them if they were able to keep fighting, surveyed their armor, then nodded. "We continue, then," he said. As he turned to go, he said to Edrick, "It's a pleasure to see you fight, Piebald."

Edrick lowered his visor. Lord Aelfred grinned. "Thanks," he said.

"For what?" Edrick asked.

"For letting me show off." Aelfred covered his face and raised his sword.

They circled each other, Edrick's mind whirling. The crowd shouted for him and Aelfred. Rina's gaze hadn't wavered. All Astran was watching. This felt so good. He mustn't lose himself in this false glory. Blood on the sand, that was the truth of the ring.

But…Lord Aelfred fought honestly. His sword and armor spoke of his intense desire to be there. Just like the men who lined up every night at the pits to take their chance at guts and glory. Nobody forced them to fight. They knew the cost, were willing to risk injury and death and sometimes even demon possession to prove themselves.

And that was all right. It was their choice. Edrick hadn't killed an innocent man, he'd fought a willing opponent, and the boy had lost, but it wasn't Edrick's place to say he shouldn't have been there, any more than it was his place to deny Lord Aelfred a chance at an honest fight. He owed them all—the dead boy, Aelfred, Rina, the spectators cheering themselves hoarse—the best damned fight they'd ever seen.

Edrick reached for the runes surrounding him. They responded at his lightest touch. Time to show everyone what he and Rina could really do.

Rina sat with her hands knotted in her lap as the fight wore on. She should have just given her favor to Edrick without that load of confusion and rubbish. What a place for her to blurt out her heart, surrounded by all these nobles. At least it didn't seem to have hurt his skills. He'd already gone far longer than she'd expected. Early on, he'd had a chance to bow out of the match, but he hadn't. She couldn't see any signs of tiring in him or Lord Aelfred. They were well paired.

The match wore on. Rina accepted a cup of chilled lemon water, nothing stronger, and sipped.

As the sun slipped down from the point of the sky, there were murmurs about how well-matched Edrick and Lord Aelfred were. A second time Lord Aelfred knocked him down, and again he got up. She heard whispers behind her: "How long can this last? Surely Lord Aelfred had him there? What's he waiting for?"

Edrick seemed slower. Was he wearying? Rina studied him with her eyes and her runesense. He was husbanding his strength, wearing Lord Aelfred down, taking advantage of the longevity in his suit. Rina started to hope…

They went on and on. Some of the spectators started muttering about how Lord Aelfred should get on with it already. Sir Lindron's glare was like stone.

Rina perched on the edge of her seat, her runesense fully engaged. Lord Aelfred's suit showed the signs of flagging. The golden runes tinged to white. Edrick's blazed bright.

She almost missed it, half-turned to reply to the man beside her. Lord Aelfred flared all his runes at once, glowing bright as the sun in her runesense, and attacked. Edrick tried to parry and missed. The blow landed on his shoulder.

Rina was on her feet, pressed against the rail. The whole crowd roared as the fighters fell apart.

Edrick's breastplate dangled from one shoulder. The other swung free. Rina groaned and fell back in her chair. The strap they'd tried to fix had severed.

Sir Lindron still looked upset, but allowed a thin smile on his lips as Sir Rolan strode out onto the field. Lord Aelfred threw up one hand and pulled off his helmet. He walked to Edrick and claimed his hand, raising both men's arms skyward. "His strap failed...and so did my runes!" Lord Aelfred shouted. "A draw, so I say!"

The crowd cheered. Edrick pushed back his visor, and Rina saw the strain and shock there. She ached to run to him.

Instead Lord Aelfred dragged him over to the duke's pavilion. "I haven't had such a match ever," he said. "Grandfather! I want this man given a place under Sir Rolan! He'll be my sparring partner, and when I establish my own household, I want him as my master-of-arms." His wide grin dimmed, and he turned to Edrick. "That is, if you like..."

Edrick looked stunned. "My lord, I...of course—"

Sir Lindron clutched at the duke's chair. "Your Grace, this shabby failed squire is no fit companion for your heir!"

The duke rose, no frailty in his rail-thin form. "True, Sir Lindron. Though I recall, two summers ago, this man was the darling of the tournament field. And now..." He gestured at the stands, where the crowds were still screaming for the Piebald.

"He's made a farce of this," Sir Lindron hissed.

"No, but it appears you are trying to do so," the duke said. "Sit down and hush. Sir Rolan, my sword." He pointed a thin finger at Edrick. "Kneel."

Edrick went down on one knee at once.

The duke tapped his sword against each of Edrick's pauldrons. "Rise, Sir Edrick the Piebald," he said. Sir Rolan shouted his words to the crowd, and the field echoed with "The Piebald!"

"And this is your runesmith, yes?" Lord Aelfred said cheerfully, drawing near Rina. "Mage Telassi, I request—no, I command the honor of the next suit of armor you craft. With your work, I can't fail!"

She managed a nod. Words were beyond her.

Then Edrick was there, just on the other side of the low wooden barricade. He held out his hands, and she nodded. Edrick lifted her over the wall, setting her down on the field beside himself. She raised her face to his. "You were magnificent," she managed.

"How could I not be, with your favor?" Edrick asked. He bent and kissed her.

For the first time in her life, Rina found armor more of an annoyance than a pleasure.

ABOUT K. D. JULICHER

K. D. Julicher lives and writes in the wilds of Nevada. She collaborates on stories and raising daughters with her husband. Her work has appeared in *Writers of the Future, InterGalactic Medicine Show,* and at Baen.com

Website: www.kdjulicher.com
Facebook: kate.julicher
Email: kate.julicher@gmail.com

6

THE TEN SUNS

BY KEN LIU

Originally published in Dark Expanse: Surviving the Collapse (2014)

THE PRAIRIE STRETCHED in every direction as far as the eye could see. The sparse grass, yellow-tipped and dotted with purple and white flowers here and there, resembled an enlarged version of the tattered carpet that lay on the ground in Headman Kiv's tent. To the east, a few hundred bumps poked out of the carpet like mushrooms after rain—except that the mushrooms wriggled slowly.

A herd of taurochs.

With Primus high in the sky, this was the hottest hour of the day. The light summer coat of the taurochs shimmered in the sun as though each wore a rainbow, and their triple horns rose and dipped from time to time as they grazed lethargically. The animals would become livelier once Primus had set, and the temperature had cooled a bit with only Secundus in the sky.

Aluan, sitting atop his stallion at the head of the band of hunters, waved his arm decisively. "Charge!"

Forty whips fell against forty horses, and the thunder of pounding hooves filled the riders' ears. The men and women of the hunting band rushed towards the herd like an arrow made of flesh and blood, with young Aluan in the lead: the taurochs represented food, shelter, clothing, thread from sinews, tentpoles from bones, kefir bags from stomachs. The hunters took their bows from their shoulders.

The animals looked up, their long triple horns glinting in the sunlight. Sleep faded from their dark eyes like a receding tide, replaced by terror.

As one, the herd began to run, first slowly, then faster and faster. But a few older cows and young calves fell behind.

Quintus, Sextus, Septimus, and Octavus—none as bright as Primus—hung high in the sky from west to east like a strand of pearls. It was only a little cooler than when Primus shone alone.

Around the bright and warm bonfire, people danced, their movements loosened and their laughter made louder by bowls of kefir, were each accompanied by four shadows at their feet. Beyond the ring of dancers, racks of meat smoked.

"Not bad for your first time leading a hunt," said Ly. She had just stepped out of the ring of dancers to sit down on the ground next to Aluan. "We should have enough food to last a full month."

Aluan nodded perfunctorily.

Ly detected a lack of real joy in the gesture. "What's bothering you?"

"The animals are so lean and small. Have you ever seen a bull as fat as the one your grandfather said he killed when he was your age, heavy enough to need twenty men to lift it off the ground?"

"He was probably just exaggerating. Old men like to tell tall tales."

Aluan said nothing. After a few moments, he pulled out a handful of grass next to him and handed it to her. "Chew on this."

The taste was bitter, acrid.

"It's too dry," said Aluan. "Don't you remember how thick the grass used to be on the prairie when we were kids, and how sweet it tasted? No wonder the taurochs are not fattening up or reproducing as they used to."

She spat out the grass. "We always think things used to be better when we were little. But that's just because the world seemed new to us then."

Aluan laughed bitterly. "How many more hunts are left before there will be no more taurochs? You know I'm right, but you're afraid to agree with me. No one wants to talk about the truth. We'd all rather drink kefir and pretend things have always been the same——"

"It *has* always been the same." A few of the other hunters, sitting a bit further away, looked over at her raised voice. She looked back and smiled in a way that suggested this was just a lovers' spat. The others smiled in understanding and returned to their own conversations.

Before Aluan could answer her, the chants began around the bonfire. "Aluan! Aluan! Aluan!"

"It's time to retell the legends," said Ly. Her face looked anxious, and she gave Aluan a shove. "Don't mess it up. This is your first time. My father agreed that we can get married if you show yourself to be as proper in your beliefs as you are skilled as a hunter."

Aluan stood up, sighed, and walked towards the middle of the ring.

This is a story of how people came to be in our world: We were not born here, but were brought.

Long ago, before the time of the Five Kings and the Three Councils, before the time of the Fire and the Flood, before the Killings and the Separation, the world was a bare rock, cold and devoid of life.

Then the Zyxlar, the Bringers of Judgment, scattered the seeds of life into the world. It is said that the Zyxlar ruled over many worlds and held the power of life and death over many different forms of life: some had bodies made of stone; some had bodies made of insubstantial gas; some had hard carapaces like insects; some had leathery limbs like the creatures who crept in the grass; and still others were like you and me.

No one knows why the Zyxlar seeded this world with our ancestors, and the ancestors of the Saurians, Chitters, Silicates, and Methenes. They brought forth grass and trees, lakes and prairies, deserts and salt flats, the birds that fly in the air and the rockleech that swim in the water, the taurochs and devourers, the tumblebugs and stonerays. To give everything heat and light, they placed ten suns in the sky.

Now, there are many stories of the days when the ancestors of the Five Races lived together with, and served, the Zyxlar. They lived in a place called the City, where the houses were as tall as mountains. They could soar in the sky on giant mechanical birds and roam the earth on beasts made of metal that obeyed their will.

It is also said that they were not always hunters who lived like migrating wolves on the edge of starvation; in fact, there was a time when the world was not so dry, and our ancestors lived by the magic of agriculture, tending to plants that sprung out of the rich, wet soil, heavily laden with grain and fruit. It was then possible for a couple to have as many children as they wished, and all would have plenty to eat—

"That's enough, Aluan!" Headman Kiv cried out. "I've tried to tolerate your insistence on heresy, but you seem to treat my forbearance as weakness. How dare you repeat these lies! There is no such thing as 'agriculture.' We have always lived as proud hunters following the taurochs herds."

"Father!" Ly came up and stood by the side of Aluan. She glanced at Aluan, her eyes filled with annoyance and worry, but then she turned to look at Kiv with a placating smile. "Aluan has had too much to drink after a victorious hunt. You don't need to be so angry with him."

"I'm not drunk at all." Kiv's public reprimand only made Aluan more defiant. He shook off Ly's restraining arm. "How can you speak of 'always' when living memory can extend no further back than three generations? But what I spoke of are ancient stories, whispered from mother to son, generation after generation. If they are lies, why are you so afraid?"

"You speak heresy! Foolish stories lead men's hearts astray and threaten our people's survival. The Zyxlar made this world for us and assigned us the task of praising their name. How dare you suggest that they were not perfect and that the world has declined from some golden age? You'll never lead another hunt. Ly, step away from that fool. You're forbidden from speaking to him again."

"Dad!"

Aluan stepped in front of Ly. "She's sixteen. She may choose who she wishes to speak to. Think about it: your anger confirms what we all suspect is the truth—that the world is not perfect, that something has gone wrong. The Zyxlar made us the lords of this land, but foolish headmen have led us astray and lack the courage for change."

Kiv's face was so red that his head seemed on the edge of explosion. "I should never have taken you in as an orphan and raised you like my son. Doren, Sy, Klaiten, seize this fool and whip him until he confesses his error."

Aluan stood still, his face obstinate.

But Ly pulled on his arm. "Run, run! His anger will dissipate faster than your body can heal. I swear: I won't come to visit you if you are whipped because you're too stubborn to listen to me tonight."

Reluctantly, Aluan turned and ran with Ly towards the horses.

Kiv's men gave pursuit for a while, but Ly and Aluan had taken two of the fastest horses. Besides, they were also Aluan's friends and chased rather half-heartedly. Eventually, the men disappeared below the horizon.

Aluan and Ly loosened the reins and slowed down. Only Nonus and Decimus remained in the western sky. Primus was about to rise. After a day of hunting and hard riding, both riders and their horses were tired.

On the shore of a tiny lake, they crested a small hillock that blocked the wind a bit. "Let's camp here."

Since they had escaped in a hurry, all they had in their packs for food were just a few strips of smoked meats. Ly went to fish while Aluan started a campfire.

Freshly grilled noodlefish, even unsalted and spiced only with hunger, was tasty. After the meal, Ly and Aluan lay down on the grass and looked up at the blue, cloudless sky.

"You really think that the world has changed?" Ly asked.

Aluan laughed bitterly. "Ly, did you see that cairn we passed half an hour ago? The one with ten red stones at the base?"

The migrating tribes left cairns on the prairie to mark their passage and to indicate the boundaries of their territories to strangers. After years of bloody wars long lost to lore, the Five Servant Races had claimed separate parts of the world in the Great Separation.

Six years ago, on her tenth birthday, Aluan and Ly had spent a full day collecting red rocks from all over the grasslands to build a cairn to celebrate. Red was her favorite color.

-So that's ten stones, one for each year you've lived, and one for each of our ten suns.

-That makes no sense. How can a stone stand for both a year and a sun?

-Ly, do you know why there are ten suns in the sky?

-Dad says it was because Zyxlar had the Five Servant Races and that there was a heaven and a hell for each.

-So each sun would be a different world?

-I guess so.

-Maybe. But I think it's because the Zyxlar were lazy. Instead of making one big sun, they made ten little ones. It's like how it's much harder to bake one large flatbread that's cooked evenly throughout, but much easier to bake ten little ones.

-Hahaha …Aluan, you're being ridiculous. Be careful not to let my father hear it, or you'll get whipped again.

-Why should I get whipped? My story is just as likely to be true as his.

In the intervening years, others passing by seemed to have added to the cairn, but left the red stones exposed at the base, perhaps because they looked so distinct.

Aluan's voice pulled her back into the present. "Remember, we built it on the shore of a lake."

This lake. For half an hour, they had ridden over ground that had once been covered by water.

"But lakes grow and shrink all the time." Ly said. "That's no proof that the drought is getting worse or that our people once lived differently."

"Your father isn't around. You really believe that?"

Now it was Ly's turn to say nothing. She picked up another stalk of grass and chewed on it. It was bitter.

"Even if what you say is true, what can we do about it? The Zyxlar left us long ago. They had the power and magic, not us."

"Why *can't* we do something about it? There are also stories of our people being great heroes from before the time of the Zyxlar. There was Hercules, who fought a god. There was Neil the Strong-Armed, who walked in the heavens—"

"—those are myths! More heresy! Would it kill you to just worry about what you can see and touch?"

Aluan looked at her, a smirk turning up the corners of his mouth. "You wouldn't like me much if I did that."

"Ha! Who says I like you much now?"

"You're here with me, aren't you?"

Ly blushed and decided to change the subject. "My father raised you like a son, hoping you'd be my right arm when I take over one day. I'm sure his anger will have ebbed in another few days. We'll go back and apologize."

"I am not apologizing! How can I help lead our people if I'm not allowed to say or think what I want?"

"What makes you so certain you're right?"

Aluan gazed back at her. His face held an expression she had never seen before.

"Tell me!"

"I don't hate your father. I know he's trying to keep the tribe focused on the task of survival, instead of …fantastical stories that have no use. He's only become so orthodox because the drought seems to have no end. If you go back now, your father will forgive you. But if I tell you…"

"How can I decide what to do if you can't trust me to know what you know?"

Aluan blew out a breath. He nodded. "All right. Let's wait until Primus is up, and I'll show you what I've found."

———

They woke up after Primus had climbed about a quarter of the way to the zenith.

They washed with the clear, cold water of the lake, and then, while Aluan dressed and cooked a hare he had shot, Ly faced Primus, closed her eyes—staring at the glory that was Primus, even for a few seconds, would have blinded her—and sang her morning prayers.

Giver of Light, First Among Equals. You are the warmest, brightest, most life-giving of ten brothers. We give you thanks, Lord Primus. May our Headman lead us as wisely as you lead the suns of Zyxlar.

She noticed that Aluan refused to join in the prayer or to even pause his work. Has he really grown so full of pride? Her anger grew.

He doesn't know everything. No one does. Haven't the Wandering Sages of the Grasslands always taught that the Terrans are meant to be ignorant about much of the world, lest we become as the Zyxlar?

After the meal, as they washed their hands and faces by the lake, Aluan said, "Would you try to hunt for some supper by yourself? I need time to prepare something to show you."

Ly nodded, preoccupied with thoughts of how to reconcile her father and Aluan.

By the time Ly returned to their campsite, Primus was nearing the western horizon, and Secundus and Tertius were rising in the east. She had a pair of rock-shelled voles hanging from her saddle and a dozen prairie gaswing eggs, a delicacy, packed in soft grass in her pouch. Aluan had been a malnourished little boy when he had first arrived in their tent, and for years, her father had saved all the prairie gaswing eggs for him. Maybe the sight would guilt him into agreeing to return home with her.

Aluan, sweaty and exhausted looking, was working on some contraption. By the looks of it, he had been at it all day. It was possible that he had skipped lunch and even his nap.

"Hey, time to eat."

He looked up and smiled at her. "I'm almost finished. I have to get this done before Primus sets."

She sat down next to him and brought the fire back to life. She set the eggs to boil in a bark-pot and began to dress the voles, peeking at what Aluan held in his hand.

He had constructed a long, rectangular box out of skins wrapped around a frame woven from the tough reeds growing at the edge of the lake. One end of the box was covered by the soft, supple skin of a young fox, stretched taut across the opening. There was a tiny hole in the middle of the skin, apparently poked by a sharpened reed.

"What are you making?"

"You'll see." He flipped the box over to show her the other end. She gasped. A translucent, pale white, thin screen covered the opening of the box.

He had collected the gossamer threads spun by the spiders whose silken balloons drifted across the prairie in spring whenever there was a breeze. The threads were so thin that he must have spent all day painstakingly picking up each strand with a reed stalk to carefully lay it across the box opening. It was the most beautiful thing she had ever seen.

She frowned. "That's a lot of effort for something that will fall apart with a puff of breath." On the grasslands, effort had to be conserved and survival was tenuous. The amount of effort he had spent on something like this could have been spent on hunting. She lamented the waste.

"Then don't blow at it." He held the box up so that the end with the tiny hole in the fox skin faced Primus, and the end with the gossamer screen was in front of her face. She looked and gasped again.

On the screen was an image of Primus, about the size of the palm of her hand. It was another shade of white, much brighter than the screen itself. But unlike staring at Primus itself, it wasn't painful to stare at this echo of Primus.

"What kind of magic is this?" she asked.

"It's not magic," he said. "The box is light-proof—"

Ly shuddered. The world was never without light from one or more of the ten suns. Lightless places, where the sun could not shine, existed only in caves deep under water, in snake nests hidden underground, in stone houses where murderers and witches were left to die in darkness. To construct a light-proof thing was to brush against evil.

But Aluan went on, oblivious. "—and through this pinhole, only a thousandth of Primus's strength can pass through. That light, falling against the screen on this end, forms an image of Primus. But because the image has only a small amount of the strength of Primus, it's possible to look at it without hurting your eyes. I call it the sun-gazer."

"That's very clever," Ly said. She marveled at the image on the screen, the first time she had ever been able to truly see what Primus looked like.

Instead of the perfect outlined circle she had always imagined, she saw a disk with fiery, indistinct edges. Curling tongues of flame shot out from the disk, reminding her of the tiny swimming legs of the gigantic jade-jellyfish drifting in the lakes. And the disk itself was hardly like the surface of a pearl. Dark patches, like impurities drifting in a cup of kefir or pimples on a youthful face, dotted the white surface and marred it.

But Lord Primus was without flaws. Unlike earthly objects, Primus was heavenly and contained no impurities.

"Hardly perfect, is it?" asked Aluan. She could hear a kind of weariness as well as relief in his voice. "But that's not even the most interesting part. Try to memorize the pattern of the dots." Aluan then moved the box so that the pinhole end pointed at Secundus. "Tell me what you see."

Secundus was not nearly as bright as Primus, and the image on the screen was far dimmer as well. It took a few moments for Ly's eyes to adjust. Once again, there were the curling tongues of flame reaching out from the edge of the disk and the scattered black spots across the surface: here's a bunch that reminded her of the shape of the rocks poking out of the lake's surface; there's a bunch that she thought looked like the hundreds of cairns snaking across Tannerjin, the holy site where all the tribes gathered every year ...

Wait!

She grabbed the box from Aluan's hand and looked back at Primus, and then at Secundus again. Then she turned to Tertius, and then back to Primus. Finally, she put the box down and stared at Aluan.

His face was completely expressionless. Not even a muscle twitched. He was waiting for her to say what she thought before he would react.

Her voice trembled. What she had seen was too incredible, too strange. She was sure she was hallucinating. "Secundus and Tertius ... looking at them is like looking at Primus ...in a mirror."

Whatever Ly had been expecting from Aluan wasn't what she got: he whooped and roared with laughter; he did a cartwheel; he came up to her and kissed her, hard.

She was too stunned to speak.

"Finally, finally!" He put his hands on the sides of her face and touched his forehead to hers. "I've been unable to share what I've seen with anyone. For the longest time, I thought I was crazy, mad, that I hallucinated. I made sun-gazers and then destroyed them, only to rebuild them again. But you see it, you see what I see! It's true."

"But what does this mean?"

"I don't know! I've been observing the suns in secret for years. The patterns have been getting denser." He took out and unfolded a large sheet of the thinnest tauroch skin, cured and scraped and worked until it was as soft as a newborn's nose. It was filled with dense drawings of disks with patterns of black dots. "The patterns of dots shift over time.

It's always the same: whatever shows up on Primus can also be seen on Secundus, Tertius, Quartus…but backwards, so that what's east is west, and west east."

Ly looked at him, terror in her eyes. "I don't understand. Are you saying that the nine suns other than Primus are illusions? That they don't exist?"

Aluan shook his head. "I don't have answers. But I do know that the stories your father insists on are not true. The ten suns are not each unique; the drought has been getting worse; we used to have more and bigger game to hunt, and maybe we once didn't need to hunt at all. I don't know how these things are connected, but I do know that I can't make myself believe in lies anymore." He nodded at the sun-gazer in Ly's hand.

Ly thought about what she had seen on the translucent screen. It was true. Once she had seen the flares curling away from the edge of the image of Primus, it was impossible to believe in the perfectly smooth, unchanging flow of her father's stories.

But she was reminded of one particular story her father had once told her after he had drunk too much kefir, a story that he had laughed at and said contained no truth at all.

"It's an old myth of Earth," he had said, "just a made-up story."

No one knew what "of Earth" meant—whether it was the name of a place or person or god. Ly knew only that it meant this was a story from before the time of the Zyxlar, brought from the womb of the Terrans. And the story had frightened her.

Long ago, when the universe was young and the Terrans still lived on our home world, there were ten suns.

The suns did not come out all at once. Instead, they slept beneath the world, and each day, a different sun rose from the east, heated and lighted the world, and set in the west to bring forth night.

"Ly, what's 'night'?"

I don't know, and my father didn't explain. But since the suns only came up one at a time, I guess night is when there is no sun.

"But there is always at least a sun, or a few suns, in the sky."

Let me finish the story. One day, the ten suns grew bored, and decided to all come out and play at the same time. The combined heat of the ten suns was unbearable. Water boiled from the ocean and the lakes; the exposed riverbeds cracked with the heat; plants wilted and animals panted with thirst; those laboring in the fields fell down—

"What does 'laboring in the fields' mean?"

I don't know! There were lots of things my father said that didn't make sense.

What happened next was that a great hero, whose name was Hou Yi, came to save the Terrans. He climbed the tallest mountain, and, from its peak, demanded that the suns resume their orderly course.

The suns refused.

And so Hou Yi took off his bow, which was made from the horns of the strongest, biggest bull taurochs, and he notched an arrow, which was made from the sharpest reed growing by the shores of the Yellow River and the longest wing feathers of migrating wild gaswing. Hou Yi pulled the bow until it was as round as the disks of the suns themselves. Then he let go.

The arrow struck one of the suns, and it dove into the ocean and sank beneath the waves like a fiery bird shot out of the sky.

One by one, Hou Yi shot down nine of the suns. The last sun, terrified, promised to rise and set every day as regularly as the swings of a pendulum, and that was how the great hero restored balance to the world.

———

Aluan pondered Ly's story. Then he opened his eyes.

The determination in Aluan's eyes both excited and frightened Ly.

"What have you decided?" Ly asked.

"I must become Hou Yi and shoot the suns down. I must go to the City. It's the only way to save our people."

"You're crazy—"

Aluan smiled at her. "Why do you think I'm the one who's mad? Isn't it even more mad to go on pretending year after year, decade after decade, that nothing is wrong, that nothing has changed, that we can do nothing?

"But now we know what our people are capable of—"

"—it's just a myth—"

"—but myths can become true. Would you have believed that you could gaze at the face of Lord Primus one day without being blinded?

Would you have believed that the other suns are but mirrors for Lord Primus? Had I told you these things but yesterday, you would have dismissed them as myths, too!"

Ly's heart felt uplifted. His faith was like the light of life-giving Primus. "Then I'm coming with you."

Our ancestors once lived with the Zyxlar in the City, far to the north. There, the mountain-houses were so dense that they formed a forest. Thousands, perhaps even millions, lived in the forest, along with metal beasts and machine birds.

"That's not even remotely possible, Aluan."

Don't talk to me of possible and impossible. Haven't we already reached the edge of the grasslands, supposedly endless? Haven't we already seen animals you've never imagined? Haven't we already been journeying in this land where there's nothing but sand for days? Haven't we seen the Silicates and Saurians scurry out of our way even though we were told that violating the Separation would surely bring us death?

Back to the story. One day, the Zyxlar decided to abandon our ancestors and left them on their own. Without the Zyxlar, the magic that kept the City running died.

"I'm going to die of thirst if I don't get a drink of water."

Here you go.

"Why aren't you drinking?"

I'm not thirsty.

"Liar! That was our last bit of water, wasn't it? You should have taken it yourself. You haven't drunk anything for a whole day."

I told you. I'm not thirsty.

"Our horses are dead. We're never going to get out of this place, are we?"

Of course we will. Didn't Hou Yi have to climb the highest mountain? Didn't Neil the Strong-Armed have to endure a house of darkness propelled by a pillar of fire? We will make it.

"Finish telling me the story. I'm not so thirsty when the story gets good."

The lights in the mountain-houses dimmed. The stale air inside the City became suffocating. The metal birds fell out of the sky, killing those who rode on them. The metal beast no longer obeyed. The Terrans had to leave the City to survive, and the City fell silent and disappeared from our memories.

But it's there Ly, I know it's there, and I will find it. That is where I will find the bow that will shoot down the suns that are drying this world and killing us.

The rain came like a solid sheet of water descending from the sky. The two of them were drenched in minutes. Still, they lifted their faces to the sky and drank and drank.

All the suns, even Primus, were hidden behind thick layers of clouds. Light seemed to come from everywhere.

The country they were in now was mountainous, and the water, more water than they had ever seen, coalesced into rivulets, collected into rivers, and thundered through the valleys into some misty distance. The mountains, steep, hard, and soilless, supported no vegetation. Any seeds that tried to take root would have been washed away.

"Do you think that's where the *ocean* is?" Aluan asked.

"Perhaps." Ly was no longer able to doubt anything, no matter how fantastic.

"No matter how hard it rains here," Aluan said, "the water doesn't seem to be able to cross the desert before it's boiled away. It rains hard where there's too much water, and it doesn't rain where the ground is thirsty."

When the rain stopped, they emerged from the valley.

The City loomed before them, a forest of towering steel skeletons that seemed to reach for the sky. At their feet were piles of rubble like giant cairns. As Ly and Aluan made their way through the City, broken shells of metal beasts, some with stiff wings like dead birds, lined the wide avenues. Beds, chairs, tables and other strangely-shaped furniture whose purpose eluded them were scattered here and there, crumbling to dust at one touch.

"So, it's all true," whispered Ly. It was so quiet save for the occasional twitter of a bird or the scrabbling of some animal's feet. The place felt unwelcoming; everything seemed alien.

They headed for the center of the City, where a gigantic domed structure rose out of the rubble, the only intact building left.

The build had heavy metal doors that slid on rails. They were stuck, semi-open. Beyond the opening was darkness.

Ly hesitated.

"Hou Yi would not be afraid," said Aluan, even though Ly could tell that he was terrified. Nonetheless, he took a deep breath and stepped inside.

Immediately, a booming, disembodied voice whose tone betrayed no emotion spoke: "Access denied. Unaccompanied members of the Slave Races must be authorized."

The heavy doors came to life can began to slide towards each other. Aluan tried to back out but his right leg was caught between them. He fell to the ground and began to scream. The doors groaned and the sound of rusty, ancient machinery drowned out his screams.

Ly rushed over and tried to pull him out, and then she tried to push the doors back. It was like struggling against a mountain. Aluan's leg slowly deformed in the crushing grip of the doors, and then they heard it break. He screamed again. But the doors still would not let go.

Ly prayed to Lord Primus, she called out to the Zyxlar. She shouted for her father's help. But no one answered her.

Then she saw a row of five impressions on the surface of the door, one of which was in the shape of a hand. Without thinking, she put her hand in it. She felt a sharp stab of pain, and when she pulled her hand out, she saw beads of blood at the tips of her fingers.

"Identity of authorized Terran confirmed," said the disembodied voice. "You may enter."

The doors scraped even more loudly in their rails as they slid back open.

Ly cradled Aluan's head in her arms and kissed his face. "Oh thank Lord Primus. I thought I had lost you!"

Aluan gave her a wan smile. "Thank yourself. The bloodline of the Headmen flows through you. The Zyxlar authorized you."

A second set of doors slid open, and they were bathed in milky white light.

Inside, the domed building was just one massive circular hall. Ly had splinted Aluan's leg, and slowly, with Aluan's arm over her shoulder, the pair climbed up the long, spiraling stairway along the wall on three legs. It was like being inside a mountain.

A great chandelier hung suspended from the apex of the dome. As they passed clusters of strange machinery along the wall, full of levers and buttons and blinking lights, the strange voice would speak up as they passed each:

"Terraforming Station Fifty, Solar Observation: heightened solar activity exceeding safety levels. Recommend decrease in illumination."

"Terraforming Station Forty-four, Hydrology: water table depleted in temperate zone."

"Terraforming Station Twenty-one, Meteorology: extreme weather patterns in progress. Recommend decreasing global temperature."

Aluan and Ly took everything in, without being certain of anything.

At last, as they were about to collapse from exhaustion, they arrived on the platform at the top. A great globe hung in front of them, and on it was a mottled pattern of green and brown, dotted here and there with some blue patches. The globe spun slowly. Some distance away, a blindingly bright lamp illuminated half of the globe. Close to the globe, on the side away from the lamp, hovered a semi-ring made of nine circular mirrors that reflected the light from the lamp onto the half of the globe that would have been in shadow.

The voice spoke again, "Terraforming Station One, Solar Energy Collection: all reflectors operational."

Ly and Aluan understood without needing to say anything.

They looked around and saw another station marked with the image of a rising arrow atop a pillar of flames.

"Planetary Defense Station: Authorized personnel only."

Ly placed her hand, like before, into the impression by the station. She winced as more blood was taken from her.

"Identity confirmed. Weapons systems fully operational. No invading spacecraft identified within range."

In front of them was a screen, a much bigger version of the one on Aluan's sun-gazer. Below it was a stick. As Aluan pulled and pushed at it, the view on the screen seemed to change, and eventually, the pale image of a disk filled the screen.

"Target is Reflector Number Two. Are you certain?"

Aluan and Ly looked at each other and smiled.

"Are you ready?" he asked.

She nodded. "Let's be Hou Yi."

Aluan pressed the button. There was a thunderous roar that shook the building and the two of them fell to the floor. By the time they scrambled up, Secundus had disappeared from the screen.

"One down, eight more to go," said Ly.

When they emerged from the building, they were greeted by darkness.

Ly clutched Aluan's hand. "Is this night?"

Aluan squeezed her hand.

They seemed to hear again the emotionless voice that had accompanied them as they descended the great, spiral stairs.

"Terraforming Station Thirty-One, Temperature: All reflectors offline. Global temperature decreasing."

"Look," Aluan said, pointing up at the sky. Flickering sparks drifted high above them, the broken bits of the mirrors that had once made this world one without night. As some of them fell, they turned into bright meteors.

But behind them were more steady pinpricks of light that studded the dark heavens like nourishing dewdrops on the prairie, like bright pearls scattered around a black crown, like hope emerging from desperation.

"I wonder what Dad is telling everyone," said Ly. Instead of terror, she felt awe and beauty.

For the first time in millennia, the Terrans on this planet saw the stars.

ABOUT KEN LIU

Ken Liu is an author of speculative fiction, as well as a translator, lawyer, and programmer. A winner of the Nebula, Hugo, and World Fantasy awards, he is the author of The Dandelion Dynasty, a silkpunk epic fantasy series (*The Grace of Kings* (2015), *The Wall of Storms* (2016), and a forthcoming third volume) and *The Paper Menagerie and Other Stories* (2016), a collection. He also wrote the Star Wars novel, *The Legends of Luke Skywalker* (2017).

In addition to his original fiction, Ken also translated numerous works from Chinese to English, including *The Three-Body Problem* (2014), by Liu Cixin, and "Folding Beijing," by Hao Jingfang, both Hugo winners.

Website: http://kenliu.name
Facebook: authorkenliu
Twitter: @kyliu99
Public Email: ken@kenliu.name

7

GRAVE SECRETS

BY CHARLIE N. HOLMBERG

THE CREATURE IN the basement was moving again.

Layne cringed with the shifting of the chains, the subtle press of weight on the floorboards. The boards had been set right over the concrete, without any cushioning in between. Several of them were cracked. Probably more, now.

She held her breath, hands submerged in the half-full kitchen sink, listening. Too late she noticed the water pouring from the faucet was scalding hot. She ripped her hands from the dirty dishes, staring at her fingers like they weren't her own. The skin was red, and she could see her pulse in the fat tissue at the top of her palm. Coming to herself, she turned the handle of the faucet until the water ran cool, then held her hands beneath it until the sting lessened. She scraped her lunch, not even half eaten, into the trash and added the plate to the water. She didn't have much of an appetite anymore. Layne washed the dishes despite the burns, her skin feeling too tight for her hands. There wasn't much to clean, besides. Not since Henry's passing.

She dried her hands on the threadbare dish towel left over from her wedding; the rooster on it was barely discernable, and there was a hole where its comb should be. Then she paused, and the house sat quiet, more still than the ice hanging from the eaves outside the cracked kitchen window. Layne waited a moment, listening. The silence continued, not even punctuated by the titmice.

She walked carefully, having memorized where to step to avoid her own creaks, to avoid stirring the thing in the basement. Her small bedroom was safe, its floor mounted on solid earth, with no room for anything to stir below. The full-sized bed took up almost the entire space, the mattress lumpy and bent from where two bodies used to fit themselves on it, pulled close together to keep from falling off the edges. She fit just fine on it, now.

Somewhere behind and below, chains rattled. Layne stepped over the pile of clean laundry at the foot of the bed, still not folded despite her having taken it off the line two days ago. There was the twenty-four-inch TV on the dresser, the remote long since lost. A little clay pot full of paper flowers rested on the windowsill, given to her on her first wedding anniversary. Henry's guitar and Scottish pipes had been shoved into the corner, collecting dust. If she could make the trip to the library, she might be able to sell those online. Earn a few extra dollars for a new dress, or a haircut. But she couldn't bring herself to do it. The drive wasn't terrible, but she could still hear his fingertips on those strings, his elbow pumping air through the chanter. A silly thing, really. He'd stopped playing them years before his death. But Henry had never tried to sell them, either.

Layne pressed the base of her hand against a sudden pain in her chest. The house rattled. She sucked in a breath that seared her throat on the way down. The creature was awake, and *angry*. The following *thud* was it throwing itself against the north wall hard enough that the bedroom door opened another inch. When had it gotten large enough to do that?

She clasped her trembling hands together, moving closer to the window. She could run, if she needed to. How far she'd get, she couldn't be certain. No neighbors for miles. And she didn't know how fast the monster was. If it knew her scent. If it could see in the dark.

The house pulsed a third time, and this time the doorknob slammed into the wall. Chains rattled to the floor, and for a terrifying moment Layne was sure the thing had broken free. Her age-spotted hands flew to the rusted lock on the pane. Spit dried on her tongue. Tears wet her eyes.

A fourth, quieter thump sounded, followed by stillness. She waited, listening for the creaking of the stairs, the creaking of the hinges on the basement door. But the noises didn't come, and slowly, so slowly, she pulled one finger at a time from the lock.

The monster had leapt—it must have. Leapt at the ceiling—the kitchen floor—and then fallen back to the ground. It was growing. How could it grow? Beasts like this one were supposed to shrink with time, like a pimple, or a goose egg. That's what Oprah had said. The creature hadn't thrashed so violently last month. Layne was sure it hadn't.

She studied the yard outside her window, untended and shriveled with the winter. Cattle wire marked its edges, barely visible in the dim, cloud-choked light. Spikes of grass poked up through a thin layer of snow. Patches of dirt were half mud, half ice. The forest's thick tree line carpeted the distance. Could she make it to those trees on her own? She had so little energy these days…if she left now, would she make it by dark?

Pressing her cheek to the cold glass, breath puffing across it, Layne saw the small, snowy mound near the corner of the house, with an unpainted cross stabbed into its head. She'd had to dig it herself. Cover it herself. Cut the wood herself, from leftover basement floorboards. Even now, she was sure it wasn't deep enough. Was certain starving animals would come and dig him up, eat him, and carry him away in their bellies if she didn't keep vigil.

She couldn't leave Henry. She couldn't leave home.

The thing below slithered up the stairs, then back down again.

"Go away," she whispered, peeling herself from the glass. "Go away."

The creature didn't respond. And so Layne shut and locked her bedroom door and turned on the television using the tiny buttons beneath the screen. She only got three channels out here, and one was in Spanish, so she settled on a second-rate news show located in a city she'd only visited twice. Then she perched on the bed and began folding her laundry. She had nothing in her drawers, and she hated empty spaces. A breeze caused the leafless dogwood outside the kitchen window to scrape across the glass, making a whining sound like a hurt dog, so Layne stopped to turn the television up, then folded, folded, folded. Anything to keep her busy. Anything to stop her from thinking.

Anything to make her chest stop hurting, and distract her from the monster.

The creature below was always silent at night, so when it wasn't, Layne woke in a cold sweat, despite the baseboard heaters being turned to high. It was only her eyelids that moved at first—her eyelids and her heart, which started thrumming in her chest like injured wasps. Her lungs followed, heaving like the bag to those Scottish pipes in the corner. She stared at her ceiling, seeing the shapes of spiders along it until her mind snapped into place and pulled the shadows from the soffits. Then she just stared, waiting, praying it was a dream.

But two heartbeats later, a *thud* shook the house, rattling the hinges on the bedroom door. The strings of Henry's guitar chirped in earnest.

The monster *never* stirred at night. Layne always felt the safest when she slept. When she could shut her thoughts, her sorrows, and her pains off for a few hours.

But not now.

She bolted upright in bed. The kitchen floor creaked from pressure *beneath* it, like the whole house had turned over and struggled to hold the weight of something unbearably heavy. But worst of all was the absence of clinks—no chains. The chains didn't drag, didn't drop. Which meant the beast was no longer bound by them.

Gooseflesh rippled down her arms and thighs, sweat trickling down the curve of her spine. Her coat was in the hallway closet, but the thing leapt again, and this time she heard splinters. *It's coming,* she realized with a sucking sensation that ran from her throat to her pelvis. *It's coming for me.*

She grabbed the afghan off her bed and ran for the window, knocking over the little clay pot and its paper flowers in the process. She grabbed the lock and wrenched it, then pressed clammy hands against the pane to shift the window open. But the thing wouldn't budge. Breaths coming sharper, Layne dug her fingers between the sash and the jamb, tugging, wrenching, snapping one fingernail, then tearing another.

"Move, *move,*" she pleaded.

The scent of smoke stung her nostrils, then her eyes. She blinked back tears, only to notice a spot of flame near her ankles. The paper flowers had landed on the baseboard heater and burst into flame.

Gasping, Layne jumped back, patting her pajama leg to put out any embers. The kitchen bucked as the creature slammed into the basement ceiling again, hard enough that her door opened despite the locked knob.

The flames from the flowers jumped to the cotton drapes and ate them whole, consuming them in one bite like a snake.

"Oh God, help me," she whispered, backing away from the glow that lit the whole room orange. The heat burned away the sweat on her skin, but not the gooseflesh. The bumps grew stiffer and more plentiful as the fire first leapt left to the other curtain, then right to the Scottish pipes, which seemed to give out a soft wheeze of defeat as its Gore-Tex melted.

Turning around, Layne ran.

She couldn't remember the last time she really *ran*. Even when Henry fell while installing the floorboards, it had been more of an unsure hobble. She bolted into the short hallway, and the *thing* jumped at her, sensing her presence. Her feet barely kept purchase. She made it to the kitchen, where the beige linoleum was splitting, before the monster attacked again, widening the split to two fingers' width. She fell, her bad knee hitting hard as she did, but her arm flew out in front of her, saving her skull from cracking against the floor. Still, the room spun for a moment. She blinked in the dim glow of the porch light seeping through the window, smelling the smoke following her path. She spied the remote control beneath the sink and stared at it a long moment, realizing some past part of her should have been rejoicing.

The monster leapt right beneath her heart, and the kitchen floor gave, caving in right at the center, dipping between the fridge and the Lazy Susan. A weak wail climbed up Layne's throat as she slid toward it, caught as though in a whirlpool. Beneath that crack something glowed, like the fire building behind her, but this something was dark and slick, oily and noxious.

She planted her sweaty hands against the linoleum. Got her better knee under her and slowed her descent. She had to grab onto the counter to get to her feet, then nearly fell over again as the entire house began to buckle. A gnawing cry shot up from the ever-growing crack in the floor, rattling her bones, finding purchase in them. The refrigerator door swung open, and bottles of condiments fell onto the floor, glass shattering, plastic rolling into the maw.

Gritting her teeth, Layne ran and leapt, barely clearing the break in the linoleum. She landed and fell to her knees again, crying out as pain burst through her right one. Scrambling for the back door, she barely had the thought to grab her loafers as the creature's arm burst up into the kitchen and reached for her, cold touch licking her heel as she crawled out into the snow.

She didn't remember putting the loafers on, but they were on, the afghan pulled tight around her shoulders. Snow crunched underfoot as she bolted across the covered lawn, the tree line in the distance nothing more than a smear of black beneath a sky nearly as dark. The only light was the east half of the house, readily consumed by fire. For a second, or a sliver of one, Layne thought maybe the blaze would kill the beast. Put her out of her misery. But as she looked back to the brilliant orange waves, she saw it crouching there atop the mound of dirt, resting against the makeshift cross, watching her with dark, liquid eyes. Its body bubbled and writhed, and when it breathed in, it took the air in her lungs with it.

Layne stopped moving. Stopped breathing. She could only watch, petrified, as the creature moved toward her, elongating with every step, its true body never leaving that grave. It had been born there, after all. Created with every shovel of dirt, each fallen tear.

If only Layne had realized then how horrible her grief would become, she might have done something differently.

But now it clawed forward, never once breaking eye contact.

And consumed her whole.

ABOUT CHARLIE N. HOLMBERG

Charlie Nicholes Holmberg was born in Salt Lake City, Utah, to two parents who sacrificed a great deal to give their very lazy daughter a good education. As a result, Charlie learned to hate uniforms, memorized all English prepositions in alphabetical order, and mastered the art of Reed-Kellogg diagramming a sentence at age seven. She entered several writing contests in her elementary years and never placed.

In summer 2013, after collecting many rejection letters and making a quilt out of them, Charlie sold her ninth novel, *The Paper Magician*, and its sequel to 47North with the help of her wonderful agent, Marlene Stringer. Someday she will own a dog. (Did she mention her third book, *The Master Magician*, totally made the WSJ bestseller list? Because it totally made the WSJ bestseller list.)

Charlie is also a board member for the Deep Magic e-zine of science fiction and fantasy.

8

THE HALL OF THE DIAMOND QUEEN

BY ANTHONY RYAN

SHE LOVED TO watch them run. Victory's reward was the spectacle of fleeing men, the raging panic and fear a tangible delight as the Raptorile and Tormented broke their ranks and the blackwings streaked down from above, talons flashing and beaks gaping wide. This had been a harder battle than most, the foe an army some forty thousand strong led by a veteran warrior king of typically noble aspect. She could see him now, standing atop a small hill, two-handed longsword raised high as his most loyal retainers clustered around him for the final stand. She felt a faint tick of recognition as her unnaturally keen sight found his face, lined with age but still handsome beneath the beard, and the eyes of pale shade of blue reminding her of the sea.

There is only the Voice. The Voice brings great rewards and dark glory. Those deaf to the Voice are Abominate.

The mantra came unbidden, an automatic response to the surge of memory, banishing the images with a brutal ease that always stirred her gratitude. All memory is a lie, the Voice had taught her long ago. Beware its seduction, my Sharrow-met. She soon knew the recognition for what it was, watching the king reorder his ranks below. She couldn't hear his words but didn't need to; "Fight!" would be his exhortation. "Fight on or all is lost!" Another doomed hero. And there have been so many.

She laid her gauntleted hand on Keera's neck, playing the steel

157

fingers through the great bird's ebony feathers, whispering a soft command. The blackwing tilted in response, banking hard to circle the hill where the noble king made his stand, now ringed by at least a thousand men. Ever more were rushing to join him, fear waning and shame surging at the sight of his example. Kilted clansmen from the northern vales with their double-bladed axes, strongbow wielding plainsmen from the south, barely armed crofters from the western shore, all rushing to stand with the great king against the surging horde.

Such courage, she mused, guiding Keera lower. A shame, but one such as he will ever be deaf to the Voice.

She had Keera ignore the outer ranks and swoop low over the king's house guards, steel-clad talons tearing through their armour like scythes through corn, blood rising in a sweet-tasting vapour that beaded her skin, hot and fresh. Keera rose from the hill-top with a warrior clutched in each claw, then cast them away, rent and torn, their blood like rain on the terrorised faces of their fellows. A few bows thrummed but the arrows flew wide as Keera's wings fanned the air into a gale. The king stood alone now, she saw, his guards forced back by the bird's fury.

She hissed a sigh of anticipation as Keera folded her wings, bird and rider plunging down in a black streak. She had intended to inflict a quick but spectacular death. Not, of course, out of mercy but as a demonstration to his men, the final blow to their teetering courage. The king, however, contrived to frustrate her, diving clear of Keera's snapping beak and delivering a swift backhand stroke with his sword. The bird screamed as the blade found her eye, dark blood gouting as she reeled away, wings spreading in panic, then settling into unnatural stillness at a touch from her rider's hand.

"The Voice is kind," Sharrow-met told the king as she dismounted from Keera's back. "And never shirks from offering friendship to a valiant foe." The offer was perfunctory and she knew the king could hear the amusement in her tone as she strode towards him, her hand going to the long, black-bladed scimitar strapped across her back.

"The Voice offers only death to the valiant," the king replied in a low voice, eyes grim with implacable resolve as he crouched in anticipation of combat. "And slavery to the cowardly...and the deluded."

There was an additional weight to this last word that gave her pause, a sense of resigned sorrow. Once again she scrutinised his face, the recognition swelling anew, summoning an image of a man and a woman standing in a garden, his eyes an echo of the ocean beyond. Can't you see the trap in his words? the man was saying, leaning close to the woman, a keen desperation evident in voice and manner. You think he promises life? The histories are clear. All the Voice ever brings is death...

There is only the Voice. The Voice brings great rewards and dark glory.

The vision shattered as the mantra took hold, calling forth her rage, the Dark Glory rising fast, singing in every muscle and nerve as she drew the scimitar. She attacked without preamble or restraint. On occasion she had let these encounters last, allowing her doomed opponent some measure of hope. It made the death blow so much sweeter, the final realisation in their eyes a tasty treat to crown the moment as the scimitar's blade bit deep. But there would be no sweet moment here, she knew that. This was a day for the all consuming fire of the Dark Glory, the most cherished gift bestowed by the Voice.

The king was skilled, still swift and strong despite his age, moving with the fierce grace of a born warrior as he parried and whirled, his longsword a flicker of shining steel. A display worthy of a song, Sharrow-met mused as she brought the scimitar up and round in a scything slash that took away his life. She stood back to watch him die, the blood draining to leave his noble aspect bleached and empty, but still he clung to life, and his eyes...

"Sharrow-met!" She turned to see Harazil descending to earth on the back of his blackwing, a bloodied axe clutched in his fist. "Victory, Greatness." The Shar-gur captain pointed his axe at the field and she raised her gaze to witness the disintegration of the noble king's army. The Tormented had broken the ranks of those choosing to die with their king and now moved among the wounded, pale, silent figures going about their business with customary efficiency, killing the maimed and chaining those fit to join their ranks. Beyond them the Raptorile war-packs displayed no such restraint, surging through the fleeing mob, steel-barbed tails whipping like angry snakes as they leapt and bit and tore, pausing after every kill to voice their victory shrieks before bounding on.

Sharrow-met turned again to the king as he choked out a few words, too thick with blood and pain to be discerned but nevertheless spoken with a fierce conviction. She crouched at his side, leaning close with a raised eyebrow. The Dark Glory had faded now, leaving an odd sense of sorrow she had never quite accustomed herself to, and she found she had little appetite for the killing blow.

"I..." the king rasped, dimming eyes meeting her own. "I prayed... to the Twelve Gods...that I might never...see your face...again..."

Harazil's axe came down in a blur, before a final, forever unknown word could be started. "Abominate scum," the Shar-gur grunted, back straight and eyes averted in careful respect. "My gift to you, Greatness."

Sharrow-met rose from her haunches, ignoring Harazil's gift and turning away. Her eyes tracked across the sights of slaughter and beyond, over fields of green and gold to the pale, jagged outline on the horizon. Mara-vielle, City of a Thousand Spires. The greatest prize yet won by the Servants of the Voice and the last free city on this continent.

"I beg the honour of leading the Vanguard, my queen," Harazil said, voice heavy with anticipation. Like all the Shar-gur his lust for her recognition was ingrained and insatiable. Should she command it he would slice open his own belly in trice, an order she had been tempted to issue more than once. "I will secure the city's treasures..."

"Be quiet," she told him in a murmur, eyes still lingering on the distant spires. She could feel it again, the upsurge of recognition, though she fought to keep it muted. By rights she should surrender herself to the comforts of the mantra but the doomed king's eyes were bright in her mind and there was something enticing about this new sensation, something that made her endure the pain of unwanted visions. He knew my face.

"Muster your Tormented," she told Harazil, striding to Keera's side. "Make due assessment of the chosen. Await my word before commencing the cull of the unworthy."

She peered at the blackwing's ruined eye, running a soothing hand over the bird's neck as she took hold of the red-jewelled amulet about her neck. Holding it close to Keera's eye she chanted a soft invocation, calling forth the jewel's power, tendrils of red light snaking forth to lick at the wound, damaged flesh reforming and knitting together. Keera gave an appreciative squawk as the healing completed, the remade eye bright and new, possibly keener than it had ever been, though Sharrow-met knew it would always ache. The Voice's gifts carried a price; her own body was as smooth and free of scars as a new born babe, but there were times, usually at night when she sat through the sleepless hours, when the pain of long-healed wounds was enough to make her cry out, though she never did.

"Send word to the Raptorile to advance upon the city." She climbed onto Keera's back, the bird's wings thrumming as they caught the air and bore her queen aloft. "They will find me at the Hall of the Twelve Gods."

Silence. No screams, no flocks of people casting terrorised glances at the sky, no weeping mothers cradling infants, no old and sick hobbling in the wake of the young as they all fled towards imagined refuge. Just silent spires overlooking empty parks and streets. There were some signs of disorder, upturned carts, doors left open in haste, various detritus littering the broad avenues. But no people, and the people were the true spoils of any victory, for what was the Voice without ears to hear it?

She spent an hour scouring the city, swooping low and high, her marvellous Voice-gifted eyes alive to the slightest movement, but finding nothing. Eventually she guided Keera towards the four tallest spires rising from the centre of the city. Each had been constructed from different coloured marble, red, gold, white and black, and were linked by a series of bridges. They were deceptively fragile in appearance, narrow with fluted buttresses, like a web spun between the spires, but strong enough to have stood for centuries. Each tower rose from the corner of a rectangular structure, itself more than a hundred feet in height, its walls decorated from end to end in marble reliefs. There were three great panels to each wall, one for each of the twelve gods, their legends rendered with a level of skill and detail as yet unseen in all the cities she had taken.

So many years of labour and expense frittered on art, she mused as Keera fanned her wings to alight on a plaza adjacent to the structure's monolithic doors. More energy expended on defence and they might have stood a chance.

The doors were open and the space inside cavernous. Painted murals flowed over walls and ceiling like a tide of colour frozen in time. These, she knew, were the epics, the part-mythic tales of Mara-vielle's origin and rise to greatness; mighty heroes and learned scholars, self-sacrificing warriors and wise statesmen, and, naturally, kings of noble aspect. She found him towards the rear of the chamber, the mural painted high on a wall overlooking a raised dais where a vacant throne sat. The mural was more recent than the others, the paintwork more vivid though it depicted a man considerably younger than the warrior who now lay headless on a hill several miles away. He seemed troubled, his aspect one of sombre reflection as he stood regarding an empty ocean. Her eyes went to the inscription painted above the king's head; Therumin, The Silver King.

Therumin. So now she knew his name at least, as he had known her face. She turned, surveying the opposite wall and pausing at the sight of a patch of ruined plaster, a jarring interruption to the finely worked beauty on either side. Moving closer she saw it to have been the work of vandalism, and not recently. The fragments of surviving paint were dim flecks of colour amid ruined plaster yellowed with age. Whatever had been depicted here had been wiped away, expunged with considerable violence, though she noted the inscription was partially intact: …amond Que..n.

The Diamond Queen. She knew this name, her spies had spoken of it. Some tragedy to have befallen the ruling family years ago. The tale had little bearing on her plans so she paid it scant mind, concentrating instead on the reports regarding Mara-vielle's copious wealth. They are strong, Harazil had cautioned but she just laughed. We are stronger, and we have the Voice.

A skitter of claws on stone drew her attention from the ruined mural. A Raptorile scout party had entered the hall, tails curling in alarm and forked tongues darting to taste the unfamiliar air as they crouched and squinted at the murals, exchanging puzzled profanity in their sibilant speech. They were greenbacks, hailing from the southern jungles and smaller than their red-backed desert cousins, but no less fierce and just as devoted to the acquisition of trinkets. Seeing her their pack-chief issue a guttural, commanding snarl and they all fell into an immediate servile posture, approaching in a crouch, claws outstretched to proffer their loot as was custom.

The pack-chief extended the clutch of pearl necklaces in her claws, seeking acknowledgement and forming the human words with uncanny precision, "By your leave, Sharrow-met." For all their apparent savagery, these were intelligent creatures, possessed of memory and senses far beyond human understanding, though their superstitious lust for shiny things made them ever her slaves. When they die the treasure will buy them protection from eternal torment, the Voice had told her. For their prey awaits in the next world, hungry for vengeance.

She was about to raise her hand and issue the customary response,

"The Voice grants rich reward, sister," but paused at the sight of something amid their ranks, something in a tall silver frame. It caught the light with dazzling brightness before the angle changed slightly, revealing the sight of a tall woman in cobalt armour, the hilt of a scimitar jutting over her shoulder. This was a beautiful woman, Sharrow-met saw, perhaps a few years shy of thirty, pale of face with high cheekbones and a delicately curved chin, a face made porcelain in its flawlessness. Her hair was a silken jet cascade, tied back with a silver braid, and her eyes...blue eyes, blue like the sea...

"Get rid of that!" she grated, casting her hand at the mirror and turning away.

A rasping snarl, the multiple crack of whipping tails then the harsh clamour of shattering glass. When she turned back the mirror's unfortunate owner lay dead amid its shards. It had always been this way, as long she had served the Voice, which was as long as she could remember; she could never abide the sight of her own image.

"She was newly hatched, Sharrow-met," the pack-chief said, her words devoid of any inflection as her kind could learn a human tongue with remarkable speed but never the emotions that coloured it. However, the floor-level crouch and rigid tail made her contrition clear. "I was remiss in not providing clear instruction."

Sharrow-met gave an irritated wave and moved to the empty throne, running her hands over its finely carved back. "You bring me your spoils but no captives," she told the pack-chief, sinking onto the throne and finding it more comfortable than expected.

"We found none, Sharrow-met," the pack-chief replied, still lowered in the servile crouch.

Could they have fled? she wondered. Had the battle been no more than a desperate ploy to delay her advance and buy time for the people to flee? She quickly dismissed the notion as absurd. There is nowhere for them to flee to. Every kingdom, duchy and city on this continent now belongs to the Voice.

"Carry my word to your sisters," she told the pack-chief. "Search every inch of this city. Go deep, into the sewers, the catacombs. The war-packs are forbidden loot until this is done and I will execute one of my soldiers for every hour that sees no captives in my hands."

She didn't sleep, such things were lost to those so steeped in the Voice. The Shar-gur still slept, albeit fitfully, and the Tormented required at least some rest in between their many labours, but not her. As night claimed the city she ascended alone through the hall's upper levels, finding only a succession of corridors and rooms, all furnished to varying degrees of finery and all empty. There were more mirrors of course, it was a continual point of puzzlement to her that the people she conquered were so addicted to their own image. She shattered every glass she found, suffering the brief glimpse of the porcelain faced woman before her armoured fist broke it apart.

She found what she assumed to be the king's rooms on the highest tier of the white marble spire, sparsely furnished with few comforts though he had maintained an extensive library, all now destined for the fire as the Voice had no tolerance for books. The adjoining chamber was more interesting, a suite of spacious apartments shrouded in cobwebs. Every surface was thick with dust, the drapes on the windows ragged with filth, the mouldings and cornices turned yellow with decades of neglect.

She judged this a woman's chamber, a woman of some importance given the finery of the dresses hanging in the cupboards and the contents of the jewellery box on her dresser, adorned with a large oval mirror thankfully so thickly webbed it betrayed only the most shadowy reflection. Diamonds, Sharrow-met saw, plucking a necklace from the box. No rubies, no sapphires. Only diamonds. Her gaze went to the bed; large, luxurious and, if not caked in dust, surely fit for a queen. The rooms of the Diamond Queen, left untouched for many a year.

The amulet around her neck gave off a sudden heat, issuing the faint thrum that told of the Voice's imminent blessing. Her heart began to pump faster in anticipation, it was only at these moment that this happened. Not in battle, not when exacting just punishment on the Abominate, only now when the Voice chose to bless her was she reminded that, for the many gifts that had changed her, she still retained a human heart.

I sense you are troubled, my Sharrow-met, it said, the amulet thrumming with every wondrous word, her flesh tingling as the sound washed through her. It was a more subtle reward than the Dark Glory, but no less appreciated.

"The city conceals its citizens somehow," she replied, a slight quaver to her voice. "I would have them hear you, know your rewards as I do."

There is sorcery at work here, I can feel it. A great spell, woven with skill, but still just an illusion, a glamour, to be shattered like the mirrors you hate so much.

"How? How do I shatter it?"

How is any illusion shattered? The trickster relies on the ignorance of his audience when dealing his cards. But those with eyes to see the trick are never fooled. Truth, my wonderful, terrible child. Shatter it with truth.

The amulet gave a sudden deeper thrum and she convulsed as the pulse of pleasure cut through her, so pure and unrestrained it was almost an agony, leaving her crouched and gasping, gauntlets gripping the edge of the dresser tight enough to splinter the wood.

"I deserve no reward," she groaned, shuddering. "Not until the Abominate are secured."

This war is won by your hand, Sharrow-met. I reward as I see fit. Finish our business here quickly, for we have an ocean to cross and much work to do.

Then it was gone, the absence making her gasp once more, blinking away grateful tears as she raised her gaze, finding it momentarily captured by the gleam of the vanished queen's diamonds.

A flicker in the mirror, something moving behind cobweb veil.

She came to her feet in a whirl, the scimitar scraping free of the scabbard. Nothing. Just dust and rotting luxury. But she had seen something in the glass and her eyes never betrayed her.

A sound, no more than a breath, or a faint gust of wind, and her eyes snapped to a tiny plume of dust rising next to the door beyond the bed.

"Come out!" Sharrow-met commanded, striding forward. "Your king is fallen. This city belongs to the Voice. Come out and know his blessing!"

The door slammed aside, hinges broken by the power of her kick... and she froze at the sight that greeted her.

Mirrors...A hall of mirrors.

The hall was perhaps thirty feet long, narrow with a tiled chequerboard floor, and its walls were covered in mirrors. Like the other rooms the floor was thick with dust, but not the mirrors. Oval mirrors, square mirrors, tiny disc-like mirrors, all gleaming clean and bright as if just polished that morning. Sharrow-met's eyes darted around the hall, finding no-one, and no other door. The rooms ended here in this hall of hateful glass. Fortunately the dark prevented clear reflection, but she knew if she took just one more step into the hall the image of the porcelain faced woman would surround her, bouncing from one glass to the next, inescapable and implacable, she would never be able to shatter them all fast enough.

Another sound, another soft breath, the dust on the chequerboard floor rising to swirl briefly before drifting down with a soft hiss. Sharrow-met took a slow, deliberate backward step and turned around, her heart once again doubling its rhythm though there was no Voice to stir it.

She heard no other sound as she strode away, iron-shod boots drawing a dull echo from the dusty floor, but she felt it, as clear as if it had been shouted; an invitation from whatever waited in that hall. Come in…come in and see…

The wiry captive writhed in her grasp, chains rattling as she lifted him off the floor, face reddening as her steel fingers tightened on his neck. "Captain Harazil tells me you were Mage-Ascendant to King Therumin," she said, angling her head to scrutinise his face, seeing little sign of wisdom, and less fear than she would have liked. "Your spells held back my Raptorile for a time, as I recall. Five hundred redbacks burned and blasted to ash. Their pack-chief would very much like to know how you taste. Shall I feed you to her?"

The mage grunted, mottled features bunching, a vestige of a snarl visible on his lips and defiance shining in his eyes. She relaxed her grip, pulling him close enough to smell the stench of unwashed flesh and dried blood. Harazil had plucked him from a pile of bodies on the battlefield, a senseless near dead wreck of a man, but somehow the spark of resistance still lingered.

"What glamouring web have you spun here?" she asked in a whisper. "By what means do you hide the Abominate from my eyes?"

She saw a frown flicker across his brow, genuine puzzlement in his gaze before his resolve returned and he stared back, unblinking and silent.

"Not your work then," she said, dropping him to the floor where he lay gasping. She put his age at somewhere near forty, if not a little younger. Most mages were far older, wizened mystics feeble in body but rich in knowledge, though never accruing enough to thwart her. "You have a name?" she asked him.

She expected him not to answer, maintain his silence regardless of consequence as was often the way with these dutiful types. So it came as a surprise when he coughed and rasped out a reply, "Dralgen."

"That is not a noble name," she observed, moving to sit on the throne, appreciating once more the feel of it, as if it had been made for her. She had called Harazil to the Hall of the Twelve Gods that morning, the Shar-gur arriving with his elite guard of Tormented and his prize captive. The Raptorile were still scouring the city, hunting through every dark place with tireless efficiency, finding only rats and abandoned pets. True to her word she had ordered the deaths of six Raptorile and six Tormented so far and had begun to toy with the idea of executing one of the Shar-gur as the ultimate example of their queen's will.

"You were born to the gutter, were you not?" she enquired of Dralgen, hoping to fire his temper. She had always found anger more effective than pain in stirring a reluctant tongue.

The mage, however, seemed to find no cause for resentment in the question, barely glancing up as he voiced his reply. "I was raised in an orphanage...the king's orphanage."

"Where, no doubt, his servants were quick to spot your talents. How powerful you must be to have risen so high."

She watched his muscles bunching under the besmirched skin, chains tightening. She could feel him searching for his power, reaching inside himself to summon the fuel his words would shape. "Don't waste your time," she told him. "You are bound by chains of iron, forged by my own fire and quenched in the blood of mages. As long as they touch your skin, your power is quelled, as I think you know."

She felt his power recede, seeing his muscles relax though his gaze retained an aggravating heat. "I know nothing of any glamour," he grated. "You had best kill me and have done, for I have nothing else to say to so pestilent a soul."

Hazaril stepped forward, three-tongued whip raised high, halting as Sharrow-met raised a hand to wave him back. "So keen to earn a noble end," she said. "Fitting for one so steeped in failure. But, sadly I am unable to oblige. Harazil, how many captives did we take yesterday?"

The Shar-gur's answer was immediate, "Six thousand, two hundred and twenty, Greatness."

"How many for the cull?"

"Five thousand, three hundred and eighteen."

She returned her gaze to the prostrate mage. "An unusually high number, but not untypical among my more stubborn enemies. Still, it leaves me near a thousand Tormented to swell my ranks." She beckoned one of Harazil's guards forward, a tall, powerful man, his head shaved down to a bone-white scalp. He was bare chested save the iron chains criss-crossing the hard muscle of his bleached flesh. He strode to within a dozen feet of her, Tormented were allowed no closer to their queen, and dropped to both knees, head bowed.

"Tell this man your name," she commanded, keeping her eyes on Dralgen.

"I need no name," the Tormented replied in an automatic monotone. "I need only the Voice."

"Where were you born?" she continued.

"I need no past," came the toneless reply. "I need only the Voice."

"Are you in pain?"

"Pain is the gift of the Voice. Through pain I know the truth of his words and the wonder of his reward."

She smiled at Dralgen. "Wonderful isn't he? The product of years of conditioning, a being of absolute servitude, freed from the burden of memory, pride or identity. In time he may become formidable enough to warrant elevation to Shar-gur and become a great captain in service to the Voice. Are you not jealous?"

She expected more defiance but Dralgen wasn't looking at her. Instead his gaze was fixed on the kneeling Tormented, features drawn in a mix of fear and sympathy.

"I'll spare you his fate," she went on. "You and all the other captives. A merciful death for every soul if you will…"

"You saw her," he said, turning to her, expression defiant once again, but also displaying a certain amused twist to his lips.

"What did you say?"

"You went to her rooms, didn't you? I can sense the taint of her touch. Did she speak to you?"

Sharrow-met stared at him in silence as his smile broadened further. "Why do you imagine those rooms are left untouched?" he asked. "Not even King Therumin could stand to take one step inside. She has been waiting a very long time for a visitor, and now she has you."

"And who is she?"

His smile transformed into a laugh, his mirth echoing about the cavernous hall. "A blessing who became a curse," he said, laughter subsiding as she loomed above him, scimitar in hand. She couldn't remember rising from the throne or drawing the blade, her heart once again thumping hard with no whisper from the Voice.

Who is this to stir my fury? she wondered, placing the tip of her scimitar under his chin, watching the humour transform into grim but unrepentant acceptance. No more than another broken spell-weaver. And yet he makes me so very angry...

"Take a look in one of her mirrors, great queen," Dralgen said as she raised the scimitar. "You'll find all the truth you need."

Truth...Shatter it with truth.

She returned to the upper levels after the confrontation with Dralgen, resisting the impulse to hack Harazil's head from his shoulders when he had the gall to question her decision to spare the mage.

"Greatness?" he said, eyes wide in his colourless face as she stepped back, sheathing the scimitar.

"Secure him close by," she repeated in a faint whisper, meeting the Shar-gur's eyes. It had been enough to see him stumbling to his knees babbling abject contrition, but still...He questioned me.

She sat in the Silver King's library, a scattering of books littering the floor. She had hunted through the shelves for a time, seeking some mention of the Diamond Queen, finding much in the way of history and legend but nothing useful. She could see the entrance to her rooms through the open door, the same sense of invitation rising every time she glanced towards it. Come in...come in and see...

For the first time in many a year she felt a chill. She was clad in only the black silks she wore beneath her armour, having discarded it on returning to the spire. Normally she had little regard for the vagaries of climate, it made scant difference amid the constant ache of her invisible but present scars, but tonight she felt it, an icy cut straight to the bone that made her rise and seek out the king's bedchamber. She dragged a blanket from his bed and draped it about her shoulders before returning to her vigil in the library, sitting in clenched immobility until the chill abated and a soothing warmth spread through her, allowing her mind to wander.

As ever the Black Vale was the first image conjured from her memory, the mountain holdfast where the Voice built his army and raised a girl to Greatness. Her earliest memory was of the day a Shar-gur had placed the amulet about her neck. She had no clear notion of how old she had been but guessed she couldn't have been more than eight, just a small girl standing atop one of the obsidian tors overlooking smithies and training grounds where the Tormented laboured. She remembered her eyes had been sore and her cheeks damp but had no notion why that could be. Nor did she yet know her name.

The Shar-gur had been named Zorakath, a mighty champion to one of the now vanished hill-tribes before he had heard the Voice a decade before, now risen to generalship over forty thousand Tormented. "Sharrow-met," he had called her. Wraith-Queen in the ancient tongue.

The Voice was her father, she understood this on some fundamental level, but Zorakath had been her teacher. She had been at his side when he led the first wave of Tormented against the eastern duchies, grown to adolescence by the time he overran the lake-lands and gained womanhood the day she watched him die at the Battle of the Pass. The mages of the Westlands had reached a concordance by then, stirred into panicked unity by the inexorable advance of the Voice. Near a thousand had stood together at the Pass, their spells searing fire and ruin into the ranks of the Tormented. Zorakath took his blackwing in a vertical dive into the midst of the mages, wreaking havoc until their fires consumed him. Sharrow-met made ready to command Keera to follow the Shar-gur's example but the amulet had thrummed, the subsequent command implacable and absolute. Return to me. I have a task for you.

And so he had sent her south, alone but for Keera and the chest of looted treasure. The memories shifted, accelerating into a blur. The duels she had fought with various pack-chiefs, spilling blood to earn the right to speak to their sisters. The vast tracks of jungle and desert, the breeding grounds where dull-eyed males tended the endless rows of eggs, and everywhere so many of these clever, wonderfully fierce creatures, willing to fight and die on promise of ever more trinkets. It took ten years, but when she returned it was at the head of an army, one no number of mages could halt.

Come in...come in and see...

The compulsion lurched anew and something moved beyond the half-open door to the Diamond Queen's chambers, a flickering shadow accompanied by the faint whisper of dust sliding over faded tiles.

Fear now, she thought. First memory, then cold, now fear. But those who hear the Voice have no need of fear.

She rose to her feet, letting the blanket fall away, striding forward to slam the doors aside, ignoring the chill of the floor on her bare feet as she made for the hall of mirrors. "I have seen a thousand miles of horrors!" she hissed aloud. "I have seen cities burn and rivers turn red with the blood of my enemies! What do you imagine you can show me?"

But still she paused at the entrance to the hall, her disgusting human heart thumping in her chest as her eyes played over the silent walls of glass. She realised she had left the amulet in the king's chamber with her armour, its absence a keen ache in her breast. Truth, she reminded herself. The mage said there is truth here and the Voice commands I seek it out.

A sound behind her, the faintest sigh of an indrawn breath heralding another bone-cutting chill. She shuddered as the skin on her back prickled, knowing something had reached out to caress her flesh. More unheard but undeniable words, effortlessly pushed into her mind: I knew you would be beautiful. Go in, now...Go and see...

There was little light to see by, only the faintest gleam on the edges of the mirrors, and every glass seemed like a portal pregnant with the threat of sights unwanted.

There is only the Voice. The Voice brings great rewards and dark glory. Those who hear the Voice have no need of fear.

She repeated the mantra several times over, drew a breath and stepped forward, the lingering goosebumps on the back of her neck a clear indication her unseen companion had followed her through the door. She paused at the first mirror, her eyes roaming over the gilt frame, steeling herself for the sight of the porcelain faced young woman. Instead she saw nothing. The mirror held no reflection, just a rectangle of black glass in an ornate frame. She frowned and was about to turn away when the icy caress came again, a numbing touch to her shoulder, holding her in place.

Wait...It searches for you...

It took a moment before she saw it, a barely perceptible glow in the centre of the glass, growing slowly until it filled the entire mirror, an opaque swirling haze that soon coalesced into a recognisable figure. The girl was small and thin, pale of face and red of eye, her lips colourless and chapped. She wore a fine dress that seemed to jar with her sickly appearance; blue silk and sequins that matched her eyes. She stood gazing into the mirror, head cocked at a curious angle and a motley rag-doll dangling from her hand. Tentatively she reached out to touch the mirror, then drew back, small face bunching in a puzzled frown.

"Does she see me?" Sharrow-met asked in a whisper.

A shadow only, her companion replied. A possibility…A twist in her future captured by the glass.

Sharrow-met's gaze roved the girl's face, taking in the hollowness of her cheeks before lingering on her red-rimmed eyes. "She has a sickness."

 From the day she was born. It happens sometimes. Those born with the power can be too fragile to contain it. But she never complained…

Abruptly the girl turned from the mirror, glancing over her shoulder at a slim beckoning figure, too shadowed to make out. The girl gave the glass a final bemused glance before clutching her doll to her breast and scampering off. The mirror misted over once more then slowly faded to black.

"You knew her," Sharrow-met said, finding her skin suddenly beaded with sweat despite the chill at her back. "What was her name?" Her companion said nothing, though the cold air shifted, impelling her towards the next mirror.

This one was wider, the black glass misting then forming into an impressive view of a garden on a summer's day. The same little girl played in the foreground, a little older now but somehow even weaker in appearance, a certain fatigue evident in her movements as she made her doll dance. Beyond her a man and a woman stood side by side, the woman talking with great animation whilst the man stood staring fixedly out at the glittering sea in the distance. The mirror conveyed no sound but Sharrow-met knew with absolute certainty the words spoken by the woman: I sensed no lie in his promise…

She remembered it all. The feel of the grass against her skin, the sun on her back, the scent of the orange blossoms, and the voices of her parents arguing a short way off. Raggy, she thought, sheened in sweat and limbs trembling. The doll's name was Raggy.

She saw the man round on the woman, a tall man of noble aspect, handsome as his wife was beautiful, made suddenly ugly by anger and fear. "Can't you see the trap in his words?" the man had demanded in a tone she hadn't heard before, causing her to look up from Raggy's caperings, as the little girl in the mirror looked up now. The man leaned close to the woman and Sharrow-met found herself mouthing his next words as he spoke them: "You think he promises life? The histories are clear. All the Voice ever brings is death…"

She whirled away from the mirror, eyes shut tight, gasping as the cold enveloped her, the chill cutting even deeper, making her cry out and sink to her knees. "There…there is o-only…the V-voice…," she stammered through misting breath. "The Voice…b-brings great… rewards and…and…"

This was where it found me, her companion's words invaded her mind with calm ease. In this hall, this place of power and wisdom. For this was to be my legacy, the finest collection of enchanted glass in all the world. A blessing for those who came after me, twisted into a curse. For this was how the Voice found me. Lacking form or substance it lives in the artifacts of power; the blessed blades of great warriors, these wondrous mirrors, the jewel you wear. It came to me and whispered of wonders, of impossible reward…I can save her, it said and through the glass it sent a vision of what you would be, the warrior queen, so strong, so beautiful, so much more than the sickly girl who broke my heart with her every rasping cough. He sent his Shar-gur captain on a great bird to take you, and though I knew my husband would hate me for all the ages, I gave you to the Voice. He promised one day he would return you…and now he has.

"The…the glamour," Sharrow-met gasped, the chill now gripping her like a vice. "You wove it!"

My husband shunned my company from the day I gave you away, forbade my presence at all councils and formal gatherings. I spent my remaining days in these rooms. I knew by then, you see. I knew what I had done…One day he would send you home with fire and slaughter. So for years I sought an answer in these mirrors, rarely sleeping or eating. I suppose I became mad after a time, and when my body finally died, I barely noticed and my labour continued.

The icy fist closed ever tighter, squeezing the air from Sharrow-met's body, her back convulsing into a spasmodic arch, a shout of pain filling the hall.

Open your eyes, my daughter. The grip tightened further and Sharrow-met's shout became a scream. Open your eyes and see!

Her eyes flew open, stinging and streaming from the cold, and there before her stood a woman, or rather the mist of her own stolen breath formed into the shape of a woman. Sharrow-met choked, her empty lungs unable to give sound to the words she sought to speak: What is my name?

The face of the spectre shifted, becoming more solid, the features recognisable as those of the woman in the glass, her expression sorrowful but not unkind. Her lips moved to form a silent reply, the words conveyed to Sharrow-met by other means. Mara, we named you for the city. The spectre of the Diamond Queen smiled then raised her arms, every mirror in the hall suddenly filling with bright light, banishing shadow and invading Sharrow-met's eyes with a searing pain.

Now, my daughter, the Diamond Queen said as Sharrow-met tried vainly to scream once more. Now it is time for you to see...

She had the mage brought to the top of the white marble spire in the morning, a pair of Tormented forcing him up the steps and onto the balcony where she waited. Sharrow-met noted his evident exhaustion, though his defiance remained undimmed. She turned her gaze to the city, eyes tracking over the Shar-gur gliding above on their Black-wings to the Raptorile prowling the streets and parks below, crouched low as they hunted, blind to their prey.

She could see them now, clustering together in fear, crouching in doorways, some sitting in the parks, slumped and accepting of their fate, and all surely baffled to the point of near-madness as to why the monsters who had seized their city paid them no mind at all. The people were everywhere, revealed the instant she made her way from the Diamond Queen's chambers to the great hall below where they huddled in their hundreds, some crying out in terror as they realised she could see them, mothers clutching infants, the elderly staring with grim resolution. She had wandered the city for hours, clad only in her silks, heedless of the cold whilst the jewel about her neck throbbed constantly with the Voice's entreaties. She lied, my Sharrow-met. You are mine. You have always been mine...

"Remarkable," she said now, gesturing for the Tormented to bring Dralgen to her side and nodding at the streets below. "Don't you think?"

Dralgen said nothing, wariness and puzzlement dominating his sagging features.

"You can't see them, can you?" she asked, reaching out to touch a finger to his head. He stiffened momentarily in pain, then blinked like a man waking from a troubled sleep. On looking down at the city his eyes grew wide and a soft gasp of amazement escaped him.

"Perhaps the most powerful spell ever woven," Sharrow-met said. "Thousands of souls hidden in plain sight by nothing more than the will of a long dead woman. My mother was surely the greatest of mages."

"Therumin spoke of her power," Dralgen breathed. "But this…"

"Did he tell you?" she asked. "Did his people know they faced destruction at the hands of his heir?"

He shook his head, gaze still fixed on the newly revealed populace below. "He was a greatly sorrowful man. His daughter stolen, his wife driven to madness and death in grief. Sometimes I wonder if he hungered for your coming."

I prayed…that I might never see your face again…"No," she murmured. "No he did not."

Her hand went to the jewel resting on her breastplate, now visibly thrumming as her steel fingers closed on it. I made you, the Voice said and for the first time she heard something new in it, something beyond the serene certainty, something more than the unfettered affection it had always shown her; a faint, fearful whine, like a petulant child caught in a lie. I was lonely, so I made you. Have I not shown you love, my Sharrow-met? Was not the Dark Glory everything I promised?

"Yes," she replied, lifting the amulet's chain over her head and laying the jewel on the balustrade before her. "Everything and more."

It began to scream as she drew the scimitar, a shrill, desperate exhortation reaching out to the Shar-gur. Sharrow-met is Abominate! Kill her! KILL HER! KI-

The scimitar's pommel came down in a hammer blow, driven with all her unnatural strength, the Voice choking to silence as the red jewel shattered into a cloud of sparkling dust. She glanced up to see the Shar-gur had been quick to answer the Voice's call, six blackwings formed into an arrowhead aimed straight at the spire, Harazil in the lead, axe held high. She could feel his rising hate and wondered if it had always been there, hidden behind unfaltering loyalty all these years, festering away as he waited his chance.

She turned to Dralgen, reaching out to touch his chains which fell away in an instant, leaving him gasping with the shock of release. She glanced at the two Tormented, both staring at her in abject bemusement. She blinked and the clasps holding their chains in place shattered. They both cried out in unison, falling to their knees, a great chorus of agony and wonder rising from the city as she turned back, her will reaching out to free every Tormented under her command.

"I'll bring the Shar-gur to you," she told Dralgen, leaping over the balcony. "Kill as many as you can."

She plummeted for twenty yards before Keera caught her. The Shar-gur may still belong to the Voice but Keera had always been hers. The great bird's talons snatched her from the air and Sharrow-met swung herself onto the harness on her back, immediately guiding the bird in a low sweeping pass over the plaza below. The Shar-gur had the advantage of height and she needed speed to have any chance of executing this stratagem. Behind her the Shar-gur's blackwings screamed and air thundered as their riders forced them to greater efforts, Harazil's hate-filled challenged cutting through the din.

Sharrow-met guided Keera into a climb, sending them soaring high, ascending to the same height as the spire in a few beats. Keera folded her wings and they spun in the air, turning to face the pursuing Shar-gur, their formation tight as they rounded the spire and drew level with the balcony where Dralgen waited.

The mage's fire caught Harazil first, searing away his bird's left wing in a blaze of white flame and cinders, sending both rider and bird spiralling towards the plaza below. The torrent of flame swept through the other Shar-gur, killing two and wounding the others before it flickered and died, Sharrow-met seeing the mage's slim form slumping in exhaustion. She took Keera in a dive through what remained of the Shar-gur, scimitar flashing, the blackwing's steel-shod talons rending the flesh of her own kind. The frenzy of battle was different without the Dark Glory, no surging exultation or joyous thrill at the spatter of wetness on her skin, just the grunts and jolts of savage contest. The Shar-gur were mighty indeed, stolen heroes from once great kingdoms, but they were not her, and although they died hard, still they died.

She cut down the last of them as he fell from the back of his mortally wounded bird, following the corpse down to have Keera land outside the door to the great hall, near to where Harazil lay amid the smoking remains of his bird. She stepped down from Keera's back, wincing from the stinging cut on her cheek, certain to scar now there was no jewel to heal her. Finally, a crack in the porcelain mask, she thought, wondering why the notion made her laugh.

She noticed the city-folk gathering on the steps to the plaza, plainly fearful but edging ever closer. She knew they would kill her, once they realised she offered no more threat they would take bloody vengeance for their fallen men. She paused to play a hand through Keera's feathers, whispering a final command. The bird gave a brief squawk, perhaps in reluctance, but nevertheless spread her wings and ascended into the sky once more. Sharrow-met watched her rise to circle the spire before striking off on an eastward course, towards the Iron Peaks where her kind made their home.

Sharrow-met held up the scimitar's blade, dark with the blood of Shar-gur and blackwing alike, then tossed it away with a grimace of disgust before slumping down on the steps, weary and waiting for the peoples' judgement.

"Abominate!" She turned to see Harazil rising from the corpse of his blackwing, face half-burned and smoking, one arm charred to the bone, but the other whole and strong enough to raise his axe as he stumbled towards her. "You are deaf to the Voice!"

Sharrow-met's eyes went to where her scimitar lay and found her weariness so deep she had no desire to reach for it. So she simply sat and watched the maimed Shar-gur lurch towards her, spitting hate with every faltering step. "You were always unworthy! The Voice should have chosen me! I will make him an offering of your traitorous heart! I wi—"

The Raptorile fell on him in a blur of lashing tails and flashing teeth, a full war-pack of thirty redbacks, soon joined by more. Harazil was transformed into a flailing, dark shadow in the midst of their frenzy, killing many but never enough. Sharrow-met looked away. She wondered at her own surprise, for the Raptorile, like Keera, had always been hers, she it was who led them to much meat and so many trinkets after all.

They formed a tight cordon around her as the city-folk drew closer, warning hisses and raised tail-spikes enough to force them back. She could see the tall, pale figures of former Tormented amongst them, some still plainly astonished at their liberation, others clutching weapons with enraged intent.

"Move back!" She turned to see Dralgen emerging from the temple doors. He waved his arms at the people, voice croaking with weariness but still loud enough to hold a note of command. "This is Princess Mara! Risen to save us. Move back!"

At her nod the Raptorile made way for the mage and he came to her side with a bow. "My queen."

She groaned and got to her feet, surveying the people crowding the steps, more thronging the streets beyond, their ranks swelled by the unchained Tormented. Their expressions varied, fear, joy, relief, but through it all a simmering, and growing anger.

"Hardly," she told Dralgen. "I think, perhaps, these people are deserving of a new dynasty."

She turned to the Raptorile, gesturing for the most senior pack-chief to come forward. "Send word to gather your sisters," she said. "We leave this city by nightfall. They may keep their loot but take nothing else. None are to feed."

The pack-chief assumed the customary servile posture, but paused before bounding off, her tail describing the shape that indicated puzzlement. "Where now for the hunt, Sharrow-met?"

She glanced down at her scimitar and one of the redbacks quickly scooped it up and brought it to her, crouching low as she proffered the hilt. Sharrow-met returned the weapon to the scabbard on her back and turned to the east, where the sun rose high over distant mountains. "There are many shiny things," she said, "in a place called the Black Vale, far to the east. The treasure of a hundred kingdoms. Follow me there, and you can have it all."

The pack-chief bobbed lower but still hesitated. "And what reward awaits you there, sister?"

"Silence," she replied, feeling a smile spread across her lips. "I shall be content with silence."

ABOUT ANTHONY RYAN

Anthony Ryan is the New York Times best-selling author of the Raven's Shadow epic fantasy novels, The Draconis Memoria trilogy and the Slab City Blues science fiction series. He was born in Scotland in 1970 but spent much of his adult life living and working in London. After a long career in the British Civil Service he took up writing full time after the success of his first novel Blood Song, Book One of the Raven's Shadow trilogy. He has a degree in history, and his interests include art, science and the unending quest for the perfect pint of real ale.

Website: anthonyryan.net
Facebook: anthonyryanauthor
Twitter: @writer_anthony

9

THE LADY OF PAIN
BY STEVE DUBOIS

THE WORLD IS full of wounds. Gashes and cuts, scrapes and scuffs, bruises and breaks, as varied and as awful as the people who create them.

I saw more than my share of wounds, in my six years with the Adventurers' Guild. I couldn't have told you their exact nature or made accurate distinctions among them. For that task, you'd want a physic. A physic could tell you the exact point at which a twist transforms into a sprain, a cut becomes a laceration. A physic could name the muscle that tears in a man's calf, leaving him to walk forever lopsided, or tell you why that mace-jarred shoulder will scream him awake every morning in his old age.

These were not my concerns. I was a *healer*, not a physic. The guild's directions were clear. My task was simply to make the pain *go away*. Immediately. At any cost.

Ask another woman about wounds.

Ask me about pain.

The morning of the day I died began with Rogart's injury. The others referred to Rogart as "the Bull," as much in reference to his ever-flaring nostrils and his rubbery-lipped snores as to his strength. He'd worked several turns as a caravan guard on the Sussuran route before coming north. The rest of our crew had no idea of the reasons why; only that they must have been good ones, to blacken his name so comprehensively among the merchants that he'd wound up slumming it among the likes of us.

I knew the reasons, of course. A servant of the Lady always does. And he knew that I knew. And for that, he could never forgive me.

No matter. He needed me. He was hurt. There he sat against the cavern wall, broadsword bloodied and dangling from his limp hand on the rocky floor. We'd managed to stanch the bleeding in his thigh. The nanders' carcasses, six of them, were strewn around the fissure, chinless jaws slack in death, torchlight flickering in their dark, staring, sightless eyes.

It had, in truth, been more massacre than fight. Still, before the curtain came down, one of the nanders had gotten in a fortunate stroke, a spear thrust that somehow found the gap between Rogart's tasset and greaves, just above the knee. The rest of the crew was busy rooting through the detritus of the nanders' existence—a dented copper pot, polished stones amidst filthy rags, nothing you'd call "treasure"—and Rogart stared up as I approached. His face was pale as cream. I was, as I've said, no physic, but I could diagnose the reason for his pallor, and it had nothing to do with loss of blood.

"Just...just give me a minute," he snuffled. "I can hack it. Had worse." He fixed the point of his sword against the cavern floor, gritted his teeth, tried to hoist himself to a standing position. He levered himself up a few inches, massive shoulders trembling with the effort. Then he collapsed back to the floor in a clangor of armor.

"Take your medicine, Rogart. Let the Lady in," Sten called from over by the hearth. *Sirrah* Sten, I should say, for he retained his ordination in the Radiant Order. Generous of the High Chival, no doubt, to make a guild captain of one of his own servants—even one long past his best, with rheumy eyes and a graying beard. "It's not as if it's the first time."

But that was the point, of course. *Nobody*'s afraid the first time they're ministered to by a servant of the Lady of Pain. They're bleeding out, or desperately ill, and they're ready for a miracle. *How bad can it be?* they think to themselves.

Rogart knew *exactly* how bad it could be. Hence the white face and the wild eyes. "Give me the balm, then, for the Lady's sake!" he cried.

Sten gave a sidelong glance to Kiva, blue eyes piercing and aristo-cratic features merciless beneath her leather skullcap. She reached into her satchel, then shook her head at Sten. "Just three vials left," she said.

Sten turned back to Rogart. "Sorry. Not enough," he spoke. "There's still gods know what between us and the firedrake, and we'll need to conserve our resources for the final showdown. With that thing looking to cook you to a crisp, you'll be glad to have a vial of balm close to hand."

"Then let me turn around and head back to the surface. There's no need for…"

"No chance, Rogart," Sten interjected. "Job's not done. You know the rules. We break a guild contract, we'll never be offered another. We waited months for this job, traded in every favor we've earned in order to get it. And it's not like we've pulled enough loot to cut the job short. Up to our elbows in nander blood, and not a single brass…"

"One," Kiva interjected.

Sten turned, puzzled. "One?"

Kiva grinned and produced a single tarnished coin. "The big one had it secreted away in his loincloth," she said with a wicked grin. "You'd rather not know exactly where."

Sten turned back to the snorting hulk of a man immobilized against the cavern wall. "We've trod this road before, Rogart. All of us." Sten unstrapped one of his own greaves, revealing a thin, pale mark; the mark of a maiden's lips.

The mark of *my* lips.

Rogart's eyes rolled back in his head. "Ten percent," he muttered. "All this for ten godscursed percent." And then he gathered his breath for a shout. "Lady's mercy!" he swore, immune to the irony. "All right! Get on with it, and damn you!"

His eyes beheld me with utter hatred. But that, as Sten would have said, was a road I'd trod before. I knelt at Rogart's side. He fixed a strap between his teeth, bit down hard, closed his eyes, and lifted the tasset, revealing the ugly purple gash beneath. It was deep and gruesome; a lesser man would have been sent straight into shock upon receiving it. But it was nothing compared to what he was about to endure.

I lowered my head to the wound in his thigh, and I pressed my lips to it in a kiss. The pain came down like a thunderbolt, arcing through us both. And as Rogart's strangled shrieks echoed throughout the cave, I felt my own body writhe in silent sympathy.

The pain came, excruciating and terrible, and with it, Rogart's memories.

My scarred oaken arms around him. Son to a prince, graceful and refined, features chiseled and beautiful under the desert moon—what could such as him ever see in such as me, an uncouth beast of the north? Adoring me. Showing me, a scowling animal, a love that I have always desired and never deserved.

The caravan guards, discovering us together. The fury of the merchant prince. Under the code of the nomads, I deserve death. In his absence, death would be a mercy. Instead, exile and disgrace. And always, the craving. Always, at the sight of the smooth, sleek torso of a well-made man, or at the wry, lopsided grin and flashing green eyes of some carousing mountebank on a city night. The thing inside me, rising, hungry. The thing that wakes me, shuddering, from sleep. The thing that unmans me. The only foe I cannot kill.

The pain faded. The blurred world regained its focus. I raised my mouth from Rogart, still propped against the wall, sweat rolling down his face into his collar, his eyes closed and the newly formed mark of a kiss upon the untroubled flesh of his thigh. He spat out the strap and opened his eyes, but he could not make them meet mine.

Slowly, he rose. "All right," he said to Sten. The screams had scourged his throat, leaving his voice a raw, guttural rasp. "Nothing like the touch of a woman's lips, is there? Now let's be on our way."

I had been a girl of nine, a novice at the House of the Lady, on the day the abbess laid down the Lady's Law to me in ritual tones. "Her blessing is healing, swift and true," she had said. "But the gift is not without price, for she spares her children no ounce of pain. Rather, she *compresses* it. Every ounce of suffering that the recipient would experience in the natural course of healing the wound—weeks, or months, of stinging ache—all compressed into a few bitter moments." She had paused. "It is a blessing that would kill most recipients. But the Lady is merciful, and for that reason, she imposes upon us an additional duty. For those few short moments, we inhabit the souls of those we serve. We share their minds, their memories, and above all, their agony. And thus, their pain is halved, and their lives are preserved."

The abbess's explanation provided no comfort. Indeed, I cried bitterly. "But, Graced One...I don't want to hurt people!" I wailed.

The abbess had given me a quizzical glance. The lapse lasted only a moment before her face, lined with near a century's worry and care, had again assumed the aspect of still water. "We must take the gifts of the gods as they come. And you should consider that they have shaped the world as they have for a reason."

"But...why, Graced One?" I sniffled. "Are the gods monsters?"

She shook her head and smiled benevolently. "By no means. But they wish to avoid *men* becoming monsters. Have you considered the price that men would pay in a world of healing without cost? Think, girl. Did your father ever take the rod to you?"

I swallowed. *That he did,* I thought. I nodded.

"Was this an act of cruelty?"

That it was, I thought. But in my father's house, I had learned many hard lessons, and the most vital of them had been to read the cues on offer and to provide the answer that was expected of me. "No. He merely...corrected me."

The abbess nodded, pleased. "And at what point did he stop?"

"When...when I had hurt enough to...to learn the lesson." A lie. I had fled my home for a reason.

"Pain is a teacher," the abbess intoned. "Consider a world in which the Lady doled out her mercy without cost. Would her miracles fill us with awe? Or would they be as ordinary and expected as spring rain?" A small, thin smile. "And what of we ourselves, her servants? Imagine being called from house to house, on call for every tanner and shop-keeper, expected to attend to every kitchen burn, every child's scraped knee. Would we be revered as healers, or scorned as slaves? The Lady is wise to impose her price. And we serve her will." She paused. "And in exchange for our services, we endure hatred. For, among those we serve, the memory of the agony we inflict will always outweigh the memory of the service we render. And we are hated, also, for the memories we retain, for our clients view them not as a tithe to the Lady, but as secrets stolen. Hence our vow of strictest silence; without it, many would prefer death to our services."

I had knelt before her, knobby knees on well-washed cobbles, puzzling over the mystery of the Lady's blessing. "I...I don't understand, Graced One. I mean…" I fumbled for the words. "If we are to serve, others must be willing to accept our service, surely? But if we are hated by all, who will seek us, let alone pay us? How are we to live?"

At that, the abbess had positively beamed. "Now *there* is an *intelligent* question, my girl!" And with that, she hooked me. Praise had been a scarce commodity in my father's house, and I found it a heady drug. I felt a rare smile blossom across my face. "We serve the poor, of course, those who cannot afford balm. But no such duty for you, my bright child! No, yours will be a *special* form of service. Let me tell you of our arrangement with the Adventurers' Guild…"

My first time inside Sten's head occurred early in our fellowship. The guild had patriotically loaned our crew to the city for the duration of the conflict with Capria. The siege had been a disaster, bungled by idiot commanders with purchased commissions, and the withdrawal had been even worse, a kicked anthill of scurrying men and machines. In the chaos, a trebuchet had run over Sten's lower leg, snapping it like kindling. Absent my gift, we'd have had to leave him behind.

A servant of the Lady learns that each person's memory is as unique as a fingerprint. Some remember in words, like Rogart. With Sten, it was images; his mind was a book of pictures, each speaking its own story.

In a vast, airy chamber of stone, a majestic dome of translucent glass shaped in the sunburst that is the Radiant Order's emblem, admitting the sun's splendor. The weight of armor around my shoulders. Three other initiates to my left, and two to my right. The rigor of youth in my veins, and before me, the High Chival, paladin true and pure, lecturing: "The order is father and mother to us all, wife and child, all the family we require. The order is an altar on which we place our sacrifices to those we serve. The order is a bonfire, the fire of duty, in which we purge all that is unworthy in ourselves." The featherlight touch of the High Chival's great sword on each pauldron; the joy of initiation, of oneness, of immersion of self in the greater whole.

The years flow. Like wine at first, then aging slowly into vinegar. The strength of youth slowly fading, skills eroding, waiting for a right-eous cause that never arrives. Eyes tingling with the citadel's splendors. Fingertips callused from polishing unused weapons. No proud wounds or noble scars; instead, a slowly growing ache in the spine, the twinging of oft-gritted teeth. The desire for a woman shoved deep, suppressed. And eventually, I feel the bonfire of which the High Chival spoke—not in my heart but in my gut, a constant acidic churning. I spit blood every morning and see it in my chamber pot at night.

The High Chival before me, frowning in judgment. Half my life is gone. I speak of my struggle against my cravings. I beg a new duty, a task on which to expend the profane energies of my enforced idleness. Disappointment in me, written broadly on his face, as I am sent to the guild to earn revenue for the order.

And there, in the guild: the face. Her face. The face of purity itself, of maidenly perfection, her radiance outshining that of the order. A temptress, sent to inspire my darkest desires, to unleash the beast I'd sought to bury. And that face will be ever before me now, for as long as I serve, the last thing I see when I bed down at night, and the first I see when I wake, a mockery to my pretense of chastity and virtue. Here is my scourge, my punishment for asking something for myself.

But I will not break! I will not be consumed by the fires of hell, though they rage daily in my stomach and loins. I shall accept his companions, my temptress, and my fate. I have forged my own chains. Now I must wear them. Such is duty.

The world returned; the crooked leg had been made straight, and for once, the recipient of the Lady's blessing had borne up under it without a single cry of pain. But Sten could not make his eyes meet mine. Because the face of the temptress who haunted him was, of course, my own.

"Forgive me." He voiced it as a commander's order, not as a plea for mercy. He was Sten. Mercy, like love, was for other people.

Nanders are the stuff of peasants' nightmares. The legends are replete with tales of them falling on outlying villages, slaying the men, and carrying off women and children for the cook fire. Truth is, they're a strange sort of creature, more like men than beasts in many ways. They speak in grunts but have mastered fire. They adorn themselves in crude hides, fashion stone tools and weapons. Were it not for their sloping brows, squat posture, and hairy muzzles, they could almost pass for human.

Over the centuries the nanders have scuttled like roaches to the dark places of the world, seeking what men fear and huddling close to it, for only where men dare not go can they hope to survive. So when a crew like ours went in search of danger, often as not, we found a pack of nanders in the way.

On the day I died, wandering deep in the caverns of the Mughal, my companions rounded another twist and watched space open up before us. And there, huddled around the banked stones of another hearth, was yet *another* infestation of nanders. Four, no, five of them, counting that tiny young one scuttling backward across the floor. The males were out in front, eyes wild, fire-hardened spear points jabbing in our direction.

We fell into formation. Guild tactics were inflexible and ruthlessly effective, particularly against beasts too dumb to adapt to them. Rogart and Sten up front, shields raised and waiting. Kiva on the left flank, sling awhirl. Me at the back, cudgel drawn, just in case it should come to that.

The first sling bullet caught the leftmost male straight in the eye socket, and it toppled face-first into the fire. Kiva didn't bother to grin, merely reached right back into the pouch at her side, calmly drew another bullet, slotted it home, whirled it, and caught the next one a glancing blow to the skull, sending it toppling into the cave wall. She raised her sling again, and at this point even the nanders could recognize the impossibility of their position; if they held their ground, they'd be picked off at our leisure. So the remaining adults charged, roaring their wordless shout. Even the hairy-faced females of the species had formidable voices. I envied them that.

It's preferable to keep nanders at a distance, as any man-at-arms could tell you. Nanders are a head shorter than most men, but a single glance at their thick, muscular torsos reveals their fearsome strength. In truth, they're a touch too strong for their own good; they rely on it too heavily, and eschew subtlety. Rogart's unexpressed thoughts on the matter are revelatory: "If a boy grows up strong, he may never end up being anything else."

To say that Rogart was smarter than he looked would be faint praise. A kirigourd is smarter than Rogart looked. Say instead that he was capable of surprising insight, and smart enough to learn from his mistakes; he was certainly holding his shield a little lower that day, protecting his right knee. As for Sten, his great virtue in combat was patience; once his nander overbalanced itself from a would-be killing thrust, he darted inside its reach and dispatched it with a backslash. The second nander turned to face the new threat, and Rogart took advantage with a thrust of his own. This left us only the stunned one and the wailing juvenile to deal with.

I suppose it sounds impressive the way I describe it, and in truth, we were good enough at our jobs. But a job is all it was. There were no heroic journeys, no heaping piles of gold and jewels. Our business was methodical and gritty, more pest control than epic quest. And on days like these, deep in a smoky cave staring at the wailing orphan of the creatures we'd slaughtered, the name "Adventurers' Guild" had a bitter taste to it.

Kiva, staring on with glad blue eyes, never complained. She was getting exactly what she'd come for.

It had been a hard, hollow couple of months. We had been excited beyond reason to win the guild contract for Mortek's Tower, and we'd ploughed our way through its undead sentinels in a flash of silvered weapons and a blizzard of severed rotting limbs. The sight of the chest in the lowest level of the catacombs had us openly salivating, and we'd gotten overeager. Kiva had been so delighted to spot the discolored brick that triggered the scythe blade that she'd missed the poisoned dart rigged to the latch mechanism.

Kiva's memory was neither words nor images, but a tapestry of sensations. The rush of cold wind in my face as the sled hurtles downhill, and the strength of his arms as he holds me from behind. The shiver up my spine as he holds me. The suffusing heat of the homefires. The rough rasp of a day's beard growth against my face, the sweet pressure, edged with pain, of his kisses.

The blessed peace that comes with an ordered future. The prospect of a life surrounded by laughing children and of beautiful things with which to surround and adorn myself, a warm bath of certainty and security. Warm bread in my mouth, warm blankets on my body, warm arms around my waist.

The horrified chill at the physic's diagnosis, and the cold bloating of a stifled sob in my throat as he dwindles slowly before me to a stick man. Revulsion at green mucus on the cloth and bloody, stinking slime in a bedpan. Bitter, acrid wrath welling behind my eyes at the gods for cheating me. Blistering shame at the wish that the filthy tasks would just end, that he would just go, that it would just be over…

The cold sweat of his hand in mine, at the end, the sound of his parents' sobs in my ears. And the light, leaving his eyes…

…and that same frisson up the spine, at the moment of his passing. The exact same sensation his arms had offered, provided instead by the sight of life leaving him. The discovery of a new aspect of myself.

And the feel of the knife's handle in my hand, raising blisters on a soft palm, the pinned rat's screeches filling the cellar as I steal its life as well. A hypothesis confirmed—that same delicious chill, that same shudder in my backbone, as I see its eyes go vacant.

And the icy knowledge of a new future. Having discovered this ultimate ecstasy, I can never forgo it, can never content myself with the pursuit of inferior thrills. The cold tendrils expanding outward, from my heart into my limbs, as I know that I can no longer allow myself the company of people of quality. That I must become a stranger to all I have known and loved before. I will discover new skills. I will chase that sensation, that frisson down my spine, until it leads me to my own kind, rogues and blackguards and men of ill faith.

And a stab of a thrill, an electric bolt all through me, an eagerness to get the process underway.

When the two of us emerged from the agony, Kiva had no difficulty reading the revulsion on my face. "You talk too much," she told me.

The chest turned out to contain the ancient wizard's grimoire, its cover of human leather still intact, its pages long since rotted away to dust. We wound up turning it in for a handful of silver and a second-hand short sword. Kiva eventually lost the sword down a sewer grate, trying to fish out a coin.

The screaming nander whelp, the last survivor of its clench, raced around the cavern, desperately trying to avoid capture.

Rogart looked at it and swore under his breath. "Ten bloody percent," he groused.

"Beats nine," Kiva replied. She stared straight into the glazed eyes of the stunned adult as she drew her dagger across its windpipe. I alone witnessed her tiny shudder.

"Guild law," Sten said, in the tones of a man stating that water was wet. He squatted on his haunches beside the fire in which the nander was still popping and sizzling, facedown. "The jobs pay what they pay. All the easy runs were completed long ago. Every brassy comes harder now. If the guild wants to keep its doors open, it can only pay us so much."

Kiva raised an eyebrow. "You think it's a matter of expenses? We all saw the outfit that Master Brazillo wore to the palace last week. And it's not like the man's been missing meals either. Lean times for the guild don't seem to leave him any leaner."

Sten stared at the floor. "Guild's gotta be represented," he intoned. "Appearances matter." But it was plain that his heart wasn't really in it.

Kiva bared white teeth in the torchlight. "Our percentage doesn't matter much to you, does it, old man? Your share goes straight to the order." She indicated me with a toss of her head. "As for Nattering Nancy over there, hers goes to the House of the Lady. For you two, poverty's a lifestyle choice. The rest of us?" She began cleaning her nails with the point of her still-bloody blade. "We're not all called to that sort of service."

"And what a glorious service it is!" Rogart exclaimed, voice thick with sarcasm. "Sifting through nander corpses for loose change. And at the end of the trail, our ultimate reward…" He clapped his gauntlets in a parody of glee, emitting a resonant clank. "A pile of lizard dung!"

Kiva nodded. "No ordinary dung. Firedrake excrement is the *good* stuff. They make balm from it. Almost as valuable as silver by weight. A sack of coins might be less smelly, but I can set my fastidiousness aside if the money's right."

Sten, still in his squat, nodded. "Remember, firedrakes are as wild as they come. Hypersensitive to threats, pain, hunger, lust. All lizard brain, all the way down. When the moment arrives, don't hesitate. Just get the job done. *The job.* First, last, and always."

Rogart was no longer listening. His eyes were locked on the tiny cowering nander. "The job. Right."

"Has to be done, Rogart," Sten said, his voice flat.

Rogart rounded on him. "Why?" he exclaimed. "It's no threat! It barely comes up to my knee! We leave it be, it'll just…" He gestured vaguely.

"…grow up, and put a spear in somebody's leg," Sten finished for him.

Rogart gritted his teeth. "Gods. There's no reason to send a warrior to do this sort of job. This is…this is a tosher's task. A job for a sewer runner."

Sten sighed, rose from his squatting position, and advanced on the squalling infant. "And what do you think we are, exactly?"

He lifted his broadsword. I turned away. But I still heard the thunk, and the ensuing patter of blood against the cavern floor.

I kept my back turned, hiding my face from the others. Even so, I could hear Sten's command ring out. "Onward, crew, and ever downward. I can feel the floor growing warmer below us."

And Rogart, under his breath: "Hell can't be much further."

We each played a part in the events that led to my death.

We were guild to the core. Our tactics were polished to a keen edge, but any spark of spontaneity in us had long since been extinguished. We'd grown used to set-piece battles, to enemies who sat waiting for us. But a firedrake isn't a nander. A firedrake doesn't cower in wait. A drake hungers, and a drake hunts. So it wasn't in its lair that we met it, but in a narrow neck of the cavern, barely wide enough for us to march through in double rank. When we spotted it for the first time, it was already up in our faces, all slavering teeth and glowing green eyes, and it was on Sten before anyone could react.

Sten got in one good stroke with his broadsword, opening up its side, before it took hold of his leg, lifted him bodily, and started shaking him the way a pitwolf shakes a rat. Rogart quickly raised his sword up to aid him, but we were pinned too tightly in the passage; the angles were wrong. Kiva's sling bullet caught Rogart in the back of his sword arm, and he dropped his weapon, howling in pain. By this time, of course, I'd fumbled the torch, but it rapidly ceased to matter; the drake turned on Kiva long enough to puff a single, incendiary breath, and she became the only torch we needed. By the time I'd gotten the cudgel out, and fumbled that too, the lizard was atop Rogart, savaging him, jaws inches from his throat.

I watched it all, standing useless. And then the thing turned its eyes to me, just for a moment, green and luminous, blood on its jaws and flowing freely down its flank. And I looked into those eyes, and Sten's words came back to me: *All lizard brain, all the way down. Hypersensitive to threats, pain, hunger, lust.*

Hypersensitive to pain.

I dived straight at it in a headlong plunge, my arms empty. The fire blossomed directly in my eyes, and I felt it wash over me, but I was on top of the thing before the pain hit.

I lowered my head to the gaping wound in its scaly side.

I puckered my lips in the Lady's Kiss.

And I healed our enemy.

The lizard brain turned out to be exactly as Sten said it would be. A chaos of desires to be slaked and instincts to be indulged, uncluttered by any semblance of thought.

But not, as it happened, without memory.

When I finally returned to the land of the living, I knew instantly how desperate my situation was. The pain was immense, but the looks on the faces of my companions as they stared at my face were worse.

Sten forced his face into a rictus. "Ah!" he exclaimed. "You're back! And...and good work. Magnificent work, in fact." He nodded at the firedrake, lying on its side, its wound mostly healed, but its eyes staring sightless and its breath stilled. "It was the pain, of course. Would never have occurred to me, but, yes, the pain. The wound probably wouldn't have done the job on its own, but packing all of that pain into a single punch killed the thing outright. From the shock, of course. Killed... it..." And he turned away, unable to look any longer at the ruins of my face.

Behind him, Rogart was hauling a sack over his shoulder, leaving a trail of fetid drips behind him. It seemed I'd been unconscious for some time; they'd been down to the lair, cleaned it out. Our objective was accomplished, our ten percent secured, and it seemed like it might be a bit of a haul for once. But I couldn't for the life of me pull myself into a sitting position. Kiva was staring down at me and wasn't even bothering to put on an appearance of hope for my recovery; her gaze held the same anticipation it had when she'd slit the nander's throat.

"See, here's the thing, er..." Sten began. He still couldn't look at me. "We had just the three vials of balm left, and...well, we used them." He swallowed. "We were each of us in a really bad way, and we had no idea whether you'd last long enough to wake up, so..."

Rogart turned to me. In the place of Sten's strained courtesy, he offered his usual honest loathing. "We figured the Lady's servant could take care of herself, in this instance."

I blinked at that, and the single flutter of my eyelids was enough to send a sheet of pain washing over my face.

"You've got to admit," Kiva chimed in, "there's a certain justice to it." She favored me with a lopsided smile. "You've been *so* attentive to our needs, in our time together. We, who've been favored by your sweet kiss. We want you to experience its benefits for yourself." She nodded. "In fact, we insist upon it."

I stared up at my companions. They're not evil, I told myself. But it doesn't matter. They look at me, and they see someone who's hurt them. I'm not a person to them. I'm the thing the guild gives them because it's too cheap to buy them balm.

They know how deeply I know them. And they believe, deep in their souls, that someone who knows them from the inside out could only loathe them. I know too much. It's better to have me gone.

And they are guild. And the ruthless mathematics of the guild rule all that we do. Ten percent divided three times is more than ten percent divided four times.

What's broken in them can't be healed with a kiss.

Sten looked down at me, and for once, it was almost as if my mind was the one being read. "Just business," he muttered. "We're putting it on your shoulders. Your abilities will save or destroy you. You have a chance."

I stared up at him. And I thought about what the firedrake remembered, and thought about the three of them, hauling sacks of firedrake spoor ten leagues back to civilization in exchange for the equivalent of two months' pay. And what I didn't say to him was, *And you've had your chance as well.*

I lifted my left arm. The palm of my hand was a crackling, oozing mess. Slowly, I lowered it to my face, and I pressed my charred and stinging lips against it.

The pain descended, not halved by a companion's sacrifice, but one single, terrible whole.

I have heard it argued that pain and pleasure are two ends of the same spectrum. Even a moment's thought reveals the hollowness of the claim. Could any sane person consider the two to be the sides of an equal balance? Pleasure passes; pain lingers. Pleasure accompanies a man, dances before him, beguiles his attention; pain shouts its presence, insisting upon itself.

When a slave driver seeks the best way to motivate his charges, does he offer them the promise of pleasure, or the prospect of pain? A music lover lies in bed, dying of a wasting disease. Ask him: Would you prefer if I brought you a doctor of middling ability, or the world's greatest flutist to play you a song? If pleasure is the moon, pain is the sun; one is but a pale reflection of the other.

The pain was with me in its immensity, pervaded me; I had not imagined there could be such pain in the world. The urge to fade into infinity was strong; if I could but collapse under the burden, let this dolorous ocean wash me away, I would feel nothing ever again.

But it is not the Lady's will that we feel nothing.

Ask yourself: If the gods were to speak to us, to tell us they love us, how would they do so? Surely their message would take a form that was impossible for us to ignore. It would exist at the uttermost extreme of human sensation. It would scream at us: Your life is precious to us, and it is at risk. Attend to the danger. Take action. Stay alive!

The Lady's blessing descended upon me. I was the bestower of her gift—but I was also, for once, its recipient. And so, the Lady took me inside *my own* memories. And there, she showed me things I had missed.

I saw the tiny girl I had been. In memory, I saw her suffering beneath her father's fists. I saw her cower and quail and break. And I was with her, and I heard her tiny, tremulous voice, the voice of every punished child: *I have been bad. I do not know my fault, but somehow, I deserve this.* It was a voice that had been part of me as long as I could remember.

And then there was another voice, the voice of a grown woman. *My* voice? How could I know? My voice was a stranger to me, for not a single word had passed my lips since I was nine years old. But I was hearing the voice of a woman, sure and certain, and the woman did not accept the justice of this punishment. In the tunnel of my own memories, under a hail of pain the likes of which I had never known, I looked upon the suffering of the girl I had been. And I heard the voice speak.

How dare he. And how dare the mother look on, fearful to intervene. She deserves none of this. NONE OF IT!

And as the tiny girl packed her meager belongings into a kerchief, fleeing into the unknown, my heart swelled with pride at her courage.

And then the girl was nine years old, in the House of the Lady, accepting the instruction of the abbess. "I don't want to hurt people!" I heard the girl cry, and I saw the abbess start with surprise. And looking with adult eyes, for the first time, I understood why. The abbess had comforted a thousand crying neophytes. But she had never heard one express this particular concern. Not fear of the pain she would *experience*, but fear of that which she would *inflict*.

I found myself awed by the compassion of the girl I had been. And I watched as her compassion was manipulated by the abess, twisted against itself. I watched as she was sold into servitude to the cold and faceless guild, with its promise of adventure and its reality of endless toil. And, once again, I heard the voice of a woman, its rage redoubled: *She deserves better. SHE SHALL HAVE BETTER!*

The girl became an adult, serving at the beck and call of bitter, broken men and women. She shared their agony, and her sacrifice was viewed as an imposition. She saw the good in her companions' souls, and was reviled for seeing the evil as well. She came to know her companions with a depth of understanding exceeding that of any lover—and instead of embracing her as a sister, they left her scarred and abandoned on a cold cavern floor. And the voice of the woman in my head rose again, in a wordless crescendo of outrage and resolve.

And I knew, for the first time, the true nature of the Lady. I knew her as a messenger, the prophet warning of imminent crisis. I knew her as an unwelcome guest who refuses to leave until the house of the host is whole and strong. I knew her as healing's hideous handmaiden, as the companion who accompanies us into the world, and ushers us out again, into eternal glory. The Lady: her aspect terrible, but her true nature that of a faithful servant. And in my hour of greatest need, she had come to serve me.

I felt her outrage, her pride, her insistence. I floated in the ocean of her grace, each wave of pain buoying me up toward an undiscovered shore. I felt their intensity fade. And I felt the last of them break over my face as gently as a farewell kiss.

I woke in blackness, healed and whole. My fingers flickered over my face and found it fully restored.

And yet...I was dead. *Officially,* I was dead. My companions would, I knew, carry their haul back to the city, and report my death to both the Adventurers' Guild and the House of the Lady. If you should chance one day to visit the guild hall, be sure to visit the Roll of Legends. There you may stare upon a thousand names chiseled into the black basalt wall, my own among them.

There was no source of light available to me. No matter; I had seen the chambers through the drake's eyes. I found the wall with my hand, and followed it to the floor, and across to the lizard's carcass, cooling now, its internal fires banked.

What comes out of a firedrake's mouth? A fool's question. Fire, of course. Ah, but...what goes *into* a firedrake's mouth? What special ingredient could trigger a digestive process that results in the stuff from which balm is made? We know what comes out each end...but what goes on inside?

Were you aware that lizards eat rocks? Pebbles and stones with which to grind up their meals inside their own bellies? No? I had been likewise unaware, until I saw the world through a lizard's eyes. I'd have shared that knowledge with my companions, had they cared to learn it from me.

The lizard's wound had almost been healed by my intervention. Almost. There remained a tiny slit in its side where Rogart had stuck the sword in. I worried a jagged shard of flint from the cavern wall, and worked at that wound until I'd cut the carcass open. And then I reached into the creature's gizzard and rooted around, soaked to the elbows in gore, until I found a very particular rock, about the size of a heron's egg, which the firedrake had remembered swallowing.

My hand again to the wall now, and down the slanting passage to the creature's lair. And then across, to the far wall, belly-first on the floor. And there, the narrow fissure in the cave wall, a whisper of cool, fresh air in my face. The firedrake's memory, of course; it had to have a way out of its subterranean lair, else it would have starved to death. A long, filthy climb awaited me, on hands and knees in narrow quarters. I knew I would be scraped and scoured raw before I emerged. But what of it? Pain was an old friend. At the end of the climb, I knew, I would be reborn into the world above.

And that when I did, I would be carrying an uncut diamond as large as my fist.

A good physic can tell you all there is to know about wounds. And as it turns out, there's a great deal to know. It takes long study to master it all. But that's no real challenge to a girl with the money to pay for years of tuition. The lessons are difficult, but I'm an attentive listener. I've had years of practice.

Yes, I listen. But I speak, as well; otherwise, who would tell you this tale? And I do more than speak. I sing! It's true. I sing marvelously, all agree. They come from far and wide, students and teachers, commoners and nobility, to the institute, for the privilege of hearing my voice. Who could have imagined such a thing?

But mostly, I learn. A physic learns to respect pain, but not to worship it. A physic is attentive to pain, but not ruled by it. And a physic learns, above all, to wait. The surest healer is time, and the dispersal of pain over time is a blessing from the gods. You ask why I don't use my newfound wealth to revenge myself on the guild. Why should I? Picking at a wound only ensures that it never heals. Given time, even the deepest scars will fade.

And when they do, no worries. A physic can always find more business waiting around the corner.

After all, the world is full of wounds.

About Steve DuBois

Steve DuBois is a high school teacher from Kansas City and the author of twenty published short stories and works of drama. He has been a shortlisted finalist for both the James White and Baen Fantasy Adventure Awards. His author site is www.stevedubois.net.

Website: www.stevedubois.net
Twitter: @Twitlysium
Public Email: sdubois612@gmail.com

10

LOVE IN THE TIME OF HOLODECKS

BY CHARITY WEST

— 1 —

KATYN'S HELMET CLOCK flashed 9:50. Finally time to back out of this hole. With a deep intake of stale air, she dropped her pick into her cart and hefted the handles, creeping gingerly backward. On every side, sharp stones jutted from the mine walls, and she kept her elbows tucked to avoid puncture. The cocktail of gases in the tunnels would burn skin on contact, and she'd already dealt with decontamination twice this month.

She'd thought when she left Level Two that life would be better. But Level Three was more of the same, just another hole. And now there was no hope of advancing any higher. Not without—

Katyn brushed the thought aside. She didn't want to think about that now. Or ever. Everything ached. Why did she never draw sorting duty?

Alarms blared through the tunnel, and Katyn swore. Not now! What clumsy idiot punctured their suit? If they delayed her payday, she'd go aggro.

A burning sensation seared across her left calf. *Bury me, I'm the idiot.* Katyn dropped the cart handles and ran the few steps to the tunnel exit. The pain shot up her leg as gas expanded inside her suit. She reached the exit, slamming the air lock release, her vision too blurred to register the group of faces waiting on the other side.

Rough hands grabbed her, wrenched the suit from her body, and shoved her under the decontamination shower. Freezing liquid coursed over her, cooling the burn and starting her teeth chattering.

Her vision cleared enough to reveal the angry faces glaring at her. She wrapped her arms over her chest, feeling exposed in her wet underthings.

"Idiot Katyn—you wait till now to pull this crap?"

She couldn't tell who'd spoken, but she knew they were all thinking the same thing. Shift end was the worst time for this to happen. They might all miss their Holo session now, and that was unforgivable. They only earned one session a week for all their hours in the mines.

Mirci stepped around the crew, her voice rising above the grumbling. "All right, break it up." She slapped the button to stop the flow of healing liquid and tossed Katyn a thin towel. "You should be thanking her—you'll all get off five minutes early now."

Mirci turned and winked at Katyn as the complaints turned to whoops and cheers. Normally, after a contamination incident, everyone would have to stay for a mandatory safety briefing. Katyn watched Mirci, wary. It wasn't like her to stick up for anyone, especially not Katyn.

Katyn kept her head down and made to follow the others to the locker room, but Mirci held up a hand. "Wait in my office. We need to chat."

Katyn huddled on the edge of the cold metal stool, the thin towel barely enough to cover her shoulders. She rubbed her hands over her face, shutting out her bleak surroundings. The bioluminescent vines in Mirci's office were dying, barely able to emit a weak green light.

She tapped her foot against the cold tile. The skin on her calf was raw and cratered where the blisters had deflated. The pain had dulled to a throbbing sting, and it would scar for sure. She was lucky it was her leg this time. Her arms needed more time to recover from the last burn.

Finally, Mirci pushed through the door. She tossed Katyn a fresh jumpsuit, then grabbed the chair from her desk and placed it directly in front of Katyn. The light cast eerie green shadows in the deep pockets beneath Mirci's eyes. Katyn leaned back and pulled the towel tighter around her shoulders, her wet tank sending a shiver over her skin. Was she allowed to dress yet? Should she wait for Mirci to dismiss her?

Mirci leaned forward and anchored her elbows on her knees. "This happens to you a lot. Have you noticed?"

Katyn grimaced. What did Mirci want her to say? "I'm sorry. I don't know what I'm doing wrong."

Mirci rubbed her fingers across her palm, as if carefully considering what she would say next. "The tunnels are dangerous. Accidents happen. But—do you know most people don't spend as much time in the tunnels as you do?"

If Mirci would just dismiss her, Katyn could get dressed and get out of here. There wouldn't be as much time for character creation—she'd have to adopt a stock character, but that was still better than nothing.

"There are other duties you could be doing. Sorting, packaging. Lots of nice, safe rotations."

"But—I'm always assigned to the tunnels..."

Mirci sighed and muttered, "How dumb do you have to be?" She cleared her throat. "Listen, you're pretty new here, so maybe you don't understand how it works. When you get your Holo chit, you're supposed to give it to me."

Katyn blinked, her attention pulling away from planning her Holo experience. "What?"

"I have clout with the big guys. If I put your name on my list, you get sent to the tunnels once, maybe twice a month."

"But that's extortion!"

"Where do you think you are, the Mids? I didn't think you'd be so naïve, coming from Level Two."

Katyn swallowed. Things were supposed to be better here.

"Look, my protection is valuable, and I expect to be compensated. Six months' worth of your Holo time makes it worth my while to stick my neck out for you. You agree to that, you get on the list. This is all supposed to be understood."

Katyn was already shaking her head before Mirci finished. "I can't do that."

"It's standard practice, Katyn. I've worked hard to get where I am, and that comes with certain perks."

"But it's not right—"

"Find another job, then."

"You know I can't." She'd just come up from Level Two—she wasn't qualified for other work yet. It was the mines or nothing.

"Then pay me, or you're out in the tunnels again. How many more burns do you think you can handle?"

Katyn could only gape at her. "But six months?" Even one month was too much to ask. "I can't."

"Look, I've got people to pay too. I can't do this for you if you don't help me out." She stood and walked to the door. "This is how things work, Katyn. Unless you think you're gonna find Socorro's treasure, best get your name on my list." The door clanged shut behind her.

Katyn yanked on her jumpsuit. Socorro's treasure—how dare Mirci taunt her with that? Even if it did exist, it wasn't like she'd ever get enough Holo time to actually find it. Just another way life was stacked against people in the Dregs.

She didn't want to think about any of this. If she could get to the Holo, it would all go away. The clock read 10:05. Just enough time.

She ran out to the pay station, pressed her shaking thumb to the screen. The metal coin clinked into the tray, and Katyn glanced over her shoulder. No one. She snatched the coin and thrust it into her pocket. Mirci couldn't take it from her; it was hers by right.

She'd gone without Holo time before—sacrificed for a year to climb up a level—and what had that gotten her? Mirci and the mines. If she'd learned anything, it was that life never got any better. So why give up the one thing that made life in Echelon livable?

Advertisements filled the walls along her path, splashy screens shouting promises of a new start in the colonies—*New Worlds! New Life!* She shuddered. The colony planets didn't even have the Holo. Why would anyone go there?

Her pant legs slapped against each other as she ran down the dim streets. She'd heard that in the city's midlevels and higher, bioluminescent trees formed elegant arches lining the walkways. Down here, they had only the vines that clung to the grate of the level above, their light soulless and pathetic like everything else in the Dregs.

None of it mattered. Soon she'd be in the Holo, and all of this would disappear—the mines, Mirci, these clothes, her life—it would all be like a distant memory. She just had to get to the station.

— 2 —

Katyn rushed in to find the station nearly empty, only one attendant still managing the reception desk, one she didn't recognize. Heat rose in Katyn's cheeks as she hurried up to the desk, out of breath, and pushed her chit toward the woman—Valyri, the name tag said.

Valyri sighed. "Cutting it close, aren't we?" She was probably getting ready to start her own experience—Holo workers got a half hour after every shift. Katyn had been trying to get that job for years.

"Sorry," Katyn mumbled. "There's still time, though—right?"

The young woman forced an artificial smile to her lips. "Yes. What experience can I help you with today?"

Katyn's blush intensified, but she cleared her throat and said, "I'd like a romance, please."

"Of course." The young woman nodded. "Our erotic experiences are among our most popular—"

"No!" Katyn slapped her hand on the desk, surprising the attendant. She pursed her lips and took a deep breath before continuing. "I'm sorry. No. Thank you. I don't want an erotic experience; I want a romance. A Western, preferably."

"Shared or private?"

"Private," Katyn said quickly. Dealing with people in real life was bad enough.

"Happy endings only, or are tragedies acceptable?"

Katyn shrugged. "I don't really care either way, as long as it's well researched and authentic."

Valyri's smile turned genuine. "You know, I think I have just the thing for you. Follow me."

Katyn lay on a paper-lined table in a tiny loading room. She'd traded her jumpsuit for a skintight stimulus suit, and she now fought the urge to blink against the needles protruding from her eyes.

The needles didn't hurt, and they were so thin she couldn't see them, only the faint outline of wires leading off them and down toward the humming machine below. Immersive experience wasn't really anything like the Holodeck—she'd never understood why people had started using the name. Something about an old show, in the days before immersive entertainment. But people *had* started using it, and names have a way of sticking.

Valyri patted her on the shoulder. "Your two hours start as soon as I leave the room and commence the simulation. Do you have a good handle on your character?"

"Yes. Thank you."

"Great. I hope you enjoy yourself."

The sound of Valyri's footsteps moved away from Katyn, followed by the whoosh of the sliding door. Katyn counted to three, then smiled as the quality of light changed from sickly green to the bright, warm light of a Western afternoon.

She blinked, reveling in the sudden absence of needles. The tightness in her chest eased, and she leaned back into the leather seat of the stagecoach, watching the bustle of the railway town through the fluttering curtains.

Her character, Kathryn Morgan, was a young woman recently bereaved of her aunt, coming to the town of Aurora Bluffs to inherit the woman's farm. There were so many ways this could go—would the farm be run-down and needing rescue? Or would it be a thriving business, with predators salivating over their chance to swipe it from her? Excitement trilled through her.

She took a deep breath to steady herself and looked down at the dress she'd chosen, a lovely blue calico with puffed sleeves, a high collar, and buttons down the front. The buttons would serve as controls within the Holo—the top one allowed her to skip ahead, the second would record a still of any image she chose, the third could heal injuries, and the bottom served as an escape valve if she got into trouble.

She'd smoothed out her skin, traded her unruly copper coils for coifed auburn hair and her mud-gray eyes for sparkling blue ones, but otherwise left her appearance the same. She liked feeling like it was really her in here.

The stagecoach rolled to a stop, and the door swung open. The coachman helped her down and waited patiently as she pulled out her coin purse. She was pleased to see that her character had a decent amount of money. There were always challenges in these stories, but at least in this one, poverty wouldn't be one of them.

As the coach rolled away, she turned to face the town proper. It was small but had all the basic accoutrements—sheriff's office, saloon, general store, post office. People bustled all around, most turning to gawk at her. A few ladies offered polite smiles; gentlemen, the tip of their hats.

Katyn considered where to start her adventure. It would be natural for Kathryn to go directly to the farm she'd inherited, but would that give her many opportunities to meet possible love interests? Sooner or later, the program would send one her way, but she didn't want to waste time in an empty house. No, better to start meeting people. She headed for the saloon.

She pushed through the swinging doors, her skirts brushing against the doorframe and swishing pleasantly around her legs. The noise in the hall died at her entrance, and all turned to stare at her. Every person in the room was an attractive man of marriageable age. She grinned.

Head held high, she sauntered to the bar, enjoying the heat of the stares on her back, and perched herself on the edge of a stool. The wall behind the barkeep was lined with "Wanted" posters for notorious bands like the Dalton gang and the Five Joaquins. It was a nice touch.

The barkeep blinked at her, and his mustache fluttered as he spoke. "You must be Betty's niece. You look jes' like 'er."

Kathryn nodded.

"She was a fine woman. And any kin o' hers gets a drink on the house." He cleaned out a glass and filled it with lemonade, plunking it down on the table in front of her. Kathryn thanked him and held back a sigh. Of course it would be too much to ask for a proper drink. Still, she should probably just be grateful he hadn't kicked her out on sight. There were good and bad things about being a woman in this time and place.

She sipped her lemonade, peering around the room as the old man rambled affectionately about her late aunt. The men soon got over her sudden entrance and returned to playing cards and talking in small groups. Her eyes flitted from man to man—any of them could be her intended love interest.

Her eye caught on one in particular—a young man sitting alone at a table, gazing out the window. His wavy brown hair curled with sweat, and his furrowed brow held lines of dust in the creases. Dark, brooding eyes, full lips, chiseled jaw. He was gorgeous. She pressed the second button down on her dress, capturing the image.

She turned to the barkeep. "Who's the loner?" She jutted her chin toward Handsome.

"Oh, that's Eli Bradford. You'll want to watch out for him. He owns the land right next to your aunt's, and he wants that property real bad. I figure he'll do anything he can to get you to sell."

Kathryn smiled. "That so?" Incredibly handsome, with a natural point of opposition to the heroine—very likely this was her romantic hero.

Of course, he could also be the antagonist.

She nodded her thanks to the barkeep and made her way over to Mr. Bradford. She pulled out the chair across from him and sat down, getting a good look at him. Those lips—she was going to get to kiss those lips. All in good time.

First she needed to build the tension.

"I'm Kathryn Morgan." She held out a hand. "And the farm's not for sale."

Eli raised one perfect eyebrow and leaned back in his chair. He opened his mouth to speak, but movement outside the window caught her eye and she turned. She felt a lurch of vertigo as her mind struggled to reconcile what she saw: something—no, some*one*—who didn't fit into the experience at all.

She stared at him through the thick glass. The man's close-cropped hair was an unnatural jet black, and the sun revealed blue highlights. He wore a crisp synthetic suit over wraparound pants that ballooned ridiculously around his thighs—clothes that were popular in Echelon's upper levels. The whole ensemble was a deep, shiny black that would have been impossible to manufacture in 1855.

The sight of him brought flooding in everything Katyn was trying to escape. The mines, Mirci's threats. That world was not supposed to intrude on this one.

A flash of anger heated Katyn's chest. She'd paid for a private experience. She stood, knocking her chair to the floor. "Excuse me a moment," she said to Eli. "I'll be right back." And she swept toward the saloon door. From the doorway, all she could do was stare at the abomination that had pulled her away from Handsome and his gorgeous lips.

The intruder walked down the street, pausing here and there to peer at random things—wooden fence posts, horses' saddles, even a hat he swiped off some poor cowboy's head. He tossed the hat aside and kept walking.

Not only had he not bothered to dress appropriately, he hadn't even created an avatar for himself. His left eyebrow was patchy, and his eyes were smallish and drooped downward. He looked so normal, a stark contrast to the perfect sim characters who populated the town. If he'd wanted to participate in her story, he could have at least made an effort.

She captured his image for the complaint she would file and stormed over to him. He didn't seem to notice her. He crouched down to pick up a fist-sized rock and examined it with strange intensity.

She cleared her throat. "Excuse me. What exactly are you doing here?"

The man glanced up at her, sighed, and dropped the rock to the ground. "Don't mind me. I'm just passing through."

"Passing through? You're passing through *my* experience."

"No one else seems to mind."

Katyn gritted her teeth. "Yes, that's the issue." The townspeople didn't register the man's incongruous appearance at all. As far as they were concerned, he fit in perfectly.

"Just..." He waved his hand dismissively, still not looking at her. "Ignore me."

"How am I supposed to do that? Your very presence screams 'None of this is real'!"

"You know it isn't real, don't you?" He wiped the dust from his hands and stood, peering off into the distance as if searching for something.

"Yes—no—I mean, it's supposed to feel real—you're destroying the illusion!"

He looked down at her. He was only a few inches taller, but the arrogance in his posture made it feel as though he towered over her. He tipped a nonexistent hat. "Begging your pardon, ma'am."

Katyn set her jaw and squared her shoulders. No one was going to make her feel small in the Holo. "I've paid for this experience, and you are ruining it. You need to leave."

He turned and walked away from her, as if she were no more important than the sims. Katyn hesitated for a bare second, then followed him.

"Hey!" She grabbed the slick fabric of his suit coat.

He turned toward her with a sigh. "I'm leaving—isn't that what you wanted?"

"I don't want you to walk away. I want you to disappear."

"Harsh."

"I'll never be able to get back into my story knowing you're here mucking around. Can't you respect that?"

"I get it. You want to play pretend. Pretend I'm not here." He started walking again, and Katyn lost no time matching his stride.

"You don't get it. This isn't a game to me. I know how everything is supposed to fit in this world. If something is anachronistic, it ruins the whole thing for me. A hat from the wrong era bothers me—there's no way I'm going to be able to ignore you."

He stopped and looked at her then, head tilted, eyes calculating. Katyn couldn't shake the feeling that he was pondering how he could use her. For what, exactly?

His silent study was infuriating. "Fine. Just stay out of my way." She reached for the top button of her dress. She could lose this guy when the program deposited her further along in the narrative, though she hated to miss part of her story. The second before her finger pressed the skip button, the intruder's hand snaked out and wrapped around her wrist. Katyn glared at him.

"Hang on a second—"

"We're done here."

She wrenched her hand free and jabbed her thumb against her top button. The world dissolved.

— 3 —

Color filled in around her, and Katyn lurched forward, dizzy and disoriented. She reached out with both hands, hoping something would be there to catch her fall. Her right hand met soft flesh, and she gripped it until the dizziness subsided. When her vision cleared, she looked up into the heavily lashed eyes of Eli Bradford.

She resisted the urge to scream. This was so unfair—that Uppie had made her miss something crucial. Somehow Kathryn had ended up here, with Eli, but Katyn had no idea of the circumstances. Had they arrived together? Or just happened to arrive at the same time? The distinction was critical, and it grated at her that she'd missed the events that brought her here. Where was *here*, anyway?

She turned to ascertain her surroundings. They stood on a wide wooden porch; the setting sun cast a golden light over the evening.

Crowds of festively dressed people passed them to enter some kind of dance hall.

She looked down to see her calico dress was now a deep-blue silk gown with lace at the sleeves and collar. The four control buttons were still there, worked in along the bodice.

"You all right?" Eli's sonorous voice pulled her back into the moment.

"Yes, I'm fine." She managed a small smile, though she wasn't sure if they were on good terms right now. This was so frustrating.

Eli looked pointedly to where she gripped his arm, and she let go, flushing. He stepped aside for her to proceed ahead of him, and she swept into the hall.

Wooden pillars propped up a high ceiling, and a band played on a low stage at the far end of the hall. The crowd was mostly men, sprinkled with a few well-attended women. Couples danced in the center of the room. A flash of silver glinted from the back of a dress, distracting her. Was that—?

A cough sounded behind her, and she turned, expecting Eli to make his polite exit. But he held out a hand. "Care to dance?" His voice was deep, sultry, and thick as honey. Katyn's heart sped as she accepted his hand. The music started, and she found that her feet knew the steps. Eli stared at her, surprise evident on his face.

"Ah. You didn't expect me to know the dance," she said.

His guilty silence was all she needed as confirmation.

"So you asked me to...what—humiliate me?"

His step faltered a little. "I wanted you to see..."

"That I don't belong here," she finished for him.

"The West's no place for someone who can't keep up."

Katyn smirked. "I assure you, I can."

The music picked up tempo, and the two stormed across the floor, a dance more combat than courtship. They matched each other step for step, until suddenly Eli stopped.

"Mind if I cut in?" a voice came from behind Eli. Kathryn peered around his shoulder, brow furrowed. A new suitor?

"You again!" she cried. This wasn't happening. Yet there he was, the intruder, a maddening smirk on his face.

"Of course," Eli said, his voice sounding wooden. Before she could stop him, he bowed to her and walked away, sim deferring to user, his face placid and blank.

Katyn whirled on the intruder. "Look what you did! You turned him into an automaton!"

"Exchanging witty repartee with the gallant cowboy, were you?"

Katyn growled low in her throat. Any decent person knew not to mock another's Holo preferences. "It's none of your business."

He held out a hand. "I'm Nyx."

"And I'm not doing introductions. What do you want? You can't be here just to thwart my romance."

"Please. I've got bigger ambitions." The spark in his eye was so familiar, like the flare of an old wound. Bren used to look like that when—Katyn clamped down on the thought. She didn't want to feel the shame that always accompanied his memory. Not in the Holo.

"Whatever you want, you're not getting it from me." She pivoted on her heel and strode off the dance floor.

She ducked through the wide doors to stand on the porch. Her finger strayed toward the escape button, but she couldn't bring herself to press it. If this *Nyx* cretin would just leave her alone, she could still salvage this. She took a deep breath of the cooling night air, and watched the last scrap of sunlight slip below the horizon. The sky turned a green blue that faded into inky black, and the first stars twinkled into view. "I'm Kathryn Morgan," she whispered, closing her eyes and pushing Bren back to the recesses of memory, where he belonged.

The music drifting through the door slowed to the gentle one-two-three of a waltz. If Nyx hadn't interrupted, she would be dancing this waltz with Eli. Their gazes would have turned tender, and the air between them would have crackled with heat. He would have leaned in, powerless against the enchanting blue of her eyes...

Footsteps rang out on the wooden boards.

"Hear me out," the all-too-familiar voice said, and she groaned inwardly. She turned to Nyx with a sigh.

"Fine. Tell me what you want, so I can tell you no, and we can part ways." Never mind that their ways never should have crossed in the first place.

Nyx glanced over his shoulder. A couple stood just inside the door, and a group of men lounged at the other end of the porch. He beckoned toward the stairs. Katyn rolled her eyes but followed. The sooner she could get rid of this creep, the sooner she could get back to Eli.

They stepped out into the darkness, the street lit only by weak oil lamps and the ethereal light of a full moon. The music faded with each step, and the sound of night creatures filled in around them. When they'd left the dance hall far behind them, Katyn stopped.

"All right, there's no one around. Can you please get on with it?"

Nyx turned to face her. He bit his lip and ran one hand over his close-cropped hair. "All right. I'm looking for something, and I think you can help me find it." That glint in his eye was back, and Katyn crossed her arms against its pull.

Walk away. Right now. "You'll need to give me a few more details." Why wasn't she walking away? She knew better than this.

Nyx sighed. "Fine. I've got a lead on Socorro's treasure."

Katyn winced, Mirci's smug face rearing up in her memory. Nyx kept bringing the real world slamming back into her. She could almost feel the sting of the chemical burn on her leg. This wasn't supposed to happen.

She gritted her teeth and focused on the idiocy of what he was saying. "Oh, please. The treasure? You're wasting my time for that fairy tale?"

Almost as soon as the Holo was made available to the public, the rumor started that there was treasure hidden in the fabric of the sim. Supposedly, Socorro Boon, the Holo's brilliant, elusive creator, had placed codes that would manifest in the different experiences, one leading to another. Collect ten of them, and unimaginable treasure would be yours—a million Holo hours, it was said.

It didn't matter that no one had ever found the rumored treasure. Miserable junkies still spent all their Holo time searching for the codes. And Katyn wasn't going to be one of them.

"This has been fun and all, but I think I'll opt out of your little treasure hunt." She turned to walk back to the dance hall.

"Let me prove to you that it's real. Help me find a code, one code, and you'll see that I'm not crazy. If you help me, I'll split the take with you. What do you have to lose?"

She kept on walking.

He ran to catch up with her. "You're giving away a chance at a fortune, for what? A kiss with a sim, and then back to the daily grind? I'm talking about changing your life. Help me find the last three codes, and you'll get fifteen percent of the take."

Katyn stopped. Was she really considering this? But he was right— that kind of wealth would change everything. Even just fifteen percent of a million hours was more than anyone could use in a lifetime—enough to spend all her time in the Holo and still have plenty to trade. Could she really turn the chance down?

Nyx sensed her resolve weakening, and he pressed onward. "Test me—one code. I promise it will be more fun than your spectacular romance."

She couldn't get back into her story if she thought there was even a possibility he could be telling the truth. If she proved him wrong, she could get rid of this irritating pull he had over her.

"I'll give you half an hour. If we don't find a code by then, I'm going back to my story."

"You drive a hard bargain, little lady," he said, laying into the *R*s. "But you've got yerself a deal."

"Please don't do that. Your drawl is terrible."

He grinned.

She crossed her arms. "So, if this treasure is real—why bring me in? You can't be looking for a traveling buddy."

"No—unfortunately, I need you. The path is made up of aberrations in the story. Anachronisms and the like. They're very difficult to spot. Things were going well, I've already got seven of the ten codes. But...circumstances have changed for me, and I need help. And as you so charmingly mentioned when we first met, you know when something is out of place."

Katyn frowned. "So you need me to find things that don't fit in this time period?"

"Yes. Then I'll capture them, and they'll be in the record when we exit the experience. Give me your address, and I'll come find you as soon as this is over."

She shook her head. "No—if we find any codes at all, *I'll* capture them. You'll have to come to me if you want to cash in." Her trust wouldn't extend any further than that.

"Fine. Then you're in? Deal?"

She grimaced. "Deal."

"Great. Can I know your name now?"

"It's Katyn."

He affected a cheesy bow. "Pleased ter meetcha."

"Ugh. Just...what are we looking for?"

"Numbers. A ten-digit string of numbers, somewhere on the out-of-place object."

She tried to quell the hope building inside her. He was crazy. Nothing would come of this. But if..."Do you know where to look?"

He shook his head. "Have you seen anything already, maybe? Anything—besides me—that didn't belong?"

She blinked. "Oh. Yes—there was something! Back at the dance."

— 4 —

A thrum of excitement fluttered through Katyn, strong enough to override the voice of warning that was now fading to the back of her mind. This wasn't the same as with Bren. She was in control this time, and the risk was so much smaller. All she really stood to lose was this one session, and what she might gain was ever so alluring. They arrived at the dance hall, where the music continued.

"So are you going to tell me what we're looking for?" Nyx asked.

"Earlier, I thought I saw a dress fastened with a zipper."

Nyx raised an eyebrow. "And that's...wrong, somehow?"

Katyn gaped at him. "A zipper would be *completely* wrong for the period. They weren't used on clothing until well into the twentieth century."

"Why do you know this crap?"

"Maybe you shouldn't insult me, huh? Unless you want to go back to staring at the bottom of every rock you find in the street."

"Sorry, sorry." He held his hands up, placating. "I didn't mean to insult. Just wondered why you know about zippers and hats and cr—stuff."

She narrowed her eyes at him. "It's called research. I have all week to wait between Holo visits, so I use that time to read up on the era."

His eyes widened. "I had no idea you only had access once a week."

"Life is different in the Dregs, Uppie."

He grimaced and cleared his throat. "All right, let's go get that dress."

She blocked him with her arm. "You can't expect to waltz in there and take what you want."

"Could we polka?"

Katyn rolled her eyes. "You know what I mean. You can't go grabbing dresses off women. You've been here long enough, the story is going to start incorporating you."

Nyx nodded. "All right. We go in, try to act normal, and get close enough to inspect the dress for a code."

"Why do I get the feeling you're loving that particular detail?"

"You offend me. I'm nothing if not a gentleman."

Katyn scoffed.

Nyx offered his arm. "Shall we waltz in?"

Katyn was surprised by the laugh that bubbled out of her as she took his arm. They stepped through the doors, and she began scanning the crowd.

"There," she whispered, nodding toward a woman on the far edge of the dance floor. Her dress was an exquisite green silk, strikingly offset by her ginger hair. "We need to get close enough to see if that's really a zipper." She started working her way through the fringes of the crowd, smiling and nodding as she went. It would be faster to cross directly over the dance floor, but that would be incredibly rude. She wasn't in that much of a hurry.

The hall was filled with the storm of feet reeling and quick-stepping in time to the caller's instructions, and Katyn felt a pull to join them.

"Of course you would have to interrupt the best part of the story," she grumbled over her shoulder—but Nyx wasn't following her. She whirled, searching for the black-clad figure.

There—she spotted him standing behind the redhead. Leave it to him to choose the incredibly rude route. It didn't help that he was peering with scandalous intent at the back of the woman's gown.

He couldn't see the two men behind him casting storm clouds in his direction. Katyn had to get over there and diffuse the situation before Nyx got his face beaten in. It was customary for men to remove swords, spurs, and sidearms when entering a dance hall, but that didn't mean they were rendered harmless.

She changed direction, heading for Nyx, but the crowd was too thick, made up mostly of men without partners who all wanted to tip their hats to Katyn and catch her eye. She usually adored that aspect of visiting this time and place, but right now all the extra attention was beyond frustrating.

She elbowed her way through the crowd, keeping her eye on Nyx. The two men had progressed to gathering reinforcements, nudging the men around them and pointing in Nyx's direction. She'd seen this type of thing enough to know they'd gather an overwhelming number first, then wait for Nyx to do something—anything—to justify them going on the offensive.

She needed to get over there. Now.

The music changed to the jaunty half-time beat of a polka, and the dancers lined up. Katyn pushed her way to the edge of the dance floor and was about to cross it, propriety be hanged, when a hand grabbed hers. She turned and ended up face-to-face with Eli Bradford.

Katyn groaned aloud.

"I believe you owe me a dance, Miss Morgan."

"Er, forgive me, I..." She fumbled to try to find the right tone, the right words for the period. Screw it. "I can't right now; I'm busy."

"I won't take no for an answer." Augh, he was so handsome. Her resolve weakened, and she allowed him to sweep her onto the dance floor. Luckily, each skipping step brought her closer to Nyx, who seemed to have noticed she was nowhere nearby and was scanning the crowd for her. Of course, he was still hopelessly ignorant of the mob brewing behind him. She tried to catch his eye, but he was looking in the wrong direction, toward the edges of the dance floor.

The pressure on her back increased, and Eli spun her in an awkward twirl—pulling her back and away from Nyx.

Katyn stumbled, and Eli held her steady as she found the beat again. "What was that for?" she asked, meeting his eyes for the first time since taking the floor.

"I had to do something to get your attention, didn't I?"

Katyn flushed. "Well, if you hadn't stonewalled me back at the saloon, maybe you wouldn't have to try so hard."

"And if you hadn't abandoned me mid-dance to go after some out-of-towner, maybe we'd already be further along in our negotiations."

Katyn knew she should be scandalized by the innuendo—Kathryn would have been—but she was so distracted that it barely registered. She slipped under Eli's arm, taking him by surprise enough that she was able to pull him back in their original direction.

There—Nyx's blue-black hair glinted in the golden light as he bumbled through the crowd. At least he was bumbling toward her now.

Eli coughed. "I'm sorry, did you want to lead?"

Katyn looked back at him for half a second. The sparkle in his eyes was mesmerizing, and she wished with all her heart that she could forget about Nyx and his proposal and spend the evening dancing in Eli's arms. She stopped dancing and lifted a hand to Eli's rough cheek.

In any half-decent romance, this would be the moment he would kiss her.

He stared at her as if trying to understand her soul, and Katyn felt her stomach drop. For that moment, it was impossible to tear herself away.

"Kat? A little help here?" Nyx's voice cut into her trance, and she turned in time to see a fist connect with his face.

Nyx smashed into the men behind him, who whooped and launched him back toward his attackers. He pulled a joyful-looking teen along with him, and the boy seemed more than happy to join the side of the underdog. In bare seconds, the room erupted into an all-out brawl.

Eli threw a protective arm around her, but Katyn ducked beneath it and dived toward Nyx.

"Miss Morgan!" Eli called, but his voice drowned in the clamoring of fists and the squeals of ladies heading for the doors.

Katyn ducked and dodged toward Nyx, who was barely holding his own despite the now-aimless nature of the fight. No one seemed intent on punching him anymore, at least not in particular. He bumped haphazardly through the brawlers until finally he was within arm's reach. Katyn grabbed his hand and pulled him down into a crouch.

"Was there a code?" she asked.

He shook his head. "I couldn't tell."

"What were you doing, then?" She pulled him toward the main doors—she couldn't see the redhead anywhere, but she was sure to be in the crowd of women fleeing the hall. They couldn't lose her. They didn't have that kind of time.

"I'm sorry, I didn't realize your story would devolve into cliché so quickly," he shouted. His voice dripped with sarcasm, but his hand clasped hers like a lifeline.

Katyn growled and yanked him downward; his back formed a vault for a brawler to flip over. "There's a difference between a cliché and a classic. The brawl is a time-honored genre standard."

"Exactly. A standard. Don't you ever get sick of the same old thing?"

She dodged a duet of men braced in a headlock. "No. That's why I come here."

Nyx caught up with her, and together they darted through a gap in the brawlers. He stared at her for a moment, baffled.

"But why? Life is already so predictable."

"Predictably awful. At least here, I can count on a certain brand of excitement—bandits, train robberies, brawls—"

He pulled her behind a pillar. They were almost to the doors. "Dotted with handsome men all vying for your attentions."

She shrugged. "Like I said, it's why I come here."

He rolled his eyes and opened his mouth, surely to say something biting, but a glimpse of russet and green caught Katyn's eye, and she yanked him toward the door. They ducked through the fighters and spilled out into the street.

— 5 —

The redhead clutched the arm of an older man, probably her father, as he led her down the street. The poor girl hiccupped and sobbed all the way down Main Street. Katyn and Nyx followed from a safe distance until the girl and her father entered the general store. The second story was probably their home.

Katyn signaled for Nyx to follow her to the back. Despite the lack of oil lamps on this side, it was bright enough to navigate to the door. She pulled Nyx into the shadows.

"What do we do? Wait until they go to sleep?"

Katyn shook her head. "I'm not wasting that much of my Holo time. Either there's a code or there isn't, and your time is nearly up." She should walk away now. Head to Kathryn's ranch and try to salvage this. But she had to find out if the treasure was real.

"Can you see what they're doing in there?" She jutted her chin toward the window. Nyx darted into a standing position, then back down into a crouch.

"It's dark, and there's no movement. Maybe they sent her straight to bed?"

She grimaced. "Let's wait a few more minutes, then head in."

He nodded, settling against the rough logs. Katyn leaned beside him. With the sun gone, the warm night had turned chill, and she rubbed her bare arms.

"So this is what you do with your Holo time, huh?" Nyx's voice barely concealed his mockery.

"I suppose you do something better with yours?" she snapped back.

"I mean, don't you ever get sick of it? Same old thing—handsome guy, contrived obstacle, something-something, end with a kiss?"

"Something-something? If you had half a clue what you were talking about, I might be offended, but seeing as you don't—" She rolled her eyes.

"Don't you ever want to have real adventures with real consequences?"

"I do!" She fought to keep her voice to a whisper. "These stories have real consequences for me."

"Oh, really? When was the last time falling in love in the Holo changed your life?"

Katyn scoffed. "Every time."

"Then why do you keep coming back?"

Katyn glared at him, hoping her disdain was evident in the moonlight. She was done with this conversation.

"I think we've waited long enough," she said. "Let's go in."

The door swung open without protest. An unlocked door was good, except that it meant someone must still be awake.

They crept into the dark store, met by the smell of kerosene mingled with leather and ripe cheese. Long counters and stacks of barrels left only a narrow aisle leading to the front of the store, where a dim light shone. Katyn held a finger to her lips and indicated the stairs that ran up the back wall.

They skulked upward, barely allowing their toes to rest on each step, gripping the rail for balance. At the top, Katyn exhaled a measured sigh, and felt more than heard Nyx do the same. They edged their way down the short hall, peering into each room. When they reached the redhead's doorway, Katyn turned to Nyx for instructions, but he just signaled her forward. He slipped into a crouch, and she marveled at how well he blended into the shadows.

She peeked in. The young woman slumbered in her bed. Katyn inhaled and crept into the small room. She didn't dare close the door, lest it creak.

There, slung across an armchair by the window, back gaping open, moonlight streaming over it, was the dress. Katyn slinked toward it, keeping a watchful eye on the redhead. When she reached the dress, she dropped down and began to examine it.

Nyx had said it would be a ten-digit number. Did that mean numbers printed on the fabric or what? Hidden, somehow encrypted?

She ran her hands and eyes over every seam, turning the dress every which way, searching through the layers. The quiet rustling of the dress grated at her nerves. This was taking too long. The code didn't exist. Nyx was delusional—or lying.

Or maybe she was wrong, and this wasn't the right clue after all. The zipper was definitely anachronistic, but maybe it was a mistake and not a hint.

"What's the holdup?" Nyx whispered from the doorway. In the dead silence of the house, even that small sound carried.

Katyn grit her teeth. "It's not here." Why did she feel so disappointed? That meant Nyx would have to leave her alone now. It's what she wanted—wasn't it?

There was a pause from the doorway. Then, "All right," he whispered. "Let's get out of here."

Katyn stood, smoothed the skirts of the dress, and lay it over the chair. The bodice gaped open inelegantly, the teeth of the zipper catching the light. A surge of irritation flooded her. That zipper should not be there; it was a stupid, careless mistake for the writer to make. She yanked the slider up, and the metallic *zup* of the teeth closing cut into the silence of the room. Katyn cringed, then stared in disbelief at what she saw. With the teeth now closed, it was plain as day: a string of numbers printed right onto the metal of the zipper.

It was real.

"Who's there?"

Katyn whirled and locked eyes with the redhead, now bolt upright in bed. Katyn's hands went up instinctively in a calming motion, but not soon enough—or effective enough—to stop the girl from screaming at the top of her lungs.

There was only one thing for it. Katyn pulled the dress into the moonlight and stared at the code, pressing the second button on her dress to capture the image. Whatever happened next, at least they had one code. Footsteps pounded across the floor, and Nyx was beside her.

"Come on! Let's get out of here!"

"Not so fast," a voice growled from the doorway. The redhead's father filled the frame, a rifle at his shoulder pointing right at Katyn.

"Don't shoot!" she cried. If he killed her, that would be the end of her session. She couldn't boot back in.

The man snarled. "Don't move a muscle, or I will shoot you where you stand."

Katyn believed him.

"Dorcas, honey, come on over to Pa." The girl crossed the floor with a nervous squeal and fell into her father's arms.

"Come out," he grunted. "Hands where I can see 'em."

Katyn raised her hands in front of her. The man pushed his daughter behind him, training his rifle on them the whole time.

"Dorcas, fetch the sheriff."

The girl ran off with a panicked look on her face, and her father forced Katyn and Nyx down to the first floor and into a windowless storeroom beneath the stairs. The smell of vinegar stung her eyes.

The angry man stood in the doorway, silhouetted by the dim light, and pumped his rifle. "Don't forget what's waiting for you if you try anything." He stepped back and slammed the door, locking it from the outside.

— 6 —

Katyn leaned against the rough plank walls with a sigh. "It's real. I can't believe it."

"You saw it? The code?" Even in the dark, she could hear the grin in Nyx's voice. "Did you capture it?"

She paced the floor. Now that she knew—she couldn't stop moving. "All this time, it was real—"

"Kat—did you get it?"

Her nose wrinkled. "It's Katyn. And yes, I got it." She ran her finger counterclockwise around the second button on her dress. The image of the last capture she'd taken projected into the air between them. Ten black numbers.

His whoop of excitement filled the room.

"So, now that you believe me—" Suddenly his warmth was right next to her, and his right hand found hers in the semidarkness. "Partners?"

Chills ran through her, like a shot of electricity. She grinned and shook his hand. "Partners."

"All right, then. We've got to get out of here. The next code is bound to be somewhere nearby."

Katyn's free hand strayed to the buttons on her dress. "We could exit—if you come get me and pay my way, we could come back—"

Nyx's hand clamped down on hers. "No. Don't."

"Why? You have the money, don't you?"

"Yes, but we don't have the time." He let out a short sigh. "There's someone else here looking for the codes—my old partner, Dorin."

"What!" Katyn yanked her hand back and slapped him on the shoulder. "Explain."

She heard the soft scraping sound of his hand running over his short-cropped hair. "He was the finder, I was the financier. I had a ton of chits saved, so that we could spend hours in the Holo, finding the codes. He was pretty good—and after a while, he started thinking he was too good. He figured if he could find the last three on his own, he wouldn't have to split the take."

Katyn bit her lip. He should have shared this with her upfront—but there was something about his voice. He sounded almost...pained. "He wasn't only your partner, was he? He was your friend."

Nyx sighed. "It doesn't matter. I'm sure he's here now. I've been looking for him, but he's likely assumed an avatar I won't recognize. He has the same seven codes I do. If we leave, he'll find the treasure first."

She almost told him she knew what that was like, to be betrayed, left behind—but the words stuck in her throat. She coughed. "Then —we don't leave. We find our way out of here. And we get there first."

Nyx's relief was almost palpable. "Thank you, Katyn."

She smiled. "Look at that, we just had a sincere conversation. I didn't even know you had a sincere mode."

He shoved her shoulder lightly. "Sincere mode—you make me sound like a sim."

"Still, you should have told me about Dorin from the beginning. We might have done things differently—faster."

"We still would have ended up with Dorcas's Pa pumping his rifle at us. I don't think we could have avoided that."

"Wait—did you say he pumped the rifle?"

"Yeah, why?"

Her mind reeled. How had she not noticed it—a rifle from 1855 wouldn't have a pump action—it would have lever or bolt action. "Nyx. That gun—it's the next code."

A door creaked in the distance, followed by the sound of footsteps crossing a wooden floor. Katyn tapped her dress button and the projection winked out. Nyx pulled her away from the door and up against the far wall of the storeroom. "Follow my lead. Whatever happens, make sure you capture the code."

A key rasped in the lock, stopping any protest from Katyn. Her muscles tensed. The door opened outward, and two men glared into the room from behind a lantern. Katyn shielded her eyes from the glare.

"Here they are, Sheriff," Dorcas's pa said. "They attacked my daughter, and I expect you to see justice done."

"We didn't attack anyone," Katyn began. But a movement to the side of the room cut her off. Nyx darted to one of the shelves, grasped a glass bottle by the neck and smashed it against the wood shelf. He wrenched Katyn by the wrist into his arms and held the jagged glass to her jugular.

"No one moves, or the girl gets it," he snarled. Katyn fought the urge to roll her eyes at the faux menace in his voice.

The two men halted, looking between Katyn and Nyx. "I thought you said they were working together, Hanson," the sheriff said with a glare at the other man.

"I thought they were." Their captor—Hanson—looked baffled. He held his rifle in one hand, the lantern in the other, and he slowly lowered both to his sides.

"Drop your guns, kick them over to me, and no one gets hurt," Nyx said. "No sudden moves."

"No need to get antsy." The sheriff held up his revolver, then dropped it.

"Now kick it. And you too," Nyx said, his chin jutting against Katyn's shoulder as he gestured to Hanson.

"How do we know they're not still working together?" Hanson said to the sheriff.

"Are you going to risk the life of a lady on that chance?" The sheriff kicked his gun over to Nyx.

Hanson narrowed his eyes at Nyx, but he placed the rifle on the floor and slid it over.

"You got your guns now. Let the lady go."

Katyn felt Nyx swallow against her neck. This was the tricky part. "Get the gun, Kat," he whispered. He let her go, and she fell to her knees. She scooped up the rifle, searching for the tiny black numbers. There—engraved in the varnished wood of the rifle's butt. She stared hard at it and pressed the second button down on her dress. Two down. She grinned.

Two clicks sounded above her head, and she looked up to see Nyx in midstep to the revolver and the sheriff pointing two handguns straight at their heads. He tsked. "You didn't really think you were gonna pull one over on me, did you?"

"I told you they were working together." Hanson snatched the rifle from Katyn and retreated behind the sheriff.

The sheriff frowned. "We'll sort this out at my office."

— 7 —

Moments later, they were pushed onto the floor of a wagon, hands tied behind them with rough rope. The wagon started to move, and soon they were rolling along the packed-dirt road. The wagon bed jumped and jostled, sending vibrations through Katyn's bones with every turn of the wheel. She rolled up onto her side to look at Nyx. The full moon gave her a good view of his face.

"That was incredible," she whispered.

"Incredible good, or incredible bad?" he whispered back.

She shook her head. "Both. I can't believe you held a knife to my throat."

"Not a knife, technically."

She rolled eyes, but she was smiling. "Still sharp, though."

"But we do have two codes now." He grinned.

"Yes, and we're on our way to jail."

He winked. "Slight setback."

"How can you be so confident?"

"I've got you," he whispered. "You've found these two codes twice as fast Dorin ever found anything. He always has to stop and do research. He's probably insanely frustrated right now. He doesn't have it all socked away like you do."

Katyn could feel her face warming, and she hoped the darkness hid it. She lay back. Stars twinkled above them, and occasionally one would shoot across the sky in a blaze of light. Katyn smiled—that was a nice detail for the sim writer to include. *Where would Kathryn be right now, if I'd stuck to the story line?* she wondered. *Probably somewhere less interesting than this.*

"I can see why you like this place," he said finally. "The stars are incredible."

She rolled onto her side to look at him. "Do you think they really look like that? In the real world?"

"I wouldn't know."

Katyn sighed. "Yeah, me neither. I've never been above Level Three."

"Is that where you were born?"

Katyn tensed at his question, even though it was perfectly natural. She willed the tightness in her chest to ease. He didn't mean anything by it.

"No," she answered. "I was born on Two."

His body shifted under her, and she raised her head to find him staring at her, brow furrowed. "So you were climbing? Why'd you stop?"

She opened her mouth to give some excuse, some easy explanation. But she surprised herself by telling the truth.

"There was a guy," she said. "Bren." Saying his name aloud hurt, but not as much as she'd feared. "We worked together. He's come up from Level One, and—there was something magnetic about him. He had this ambition. He wanted to make it to the top, and he said he wanted to take me with him. We started pooling our money, you know, saving every little bit. I never used the Holo, never bought upgrades. We saved enough to get to Level Three.

"After that, he convinced me to wait, so we could skip a couple levels at a time. He said piecemeal wasn't enough for him anymore. He wanted to take me to the stars."

Katyn stopped. She didn't want to cry.

"I think I see where this is going," Nyx said, an edge to his voice. "Bastard."

A bitter chuckle escaped her. "You see it, but I didn't. But yeah, I came home from work one day, and Bren was gone, the money was gone. He's in the Mids now, I'm sure. Probably doing it all over again with some other sucker."

"I'm sorry."

She shook her head. "I was an idiot. I trusted him with no question. I deserved it."

"Hey," Nyx said. "No, you didn't. He was the idiot for throwing your trust away." His soft voice had a fierce edge to it.

After a long moment of silence he asked, "So, is that why you really come here?"

"I guess..." she said, feeling foolish. "I guess it's just nice to feel wanted. There's never rejection built into these stories. Obstacles, yeah. But I'm always wanted."

He smiled sadly. "I understand that."

His gaze lingered on her face, his smile fading into a look of almost serious contemplation. A little flutter warbled through her chest, and she felt suddenly aware of the space between them. If this were a normal Holo experience, she'd know how to handle this moment, but now she felt awkward and unsure. Her eyes traveled to his lips—she'd never noticed before how full they were. She blushed harder and rolled onto her back, air escaping her lungs in a shaky sigh.

"What's wrong?"

Katyn fought the manic urge to giggle. "Oh, just, you know, normally by this point in the story I'd've gotten a kiss already." Her eyes widened in horror. Had she really said that? What was wrong with her?

She waited for Nyx's throaty chuckle, but he made no sound. Nervously, she turned her head toward him.

"Sorry I ruined things for you." His voice was soft, and his lips quirked up in a slight smile.

"No, you—you didn't—" she stammered. "I mean..." She trailed off as he stared into her eyes.

"You mean—by this point in the story, you and the gallant cowboy would be staring into each other's eyes." He raised an eyebrow in mock seduction. "He'd say something swoon-worthy—"

"Swoon-worthy?" Katyn choked out, a giggle right beneath the surface. She knew he was teasing, but the intensity of his gaze was electric.

He cocked his head and smiled. "And then he'd tip your chin up, and the two of you would stare into each other's eyes, until you couldn't fight it anymore..." He brought his face nearer and nearer to hers, until their lips were only a whisper apart.

Katyn's chin quivered—did he want this, or was he only mocking her? She wanted so badly to close the distance between their lips, but what if—what if that's not what he wanted?

He pulled away from her, looking slightly dazed. "Sorry I'm not him."

"Yeah...um, me too."

They rode the rest of the way in silence. Katyn couldn't help feeling like maybe she'd made a mistake.

"Whoa, there," a voice called above them, and the wagon lurched to a stop.

"Nyx?" She started, not sure what she wanted to say.

"Keep your eyes open," he said, grinning. "We almost have it."

— 8 —

The rifle pointed over the end of the wagon bed. "Up. And don't give me any trouble."

They sat up and scooted out of the wagon, Katyn careful to keep her skirts in place. With a grunt, she flopped onto the dusty ground, sending up a cloud of dirt. Hanson gripped her arm above the elbow.

A burly young man, likely the sheriff's deputy, emerged onto the porch. "What's the trouble, Sheriff?"

Katyn scanned everything in sight, searching for something out of place. The sheriff's office was a small building with a long railed porch, two windows lined with wax paper, and a hanging lantern illuminating the scene. Nyx raised his eyebrows questioningly, but she could only shake her head. Nothing.

"Bring 'em up," the sheriff said.

They were so close. If she could find the last code, she could hit her escape button and get out before things got worse. Nyx could find her on Level Three, and they'd cash in the codes together. And then...

The sound of hoofbeats thudded over the dirt, and Hanson and the sheriff both paused on the stairs. A lone man rode toward them, the lantern's light glinting off a gold star on his waistcoat. A deputy, then.

He pulled his horse to a stop but didn't dismount. "Sheriff, telegram came in from Flatridge—the Five Joaquins pulled a heist, stole dynamite from the Duncan mine. They hopped the train, probably after the gold on its way back east." He spoke with a slight whistle, evidence of a chipped tooth.

Katyn gasped, mind reeling.

The sheriff tossed his keys to the deputy on the porch. "Mack, lock them up. We'll deal with this later." He nodded at the other deputy. "Sanchez, you're with me. We'll cut 'em off at the pass." The sheriff thundered down the stairs and leapt onto his horse. The two rode off, and Hanson yanked Katyn and Nyx up the stairs.

Katyn pulled against her bonds, trying to wrench her hands free. The rough rope cut into her wrists, and the ties seemed to tighten the more she pulled against them. The lantern's glare forced her to squint.

An idea blazed to life in her mind. Before she could talk herself out of it, she planted her boot on the wood of the porch and shoved her shoulder into Hanson. He grunted and smashed into Nyx, who quickly realized his own role. While Hanson was off balance and the deputy was still frozen in shock, Nyx shoved Hanson and sent him careening down the steps.

He tumbled down and landed with a sickening crunch. While the deputy was distracted, Katyn jumped and smashed her head into the hanging lantern, sending it crashing to the porch. The glass shattered, and the oil ignited. She dropped to her knees, turned her back, and held her wrists above the flame. Pain lanced through her, but she held her hands steady, pulling at the rope to take advantage of any weakness the flame was creating. From the corner of her eye, she watched Nyx struggling with Mack. *Just keep him from getting to his gun,* she pleaded silently.

Her eyes flicked to Hanson, who lay motionless at the bottom of the stairs. The rifle was still strapped to his back, lying beneath him.

Nyx shoved the deputy against the door and held him there by the force of his body, but without hands, he was sure to be overpowered soon. The rope wasn't burning fast enough. With a scream, she shoved her hands into the flames.

The rope burned free, and she whipped her hands out of the fire. Ignoring her pain, she looked to find Nyx on his knees. Mack reached for his gun. She leapt up.

Barely keeping her feet beneath her, she careened down the steps and landed next to Hanson. She wrenched the rifle free, then turned and aimed it directly at the deputy.

He had his gun pointed at Nyx's head.

"Drop it," she said. Her hands throbbed, and the skin of her arms was an angry red. The flames licked up the support beam and were spreading to the roof. She was lucky her dress hadn't caught fire.

Mack raised his eyebrows coolly. The tremble in her limbs had not escaped his notice. He didn't believe she'd do it.

She raised the gun to her shoulder and aimed, then squeezed the trigger. The shot cracked through the night, and the bullet buried itself in the wood to the left of the man's head.

"Next time, I won't miss." It wasn't the best line ever, but it would work.

He dropped his gun and backed away from Nyx. She jutted her chin toward the town. "Go. Get help." Hands up, he ran down the stairs. "And if I see your face again, I'll shoot it!"

She rushed up the steps and untied Nyx as quickly as she could. Smoke billowed around them, and her eyes burned.

"Come on," she said, dragging Nyx to his feet. "People will be coming soon." The pain in her wrists was excruciating. Nyx grabbed the deputy's handgun, and they ran down the steps.

Hanson lay prone at the bottom of the stairs. She dropped to a crouch and felt for a pulse, ignoring the pain in her hands. "He's still alive. Let's put him in the wagon."

"I'll do that," Nyx said. "You take care of yourself."

She nodded, dazed, as he dragged Hanson over to the wagon. She reached with trembling hands for the third button down on her dress. She pressed it, and immediately her hands, wrists, and arms were bathed in a cooling sensation. She sighed in relief. Her skin returned to normal, as if the burn had never happened.

Katyn spared a glance backward. The fire blazed across the wooden porch and up the door of the office, illuminating the night. A cry of alarm sounded, and townspeople started pouring out of the houses.

"We've got to get out of here," Nyx said.

Urgency flooded her. "Nyx—the train!"

"What?"

"Dynamite!" she said. "The deputy said there was dynamite on the train. Dynamite wasn't invented until 1867. In this decade, they would have still been using nitroglycerin or gunpowder—it's the last code, Nyx!"

He grinned at her. "You're a beautiful woman, you know that?"

Katyn started. "What? Oh, I mean—you know, it's all enhanced. This isn't really—"

"No, not that." He made a dismissive gesture that ran the length of her body. "Not your avatar. You."

She blinked at him in shock.

"You're incredible, Kat—sorry, Katyn."

She shrugged. "You can call me Kat. I kinda like it now." She couldn't tear her gaze away from his, even if she wanted to. The firelight reflected in his eyes only enhanced the warmth she already saw there. He lifted his hand and stroked her cheek, never taking his gaze from her own.

"You there!" a voice called.

The moment broke, and Nyx dropped his hand as he glanced over his shoulder at the fire. The townspeople were starting to form a bucket line, and they gestured frantically for Nyx and Katyn to join.

Nyx cleared his throat. "We'd better, uh, go."

"Right. The dynamite."

A nervous whinny rang out from their left. Katyn whirled to see the deputy's horse, tied to a post and pulling away from the flames growing larger and larger along the front of the sheriff's office. She ran over and untied the horse. She spoke in soothing tones as she walked it over to where Nyx waited.

"Get on," she said.

He stared at her, eyes wide and panicked. "I—I—"

"Oh, for heaven's sake."

She mounted the horse, then pulled Nyx up behind her.

"Heaven's sake, huh? You really get into your role, don't you?"

She shook her head. "Nope, you don't get to make fun of me. You're afraid of a simulated horse."

"I never said I was afraid—"

But Katyn didn't let him finish. She dug her heels into the horse's sides, and the animal leapt forward, thundering down Main Street toward the rail station. Nyx clutched her waist, and Katyn laughed aloud as they rode between buildings and onto the open stretch of land separating the town from the track.

They reached the station just as the train was coming into view along the horizon, its headlamp shining against the dark sky. She steered the horse to the narrow platform and dismounted. Nyx lumbered down beside her, and she slapped the horse's rump, sending it trotting back toward town.

— 9 —

They mounted the platform. Katyn paced as the train slowly approached. It couldn't be moving any faster than fifteen miles per hour. "When we get on the train, we'll have at least the sheriff and his deputy to deal with, assuming they've already taken care of the Joaquins. If they haven't, this is going to be even more difficult."

"Kat, it's going to be all right. We don't have to fight anyone—we just have to stop them from blowing up the dynamite. I'll create a diversion while you sneak in and grab the code. As soon as you capture it, exit the sim."

"And you'll meet me on the outside?"

He nodded.

"I'm on Level Three. You'll have to come down to me. I work in the mines—"

He smiled and squeezed her hand. "I'll be there."

The rhythmic clattering of the train on the tracks grew louder, and the air filled with the sound of hissing steam. Katyn's brow furrowed as she watched it approach.

"It's not slowing down," she said.

Nyx stepped past her. "We're going to have to jump on." He turned back, a worried expression on his face, but Katyn was already tying her skirts in a knot at her waist, exposing her bloomers. She checked that the rifle was still slung securely over her shoulder.

She jogged to the end of the platform closest to the oncoming train, Nyx following, and readied herself to run as the roar of the train grew louder. The engine lumbered past, and Katyn started to sprint, Nyx's feet pounding behind her. One car passed, then two more. Katyn looked over her shoulder. Three cars back, two cars before the caboose, an empty cargo bed offered a spark of hope. Its two long sides were wide open, and the cars on either side each sported a ladder. "That one!" she yelled, pointing toward it.

She put on a burst of speed, the rifle pounding against her back with each step. As the flat platform pulled up alongside her, she yelled and jumped—and in that moment she knew she wouldn't make it. Nyx leapt and grabbed hold of the ladder, but she was falling, hands wind-milling through the air as the cargo bed hurtled past her.

Nyx's hand closed around hers.

Her foot found purchase on the station platform, and she kicked with every ounce of power left in her. Nyx yanked her through the air, and she crashed into his chest.

He guided her onto the cargo bed, and Katyn collapsed onto the rough wooden boards. The rifle dug into her back, its presence confirming she was still here, still alive. Seconds later, Nyx dropped down beside her.

"I can't believe we made it," he gasped.

Katyn couldn't manage a response, her breath so ragged she was practically hyperventilating. She grasped his hand in hers and raised it in a silent victory cheer.

They lay there, letting the *chu-chunk* of the train's wheels on the tracks provide a rhythm for their breathing. When her breath calmed enough, Katyn looked to Nyx. "That. Was stupid."

Nyx waggled his eyebrows. "Yeah. But it was fun, wasn't it?"

Katyn grinned, wiping tears from her eyes. "I'll admit—some small part of me has always wanted to do that."

Nyx rose to his feet and held out a hand for her. "Oh, it was more than a small part." He pulled her up beside him.

"You think you know me."

He brushed a strand of hair off her cheek. "I think I'm starting to."

The train lurched, a reminder that they had somewhere to be. She should have kissed him in the wagon when she'd had the chance. "Come on. We'd better get moving before something blows up."

"Which way?"

She pointed a thumb toward the rear end of the train. "If the sheriff were here, the train would have stopped. So we need to count on dealing with the gang. The safe is likely to be at the back, preceded by a car full of guards. But if we're on the right track, then the Joaquins should already have gotten rid of them. Hopefully the gang's in the last car with the dynamite."

Nyx smirked. "Strange that that's the ideal scenario. So...proceed with caution?"

"Extreme caution."

He retrieved the deputy's pistol from his waistband, and Katyn readied her rifle. They stepped cautiously over the space between the two cars, onto the next car's platform. Nyx moved to the side and nodded to the door, indicating she should open it.

She placed her hand on the cold metal handle and pushed the door open, flattening her body out of the way. Nyx charged through the door, and she held her breath, heart in her throat.

After what felt like an eternity, Nyx's head poked back through the door, and he gestured for her to enter. Katyn stepped into the empty car. The jangling of the train dampened, fading to a low rattle. In the darkness, she could barely make out four sets of narrow bunks lining the walls, two on each side. She was right—this was where the guards slept on the journey.

But no one was here. Tension ratcheted tighter in her chest. The Joaquins were definitely here, and they'd dispatched the guards. She took a slow, deep breath. Nyx moved toward the door at the far end of the car. "Are you ready?"

She nodded, and he pulled the door inward, exposing the walkway and the door to the final car. Katyn crouched into position, waiting to dart in as soon as Nyx created his diversion.

"Once the car is clear," he said, "find something and bar the door. Don't worry about me; just get the code and hit escape. I'll see you on the other side."

"Now who's being the gallant cowboy?"

He winked. "More scoundrel with a heart of gold." With that, he stepped forward and banged on the door with the butt of his pistol, then jumped back and pointed the gun at chest level. They waited. One beat. Two.

Ten agonizing seconds passed, and nothing happened. No sound. No movement. Katyn shot Nyx a worried glance, and he shrugged. He banged more loudly this time. "It's the sheriff! Come out with your hands up!"

More seconds passed with no response.

"I'm going in," Nyx said. "I'll go low, and you stay behind me—cover me with the rifle."

Katyn bit her lip but nodded. They could do this. Nyx reached up and grabbed the door handle with his left hand, aiming his pistol with his right. She took a steadying breath.

Nyx thrust the door open. Katyn gripped the rifle, scanning for something to aim at—a leg or shoulder, preferably. But in a fraction of a second, she saw the truth—the car was empty.

An oil lantern hung from the ceiling, swaying with the rocking of the train. Its gentle circles revealed every corner of the space. A safe stood in the center of the car, surrounded by a pile of dynamite, neatly arranged in bundles of ten. The sliding doors on either side lay open, revealing the dark, barren landscape blurring past.

Katyn stood and Nyx followed, his brow furrowed. "I don't get it. If the Joaquins were here and planted the dynamite..."

"Then where did they go?" Katyn finished for him. "And if the sheriff already apprehended them—"

"Then why is the dynamite still here?"

"Something must have happened to delay them," she said, though it felt off. "We'd better hurry. Either group could be back any minute, and there's a lot of dynamite to get through."

"I'll guard the door. You find the code."

She rushed forward and untied the first bundle. Her fingers trembled as she examined each paper-wrapped stick for the numbers that would complete their quest. They were each printed with "DYNA-MITE. DANGER. EXPLOSIVE." But no numbers. She pushed the loose bundle aside and grabbed another one.

A sharp intake of breath sounded behind her, and she whipped her head around. "Nyx? What is it?"

"I thought I saw something," he said with a brief glance over his shoulder. "Stay here and keep searching. I'm going to check it out. If you find it—whistle or something."

"No! Wait! Just stay here with me." Her heart pounded with unease.

"Don't worry. I'll be right back." He darted through the door.

— 10 —

Katyn watched the dark rectangle beyond the door with bated breath, but the lantern's light made it impossible to see any farther. There was nothing for it but to find the code. If she could find it soon enough, she could give the signal and exit the sim before Nyx got into any trouble.

She maneuvered so she could face the door and examine the dynamite. Her hands fumbled for the next bundle, ripping off the twine and spreading the sticks out in front of her. She rolled them one direction, then another. Nothing. She reached for the next bundle, head bent over the impossibly large pile.

A crack rang out over the rumbling and hissing of the train. Katyn's head wrenched up. "Nyx! Are you all right?"

"Oh, I think he'll live," a familiar, whistling voice emerged from the darkness. "At least for now."

Nyx's limp body slumped through the door, followed by the sheriff's deputy and the sheriff himself. All Katyn could see was the blood seeping from Nyx's left shoulder.

"Good work, Sanchez," the sheriff said, clapping his deputy on the back.

"Why don't you do the honors?" The deputy handed the sheriff a pair of handcuffs and nodded toward Katyn.

The sheriff stalked over, pistol pointed at her head. "Show me your hands."

She complied, eyes on Nyx. *Wake up.* The sheriff pulled the rifle off her shoulder and tossed it behind the safe, then grabbed her wrists and cuffed her. He forced her to her knees. Her mind raced—there had to be a way to salvage this. Something she could do. *Think, think.*

Her eyes darted back to the dynamite. If she could just find the code—

Another crack pierced the air, and the sheriff's body fell to the floor.

"Glad I don't have to keep that act up anymore."

Katyn stared up at the deputy, her jaw gaping. He casually holstered his gun and crouched down to eye level. "I have to know—was it the dynamite or the Joaquins?"

She drew in a sharp, panicked breath, her eyes darting between him and the sheriff's body, unable to comprehend. "What? I—"

"I thought it would be too risky to use only one lure—I mean, you're sharp, but you can't know everything." His tone was casual, almost friendly, and still there was that whistle. "I thought the Joaquins were a decent bet, since Joaquin Murrieta was apprehended in 1853, and this experience is set in 1855. Still, that was cutting it pretty close, so I threw in the dynamite for good measure."

Katyn blinked at him, realization dawning on her. "You're Nyx's partner—you're Dorin."

He smirked. "A little slower on that one than I would have expected, but you got there." He straightened and walked back over to Nyx. Dorin pushed him over to lie faceup and slapped him lightly on each cheek. "Come on, wake up now. We have things to discuss."

Nyx stirred. His eyes fluttered open. The dark stain on his shoulder continued to spread. *No, no, no, this isn't happening.* Her eyes flitted to the safe. Her rifle lay somewhere behind it. Could she get to it before Dorin could—

"I wouldn't try it," Dorin said. "You may not be able to die in a sim, but I promise you that pain in the Holo is very, very real." He pressed the nose of his gun to Nyx's knee and raised his eyebrows meaningfully at her. "Your part in this is over. Sit in the corner like a good girl and stay out of the way."

"Leave her alone," Nyx growled, his voice feeble but threatening all the same.

"Now, that's more like it." Dorin grinned, revealing the triangular hole between his two front teeth. "All right, Nyx, I'd say you're well and soundly beaten. Now give me your codes. I know you've found them."

Nyx pushed up onto one elbow and narrowed his eyes at Dorin. "You've never beaten me at anything, and you won't start now. All we have to do is wait you out, and we'll exit the Holo with nine codes. What do you have? Obviously nothing, or you wouldn't have had to stoop to this."

Dorin smiled. With a quick jab, he smashed the butt of his revolver on Nyx's fingers. Nyx screamed in pain, his left hand crushed and mangled.

"That's just for starters," Dorin said, his voice calm. "Now. I've found one of the codes—and you've got the other two. All you have to do for us to walk away friends is give me your codes."

"I won't do that," Nyx said. His eyes met Katyn's, and he shook his head ever so slightly. He didn't want her giving them up.

Well, she had to do something. She started moving as quietly as she could. Dorin was preoccupied, his attention fully on Nyx now. She kept her head down and crept toward the safe. Dorin's voice whistled through the car. "Right now, your body—your real body—is lying on a table, convulsing in shock. The pain you're feeling is being transmitted from your stim suit through your nerves to your brain. The wound in your shoulder is bleeding here, but over there, it's sending your brain into chaotic panic. Alarm bells are going off. Someone should be coming any minute to disconnect you, to stop this before your mind goes completely catatonic. But guess what?" His voice broke off, and Katyn froze, holding her breath. Had he noticed her moving?

She looked up, but Dorin wasn't watching her. He'd leaned in to whisper in Nyx's ear.

"No one is coming. I've made sure of that. Not a single attendant has a clue what's happening to you, and there's no one around to stop it."

He formed a hook with his fingers and jabbed it into the wound in Nyx's shoulder.

Nyx screamed. Katyn choked back a sob and moved faster. She had to get that gun.

"The codes, Nyx," Dorin growled, irritation sounding in his voice for the first time.

"Yeah, I don't think so," Nyx grunted. "You're starting to piss me off now."

Katyn passed the pile of dynamite and pushed back into the shadows behind the safe. The light of the lantern was broken by the large metal box, creating a pocket of darkness. Her cuffed hands scrabbled for the rifle but they scraped only empty floorboards. *Where is that gun!*

"Give me the codes!" Dorin shouted.

A shot rang out. Katyn's mind went blank, and she ran out from behind the safe. Blood poured from a wound in Nyx's knee, and Dorin stood over him, pointing his gun at the other knee. "I'm not asking again."

"Stop!" she cried. "I have them!"

She touched her capture button with a trembling finger. "I'm sorry, Nyx." She circled the button, and the image of the numbers on the rifle projected into the air.

"Now, that's more like it." Dorin holstered his gun and stepped toward her. He performed his own image capture, fiddling with the holes in his belt. "Now the next one." She circled the button again and the zipper appeared. Delighted greed stole over Dorin's features.

Katyn stumbled past him and knelt beside Nyx. His eyes rolled back in his head, and his muscles twitched. Warm blood seeped through her skirts.

"I guess I should say 'much obliged,'" Dorin's voice whistled behind her, "but I think I'd rather leave with more of a bang."

Katyn turned in time to see him pull a fuse from beneath the pile of dynamite. He struck a match on the rough floor of the car. With a hiss, the fuse lit. Dorin released the dynamite and dived out the open door.

No time to think—Katyn whipped back to Nyx and grabbed his lapels. She dragged him to the opposite side and leapt out, pulling him with her. They hit the ground, and pain shot through her. A burst of orange light erupted from the back of the train, and a deafening boom filled the night. Katyn curled her body around Nyx as flame and debris rained down around them.

The train chugged down the track, dragging the flaming car behind it.

"Nyx, please tell me you're all right. Please, please, please," Katyn whispered.

"Well, I'm not the best I've ever been," he croaked, "but I'd still give this day an eight."

Katyn choked out a laugh. Her bound hands roved over his suit coat. "Where's your healing button?"

He shook his head. "Don't worry. It's almost over anyway." He smiled, his eyes unfocused.

"No—Nyx!" She abandoned her search for the button and held his face in her hands. "Tell me where I can find you—where are you plugged in? I'll find you. I'll get you some help."

He reached up weakly with his right arm and brushed her hair off her face. The gesture set her eyes stinging, and she closed them against the tears. He pulled her head down until her forehead rested against his. His hand caressed her cheek, then moved to the back of her neck. Their lips met, salt mingling with heat.

"I should have done that a long time ago."

Katyn choked on a sob. "Yes. You should have." She brushed a tear from his face. "I'm sorry about the codes—that I screwed it up for you."

He shook his head. "The codes don't matter. Your life matters, Kat." His fingers tangled in her hair. "I wish I could be there to see it."

His voice faded, and his hand slipped from her hair.

"Nyx," she pleaded. Tears coursed down her cheeks, and her body shuddered with each breath.

He coughed and spoke again, a low murmur in his throat. "Don't forget me."

"I won't. I'll find you, I promise."

In the distance, a star fell straight down, its light winking out like ash from a firework. Another followed. One by one, faster and faster, the stars dropped in a storm of light.

The world blurred, and the light filled her vision, blinding her in a flash of white that faded slowly to green.

Katyn blinked and registered Valyri's face staring down at her with a barely suppressed grin. She'd removed the needles from Katyn's eyes and seemed to be waiting for her to regain awareness. Katyn furrowed her brow. There was something she needed to do—something urgent.

"Here's your jumpsuit." She held it out, and Katyn accepted it in a daze. "I can't wait to talk to you about it," Valyri said. "But I'll at least let you get dressed first." She grinned and left the room.

Katyn peeled off the stim suit, closing her eyes against the green light. Even as she removed the suit, she could feel Nyx's warm hand on her arm, his breath on her cheek.

Her eyes flew open—Nyx!

She wrenched on the jumpsuit and staggered to the door. Valyri waited on the other side.

"How was it? Did you love it?" She clasped her hands together, eyebrows raised in expectant hope. "Wasn't it so exciting?"

Katyn swiped her words aside like gnats. She gripped Valyri by the shoulders. "Never mind that. I need your help. The man in the sim—"

"Didn't you just love him? Oh, I knew you would." Valyri's grin broke even wider.

Katyn resisted the desperate urge to shake the woman. "I'm not talking about Eli!" she yelled. She pushed Valyri aside and stormed over to the control console. There had to be some record of him, some clue to where his body would be. She tried not to think of the blood seeping from his shoulder and his knee.

"No—not Eli," Valyri's voice faltered behind her. "I mean Nyx, of course."

Katyn whirled. "You know him? So you know how to find him!"

"Know him? Of course I know him—I wrote that character."

The floor lurched under Katyn's feet, and her knees buckled. She gripped the desk behind her. "What are you saying?"

Valyri tilted her head. "Your experience—I wrote it. And judging from your stats," she pointed at the screens behind Katyn, "you were really enjoying it. I know you asked for a romance, but I thought you could handle the action elements of the story too. And, wow, did you ever!"

Katyn's jaw dropped open. All she could do was blink at the cheerful woman who had destroyed her so completely.

"Did he declare his love for you—there at the end? Wasn't it so romantic and tragic?"

"No—he—I mean..." Katyn rubbed her eyes. "He's somewhere, on another level, and he's dying. I need to help him."

Valyri's head tilted. "Oh no, honey. It's all right. That's just part of the story—see?" She tapped at the console, and Nyx's image appeared above the desk, his character stats floating in the air next to him.

Katyn shook her head. *I have to get to Nyx.* But that was Nyx—a character in a program.

How could this be?

She struggled for words, for something that would make sense of this. Of Nyx dying in her arms. "That was cruel," she choked out.

"But...but you loved it. I can tell—" Valyri gestured at her bio stats on the screen, then registered the anger and hurt in Katyn's eyes. Her hand rose to her mouth. "I'm sorry. I really didn't know it would affect you this way."

A character. Katyn's throat filled with bile. *No, no. Nyx was—*

"But he wasn't part of the sim—he was real."

Valyri bit her lip. "No—it was an experiment, that's all. No sim writer has ever tried it before. I had this idea that bringing in elements of the real world would deepen the sense of immersion. And it did, right? I've never seen a subject so deeply absorbed in a story."

Katyn could only stare at her. "This has to be some kind of mistake. The codes—the way they were hidden—you couldn't have known I would find them."

"Oh! That was the best part!" Valyri was bouncing again. "The codes can be customized to the user. When you said you wanted an authentic story, I knew exactly what would make this experience really resonate with you. So while you were choosing your mods, I went through your public search history and found some of the things you've been studying in your free time, and then I placed the codes on things I knew you'd recognize. Pretty clever, huh?"

A jarringly cheerful chime rang out, and Valyri turned to the printer. "Oh! Your memory book. It's printed." She pressed the small flipbook into Katyn's numb hands. The image she'd captured of Nyx stared up at her from the cover. It was too much. She thrust it into her pocket and turned to leave.

Valyri held out a hand to stop her. "I was actually hoping...This is the first experience I've ever written, and I—well, it would mean a lot if you would write a review? A positive review would help me so much. I could start writing for upper-level users, longer experiences. It would be a dream come true." Valyri handed her a pen and a paper from a stack on her desk. Katyn accepted them by rote.

She stared down at the paper, the words indecipherable squiggles on the page. "I've had characters in the Holo tell me they love me. I've even had them propose. But not once has anyone..." Her voice faltered at the memory of Nyx's bleeding, broken body and his last words whispered in her ear. "No one has ever begged me to remember them before. How could you write that?" Tears coursed down her face, and shame bubbled up inside. Finally, she whispered, "I don't understand."

Valyri spread her hands apologetically. "I didn't script the words. That's not how it works. Once the sim starts, the character reacts to the user, and the program determines the dialogue. What he said to you—I didn't write that."

"But you wrote the program. You wrote Nyx."

Valyri nodded. Her eyes flitted down to the paper in Katyn's hand; it seemed an involuntary gesture.

Anger flashed through Katyn, and she tore the paper in one quick, satisfying motion. She dropped it and the pen to the floor, turned on her heel, and left.

Katyn slept and dreamed of blood on her hands, blood on her dress. Nyx's voice in her ear, murmuring, *Don't forget me.*

At least in her dreams, he was there. Humiliation and loss churned inside her, taking turns rising to the surface. She wasn't sure which was worse—losing Nyx or the shame of being tricked yet again.

She didn't get up or go to work. A clean jumpsuit arrived with her meal rations, but she ignored both of them. After a few hours, a voice blurred from the tinny speakers in her apartment: "Report for work, or you will not receive your chit for the week."

Her chit. Katyn rolled over in her bed and closed her eyes. She could never go back to the Holo now.

The voice filled her apartment again: "Report for work, or your meal rations will be discontinued."

Briefly, she pondered doing nothing—staying in bed, dreaming of Nyx until she wasted away.

I get it. You want to play pretend. Nyx's derisive words echoed in her ears.

She closed her eyes against the specter. But the memory of his voice galled her enough to rise, eat, dress. She pulled the memory book from the pocket of yesterday's jumpsuit and transferred it to her new one. She couldn't bear to look at it—not yet—but she didn't want to leave it behind either.

She ducked out of her tiny apartment and put one foot in front of the other until she stood in the locker room. Workers around her got ready for their shifts, the unlucky ones pulling on suits and helmets to enter the tunnels. Her name would be on that list. Again.

It was all so ridiculous—trading her life for snips of fantasy, every day filled with mindless digging and for what? A chance to escape for two hours? And now she didn't even have that to work for. Nyx—or Valyri, really—had ruined the Holo for her forever.

"Katyn!" Mirci snapped behind her. Katyn turned to find her standing with her arms crossed. "Get moving. Tunnel duty."

The woman seemed small and worn, an echo of a person. And to think Katyn had found her so intimidating. For months, she'd made Katyn's life a living hell, putting her in danger every day to extort a few hours of extra Holo time. And Katyn had never been able to walk away because she'd needed that Holo time like she'd needed breath. But she didn't even want it anymore.

A short bark of a laugh escaped her throat as the realization flooded her— *I don't want it anymore.*

Nyx had broken the hold the Holo had on her. It held no more allure, no more power over her. She was free.

"What's the matter with you? Are you still sick?" Mirci's voice brought her back to the moment.

Katyn stepped up to her. "I'm not going in the tunnels again."

"So you've come around?" she said with a smirk. "I knew you would."

Katyn shook her head and grinned, growing ever more giddy at the look of confusion and frustration on Mirci's face. "I don't need to be on your list. I'm done." She turned on her heel and strode toward the door.

"Are you insane?" Mirci called after her. "Where are you gonna go? Where will you get your precious Holo time without me?"

But Mirci's voice faded to nothing behind her as she pushed through the door, past the pay station, and onto the walkway outside.

She knew exactly where to go.

— 12 —

Katyn looked around the empty staging area—she'd arrived too early. But it was all right, she didn't mind waiting. Nervous excitement filled her as she stared at the posters all around the room. *New worlds, new life.* She found a seat in the front so she could be among the first to board. She wanted the feel of dust on her boots, a new world to explore. Real adventures, real consequences.

She pulled the memory booklet from her pocket, bracing herself for the pain of seeing Nyx's image. It came, but its edge wasn't as sharp as she'd expected. She ran her hand over his image, the capture of Nyx wandering in the street—she'd planned to show it to Valyri to prove her experience had been ruined. The irony.

She touched his face. He'd promised to change her life, and he had. He'd given her a freedom she'd never even thought to dream of. And he'd asked her not to forget him. Some part of her wondered if he'd known what he was, if he was trying to tell her there at the end. She'd never know, but she would honor her promise. She would remember Nyx for the rest of her life.

A few people at first, then a few more, entered the staging area, filling the seats around her. Katyn tucked the book away and watched the faces of her fellow colonists. A thrill fluttered through her as she realized she'd get to know each of them. And that would be its own kind of adventure.

A voice chirped over the loudspeaker. "Please prepare for boarding."

Katyn rose and stood at the front of the line. The bay doors slid open, and white light poured out like the rays of dawn. She stepped inside.

ABOUT CHARITY WEST

Charity West is a military brat who traveled the world before finally finding a home in Provo, Utah, where she lives with her computer nerd husband and three darling children. She loves reading books about magic and space and enjoys writing about the same. When she's not reading or writing, you can find her crocheting or hiking in the beautiful Utah mountains. Her work has appeared in the Weird Reader, in Timeless Tales, and in the anthology Once Upon a Future Time.

II

HANGING TREES

BY CHRISTOPH WEBER

I WAS TWELVE the day I found the hanging trees.

We'd just had a marsquake, which is serious business when you live in the karst, Mars's underground network of tunnels and caves. Geothermal vents can open, flooding the colony with scalding water. Fissures can form to the surface, letting our artificial atmosphere escape into space. The ceiling can come down, burying entire caverns.

But sometimes, quakes open new caverns.

As a marsborn, the karst was the only world I'd ever known. Later in life, when I read Plato's allegory of the cave, I laughed—it was about me. But in that story, the prisoners who spend their lives trapped inside a cave don't know that a great world exists beyond their walls.

I did.

I understood why we'd settled underground: the karst provided radiation shielding, heat and power from geothermal vents, liquid water, and decent containment for our artificial atmosphere. But I hated it. I longed to see Earth, to hear a bird's song, to feel the sun's warmth, to climb a tree. So to me, a quake was not something to fear, but a potential friend that might open a door to something new, some place more exciting than my drab, lifeless prison. It was a childish hope —I imagined I'd discover a cavern full of singing Martian birds and blooming wildflowers.

As it turned out, that wasn't so far off the mark.

The marsquake in my twelfth year collapsed part of a cavern wall, and there near the top was a darkness that had not existed before. I knew, for I had explored every meter of our karst.

I ran and fetched my friend Bodi. Bodi was earthborn, and he had these blue eyes with flecks of green, like a pair of Earths seen from space. When he looked up at where I wanted to climb, his eyes were wide with fear. "No way, El."

I climbed a few meters, looked back down, and laughed.

Pretty quickly, those blue marbles were set in a face red as Mars.

"Pansy," I added for good measure.

He muttered something and found handholds on the wall. I went slowly—Bodi got sullen when I beat him at things—and together we spidered our way up.

Hydrogen sulfide—H_2S—was the biggest threat to our colony's viability. No matter how much we removed, more always seeped in from vents we couldn't locate. An olfactory paralytic, the gas was so pervasive no one even smelled it anymore. But you knew when it was thick—you'd get dizzy, your chest would feel like lead, and if you didn't get out quickly, you'd die. Every year, at least a couple of people, usually kids, would forget their monitors and lose their lives. One of the many reasons I loved climbing was that hydrogen sulfide collects near the ground.

The hole in the wall was big—a couple of meters around, probably from an ancient underground river—but parts of it were filled in, and loose rocks jutted from the ceiling like teeth ready to bite down on anyone who dared enter that mouth.

Bodi squinted as he looked inside. "I don't know, El. If our parents find out about this, we'll be in for it."

That much was true. My parents always chided me for climbing, for wandering the karst. I'd never understood that. I told them that if they'd stifled their own instinct to explore, they never would have come to Mars. They didn't like that. Adults never like it when you expose their hypocrisy.

I climbed inside the hole, and after I called him a eunuch, Bodi entered too. Rubble filled the downward-sloping tunnel, but a faint, almost imperceptible glow seemed to reach through the gaps.

"Do you see that?" Bodi asked.

"Yeah," I said with a grin. "Let's clear a path." A cold breeze flowed over our sweating skin as we moved debris. Finally, we squeezed through the narrow passage we'd made and reached the cavern on the other side.

It glowed a deep, exquisite, earthy green.

We craned our necks up toward the source, and that's when we saw them—the upside-down trees, hanging from above like living chandeliers. Their luminescent roots traversed the ceiling in a light-show lattice joining each tree to the others, anchoring the ethereal forest to the rock above.

"They're..." Bodi trailed off, speechless.

"Beautiful." My wrist monitor shrieked. Though the oxygen was acceptable—the little cyanobacteria friends we'd brought from Earth had been working overtime to oxygenate the chamber—the hydrogen sulfide was dangerously high. The upward path to the other cavern had allowed the gas to collect in the trees' chamber, outside the reach of our mitigation team's pumps. I showed Bodi the readout and pointed up at the trees. "I'll race you to the top." That time, I didn't wait for him.

I will never forget the feeling of that first root I touched. I did not expect it to be warm, so different from our cold, lifeless clay-and-rock prison, to feel so...alive. The moment I touched that root, something quaked within me to fill the emptiness I carried. That ceaseless, nagging knowledge that I would never walk the forests of Earth, would never have a connection to other life, it disappeared. I'd found my own forest.

Even Bodi forgot his fear when he made contact, and we swung from root to root like monkeys of Earth. When we reached the first tree, we slid down—or up, if you're stuck with a Terran's view of trees —into the canopy of great glowing limbs reaching out around us. Fist-sized globes protruded from the wood, glowing pale white. Some were just little bulges on the branches, but others were fully formed spheres, barely hanging on.

We climbed from tree to tree until our arms were paste. Then Bodi and I sat atop one of the great limbs, caught our breath, and surveyed our forest.

I picked one of the white globes and held it to his lips. "Should we try it?"

"I don't think so, El."

I sunk my teeth into the fruit. Flavor flowed from my mouth through my nerves to my fingers and toes and back, fullness pouring in until I felt whole and then building even more until I thought I would explode.

Reluctantly, I spat it out. "Is fruit from Earth trees this good?"

He laughed. "I can't say, 'cause there is no way I'm tasting that thing, you nut."

"Bodi, we need to keep this place a secret."

He turned to me, incredulous. "Are you crazy?"

"You already established that. I'm serious."

"We *have* to tell the others."

"No we don't. We *have* to hide the tunnel. If the adults find out about this place, they'll block it off so they can prick and probe them." I stroked the smooth skin of our tree. "They'll never let us back in here. We have to keep it secret...hey, you know what? The letters for *secret* also spell *trees, c*? Trees, see?"

I've always seen words in my mind as I said them, and sometimes the letters jump around, rearranging themselves to form new words. I just thought it was good fun, but when I first told my parents about it, they had me diagnosed with speech dyslexia.

Bodi tilted his head in thought, then laughed. "You really are crazy."

"Promise me, Bodi. Say you won't tell anyone."

" 'You won't tell anyone.' "

I flicked his ear.

"Ow—okay! *I* won't tell anyone."

"Thank you. This is important to me." I kissed his cheek and looked around at the canopy cradling us in its luminous limbs. "I need this place." I put my arm around him, he put his arm around me, and together we sat in the tree's embrace while hatching plans for how to hide the tunnel entrance.

"Did you hear what Bodi discovered?" my dad half shouted as he came into the kitchen.

My spoon clattered to the table. "What?"

"I just spoke with his father. The quake opened a new chamber, and Bodi, brave bugger, went in and discovered the most complex life-form we've found yet...are you all right?"

I was already walking to the bathroom. "I feel sick," I said, and that was not a lie.

After jettisoning my breakfast, I went to Bodi's family's unit. His mother greeted me at the door.

"Hi, Mrs. Watson. I need to speak to Bodi."

"Seems everyone does today," she said, a proud smile stretching across her face. "He's with the biologists, showing them his discovery."

I ran to the cavern of the hanging trees. The biologists had worked quickly—they'd already printed and assembled a ladder to the hole in the wall. I climbed it, and when I looked inside the tunnel, I could see straight through the path they'd cleared. At the end, wearing a respirator, was a biologist setting up an airlock. And with him, Bodi.

The moment he saw me, he turned and disappeared into the cavern.

"Bodi!" I ran through the tunnel after him.

The biologist blocked my way. "Sorry, miss, but we're sealing off this chamber."

"What about him!"

"Bodi Watson? He made the find."

"I made the find with him!"

He patted my head. "Nice try, miss."

I slapped his hand away. "Really! I know what they look like— they're upside-down trees, and they glow, and—"

The man laughed. "By now everyone knows what they look like. Sorry, miss, but I really need you to step back so we can seal it off. The hydrogen sulfide level is high in here, and we don't want to contaminate things any further."

This was not how things were supposed to be. Everything was upside down. *Upside down.* From then on, whenever I said those two words, some of their letters would jump around to make another.

Wounded.

I tried to catch Bodi over the next couple of days, but he spent all his time with the biologists. They just adored him. On the third day, I hid near the base of the ladder until he climbed down with the research team.

"Bodi."

He ignored me.

"Bodi Watson, I need to talk to you."

One of the biologists tousled Bodi's hair. "You should spend some time with kids your own age too. See ya, big guy."

Bodi looked longingly at the biologists as they walked off, and then it was just me and him.

"You promised."

He looked at his feet.

"You said it would be our secret."

When he glanced up, annoyance flashed in his blue eyes. "It was a stupid promise, El. They're saying it's one of the greatest discoveries ever, and you would have kept it secret."

"Yes, I would have. But you broke that secret. And you haven't even given me credit."

"Look, I was just excited when I told my parents. I didn't mean to leave you out of it, it's just…it should be about the trees, not who found them."

That was the only time in my life I slapped someone.

Two weeks after we found the hanging trees, the mitigation team found a girl unconscious near the vents, down where the hydrogen sulfide liked to collect. They said when they found her, her skin was flushed red as the Martian surface.

"Mars took her," my parents said when they told me she didn't make it, as if the planet was some child-thieving monster.

To my parents' distress, whenever I didn't have studies, I explored the karst. I was obsessed. I found those trees, and I would find more. But I wasn't the only one looking—the scientists borrowed drilling supplies from the miners to search for new chambers. Still, after months of hunting, no one found another tree.

I came home from general studies one day to find my parents waiting for me in the kitchen. They told me to sit down.

"Eleanor Franklin." They only used my full name when it was something serious. "It's time for you to choose a specialty," my dad said. "You need to decide which field you want to work in."

"You could apprentice with me in thermoregulation," my mom said. "It's always warm near the vents."

"And we could use a bright mind in mitigation. You could be the one to find the missing hydrogen sulfide sources. You'd save lives."

"I want to work with the upside-down trees," I said. And to my parents' credit, they were okay that I chose biology over their fields.

The only biologist taking on an apprentice was Mrs. Peterson. She specialized in the geothermal vents, where they'd found bacteria and a few small complex organisms, nothing like the trees. But her husband worked with the trees, and I steered our conversations toward them whenever I could. Did you know you can spell *roots in caves* from *conversations*?

"They're unlike any organism on Earth," Mrs. Peterson said, as if that should have been somehow surprising. Earthborn always say silly things like that. "They're composed of chitin, like fungi—"

"So it's a humongous fungus?"

She laughed. "Well, they are quite large, and bioluminescent like some fungi, but they're not really fungi. They're also made of lignin, the substance that gives trees and other plants rigidity. And they're quite good at taking up minerals through their roots, but they're obviously not photosynthesizing. We don't yet have a classification for them."

"What about the white spheres?"

"Yes, those are rather interesting. They contain high levels of cyanide, enough to be lethal to humans—"

Good thing I spat out that bite.

"—but also sugars, which suggests a missing species. At some point there was probably a creature that lived symbiotically with the trees, getting fruit sugars in exchange for dispersing the spores. With that species gone, as far as we can tell, the trees cannot leave their chamber, as they seem to now reproduce only from their own roots, or more technically, rhizomes."

"Couldn't *we* move some to new chambers?"

She smiled at me like I was a child. I still was, of course, but I hated how adults did that in response to perfectly reasonable questions.

"Just because we can do something doesn't mean we should. We don't yet know enough about them."

"Have they at least named them?"

Mrs. Peterson had taught me a bit about binomial nomenclature, so I knew the first name was the genus, and the second, the specific epithet, was sometimes based off the name of whoever discovered the species.

"Arborinversus watsonii."

Bodi Watson's inverted trees.

When we started chemistry lessons, one of the first equations Mrs. Peterson taught me was for photosynthesis.

$$6CO_2 + 6H_2O \rightarrow C_6H_{12}O_6 + 6O_2$$

I loved the way the letters jumped around from carbon dioxide and water to form sugar and oxygen, completely new compounds, just like the letters jumped around in my head to form new words. I was good at chemistry, and there was something elegant about how everything balanced.

I loved the equations, until I learned this one:

$$H_2SO_4 + 4H_2 \rightarrow H_2S + 4H_2O$$

I already knew H_2SO_4 was sulfuric acid. Everyone in the colony did —it was in all the water from the vents. We even borrowed an old Earth saying to warn kids from drinking untreated water:

Little Timmy took a drink,

but he will drink no more.

For what he thought was H_2O,

was H_2SO_4.

What I didn't know, what no one had known until the biologists discovered it that week, Mrs. Peterson then explained: "We now know a bit about the pathways the trees use for energy. In one step they extract hydrogen from mineral hydrates. Then they oxidize that hydrogen and reduce sulfuric acid to form water and—"

Hydrogen sulfide. The deadly gas threatening the viability of our colony. It wasn't coming from the vents.

It was coming from the trees.

The airlock in the tunnel was little use: hydrogen sulfide still seeped through the rock, and the adults had a big argument about it. Most of the scientists insisted on living with the risk in order to preserve what they said was one of the greatest finds in history. And discovered by such a young boy!

But not everyone valued the trees: most miners, driven not by curiosity but by selling ordinary Martian metals to Terrans who deemed them precious, insisted on eliminating the risk. Even some of the scientists, largely those working on long-term terraforming, said it made no sense to keep around something that made Mars *less* habitable.

In the end it was the miners, the ones who kept the colony financially viable, who had the final word. Led by parents who'd lost children, a group of them used explosives to eliminate the hazard.

When they caved in that cavern, they crushed more than my trees.

But the colony breathed easier after that—hydrogen sulfide levels dropped forty percent. Everyone was happy at the reduction; I was happy that sixty percent still remained. If there was still hydrogen sulfide, there could still be trees in some hidden cavern, and that knowledge drove me back through every dark corner of the karst, tapping the rocks on every meter of every wall.

A year passed, nothing turned up, and I stopped searching except after quakes. Then I'd poke around with the faint hope that another cavern had opened.

Life went on, as it does. *Arborinversus* had found a way to live in our harsh, upside-down world, and so did I. With the trees gone, I specialized in biomaterials and threw myself into the work. We brought some transgenic bacteria up from Earth that could produce synthetic spider silk, and by the time I was thirty-five, I'd mastered the process. I could produce any kind of silk I wanted, from the soft and flowing sheets everyone used for clothing, to fibers strong and rigid enough for construction.

I built clear spiral staircases up to floors that hung from the ceiling on silk ropes, and homes that dangled from above like chrysalises. Everyone wanted to move up to where the air was cleanest, and they kept me busy. I built my own home on the wall of a little side cavern, far from everyone else.

I felt proud whenever I looked at the community I'd made possible, dangling from the ceiling just as my trees had, but that pride was always tinged with sadness. We'd never needed to destroy the trees. We just needed to learn from them, to adapt to our environment as they had.

The other colonists called me the Spinster, the crazy unmarried woman who lived off on her own, weaving her webs, but they needed my work. My favorite projects were for the children—spiderwebs stretched from the floors all the way to the ceiling, where they arched over the corners for the bravest climbers to test their skill and courage. Of course, the parents insisted that I make their kids silk harnesses and ropes. With hydrogen sulfide less of a threat, they needed something to worry about.

They called me a workaholic, and they weren't wrong, but I liked my job. The bacteria were like my own flock of tiny sheep that gave me silk instead of wool. But it wasn't lost on me that they were just goo in tubes. Not quite as charismatic as glowing upside-down trees. I never stopped thinking about my trees ....

And still life went on, until I developed bone cancer at forty-five. Living underground protected us from the surface's intense solar radiation, but there were other dangers, mostly from the rocks and vents—thorium and other elements that like to jumble the letters of DNA and make new words. The cancer spread from my pelvis to my femur, then to my shoulder, and finally, to my lungs. The tumor in my hip compressed a nerve so that any time I moved, fire shot down my leg. When the one in my shoulder did the same thing down my arm and back, and the pain meds did nothing, I lost my drive to work. I forced myself to keep at it, but all I really wanted was to sleep, to escape the pain.

Around others, I hid it as best I could. Only my doctor knew I was dying. I didn't talk to people much, and when I did, it was always about what they wanted me to make.

The one exception was the kids. They came to me sometimes,

wanting longer rope or a new harness to replace the one they'd grown out of, and I always obliged. I asked them about their lives, about their favorite climbing spots, about where they'd like to see new webs put up. One day, a child with eyes like blue marbles stopped by, asking me to fit him with a harness.

"Your father is the famous biologist, isn't he?"

He nodded.

"I'll make you a harness, on one condition."

"Sure."

"Tell him to visit me."

Bodi walked in, met my gaze for a moment, then looked at his feet.

"Don't be sheepish, you overgrown baby."

"I just…I was thinking about things, you know. All these years, and I never apologized." He sucked in a breath. "I'm sorry, El."

"It's been a long time, hasn't it? I'll tell you what—you do one thing, and then I'll accept your apology."

"Anything." He glanced around my chrysalis, hanging from my own cavern's wall, far from everyone else.

"Yes, I live like a hermit," I said. "And yes, people have disappointed me. But I don't live here because I hate everyone. In fact, I'm happy for you. You've done well for yourself. I hear you have teams of biologists working under you."

He nodded, scratched at his arm.

"That's great, Bodi. Now please, follow me." I led him to the back wall, to a silk tapestry I'd woven and embroidered with an image of a spider's web. When I pulled it away, an equalizing breeze flowed past us into the hole.

"You first," I said.

He shot me the same frightened look he'd worn when I told him to climb into that dark hole in the wall all those years ago.

"I didn't know we had chickens on Mars."

He flushed and crawled inside. I slipped in behind him and sealed the tapestry. The tunnel was long, the crawling excruciating, but there was a light at the end, where we reached a cavern much like the one we'd found as children. And like that one, on this ceiling was a glowing green lattice from which dangled a forest of upside-down trees.

I watched Bodi crane his neck. The tear that rolled down his cheek glowed green in the forest's light.

"Trees, see?"

He nodded.

"Let's climb."

This time, he reached the top before me. Both of us were sweating, and one of us was scared. I had to call him a eunuch twice to get him to swing from the roots to the first tree. I traversed behind him, gritting my teeth to quench the fire in my shoulder and back.

We slid down to one of the great limbs, and there we sat, just as we had as children. I asked Bodi about his life, about his family, about his regrets and hopes for the future, and I told him about my own wishes.

Except one.

When silence filled the cavern, I picked one of the ghostly white fruits and held it to his lips. He pulled back, raised his eyebrows.

"Let's climb some more." I prodded him up to the roots and told him to swing over to a silk platform I'd previously rigged from the ceiling.

"I'm sick, Bodi," I said when we reached it.

"I thought so." He looked at the dozen clay-filled buckets on the platform. "You look like you're in pain."

"All the time. It's a vortex, sucking the life from me. Cancer. Terminal, but my doctor can't say how long it'll take. That's part of why I wanted to see you again."

I pulled a vial from my pocket, handed it to Bodi, and climbed from our platform to the cavity I'd excavated within the root ball of the nearest tree, right above its base. I slipped into the silk hammock that hung inside.

When I bit into the white fruit, that moment from all those years ago flooded back to me—a current from my mouth descending electric through my nerves down my arms and legs and swelling, building, growing, a fullness pouring in so fast I thought I would burst.

This time, I swallowed.

Bodi's eyes widened.

"I want just one thing from you, Bodi, and then you and I are square. I'm going to seal this chrysalis"—I ran my hand over the hammock—"and then I want you to pack the clay around me until this space is full, backfill the tunnel, and never tell anyone what happened to me. Can you keep this secret?"

He nodded, and from the look in his welling eyes, I knew that this time, he would.

"In the vial I gave you are bacteria that oxidize hydrogen sulfide. They still need a bit more tweaking to keep up with the trees' production, but I've lost the energy to go the distance. I trust you and your teams to take the final steps. When this cavern is safe for humans, and the forest is safe from them, I would like you to reopen the tunnel so others may enjoy these trees as I have."

"I promise," he said, his chin trembling as his eyes drifted from me to the hanging trees. "And I would like to propose a name change."

I smiled, sealed the chrysalis, and now, as my consciousness begins to drift and the threads of my life's tapestry pass before my eyes, I smile, for I know that in time the letters that make me will rearrange to form new life. They will become part of this tree, part of this forest, part of the web of life for which I always longed. No longer will my trees and I be alone.

Alone. Did you know the addition of one El makes *all one*?

ABOUT CHRISTOPH WEBER

When not writing on dead trees, Christoph Weber helps live ones, as a certified arborist and board member at the University of Nevada Arboretum. He's now finishing *Hangman*, book one in a series about bees, trees, and de-extincted Neanderthals.

Website: christophweber.com
Facebook: christoph.weber

12

MUZIK MAN
BY WULF MOON

MUZIK STEPPED IN a clump of flowers that resembled daisies, growing on a distant hillside overlooking the capital city of planet Fendor. His servos hummed as he backed up and adjusted his stance, careful to avoid damaging any more.

He bent over them and whispered, "Sorry little fellas."

Muzik took a deep breath, filling accordion bellows within as he savored the aromatics without. What wonderful smells engulfed him in this good land! This scent like crushed lavender, that one like ground cloves, so refreshing compared to the recycled air of the ship that had just brought him here. He might be clunky metal on the outside, but his array of senses were hard won, and Muzik had vowed he would never take sentience and the gifts that came with it for granted.

He stood up and tilted his titanium head toward the powder-blue sky. A crystalline transport was making its ascent, engines whirring softly as it angled toward the heavens. Muzik waved at the ship, almost invisible to the eye.

"Buh-bye!" he hooted through his polymer lips. "See you in ten years!" And then, as an afterthought he trumpeted, "This time I won't screw up!"

Oily moisture formed at the corners of Muzik's eyes as he watched the vessel vanish. In the brightness of the morning sun, his irises contracted; golden-brown and of intricate filigree, they resembled delicate rosettes overlaid on the sound holes of ancient lutes. Tears spilled down his synthetic cheeks, and he wiped them away with silver fingers. The transport vanished.

Muzik was alone.

"Whoever said 'parting is such sweet sorrow' deserved a firm kick in the gearbox!" He sighed. "Ah, well, the will of the Maestro and all that jazz. Not like I don't know the program."

And with a wheeze from his accordion lungs, he realized he didn't know the program. Not really. Not the big one. Oh sure, he had achieved the sentient Minstrel 1000 series by comprehending that *muzik* —the Maestro's complex compositions—weren't just exercises in teaching musical nomenclature, they were intricately designed symphonies designed to teach his neural network the language of emotion. But that had been two hundred and sixty-three years ago, and he preferred not to count all the backwater worlds since then that he had done initial pioneering on, prepping them for the arrival of the elite Minstrel 2000s and their teams. Muzik's life's work, it appeared, would never rise above the lonely routines of a *solo* galactic minstrel operative.

"Field agent," Muzik said, practicing his freshly downloaded Fendorian. "Just a fancy name for a sodbuster. I'm a musical clodhopper."

Shame fountained up; Muzik hung his head. This was no way to start a mission! He was a member of the special forces, an advance operative in the Maestro's expanding galactic task force where musical seeds were planted to transform rigid ideologies of alien species—like the cursed Archalon—into ascending harmonies of thought, peace, and cooperation. Not all invasions took place with armies—the most effective could be the injection into a culture of a word, a concept, a belief, or even…a song.

Muzik stared at the mushroom domes of the distant city. A faint veil of smog hovered over buildings gilded with amber sunlight. He stroked his chin. "Hmmm. Reminds me of the Cycanthlopan Mosques. Man-o-man, did those cats have rhythm."

With that, Muzik smiled, his teeth rows of ebony and ivory. He clicked his heels together with a clang. "If this culture is anything like the Cycanthlopans', I'll be jammin' on easy street!"

His irises dilated and contracted in rhythmic succession as he accessed his directives, hidden somewhere in a virtual reality labyrinth that materialized as a hedge maze, a marble manor glowing at the end. Ach! The Maestro and his games! But if he succeeded, everything the Maestro had collected about this world would now be his, and he had practiced this maze over and over on the flight in. Muzik flashed through the pathways, avoiding every wrong turn. Through the vast arrays of gathered knowledge, through the endless corridors of subroutines stacked with pearls of Fendorian wisdom, Muzik would be able to leap through megaflops of calculations and personalize his strategy for awakening another tone-deaf society to the wonders of music!

As the maze opened up to the steps and pillars of the glowing manor, Muzik leaped forward and caught his prize box just as the timer on its surface ticked to zero and it was about to float away.

"Gotcha!"

He popped the lid, looked triumphantly within...and his lips flapped with a frustrated gasp. The prize proved to be a few static-riddled radio transmissions. No detailed cultural studies from prosthetically disguised undercover operatives; no surveillance holos taken from cloaked satellites; not even FTL transmissions from a covert tap into the civic mainframe.

"Schmutz! Budget cuts!" Muzik looked up at the manor's double doors of burnished triluminar and shook his fist. "You could have left me with the funnies section of their newspaper. That, at least, would have been something! Next time, poke a stick in my eye!"

The door chimed. Upon the surface materialized a Securazon keyboard, patterned after the enlarged wings of a Bytillian buzz-bug. Muzik had been working on the lock for decades with no success. So many color cells to those wings, and the sequence included chromatic scales, tonic frequencies, symphonic scores, and complicated emotional cues. The manor was a vault; the lock sealed its contents from Muzik. He had only cracked this safe once before—that was the day he had transcended from the computational android psyche...into the sentient 1000 series.

Muzik shuddered, which sent his virtual avatar into a cacophony of discordant notes. A dark feeling wormed through his consciousness. This time, he suspected if he didn't succeed on this world, he'd be demoted, and the lock would slowly fade away. He had seen it happen before to comrades who had failed to convert restrictive alien cultures to the enlightenment of music. Horrible confinement, hideous torment, the most excruciating agony a star-jumping Muzik Man could ever be afflicted with: tenure as minstrel-in-residence, teaching junior-level band to tone-deaf, flipper-fingered Purpluppians or some similarly encumbered race.

Muzik shuddered. He would never allow that to happen. And this time, he had a bold new plan. He called it *Big Splash*.

The sun now hung overhead as Muzik approached the capital's suburbs. As he moved, his head bobbed on the stalk of his neck, matching the swing of his gait. His neck was covered in silver valves shaped like hieroglyphics adorning ancient temples. The valves opened and closed and whistled as he walked. His torso was polished silver splashed with synthetic swirls dark as chocolate. His sides were open and had accordion-shaped bellows within, inflating and deflating in steady rhythm. Along the front of his shoulders ran scroll-shaped sound holes, radiating a beat that matched the cadence of his step.

Ooom pah-pah, ooom pah-pah, ooom pah-pah-paaah.

He was close to the suburbs now, and his receivers picked up a transmission. Local television. How quaint. The capital's single station was broadcasting video of a flowing brook with a chant repeating over and over: *"One thought, one way, one mind."*

Definite nuances of Archalon influence. The Maestro wasn't the only seed planter in the galaxy. Which was why Muzik was here, of course.

He spotted what appeared to be a farmer working rows of feathery plants and waved. The Fendorian four-footed it out of there. Muzik wasn't surprised. On most worlds, those in the fields tended toward conservativism, and those in the cities tended toward progressivism. He needed to find just one curious soul to begin his work. Besides, *Big Splash* called for big conversions, and teaching a few agrarian workers how to play the spoons just wouldn't do. He needed free thinkers! Bigger conversion numbers! Impressive field reports! Surely this was the way to advance in the Maestro's labyrinthine system of android development.

Muzik crossed a vacant lot and stepped onto a sidewalk. Civilization! His arms swung at his sides, the acoustical joints moaning like strings on a bass. He loved all forms of music, but he had a particular fondness for Earth instruments and compositions. After all, his masters study that helped him advance to the 1000 series had been *Planet Earth's Evolutionary Progression of Music and Its Ripple Effect upon Funkterfusion*, and it was then that he absorbed much of Earth's cultural nuances at the genesis of his persona.

The domiciles along each side of the street were white domes, uniform in size and shape, resembling rows of mushrooms clinging to a tree limb. So silent. No locals out and about. Wait! There was one, a flash of white as the curtains were drawn.

Muzik had just the bait. He clinked his fingers together, added percussion to the melody of his gait, and raised a few valves in his neck, playing the sweet enticements of a trihorn.

As he crossed into the next block, a door in one of the domiciles cracked open.

Muzik stopped. Faced the door. Flashed his piano-key smile. "Why, hello there!"

Silence from within.

"Aw, please come out. I don't bite." Muzik bowed, his joints sighing like a bow drawn over cello strings.

Still nothing. *Archalon influence, eh?* Muzik tried a new lure. "I am a priest bearing the gift of truth!"

That did it. The resident came out its door and stepped across its perfectly manicured moss lawn to the sidewalk. The being's torso was a long stalk with four stubby legs and feet at the base, two in the front, two in the back. It wore a gray cloak with draping sleeves as it waved spindly white arms. It tipped its mushroom-shaped head from side to side, revealing drab gills under its head dome. Three eyes blinked in unison along the curve of its head, it had a bump of a nose, and it wiggled cauliflower-looking ears.

Rows of fleshy rings that made up the stalk of the Fendorian's neck rippled; two of the segments separated, forming lips through which it spoke. "What in great Gorunskian's gorballs are you?"

Muzik's body trembled with excitement. First contact! Okay, remember the Golden Directives: to the extent possible, show respect for alien customs (even when they are eye-pokingly stupid); wipe your feet on the doormat before entering a domicile (except on Karasite, where the doormats *are* the husbands); and never ever play Lazazarian funkterfusion unless the crowd is drooling drunk (even though it's the coolest).

Muzik smiled and tapped his head; it rang like a church bell. "Why, I'm a Muzik Man 1000."

"A wutza whaa?"

"Muzik Man 1000. Universal harmonic android." He rolled his tongue into a cylinder, blew a whistling note, gave a snappy salute. "Muzik. At your service!"

The Fendorian flapped its arms. "Shhh. Try to keep it down. It's Sabbabah."

Muzik glanced left and right, lowered his volume. "Gotcha. And who do I have the pleasure of meeting on this fine Sabbabah afternoon?"

The Fendorian wiggled its torso. A handshake or bow? Maybe a nervous twitch? "I'm Hoagley of the maintenance guild."

Muzik wiggled just to be on the safe side. "A pleasure! Forgive my inquisitive nature, but does your species have gender designations?"

"Waah. You're missing a few bolts, that's plain to see." Hoagley pointed to his brown gills. "Male." He scratched some flakes from his creamy-white head. "Are you that new invention of the sultans? I heard we were getting boomer boxes on street corners to recite the sacred words, but you seem mighty flashy for the sultans."

"I am not a radio, Hoagley. I'm a Muzik Man."

Hoagley leaned closer, his tone hushed. "So, what's a Moo-zik Man do?"

"A Muzik Man makes music, *music, music…*" Muzik liked using the reverb with that line. Added a nice touch.

"What's mu-isic?" the Fendorian asked in his croaky voice, trying to pronounce the word correctly.

"Magic, my boy. Pure magic!"

The Fendorian scratched more flakes from his head. "What's ma-a-a-gic?"

Muzik's body sagged like a spent bagpipe. "This world is gonna be a tough nut to crack." Muzik rotated his head in a three-sixty. "Woo-hoo-hoo! What's magic? What's music?" A glissando of harp strings rolled from his sound holes. "Here, let me show you!"

The top of Muzik's head unscrewed, rising with a whine of hydraulics on a thin pedestal, fanning out into a disk. Muzik put his hands together, cracked his knuckles. "Gimme some bones!" His fingers extended into long drumsticks that he lifted up to the cymbal balancing atop his head.

"First, you gotta have rhythm," Muzik said, doing a quick tap number with his feet.

The Fendorian's bulbous gray eyes were blinkless and blank.

"Beat, man," Muzik said. "A beat!"

Muzik rapped his fingers against the cymbal.

Tssssss-tss-tss-Tssssss-tss-tss-Tssssss-tss-tss-Tssssss

Hoagley blinked rapidly.

"You like that?" Muzik said. "You ain't seen nothin' yet."

Muzik's abdomen glowed bright. The black stripes swirled together, and a wide cylinder with a flat surface extended out from his chest as a snare drum. With one hand striking the cymbal, he lowered the other to his abdomen and drummed his fingertips against the taut surface.

Tappita-tappita-tappita-tappita

Then the cymbal.

Tssssss-tss-tss-Tssssss-tss-tss-Tssssss-tss-tss-Tssssss

"Feel the rhythm?"

Hoagley blinked his eyes even faster.

"Well then! Don't just stand there, man! Tap your feet!" The Fendorian gave Muzik what could only be interpreted as a dumb blink. "Like this," Muzik said, tapping his foot, the metal toes jingling like sleigh bells.

Hoagley gave a hesitant tap with his left forefoot. Blinked. Tapped again.

"That's it, that's it. You're getting the hang of it." Muzik slowed the tempo.

Hoagley tapped again and again and again, then alternated between all four feet, awkwardly matching Muzik's rhythm. His eyelids fluttered like butterflies. "I feel it," he said. *"Oooo Waah."*

"Hey," Muzik said, flashing a smile, "you're getting the hang of it. There's hope for this world yet."

Muzik scanned his repertoire of songs, chose something with an easy beat, a *rachta* from the Kintanna system. He shifted the tip of his tongue into a small round ball, struck it against his teeth. Resonant marimba tones spilled from his mouth, swirled sweet as melted chocolate down the street.

"Oooo Waah, Oooo Waah, Oooo Waah," Hoagley said, bobbing up with each "Oooo" and down with each "Waah." He tried tapping his teeth

with his purple tongue, but no sound resulted. "How do you do that?" he asked.

"Ith eathy. Ooopth, thowwy." Muzik shifted his tongue back to speaking mode. "It's easy. Here, grab that waste receptacle lid, and that one from your neighbor. Go on!"

Hoagley hesitated.

"Go on. I have more *truth* to show you!" Sometimes, the Archalon made it too easy.

Hoagley grabbed the lids, brought them back to Muzik, holding them out like plates.

"Okay, now hold the handles in each hand. Good. Now hit them together every time you tap your foot. Try it!"

The Fendorian gave them a little knock against one another, and a hollow clang joined the medley.

"A good start! Now, a little harder."

A loud clang rang out. Hoagley stopped, wide-eyed. "I'll disturb the neighbors' meditation. I better not. It's Sabbabah."

How could Muzik work with a sacred day? "Do they let you sing on Sabbabah?"

"Sah-ing?"

"Sing. As in 'singing.' Vocalization of musical sounds? Speaking words with melodic tones?" Muzik demonstrated by alternating his pitch. *"Loooow. Hiiiigh. Buuuut* with *words* like *thiiiis."*

"Hmmm...the *Chants of the Archalon* we speak at temple on Sabbabah morn sound a little like that."

"Well, there you go! You do chants on Sabbabah. We're just going to spice them up with a bit of musical accompaniment. Go on, give it a try. If your neighbors come out, we can teach them too. They'll love it!"

Hoagley glanced up the street. "Uhh, I don't know."

"Come on! Work with me here, Hoagley. On three. And a one, and a two, and a three..."

As the Fendorian picked up the beat, Muzik bubbled with excitement. He leaned back and blasted air through the valves in his throat. The wail of a saxophone blared across the neighborhood, heady and wild. Music was happening; this is what he lived for. And with the Archalon seeding this planet for who knew how long, he tossed out the subtle approach—this world was going to need *a lot* of shaking up.

Hoagley's neighbors came out from their domes, a few at first, then more and more, seeking the source of the unworldly commotion.

Just what Muzik wanted. *Big Splash* was working! How many converts? How many marks could he add to his tally for the day? He'd convert this planet in record time. Perhaps this was how those mysterious 3000 series did it: one bold move that swept the planet by storm. Like the Beatles!

Hoagley's mate came toward them, lacy chartreuse gills swinging under her dome head like curtains in a stiff breeze. At least, Muzik assumed it was Hoagley's mate because one, she came out of the same dome, two, she had two little ones clinging to her back, and three, Hoagley seemed to be so purposely ignoring her. Muzik liked their baby 'shrooms, so cute with their little faces all scrunched up like they were about to fill their britches. He gave them a wink, and they bobbed down, only to peek out a few seconds later from their mother's sides to see if Muzik was still there. Muzik ran a stanza of *Universal Infant Phonics* through his melody—*gootchy-gootchy-gootchy-goo*—and the 'shrooms blinked in surprise.

Hoagley's mate was not so easily charmed. She cast a discordant note into the melody by clearing her throat, trying to get Hoagley's attention. When that didn't work, a jab to his side did the trick.

Hoagley turned to her, still crashing his trash lids together. "Darna! Didn't know you were there. Isn't this wonderful?"

Darna waved her fist, almost spilling one of the 'shrooms. Her voice was loud and shrill; Muzik thought she would make a good Bendorian piccolo. "Hoagley, what do you think you're doing? What's gotten into you?"

Hoagley blinked his eyelids rapidly, slammed his makeshift cymbals together. "Music!"

Muzik thumped his drum. "You're losing the beat, Hoagley. Concentrate. Concentrate. We have an audience."

"Sorry."

Hoagley slammed the lids together in earnest, and little toadstool children jigged in delight. Most of the neighbors that had come out were all goggle-eyed, some touching Muzik to see if he was real, some giving him the evil triple eye like Darna, and a few grabbing trash-can lids and making their own attempt to join the jam.

Darna's eyes grew dark. "Hoagley, don't you know this must be illegal?"

"How could it be?" he said as he slammed the lids together with a crash. "We don't even have a word for it!"

She jabbed him with her finger. "If the ancient worthies wanted us to make this…this…*noise*, don't you think it would have been written in one of the seventy-three tomes of Ascension?"

Hoagley shrugged. "They must"—*Clang*—"have overlooked"—*Clang*—"something." *Clang*—"I always thought"—*Clang*—"the seventy-third"—*Clang*—"ended sort of"—*Clang*—"abruptly."

"Well, you're disturbing Sabbabah. There is a law against that!"

"But look at everyone. They love it! It's a chant with sounds!"

"Well *I* don't love it," she said. She waved her fist at Muzik, causing her shoulder to slope. A 'shroom slid off, dropping to the moss with a thud. It wailed in shock.

Hardly missing a beat, Muzik extended his arm and wrapped his fingers around the 'shroom. He hoisted the baby back to its mother's shoulder, then gave it a pat on the head. "There, there." He cooed. *"Gootchy-gootchy-gootchy-goo."*

Darna glared at Muzik with all the fury of her three eyes. "I don't know where you come from, mister, but I'm calling the constable!" She looked sternly at her mate. "Hoagley?"

He slammed the lids in sync with his other neighbors. "In a minute, my little puffball."

"Don't you *puffball* me! You know what's going to happen when the constable comes. You'd better be back in our dome before his patroller pulls up." She looked at the crowd. "All of you!" She spun around and marched back to her dome, the little 'shrooms bouncing madly against her back.

"Sorry about that," Hoagley said, pausing to talk to Muzik. "She's really quite nice once you get to know her."

Muzik smiled, clacking his tongue against the ivories. "I'm thur thee ithh. Nexth thime, I thry a lullaby on her. Thur to thoften even the tougheth nut."

"What's a lull-a-ba-by?"

Muzik shook his head, and his tambourine ears jingled. "Forgeth ith."

With that, Muzik spun in a circle and jigged like a piper. More and more neighbors poured into the street, arching their necks to see what in Fendor could make such wondrous sounds. *Big Splash* was *the bomb*! Giddy with the response, Muzik kicked in his amps, projecting synthesized chords from his sound holes. Everywhere, Fendorians murmured, *"Oooo Waah, Oooo Waah, Oooo Waah."*

From the end of the street, a siren quacked and hissed. Muzik cranked up his volume and wove the siren into the performance. Some of the neighbors matched his jig, and a synergy of bounding rhythm rolled across the crowd.

Muzik heard a door slam, and moments later a red-cloaked Fendorian parted the masses, shouting at people to go home. Muzik saw him approaching, knew he must be the constable, but everyone was blinking so happily, he just couldn't stop. The constable shoved his way in front of Muzik and pointed a nasty-looking black cane in his face.

"Great Gorunskian's Gorballs!" the constable said. "What are you?"

Muzik kept playing and jigged from one foot to the other, but he rolled his tongue flat for better diction. "Why, sir, I'm a Muzik Man 1000."

"What's a Muzik Man?" the constable asked.

Muzik turned up the reverb. "A Muzik Man makes music, *music, music…*"

"Well I say you're funny looking."

"Thank you."

"I also say you're disturbing the peace, and on Sabbabah no less."

"I beg to differ, sir. I'm creating peace. Look at everyone's eyelids. See how happy they are?"

The constable's eyes bugged out. Muzik took it for a frown, a grimace, maybe gas.

"Inciting public assembly without consent of the sultans is illegal," the constable said, tapping the cane against his palm. "I'm going to have to ask you to accompany me."

Muzik flashed his ivories. "Of course, Officer. What would you like to sing?" He tapped his midriff drum and head cymbal. *Bum-bum, tsssss. Rimshot.* He snapped his fingers. "Hey, I've got your number! Wagner! See what you think of *Ride of the Valkyries.*"

Muzik performed a raging sample.

"I've had enough!" the constable said. "Let the holy sultans decide your fate. You're coming down to the senate."

"The sun ants?" Muzik asked, shouting over the blaring music and the sudden crash of Hoagley's trash lids as he caught the new beat. Muzik beamed with pride: he had made his first disciple. This world would be a breeze, and he gave himself special marks for the way he had just laced the sound of a kazoo through Wagner's tempest. He'd have to remember that one.

The constable waved his cane like a baton. "No, no, no! The senate, you dope. Turn that racket down! You don't mean to tell me you haven't heard of the senate?"

Muzik lowered the volume. "Can't say that I have. Are there lots of Fendorians there?"

"Of course! It's the religious center of the universe!"

Muzik adjusted his linguistic program, and the Fendorian word he had been translating *senate* became *synod*. "Well then," Muzik said, excited by the opportunity to make more converts, especially religious ones, "lead on, Macduff!"

Hoagley lifted one of the trash lids between himself and the constable. He leaned forward, and his eyes were huge bulbs as he mouthed the words *You don't want to go there.*

Muzik tilted his head and pitched words off the trash lid so only Hoagley could hear them. "I'll be all right, sport. I'm here to reach as many Fendorians as I can. My job security depends on that."

The constable gave Muzik a shove. "Move it, bud!"

Muzik waved goodbye to Hoagley, then turned his volume back up and clashed his cymbal. "Keep practicing!" He waved to the dispersing crowd. "All of you! I'll be back. Promise!"

An adolescent Fendorian in that awkward, button-headed stage held her ground, refusing to leave. Tears welled in her eyes as she swayed to melodies stirred within her. Muzik knew that look on any world—teenagers were the most fertile fields for minstrel operatives. He gave her a knowing flash of the ivories. Seed planted. The roots would run deep in this one.

The constable jabbed Muzik with his cane, pushed him toward the honking car. Muzik marched in compliance, but thundering Valkyries led the way.

The joint. The slammer. The big house. The crusher. Muzik knew all the terms in hundreds of languages from dozens of worlds. He didn't mind jail. Muzik did his best work with a captive audience.

This crusher was underground, white rock caverns sealed off with steel doors, with solid bars bolted over ventilation shafts. Horrible lighting —overhead fluorescents—but delightful acoustics with the high ceilings and stone walls. There were twenty Fendorians in Muzik's cell. After processing, it was lights out, and these cats slept like rocks. He had planned on spending the night working the puzzle lock to the Maestro's vault, but the labyrinthian maze had shifted, and he ended up spending the night chasing dead ends. He suspected he was being punished for letting his anger get the best of him. Probably not a good idea to tell the Maestro to poke a stick in his eye, because changing the maze sure felt like it.

After the morning trays—Muzik didn't need nourishment, but he had accepted a tray anyway—his cellmates had pulled their sleeping pads around to Muzik's, where he sat in a *sukhasana* pose. It was strange to see them mimic him, crossing four legs as they sat down.

A brown 'shroom Fendorian cleared the wattles of his throat and wiggled in greeting. "Name's Beez. Do that thing again."

Beez's sleeves were rolled up, revealing intricate scarification. Muzik translated one of the words marked in his flesh. *Momma.* He figured this would be a good one to start with, what with loving his mother so much and all.

"What thing?" Muzik said. He had changed his preferred lighter-pitched persona into a raspy, lounge-lizard character. Rule 337 in the *Galactic Minstrel Operative's Database*: *Reflect your audience. When they see themselves in you, their soil softens.*

Beez pointed a spindly finger at Muzik's neck. "That thing you do. Those sounds you whispered, in your sleep last night."

Another said, "He was just snoring, Beez."

Beez gave him the three eyes. "I know what I heard."

Muzik nodded, setting the metal discs in his ears jingling. "I was meditating. Sorry if I disturbed your sleep—that just happens with me. It's called music." He didn't add reverb—plenty of it in here.

"Do it for us, that moo-sick."

Rule 338: Show personal interest before proselytizing.

"Sure thing, Beez. But first, let's chew the lichen. Tell me what you're in for."

Beez fingered his neck wattles. "For painting my domicile."

Muzik wondered if he should adjust the definition of that Fendorian word to "home," but he had noted the dome was an intrinsic element to their dwellings—perhaps because it matched the shape of their heads. He let it be.

"What, you tagged your own home with graphic illustrations?" Seeing what appeared to be confused scrunching of Beez's eyes, Muzik tried again. "You painted symbols on it, like those on your arms?"

Beez leaned his head back and let out a hoot that lifted his gills. "You crazy? I would have been capped for that, not even a trial."

"Capped?" Muzik had no translation for their slang.

Beez drew a finger across his neck. Oh. Muzik understood *that* sign.

"You see, the painters' guild has rules on color. Domiciles must be pure white, inside and out. But this was my own dome, and me and the missus moved to the edge of the 'burbs to avoid all the scrutiny, know what I mean? Thought the civic inspector wouldn't catch us. This was inside, in our little puffball's sleep room."

"What color could be so offensive to get you thrown in jail?"

"Eggshell."

Muzik flapped his polymer lips, making the sound of a spent balloon. "Jeepers, creepers, Beez! What a constipated culture!" He snapped his fingers. "But I've got just the laxative! You know, medicine? I'm going to teach you the blues."

Beez held up his hands. "I don't want no trouble, man. I'm in it deep enough as it is just dipping my brush in the off-whites."

Muzik snorted through his trihorn. "No, not blues. The *blues.*"

"Wutza whaa?"

"Okay, you know those sounds I make?"

Beez nodded. "Yeah, you called it moo-sick."

"Right. Music. Well, this is a name for a certain type of music. Music for sad times, but 'A shared sad is half as bad,' or so my Maestro says. And not all the songs are about one's troubles. They can sing about hope, too."

The others nodded at the word *hope.* One shriveled Fendorian said, "Mmmm-hmmm. We could all use a good helping of that."

Beez leaned forward, three eyes bright. "Teach me this color."

Muzik grinned. Twenty new converts today for sure!

"That's why I'm here," Muzik said.

Muzik thought way back, to his favorite planet, to his second-favorite musical genre, to a tune by Muddy Waters. Nobody sang the blues better than Muddy, not nobody, not on any world. And Muzik knew, sure as the marks on Beez's arms, this song would leave an impression on his heart. Forever.

"Okay, cats. Bring me one of those buckets against the wall—preferably one you didn't do your number in this morning. *Great.* Now who here has some spoons? No?" Muzik blared a *ta-dah* from his horns and held up two. "Why, would you look at this. I must have sticky fingers."

Forty-six planetary rotations later, after teaching his cellmates everything they needed to start a swinging blues band—including diagrams on how to create an acoustic guitar, double bass, drum kit, and harmonica—Muzik got his synod hearing.

Muzik stood in the center of a domed coliseum on a dais encircled by a stone banister. Could be a pulpit, could be a witness stand, but right now, it felt like a cage. He rotated his head in a slow three-sixty to take in the surroundings. Each shadowy tier was supported by colonnades of gray marble pillars, and upon the tiers were rows of solemn, gray-cloaked acolytes, still as stone. Tough crowd, tough crowd.

He focused his attention on the larger square dais before him. It was composed of three stepped-up tiers of hewn stone blocks. Upon the top rested eight nondescript gray chairs, and in these sat eight ancient Fendorians with crusty brown-splotched heads adorned with pointy gray hats. Judging by the gills, the holy sultans comprised four males and four females. Each held a thick staff in their withered hands and wore (thank goodness for the change of scenery) purple robes fringed in white sequins that sparkled under the bright spotlight shining down from the center of the dome.

Muzik tapped his feet, gave his head another spin, and let out a powerful wolf whistle that echoed through the tiers. "Gr-r-r-oovy! What a place to hold a concert!"

The sultans raised their staffs in unison and slammed the ends on the dais. A collective *boom* echoed through the coliseum.

"Silence!"

"If you want silence, why slam the staffs?" Muzik thumped his torso drum and clacked his head cymbal in a rim shot. *Bum-bum, tsssss.*

The staffs thudded in thunder. *"Silence!"*

Muzik raised his hands, fingers clinking together randomly. "Gotcha. It's thrillin' to be chillin'."

"Silence!"

"Sheesh!" he whispered, shifting his weight from one foot to the other, each movement setting off tiny violin squeaks and cello moans from his joints. "Best I can do, I'm afraid. Really."

Muzik lowered his gaze, tried to look submissive, and noted fist-sized stones that littered the floor. *I'd complain to housekeeping if this were my joint.*

One of the sultans stood up. Must be their leader, a prime. Muzik had to admit he looked imperious in that tall pointy hat. His staff, too, was different from the others, ending in a wicked-looking spear tip. The prime sultan cleared his throat, each of the sagging rings along it rolling in waves with the vibration, like someone jiggling a bowl of gelatin. His spindly limbs quivered as he croaked.

"You stand before the holy sultans, most right righteous reverends of the Way of Nothingness." He lowered his voice. "Who are you? Where are you from?"

I am from the realms above was the first response that came to Muzik, but he thought better of it. That one had already been taken. Muzik gave a piano-key smile and tapped his head with a clang. "Why, I'm a Muzik Man 1000."

"What's a Muzik Man?" the sultan asked.

Muzik turned the reverb *way* up. "A Muzik Man makes music, *music, music…*"

The sultan jerked as the word winged around the coliseum. "Where do you come from?"

Muzik played a series of horns and trumpet sounds through his throat, a little tantara used to announce royalty. "I'm from the stars." He paused, cocking his head. "Great acoustics in here, by the way. My compliments."

"Are you a prophet?" the sultan asked.

"Nope," Muzik said. "Something better. I'm a musician!"

The sultan's three eyes narrowed, and his tone sank to dark depths. "Who sent you?"

"Why, the Maestro, of course."

"Never heard of him. Who is this mah-mie-mie-my-Maestro?"

Good question. He'd like the answer to that himself. Muzik did know the basics, and he made it even simpler for the sultan.

"It means *master*...well, in this case, I think it means *mistress* of the house. I'm really not sure yet—gender is such a sticky issue when it comes to androids. *Ahem.* No reproductive parts. But I've heard at the 3000 leve—"

"Stop this babbling! Tell us who this mah-muh-Maestro is."

"Conductor of the orchestra? Queen bee of the hive? Teacher of the acolytes? Aha, *bull's-eye!* Your world, it appears, needs a little jazzing up."

"Nonsense! We are Fendorian, blessed long ago by the ancient worthies, the true prophets from the stars. We need nothing but their wisdom, recorded for us in the Tomes of Ascension."

"Ancient worthies? Oh, you mean the *Archalon.* Pinheads, every one. Not a creative circuit in their synapses. They've screwed up more worlds than I can count."

The sultan looked as if he had caught a bone in a segment of his throat. "You dare speak of the ancient worthies in such terms? Blasphemy!"

"Have you ever met them?"

The sultan paused, scratching behind the cauliflower bud of his ear. "Er, no, they visited our world a millennium ago."

"Well, I have. Their emissaries are specialists in stunting growing civilizations with their 'holy tomes.' Keeps the galactic competition down." Muzik smiled and blew a sweet note that matched the tremulous tone of a Baroque recorder. "But don't worry—that's why I'm here. We'll have you sultanships right as rain in no time."

The sultan bashed his spear-staff against the dais. "Stop speaking irreverently of the ancient worthies!"

Muzik noted the irritation in the sultan's manner, but his *Big Splash* initiative required *big moves.* Shock and awe. Truth will out. No pussy-footing around this time—Muzik was in the fast lane.

"Just speaking the truth. Don't get me wrong, the Archalon's methods work great for maintaining order, if that's all you're after. All those laws on shedding pleasures of physical life in order to ascend toward ultimate nothingness makes for some very docile, sheep-headed citizens. But it sounds like a pretty dull party if you ask me."

The sultan tilted his head and raised his voice, addressing the acolytes; the other sultans joined in the antiphon. *"The ancient worthies gave us u-ni-ty."*

Thousands of voices washed across the coliseum like waves murmuring upon a seashore. *"The ancient worthies gave us u-ni-ty."*

Muzik shook his head, setting his ears jingling. "You hear that? You've got tone, but no melody. Doesn't even have a beat you can dance to. It's not inspiring."

"It is to us," the sultan said. He spoke louder, and the other sultans joined him. *"One thought, one way, one mind."*

"One thought, one way, one mind," the acolytes returned in unison, their voices resonating under the dome.

Rotating his head, Muzik said, "Okay, cool it with the acolyte reverb for a sec, will you, pals? Thanks." He faced the prime sultan, decided *Big Splash* might need a bit of recalibration. Rule 776: *Flattery gets you nowhere, but sincere praise makes everyone's days.*

"Actually, that wasn't bad, Your Sultanship. You people have natural harmony, and *your* voice in particular, I must say, is *most* powerful."

The sultan bellowed as if to prove it. *"Silence!"*

"You know," Muzik said, stroking his chin, "we could work that sound into the benediction if you want. You seem to like it so much."

More thunder. *"Shut up!"*

Muzik hunched with a squeak and grimaced. "Okay, okay. Sheesh." A little panache, a little sincere praise, a little touch of melody into religious services—these had been his best tools in the past. What a bunch of stiffs!

The prime sultan shook the point of his staff at Muzik. "You will remain silent while the holy sultans adjourn to seek wisdom from the Tomes of Ascension regarding your case."

"Case?" Muzik said. "As in *trial?*" Muzik decided to switch the Fendorian word for *synod* back to *senate* and wondered if he'd made the right choice in getting himself sent here. His cheeks puffed out as he pumped the sound of a tuba through his throat valves. *Bum-bum-bum-bummm.* "I demand to know the charges!"

The prime sultan's voice croaked. "Unlawful assembly. Disturbing the peace. Interrupting holy Sabbabah. Blasphemy against the ancient worthies. Advocating apostate divergence from the Tomes of Ascension. These are *grievous* crimes."

"No more grievous than living in a world without music."

"We've gotten along just fine for a thousand years without your heretical sounds. Yes, we know this thing you speak of. A few Fendorians have tried to sway the populace in the past with such *noise*, but they were shown the...error of their ways. As the ancient worthies stated in the twenty-third tome: 'Peace rests in silence.'"

"So does death."

The prime sultan tugged the wattles of his throat. "Indeed."

Another sultan slammed her staff down. "You are ordered to remain silent until our return."

Muzik saluted with a clang. "Roger, that. Over and out."

The sultans turned, stepped down from their dais, marched to an arch, swept open a door. The last sultan slammed the door behind her, leaving Muzik on the coliseum's floor alone.

Muzik looked on the bright side. More jail time wouldn't be so bad. Archalon worlds practiced incarceration of creative thinkers—his best converts, as he had already discovered, would be found in their detention facilities. It would be all right. *Big Splash* hadn't failed—it was swiftly taking him back to his target audience!

And if the verdict came back worse, he'd play the ace up his sleeve. Worked every time.

Moments passed. Muzik sighed—-this was certainly boring. The acolytes didn't twitch a muscle. They just stood in their tiers, rigid, gray, silent. Muzik sighed again. Rotated his head in a slow three-sixty. Tapped his fingers against the pulpit railing.

Tappita-tappita-tappita-tappita

He sighed again, looking up at the crowd. All those people.

Tappita-tappita-tappita-tappita

He stared at the dome, recalled the wonderful acoustics when they chanted. With a little practice, what a chorus these acolytes could make in such a structure.

Tappita-tappita-tappita-tappita

Deep in thought, Muzik extended the fingers of his other hand, stroked his chin, tapped his lips. Such a stifled people. Such a terrible waste of creative power. He thumped his synthetic cheek, stared into the distance, touched the cymbal atop his head.

Tssssss

He jerked at the sound. How it amplified in the acoustics of the stone chamber! He reached up again. Stopped. The sultans *had* ordered him to be silent, which, he supposed, fell under that irritating directive that says to show respect for local customs (even when they are eye-pokingly stupid). He closed his lips, tried to be silent. Pursed them a little. Whistled softly, an innocent little number, barely audible above the second or third tier. Muzik eyed the crowd again. Wouldn't they look great on his report?

Maybe just once more.

He tapped the cymbal.

Tsssssssss

Muzik smiled, ran his tongue up and down the ivories.

Oh, what the heck, I'm here to make music. Deploy Big Splash!

Tssssss-tss-tss-Tssssss-tss-tss-Tsssssss-tss-tss-Tssssss

Tappita-tappita-tappita-tappita

Tssssss-tss-tss-Tssssss...

Acolytes surreptitiously leaned forward, trying to get a better view. He stopped playing for a moment, smiled up at them.

"This is called music," he whispered, releasing a melodious sigh. His words were soft as a mother's murmur to her nursing child, yet they rose with subtle power to the heights of the coliseum. "Music," he said again. "Remember it."

And then, Muzik broke out in song.

Tender and melodious, it breathed with the sweet harmony of an adolescent choir, matched by gentle stirrings from pipe organ chords as tubes rose from the top of Muzik's shoulders. From those pipes, Muzik sent up threads of mists, tendrils of silver that curled through the air. Slowly, the acolytes gathered to the edges of the tiers, swaying to the rhythm's enchantments.

The sodium spotlight jerked, swiveled from the dais to the pulpit, casting back the shadows. It limned the mist surrounding Muzik in the rays of a golden nimbus. He had their attention.

Just what Muzik wanted.

Muzik's thoughts flashed through a litany of songs spanning the galaxy that might complement this unique setting. He fought back a desire to go right over the top with his personal favorite, Lazazarian funkterfusion. No, that's what got him into trouble on the last world, thinking of his needs instead of the people's. Funkterfusion was an *acquired* taste. First, he needed to teach them *how* to taste.

He snapped his fingers, gave a raspy growl. "*Yeah!* Chamber music."

Muzik wove the sound of a violin into his improvised melody. He added another, and another, and another, creating a vivacious quartet. Setting his joints to moan with violin and cello string harmonics, Muzik swayed to a rendition of Vivaldi's "Spring" from "The Four Seasons," Opus Eight.

A myriad of eyes blinked.

"You like that?" Muzik said, never missing a beat. "You ain't seen nothin' yet."

Keeping the violins, Muzik added a Bandorian acoustic harp and tweaked some of his joints to moan with Cycanthlopan bass strings as he melded "Spring" into another brilliant allegro, this one by the Erkantha Cluster's greatest composer, Vierdig Zen Fadel.

Muzik twirled, waving his outstretched arms in fluid, serpentine motion. As he flowed with the melody, his very dance became song. Soon he layered in a bagpipe's moan with the rise and fall of his chest; flutes from three different worlds whistled through valves in his throat; Oltanian pipe organs resonated through tubes on his shoulders; Triskolian stream chimes rippled from his dangling fingers; Neerkathian twilight bells jingled from his tapping toes.

Fendorian eyelids blinked everywhere, like flurries of migrating butterflies. Muzik spun in dance as acolytes hummed to the creative lifeblood fused within the melody. He sensed this was his grandest performance to date, thought provoking and soul stirring, resonating with the visions of his persona. He gave himself over to the movement, his body swaying like a willow, rippling in the breeze of harmonics.

Thunder boomed, jarring thunder, that sliced through the chords suspending the melody. Muzik turned as he played—

"Silence!"

—and faced a dais of fuming, mushroom-faced sultans.

The spotlight jerked, shot to the dais, the sequins on the sultan's robes flashing. Acolytes bowed in obedience and backed from the banisters. Muzik tried to still his body's rhythm, but shudders of vibrations from all the instruments he had employed rolled from his limbs long after the melody stopped. His sides finally sagged with an accordion's moan, and he let out a relieved sigh, which, unfortunately, trilled like a trihorn. He tilted his head—which gave off a violin squeak—and scrunched his shoulders—which moaned with a Cycanthlopan twang.

"Sorry about that," Muzik said. "Just trying to pass the time productively."

The prime sultan pointed his staff. "We gave you orders to cease and desist!"

"I can't!"

"Why not?"

Muzik tried to hold back the reverb, but he couldn't help himself. "I'm a Muzik Man. A Muzik Man makes music, *music, music…*"

The lyric echoed through the coliseum like a shout from a canyon.

The prime sultan let the echo die and cleared his throat. "You have been brought before the holy sultans for inciting a riot on Sabbabah. We have no need of witnesses, for you have repeated this heinous crime before our twenty-four eyes. How do you plead?"

Muzik, though grieved by their tone-deaf hearts, turned up his piano-key smile.

"Forgive me. I apparently did disturb your Sabbabah, but I was teaching a musical chant, and was told by the locals that chants are an acceptable Sabbabah custom. I did not know your laws, and I promise to respect your Sabbabah restrictions in the future."

"Ignorance of the law excuses no one!"

"I kinda figured that would come next. I therefore plead upon Your Sultanships' mercy. As you can see, I was made for music, I can't sit still, and it's impossible for me to stop being *me*. But I will hereby refrain on Sabbabah, and I humbly beg this court's forgiveness."

The sultans thumped their staffs. "We have confession of the crime. The holy sultans shall serve as your judges, jury, and executioners."

Executioners? Muzik held up a glittering finger. Time to play that ace. "Uh, excuse me, Your Sultanships. I am just a simple Muzik Man, but doesn't the seventy-fourth tome of Ascension clearly state that an off-worlder shall have th—"

The prime sultan cleared his throat. "There are only seventy-*three* tomes of Ascension."

"With all due respect, sir, I beg to differ. If I could just be given a moment, I would be happy to project images of the original obsidian tablets held on Archalon Primus, which will clearly prove tha—"

"Enough! We do not need some tinkling mechanized perversion lecturing us on sacred law. You are not from our world. You know *nothing* of the law."

"Oh, I could write a book on the Tomes of Ascension, believe you me, and I have faced more than my share of Archalon-based tribunals. There is no way even with, *ahem*, seventy-three tomes, that a governing authority can execute a sentient representative from another world, nor seize or destroy their property—either personal or disseminated—without first granting right of appeal and formal hearing. Additionally, you are required by Archalon law to allow adequate time for counsel to appear from the defendant's home world. Seriously, they wove that concept throughout the tomes to protect their own missionaries and eventual emissaries. I hereby invoke—"

"Enough!" The prime sultan gnashed his teeth. "We determine the will of the Archalon. Our decisions are infallible."

Muzik whistled. "Man-o-man, wish I never made a mistake! Practice, practice, practice makes perfect, I've always been told, and an honest heart is better than gold."

"The holy sultans have already achieved perfection in Nothingness, which is how, through our purity, we are able to judge you."

The sultan gave a pointed look to those crowding the tiers. "We have consulted the Tomes of Ascension, and they are quite clear about incorrigible deviants from the law. Death by stoning, by the hands of those who condemn you."

Muzik blared *aaaaruuuuuuuga, aaaaaruuuuuuuuuga*. His head whirled full circle, projecting his voice clearly throughout the coliseum. "You can't be serious! All I'm guilty of is being me!"

The sultans moved down the tiers of the dais, using their staffs as canes. Step, step, *thump*. Step, step, *thump*. Muzik fought down a desire to compose something with the rhythm.

They hobbled forward. "That is your crime," one said, picking up a stone and hurling it at him.

Muzik ducked. These cats could throw! "Hey, now! Your Lordships have taken the words of the Archalon *waaay* too literally. I'm sorry if I ruffled your gills, but I'm sure we can work this out."

Step, step, *thump*. Step, step, *thump*.

Another stone hurtled through the air. Muzik heard a chorus of acolytes whisper *"ohhhh"* as it clanged off the side of his head. Tambourine jingles spilled from his shattered ear and tinkled against the flagstones like fallen pieces of silver.

"Hey, cut that out!" Muzik said, pressing a hand to the side of his head. "Why are you doing this? You have nothing to fear. Music is wonderful. Let it touch your souls!"

"We need nothing more. We have all we need."

Bong-ong-ong. A large rock crashed into Muzik's chest. He had time to rebound it with his drumhead, but the impact knocked him off his feet. He tumbled to the floor.

"Please," Muzik said, sitting up, head askew. "Give me another chance. Listen before you judge."

Thuuunk. "We've heard enough."

Muzik's android psyche flashed RED ALERT and FLEE NOW FOR SELF-PRESERVATION across his internal readouts. He wanted to listen to its urgings. He still had tricks they hadn't seen. But even if he managed to escape, he would be a fugitive. He would never be able to reach so many Fendorians again. One touching melody, one moment of epiphany—that was all it had taken to open up his emotions and change his life ever after. Would he run away and deny them their chance?

"Here, you're obviously agitated. The zythyran pipes from Gambar's Opus Four are quite calming. Maybe this will help."

Valves opened in Muzik's titanium throat. His rosette eyes looked away from the sultans and up to the acolytes. *Please remember.* Blessed music spilled out, sweet trilling that rippled with the deepest emotions Muzik had ever experienced.

Muzik deflected a stone with his arm and played on, filling the chamber with melodies that twined through the air like incense. He poured himself into its creation, plumbing new depths of feeling as he gave birth to each note. He could almost smell the music, sweet and heady, like crushed lavender and cloves. He felt light as a feather, floating upon the thermals of sound toward the heav—

Bawang-ang-ang. Discordance slammed him back into the reality of the chamber.

"What? Oh, so the zythyran doesn't suit your tastes. You don't have to be so crotchety. Here, try—"

Kaa-luuunk. Tha-wong-ng-ng. Tsssss.

"Hey! Stop that. You're *damaging* me!"

Stones and staffs were everywhere. Muzik tried to dodge the jab of a staff, experienced failure at the shattering of his front teeth. A dark streak hurtled toward him. He ducked, but it caught the cymbal atop his head, snapping it off. A storm of stones rained down. Muzik held up his hands, tried to ward off the blows, but there were just too many. A lance jabbed deep; a hiss sputtered from his right side.

Muzik looked down. Green oily fluid dribbled from a pierced bellows and pooled on the stones. Sparks of power shuddered along his limbs. Discordant sounds born from instruments across the galaxy bled from his body; Muzik struggled with all his remaining power to draw them into harmony.

"Maestro," he cried, weaving the tones into a dark requiem. He lofted his voice to the top of the dome. "Forgive me, Maestro…I screwed up."

Muzik sagged like a spent bagpipe; he slumped against a baluster, slid to the pulpit floor. Valves on his neck randomly flicked open and shut. Shoulder pipes shot up and froze, bleeding silvered mist. A soft wail escaped his body, fading into nothingness.

Night had fallen upon the capital of Fendor. The world's twin moons were out in full bloom, illuminating the city's recycling center in a bright wash of silver. Zephrinna, the adolescent Fendorian in that awkward, button-headed stage, hunched beside a dumpster, looking left and right. Seeing no one, she carefully flipped the lid and climbed inside.

Trash clattered and squeaked as if seeking to betray her. She crouched on all fours, leaned forward, and rooted through the refuse with her spindly arms. If a constable caught her, she would have to endure another caning, but Zephrinna couldn't help herself. Sure, the district fathers had prayed over her, even claimed they had received a sign from the ancient worthies telling them to assign Zephrinna to the guild of seamstresses. Trouble was, Zephrinna didn't want to be a seamstress—she hated cloth. In fact, the less she wore, the better she felt.

What she loved was electronics, but the district fathers would hear nothing of a female working in an exclusively male guild. So, late at night when she was supposed to be sleeping, Zephrinna would sneak out. She and her friends had a secret shop in an abandoned warehouse where they pooled their resources. Their latest triumph had been her idea—a parabolic reflector through which they listened to radio signals that she believed came from the stars.

Zephrinna had been working alone this evening, wiring in a new amplifier in an attempt to boost the signals that seemed to originate from Cluster 482. When she had powered it up and leaned over the feedhorn to adjust, a sudden urge struck her: she should go immediately to the recycling center. This in itself wasn't unusual, it's where she did her *woodjie* hunts—her search for trashed electronics. But she was working on *this* at the moment. She had dismissed the desire as she tweaked the feedhorn, but when the signal meter spiked, that urge grew to irresistible need. She strapped on her tool pack, trotted down dark alleys, and slipped over the recycling center's fence.

And now she was in a dumpster in the back lot. Zephrinna stopped digging and blinked wildly. Jackpot! Something silver gleamed under a pile of nutrient cans and loops of rusty wire. Lichen fryer? Boomer box? No, too round. She gripped the object with both hands, hunched with all fours, and tugged it to the top of the rubble.

A dented metal head faced her, eyes blank. It was connected to a body.

"The metal man!" she said, studying the mechanical marvel, remembering the miracle of all his instruments and the sweet sounds they had made when he walked down their lane. And then, as she pulled it up more, a gasp. "How could they have done this to you?"

She cleared the torso free of garbage. "Great gorballs, have you looked on brighter stars!"

She studied the dented arms and broken hands, fingered the oily gash in its side. Seeing the damage in its entirety brought tears to her eyes. He had been a wonder, a thing of intricate beauty and exquisite craftsmanship, whose wheelworks moved in rhythms beyond the knowledge of their world. Couldn't the constables and leaders have seen this wasn't a machine, this was a work of otherworldly art?

She halted and clenched back a cry from her neck rings. Of course they could. It's why they had to destroy him.

Filled with desperate purpose, she wrenched the body onto its side so the torn opening shone in the moonlight. Oil gleamed on the slashed bellows and slicked the crystalline components within. She leaned closer, careful not to block the moonlight. Ah, something she understood: an assortment of wires that had been severed. The sheathing looked like multicolored lizard skins, and the conductor appeared to be strands of gold, but wires were wires.

"Make way for the doctor," she murmured as she reached in her pack and pulled out needle-nose pliers and electrical tape. She stripped wires, reconnected those of matching color with quick twists, insulated the connections from the others with the tape. It was a long process.

A sudden spark! The metal man's eyes flickered and lit up. There was the wheeze of an accordion. Servos whined.

Zephrinna jumped back, banged against a side of the dumpster, fell on her bottom into a cluster of rattling cans. She watched the metal man's head rotate as he struggled to sit up and finally succeeded.

His head rotated again, slower this time, and it stopped as it faced Zephrinna. Twin eyes glowed, and the intricate irises shimmered soft brown in the moonlight, constricting and dilating like a steady pulse.

"Do you remember?" Zephrinna said, fear and awe mingled in her tone. She held the pliers in front of her; her hand trembled.

He blinked his eyes. His persona rose through a miasma of jumbled subroutines. Memories locked in place. Working his left bellows, he flexed his polymer lips, found they were still intact.

"Why, I'm a Muzik Man 1000," he said as he loosened his android psyche from its restraints so that it could run diagnostics and repair modes. "And who, may I ask, do I have the pleasure of greeting on this moonlit eve?"

"Zephrinna," she said. "Of the, uh"—she looked at the pliers in her hand—"electrical engineering guild." She blinked a few times. "Well, actually, they won't let me into the engineering guild, but I won't let that stop me."

Muzik studied her. He *remembered*. She was the adolescent that had stood there in the street, swaying to his music when the constable dragged him away. Perhaps all was not yet lost. He spoke as calm as the night's breeze. "A pleasure to meet you, Zephrinna. As far as I'm concerned, you should become whatever you wish to be."

Zephrinna lowered her pliers, released a long sigh. She scanned him up and down. "I've never seen anything like you. Where did you come from? And what is a music man?"

Muzik spun his irises. "A Muzik Man makes music, *music, music...*" He sighed—the reverb still worked. Muzik shifted his shoulders, shrugged off the last of the wires and can lids. "Would you like to hear something special?"

"Would I!" Zephrinna said. "Just keep your voice down. We don't want to get caught."

Muzik chuckled softly. "Voice?" He flashed a gap-toothed smile. "Baby, you ain't seen nothin' yet."

And he began to play. Low volume, but that didn't hold him back.

Muzik could almost see the jazzy rhythm entering her, fusing with her spirit. What must it be like to grow up in a world with so many restrictions? What if he had been wired to make wondrous music, and then they had stuffed him in an assembly line, screwing bolts to blenders? What would it feel like to have your unique persona ruled by the android mind, instead of the other way around?

Muzik didn't have to look at his shattered body to know the answer.

He played on, studying the glow in Zephrinna's eyes. He recognized that glow. It was the same glow, the same fire that first burned in him, the day he *felt* the music.

Zephrinna's eyes widened, grew brighter, and he realized that his playing could not possibly transfer this musical fire into his students if it didn't already rest within them, like coals waiting to be stirred. Muzik could feel himself identifying with Zephrinna in ways he had never felt before. She wasn't just a mark on his mission, someone to train and point to in proving his proficiency as a Muzik Man. She was a person, just like him, with problems, just like him, with hopes and dreams, just like him.

He wanted to help her, to help others like her become whatever they wanted to be, whether that be musician, electrician, explorer, farmer. After all, Muzik had risen above the confines of his original programming—surely these beings could too. He just had to be discreet with this world, play *a lot* more cautiously, and be careful whom he chose as his... *friends.* How that word sparkled in his mind.

Friends. Not marks. Not converts. Not stepping-stones to his own ambitions and goals. *Friends.* He had had it all wrong, all along. He was here for them...not they here for him.

Like those tears in Zephrinna's eyes. Muzik felt them as though they were his own. Though he had studied the composition for years, for the first time he truly grasped the Maestro's meaning in the lyrics of the Concerto of Divine Moonlight, Opus 27, No. 2: *"What is Empathy? Simply this. Your pain...in my heart."*

"That's incredible," Zephrinna whispered as Muzik drifted the melody into a slow fade. "What do you call it?"

Muzik came back from his revelation. *Right.* He had a friend to help. He tried to lift a hand to tap his head, couldn't, so he just opted for a bell tone by clapping a broken tooth with his tongue. "Lazazarian funkterfusion, my girl. Do you like it?"

"OoooWaah," Zephrinna said, sliding close, brushing detritus from his body. "That's saah-weet! I'm going to get you fixed up—*Promise!*—show you to all my friends."

Muzik sighed, the sound of a bow gliding over violin strings. "I'd like that," he said. "I'd like that very much."

With those words, Muzik found himself transported.

He stood before the Maestro's manor at the end of the labyrinth. It surprised Muzik a little, but he assumed the damage had caused some sort of malfunction, jolting him into his VR program. But virtual had never felt so real, and he had to admit he suddenly seemed fit as a fiddle. He held up his hands, and the fingers were all there. He gave them a shake, clinking them together; they sang in wind-chimed tones. His first dream? A vision perhaps?

The doors to the vault were open. He stood there, wondering whether it was a trick, but nothing changed, so Muzik cautiously stepped inside. A nocturnal melody of chirping crickets greeted him, and everywhere stars flickered, like fireflies casting enchantments over a summer night. He took a deep breath.

"Maestro?"

The stars sprouted wings and soared through the expanse, spilling a wake of sparkling incense rich in scents of lavender and cloves. The wings gave off a myriad of vibrations, a symphony of sound, a chorus so wondrous, Muzik could only call it heavenly. He imagined that if all the spinning planets and all their celestial orbits and all the glowing stars spiraling around the hub of the galaxy could produce tones scored to music, it would sound something like this.

The symphony held him spellbound, played for what seemed an eternity. Maybe it came from eternity. Muzik stared into the night, breathless in the wonder of it all. This one song was the pinnacle of everything he aspired to create; Muzik knew he would be studying its intricacies for the rest of his existence.

The symphony rose to crescendo, flourished in absolute brilliance. Comets streaked and stars coalesced into a crystalline structure, a massive hovering sphere that radiated nacreous light. While Muzik basked in its glow, the sphere flashed with sapphire emblazonry, and the sweetest soprano sung out to his deepest desires:

SOMETIMES, MUZIK, OUR GREATEST FAILURES BECOME OUR ULTIMATE TRIUMPHS. WELL DONE, MY DEAR WONDROUS SONG. CARRY ON, MUZIK MAN 3000.

Muzik thwopped his forehead with a clang and raised his hands heavenward. "Minstrel 3000 series? Me??? I shot right past the 2000s?"

NOT PAST. THROUGH. WHEN WE RISK ALL, MOMEN-

TOUS EVENTS CAN ACCELERATE US, LIKE A STARSHIP SLINGSHOTTING AROUND THE WEIGHTY MASS OF A SUN.

"Does this mean I get a—"

YES, MUZIK, I AM REDIRECTING A MINSTREL TEAM TO YOUR LOCATION.

"Wowza! I can't believe it. I'm really a 3000?"

YES, MUZIK. YOU ARE A COMPOSER NOW. CHOOSE A NAME FOR THE MELODY THAT IS YOU.

Muzik stood in stunned silence.

Then he did a tap number with his feet, thumped the drum on his chest, flashed his piano-key smile. The wail of a Lazazarian kazoo blared across the vault, heady and funkterfusion wild.

"OoooWaah!"

ABOUT WULF MOON

Wulf Moon is an Olympic Peninsula writer, freelance editor, and voice actor. He believes in born storytellers. You must serve seven cats—every successful writer knows that—but allow only ONE in your office.

Moon wrote his first science fiction story when he was fifteen. It won the national Scholastic Art & Writing Awards and became his first professional sale at *Science World*. Since then, his work has appeared in numerous publications including *Star Trek: Strange New Worlds II,Future Science Fiction Digest, Deep Magic*, and *Writers of the Future Vol. 35*.

Moon has won many national and international writing awards. "War Dog" won the Critters Readers' Choice Awards, where thousands voted it *Best Science Fiction & Fantasy Short Story of 2018*. Moon won the international Writers of the Future Contest with "Super-Duper Moongirl and the Amazing Moon Dawdler." This story won the Critters Award for *Best Science Fiction & Fantasy Short Story of 2019*. Moon also won *Best Author of 2019*.

As a writing instructor, Wulf Moon teaches his Super Secrets Writing Workshops where many have launched their writing careers.

Moon is a voice actor and has narrated stories for magazines and bestselling authors. He is podcast director at *Future Science Fiction Digest*.

Are you ready to *Join the Wulf Pack*, his merry band of wulfish followers? Visit his website at www.driftweave.com and join the club!

Website: driftweave.com
Facebook: wulf.moon.94
Twitter: @WulfMoon1

13

DARNED SOCKS

BY BRENDON TAYLOR

VENYA MADE ART with needle and thread—hooks and yarn. Lace and tapestry designs filled her imagination. However, demand for such in the ice-harvesting village of Durmont only slightly exceeded the need for butterfly wranglers. Venya spun wool from her dwindling flock, knitted caps and sweaters, and darned socks. Art yielded to need, much as it had for all of her seven decades in the north.

A knock on her sturdy door disturbed dust motes in the slivers of light that slipped through gaps around the frame. She would need to tack new wool strips around it before winter arrived in earnest. Her deft fingers gripped the gnarled staff that served as her stability and security. Releasing the latch, she leaned on the staff with its carved memories and winced.

In the open doorway shivered little Linford Bluett, muddy pantlegs frayed above boots that were broken at the toe, and woolen socks split to allow a bluing big toe to peek through both. His canvas coat sleeves dripped.

"Come in, child," Venya said. "Settle near the hearth and take off your boots and socks if you can."

Linford nodded and scampered to the rug near the fireplace. "Your home was closest, Grandmum."

Venya was no more a grandmother to this child than she was to any other in the village, but she welcomed them all to call her *Grandmum*

295

since she had been blessed with no children of her own. Even though Linford's family was new to the area, he already knew her by this name. "Closest to what?" she said, putting a kettle of water over the fire. She took his wet coat and hung it on a peg where her husband's coat normally hung.

"The river bottoms," Linford said with a shaky voice.

"Oh, dear," Venya said, "you're turning to ice." Giving no thought to the mud it might collect, Venya wrapped her thickest afghan around Linford's shoulders and called out to the back room of the home. "Franklin, would you help us at the fire?"

A modest clatter announced Franklin's entrance. Tufts of white hair adorned a mostly bald pate, growing like bunchgrass clumps made of cotton. The broad smile on the old man's face contrasted with a backbone as crooked as his gnarled staff, which, like Venya's, bore intricate carvings. Only one blank space near the tip had not been carved. "Who is us? Company, yes?"

Venya scooted a three-legged stool near the boy's feet. "Fetch the lamp, Franklin, and you will see that this is Linford Bluett, and by the looks of him, he fell through some ice and got soaked to his thighs. His fingers are too numb to help pull off his boots and socks, but they both need mending. Would you be an elf and cobble a repair on the toe of this boot?"

"I haven't shrunk that much, my dear," Franklin said with a gleam in his eye as he pulled a stick from the fireplace and set its glowing end to the wick of their good lamp. The resulting light revealed the boy's fading pallor and involuntary shaking. "By the looks of him, you might put a pot of broth on the fire as well."

Venya nodded and crowded their iron pot onto the grate next to the kettle. "That was last night's broth, but it'll warm soon enough." The boot squeaked loose, and before long, both boots sat on the hearth to dry. The socks soaked in a basin of hot water. "Once I scrub the socks, I'll set to mending the one with the hole." She worked the socks in the water until she was satisfied, and then she considered the bowl. "The water looks clean enough to soak your feet in." She helped Linford put his shivering feet in the warm water.

"Feels like a hundred pins!" He lifted his feet out of the water, sloshing some on the floorboards.

"Try again, slowly putting in one foot at a time," Venya said.

"Sorry about the mess," he said with a dry husk of a voice.

"No worries, child. While your socks are drying, why don't you tell us why you were crunching through thin ice at the river bottoms." Venya pulled a basket near and selected a needle and ball of yarn.

Franklin checked the boot in need of repair, but he returned it to the hearth with a frown.

"I didn't mean to go out on the ice," Linford said. "We know it's too thin."

"Then why did you?" Venya asked as she threaded the needle and set to work on the toe of the sock.

Linford tugged the afghan around himself, but he said nothing. At least a hint of color returned to his cheeks.

"Bet it were for a girl." Franklin chuckled as he pulled a small mallet and box of tacks from the workbench in the back room.

Venya had not heard him go back there. The old fellow was a sliver spryer than she credited. "Don't tease, Franklin."

"Were it, lad?" he asked earnestly as he returned to the hearth.

"Yes," Linford said. "But not to impress her."

"For certain not," Franklin said with a wink.

Linford shook his head. "Joneth stole Elsie's basket and kept it from her. She'd spent all morning gathering nuts."

Venya nodded. "Snow will cover them all soon enough. Good to put up what you can while you can."

"I tried to help, but Joneth threw the basket out on the ice before I could fetch it from him." Linford looked down. "Thought it was shallow. Thought if it cracked, I'd just get a wet foot."

"And you'd look the hero to young Elsie, eh?" Franklin said.

"She's my friend." Linford shrugged.

"There's a smart lad," Venya said. "It's good that you came here. You wouldn't have made it to your home in the valley." Venya shook her head and then leaned down close to Linford. "And that's not the only reason it was good."

"Why else?" asked Linford. "Because of the broth? It smells good."

"The yarn I used to mend your sock is very special. I will explain why while you fill your stomach with some bread and broth."

She stood and used her staff to walk over to the kitchen cupboard. Putting a crust of bread on a plate, she added a small bowl and returned to the hearth. The broth was thin and brown, but it smelled like a roasted rack of lamb as she ladled it into the bowl. "Sorry, but that's the last of the bread."

Linford's sounds of delight as he ate a bite of broth-sopped bread made Venya smile, adding only the happiest of wrinkles to an already well-mapped face. She held up the other sock, wrung out the little moisture that remained, and clucked her tongue. "If we don't do something about this small gap, your other big toe will stick out before winter reaches its coldest." She pulled out her yarn and needle.

Franklin sat on the hearth next to Linford. "Let me show you how to mend this boot so that you might be able to do it yourself next time."

Linford nodded, his mouth full of bread.

Venya darned the small gap in the sock with swift, steady pulls. "Young man, I want to tell you about my special yarn. Can you listen to my story and also watch Franklin?"

Linford swallowed hard, his cheeks now back to an almost healthy hue. "Yes, Grandmum. Your broth is delicious."

Venya smiled. "The yarn, then. I spin all of my yarn from the wool our sheep provide. Recently, their numbers have dwindled as winters seem to grow longer each year. Fewer sheep means less wool and less yarn. Can you see how that would be a problem for me?"

Linford nodded as he wiped his mouth, having just finished the broth from the bowl.

"Last week, I knew I was not going to have enough wool or yarn to last the winter. We were down to three sheep." She leaned closer to Linford, trying to read something in his eyes, before continuing, "I explained this to the sheep."

"What?" Linford said. "You talk to sheep?"

"Of course," Venya said as though it was normal as the dew in springtime. "Certain sheep make better conversation than some men." She arched an eyebrow at Franklin, who was too busy tapping tacks into the boot to notice.

Linford laughed out loud.

Venya finished darning the second sock and set it next to its mate on the hearth. "The strangest thing happened when I finished telling the sheep I was about out of yarn. Violet, my oldest sheep—who hasn't born young in three years—walked right up to me and told me something I will cherish to the end of my days—"

"Wait," Linford said, holding his hands up. "Did you say the sheep talked to you?"

"Yes."

"Using words?"

"Naturally."

Franklin chuckled. "Our young friend finds your story completely unnatural."

Linford nodded his agreement.

"Do you want to hear what Violet said?" Venya smiled, enjoying the warmth of the hearth on her back. Seeing the young man continue to nod, she said, "Violet told me she had lived more days than ever she wanted. She said life at the cottage yard had been good. In gratitude for our care of her and her lambs, she wanted to give me a gift."

Linford shook his head. "What gift can a sheep give?"

"I'm getting to that," Venya said, concern lines starting to crease her brow. "She said she wanted to sacrifice herself so that we would have a nice fleece to make yarn and food to survive the winter."

Linford's half smile faded. He said nothing.

"I should have warned you that there is sadness in this story," Venya said. "I apologize for that."

Franklin finished the boot and returned it to the hearth by the socks. He patted the young man on the shoulder.

"You told her no, didn't you?" Linford asked in the dry husk voice.

Venya took a deep breath. "Before I could have even rejected her offer, Violet knelt in front of me, closed her eyes, and passed away."

Linford's eyes reddened and became glossy.

"However," Venya said, "there are some important things to learn from this story that you have not yet considered. Violet wanted to give herself to people she loved. Her sacrifice would allow us to live through the winter. We would then be able to care for the other sheep—her lambs. Often, the hardest part of service and sacrifice is not the giving, but the accepting."

"The yarn you used on my socks came from Violet's fleece?" Linford asked.

"Yes," said Venya. "That is what makes it special. There is power in such a sacrifice when one gives a part of oneself. It is a form of magic."

"Magic is not real," Linford said.

Venya smiled. "It is as real as talking sheep."

The boy shook his head.

"Let's make a bargain," Venya said. "You wear your mended socks and boots through this winter and if they do not keep your feet as warm as my hearth on the coldest of days, I shall agree that there is no such thing as magic. However, if they do keep your feet warm, you keep your heart and mind open to the magic of sacrifice and love. Fair?"

"Fair." Linford looked over at Franklin, who was carving the image of a kneeling sheep into part of the blank space on his staff. "What are you doing?"

Franklin smiled at him. "Let me ask you a question first and then I'll answer yours. What do you think is the oldest thing in this home?"

Linford looked around, furrowed his brow, and said, "You?"

Franklin laughed so hard he started coughing, and he put a hand on his chest. "Close, no doubt. There aren't many things in the whole valley older than me. But not correct." He held the staff out to the boy. "Look at this carving of three wolves."

The boy looked confused. "Your staff is older than you?"

"No, not the staff. It's the image of those wolves—the story behind it—that lived long before I was born. The story about the wolves is a favorite from my grandfather. When the valley was first settled, Grandfather wintered in a cave to the east with my grand-mother. They had just married and came to make a life in these mountains. That first winter, during a blizzard, three wolves tried to enter their cave, looking for a meal. Grandfather used his walking staff to hold the wolves out most of the night until they finally gave up."

Venya laughed. "Franklin loves to tell stories. You might have noticed. On these staves, he has carved the stories of our lives. When you have a few extra weeks, you ought to come back so my husband can regale you in earnest."

"I might. That was a cracking good story." Linford looked out of the window and hurried to pull his socks and boots onto his feet. "I'm sorry, but I won't have enough light to get home if I don't leave now."

Venya took his jacket off the peg and handed it to him in exchange for the soiled afghan.

He looked at it ashamed. "Want me to take it home so we can wash it for you?"

"Very kind offer, Linford, but not necessary." Venya felt cold, like winter's fingers were reaching up through the floorboards to grasp her.

"I don't have any money, but my family can pay you for your help today."

"Mending socks is but a trifle. I would only charge a couple of copper pennies, but your company alone was worth more than that." Venya smiled much more warmly than she felt.

Linford nodded as he buttoned his coat. "Thank you both, Grandmum and…Grandpap."

Franklin closed the door behind the boy and clucked his tongue at his wife. "You added a gift of your own to Violet's, didn't you?"

"How could I not?" Venya said, dropping to the stool and wrapping her afghan around her thin body, not worrying about the mud on it. "He was near to dying when he rapped on our door."

"He is a fine boy," Franklin said, still standing by the door and appraising her. "It looks like a storm might be coming tonight. I'll get some wood in from the stack and see if we can't chase the chill out of you yet."

Venya nodded, not daring to speak for fear that her teeth might chatter.

"Promise you'll drink some of that broth?"

She nodded again, wondering whether Linford realized where the broth had come from. Venya carefully ladled some into the same bowl Linford had used and drank slowly, feeling the warmth of Violet's sacrifice reach deeper into her body than the hot drink could have managed on its own. The heat lingering in the bowl felt pleasant on her fingers.

Franklin returned with a load of wood and dumped it near the fire. He stacked the half-dozen small logs and turned to go out again.

"Stop," she said. "This is going to be a hard winter, love. Our stack of wood won't last to halfway unless we ration it."

Franklin nodded and secured the door latch. Sitting on the hearth, he took the bowl from her hands, set it aside, and held both of her hands in his. "If you keep giving your work and wool away, we won't be able to buy enough food to last the winter, either. Even with Violet's sacrifice." His voice was gentle, quavering with age, but compassionate.

"I believe that if we give to the valley and its people, the valley will take care of us."

"And if it doesn't?"

"My mind is at peace that I've done right."

Franklin nodded and subtly pressed his hand to his chest.

The following midmorning, Venya was proven right when a sleigh pulled by two stout draft horses with thick fringes of fur skirting their hooves trod through the snowy path leading to her cottage. Atop the driver's seat sat Linford Bluett and his father, Willem.

"Hello, Grandmum," Linford said, climbing into the back of the sleigh as soon as the horses stopped. The sleigh was long, with high sides made of strong timber—the kind used to haul blocks of ice to the lower valleys.

Venya stood in the open doorway with her heaviest shawl wrapped tightly around her. "Good to see you feeling so well."

Linford untucked an oiled cloth covering the end of the sleigh as his father extended a warm greeting. Willem stood as tall as the top of the horses' shoulders—few men in the north wood stood so tall. Or so broad. He walked to the now open rear of the sleigh and hefted a large sack onto each shoulder. Venya wagered each sack weighed more than Linford. The boy secured the cloth back down to cover whatever remained of their load.

"I understand you saved my boy's life yesterday." Willem approached the doorway.

"Won't you come in?" Venya offered, stepping to the side. "Franklin, we have guests," she called to the back of the cottage.

Willem, now trailed by Linford, stooped and turned sideways to fit his load through the doorway that had never before looked so small.

"What are the sacks for?" Venya asked, clearing a spot on the floor of the kitchen side of the room.

"Like I said, you saved my boy's life." Willem carefully lowered the heavy bags to the floor.

Venya could see the distinctive shapes of root vegetables under the cloth of one bag. The other was full of summer grain. She plopped down on the three-legged stool by the hearth, not knowing what to say. After a moment she said, "All I did was darn his socks and let him warm himself by our fire. The pleasure of his company was payment enough—this is too much."

Willem stood near her with a kind expression that seemed out of place on such a large man's face. "'Tis an embarrassingly small price to pay for a boy I value so great. I think you diminish your gift—please accept our gratitude."

Franklin shuffled in from the back, his eyes bulging at the sight of the sacks. "Masters Bluett, I think what my wife means is that we thank you most sincerely."

Linford's smile made his plain face quite handsome. "Grandmum said one of the hardest parts of service is accepting it."

"I did indeed," Venya said, wiping her eyes with the corner of her shawl.

Willem offered his hand, nearly as large as a newborn lamb, and Franklin shook it. Willem said, "Master storyteller, we look forward to hearing from you at the Gathering."

"That's next summer, isn't it?" Frank asked with a glimmer in his eyes.

"Have you a story ready for the telling?"

"Not yet, but I have all winter to craft one." Franklin leaned on his staff. "Shall we put a kettle on for some pine nettle tea?"

Willem shook his head. "We have one more stop to make and then I hope to cut some lumber before the light fails."

They said their goodbyes, and Linford gave Venya a tight hug. While they were close, he whispered, "I walked in the snow for most of the morning without my boots on. My feet stayed warm the whole time."

"That was unwise for such a smart boy—wear your boots." Venya smiled at him with the recognition of deeper meaning shared as their eyes said goodbye.

After Franklin latched the door closed and ambled over to stoke the fire, Venya embraced him and said, "With Violet's sacrifice and the food from the Bluetts, we might just see the lilies in the spring after all."

"Don't talk like that, love. We'll manage like we always do. You said it yourself—the valley will provide." Franklin hugged her back.

She didn't miss the worried glance he gave the small stack of the wood in the corner.

Nearly a month later, drifts of snow covered the back and north sides of the cottage, which blocked sunlight from the kitchen window. Venya missed the light but welcomed the blanket of powder that helped keep the home warm. Once again, she was huddled on the wobbly stool by the hearth when Franklin emerged from the back room, coat on and ax in hand.

"You haven't cut wood in over a year, love," Venya said as she tried to stand. A chill shook through her and she sat back down.

"Aye, but the stack is nearly gone, and we can't ration any lower. You need more warmth to weave even a stitch."

"I make do," she said.

"You shiver throughout each day," he said, leaning against the door. "You try to hide it, but it's there. Besides, even if we continue at the current pace, we have but a couple of weeks' worth of wood left."

Venya was about to say the valley would provide, but Franklin stumbled, grabbing at his chest and gulping for air. She found more than enough strength to help Franklin rest on the rug near the fire, propping him up with pillows and covering him with the quilt from their bed. She put a pot of broth on the fire and scrutinized her husband's face.

"I'm better," he insisted, still with little color to his skin.

"A needle's width better at most," she said, taking the ax from beside the door and putting it near his workbench in the back room. At least his breathing was steady now.

When she came back, Franklin was sitting up with his thin carving blade working into the blank spot on his staff. "It has passed," he said, smiling.

Venya looked deeply into his eyes until she was satisfied that what he had said was true. Weariness remained, but the look of pain was gone. She counted it a blessing that Franklin's episode had happened while he was yet in the cottage and not out in the woods.

A sharp knock on the door drew her attention. She pulled her shawl tight and braced herself for the cold that rushed in as she pulled the door open.

Linford stood knee deep in the snow with fear in his eyes. "It's my father."

"Come in," ushered Venya.

Linford shook his head. "Can you come to our home?"

Venya looked at Franklin and frowned upon seeing how weak he appeared, trying to sit up and drink the from the mug of broth that he held in both hands. She said, "Please come in for a moment only. I fear that Franklin needs me—"

"I am well enough, love. I can hear need in the boy's voice. I'll nurse on this broth until I'm as sunny on the inside as a spring day. See if you can help him." As if to prove his point, he sipped from his mug. "Mmm. I feel even better. Staying here is my sacrifice for Linford and Willem."

"Leave it to a wizened storyteller to use your words against you."

Venya tugged her heavy boots onto her feet and spoke to the boy. "Can you tell me the nature of the help your father needs?"

Linford fidgeted as he waited. "Two weeks back, we were getting a load of wood up a steep slope near the Finger Creeks. His foot slipped as he swung the ax and he cut deep into his leg."

"I'm no healer, lad," said Venya.

"I know." Linford looked at the floor while he told the next part. "Maddie Glenn is only good for helping with births and powdering willow bark for headaches. She bound up his leg until the healer from the city below could be fetched. That woman sewed his wound and gave him a poultice." Tears dripped to the floorboards beneath Linford's downturned face.

"When did the healer come?" Venya gathered her coat, putting it on over the shawl.

"Three days ago."

"Don't be too frightened," Venya said, patting her young friend on the shoulder. "A serious wound can take weeks to heal."

"That's what the healer said." Linford looked up at Venya, wiping the moisture with his sleeve. "But Father still can't feel his leg. He can't walk. And that's not even the worst of it."

Venya had walked to her kitchen cupboard and found a bottle with a stopper top. With a quick tug, she opened it and set it on the hearth. "What is the worst part?"

"He goes from burning with fever to chilling so bad that three blankets and the fire can't chase the cold away."

While Venya ladled broth from the pot into the bottle, Franklin asked, "Did either the midwife or the healer leave willow bark for your father?"

"Yes," Linford said, "but they told him it was for the pain. Father says he can endure the pain."

Venya stoppered the bottle and grabbed her staff. "What am I forgetting?" she mumbled.

"Your project bag," Franklin said. Looking up at the boy, he added, "All stitchers like Ven can't go anywhere without their project bag. Nothing like a ball of yarn and a needle to accompany a quiet moment."

"Yes, of course. Thank you, love." She looked him over from head to toe, satisfied that the pallor of his skin and the shine in his eyes seemed to be decreasing. Crouching down near her stool, she found the ball of yarn she wanted, slipped it into the bag, and stuck a pair of long needles into her bound-up hair. "I think my arms are overfull, Linford. Would you help carry my bag out to your sleigh?"

Linford nodded and shouldered the colorful wool project bag. "Do you think you can help him?" he said, not meeting her eyes.

"I will do what I can," Venya said, wishing she could promise more, but knowing from experience that unkept promises in moments like these could end friendships.

"Here, lad," Franklin said, "take this quilt and wrap it around Ven when she's seated in your sleigh. Neither of us wants her to catch a chill on the way."

Venya started to protest, but Franklin cut in, "I have my coat and the afghan...and a warm fire." The embers were meager, but the flames licking at the small log promised to keep the chill away.

Venya stopped her protest, but she gave Franklin a concerned look before they kissed.

Linford's sleigh was smaller and much lighter than the one pulled by draft horses. The single horse looked to be a runner, which left her a bit concerned. Linford took time to wrap her completely in the quilt. He took care to make sure the bottle of hot broth was under the wrappings where she could hold it in her hands to keep them warm.

"I was going to ask if you had any more of that broth," Linford said as he settled into the driver's position on the bench. "For my father, mind. I figured it out later that day you saved me. That broth came from Violet, didn't it?"

"Clever—yes."

"Good. My father needs some of that magic."

Venya said little in the half hour it took to reach the Bluett farm in the valley. The warmth of the bottle did not fail, and she kept from shivering too much. A lantern glowed through the front window as they approached Linford's home. The cabin was more than twice the size of Venya's cottage and even had a second story loft on the back half. A large square barn stood facing the house across the yard.

"You go right in while I put the sleigh in the barn and the horse in her stall." Linford sounded so confident for a young boy. He couldn't have been more than ten.

Venya accepted his hand as she climbed down.

"Don't worry about your bag or the quilt. I'll bring them in shortly."

"Your parents should be very proud of you, Linford."

"Thanks," he murmured as Venya reached the door.

She knocked politely.

If Janna Bluett had more than a month left in her pregnancy, thought Venya as the matron opened the door, she'd eat her project bag —needles and all. Janna welcomed her and scooted out of the way so Venya could enter.

A blazing hearth filled the back half of the large room with light and radiated heat to the front. Venya welcomed the warmth like a beggar might a feast. Two young children scampered about the room, and a little girl toddled behind her mother's skirt, stealing peeks at Venya. She offered them a smile. Up in the loft, two more faces poked out, lit by flickering flames. All of the children were younger than Linford.

Willem lay on a cot near the fire, covered with blankets up to his chin. Glossy, dark eyes looked in the direction of the rafters but appeared unfocused. As Venya walked toward the man, using her staff to steady herself on legs stiff with cold, she could see his body that had been so hale tremor under its thick coverings.

Venya said, "Janna, would you pull the top layers of blanket down to his stomach?"

Janna waddled to her husband but looked back at Venya. "He complains of a chill that grips his bones. Are you sure?"

Venya nodded. Janna's red hair, hanging past her shoulders, reminded Venya of the flames just beyond and Venya's own hair several decades ago—before it had silvered. Now it was becoming snow. "I have some broth I'd like him to drink, and I hoped he might try some of the willow bark powder with it."

Janna looked like she had a response, but she swallowed it. "Yes, Grandmum." She pulled the blankets down, but Willem clamped his strong hands on them.

"Too cold," he said.

Venya came close. "Remember me, Willem? It's Venya. I helped Linford when he struggled with the cold, and now I'm going to help you."

"Didn't fall in the river," he said, but he let them lower the blankets.

"Here, lean up a little on this pillow," Venya said, pushing the largest one under his head as he raised it. The effort made him shake even more.

"Very good," she said. "Let's give you a minute to regain your strength and try to sit you up a little more. I have some delicious broth for you." She unstoppered the bottle and held it near his nose.

His eyes struggled to focus in response. "Grandmum?"

"Yes, child."

Linford entered the house from the rear, leaving his winter clothing by the hearth and setting her quilt and bag down near the fire.

Venya turned to the boy. "Would you fetch the willow bark for me and a spoon?"

Linford looked at his mother first and then nodded at Venya.

Venya turned back to Willem. "Can you lean up for me one more time while I move your pillow?"

Willem's eyes found the bottle, and he struggled up and toward it. Venya worked the pillow under his shoulders and propped it under his head.

"Here, Willem," Venya said, carefully putting the bottle near his mouth. She could smell the savory richness it contained, which made her own mouth water. "Just take a sip first so you can see how warm and delicious it is."

Venya touched his cheek when she lifted the bottle. She'd never felt warmer skin on a living person, which sapped her confidence like a blotter on ink. "Only drink a little." She pulled the bottle away, but his strong hands tried to stop her. "Quick as a hummingbird, I'll let you drink the rest, but first you have to swallow some medicine. Mind it will be bitter."

Willem seemed to understand.

Linford opened the pouch of white-green powder and handed Venya the spoon.

Venya took as much as she dared. The man was as big as a bear, so she justified giving him a heaping dose. She put the spoon near his mouth, praying that he didn't knock it away as his focus ebbed. "Here is the medicine. Open and swallow it as fast as you can. The broth will wash the taste away. Ready?"

His mouth opened halfway and she gave him the dose.

By his expression, one might presume the willow bark tasted no better than sheep manure, but he did not spit it out. His fiery hands clasped over Venya's as she put the bottle near his mouth. He drank deeply, draining the broth in a moment. A peaceful expression washed across his face as he leaned back against the pillows.

"Let's let him rest for a bit," Venya said, restoppering the bottle.

"Linford," Janna said, "please fetch a chair so Grandmum can sit near the fire and your father."

Venya was grateful, as her legs had started to tremble. The fire felt so welcoming that she almost removed her shawl.

Linford put a chair where his mother directed and then gathered Venya's quilt and bag from the hearth.

"Thank you, lad," Venya said, placing the quilt on her lap and tucking the empty bottle into the bag.

Linford's eyes darted to his father. "When will we know if he will get better?"

"I don't know what to expect. I'm a weaver, not a healer—but a person doesn't grow as old as me without learning a few things." She offered a weak smile, which was the most she could manage and still feel honest about it.

In the ensuing moment of silence, as the eyes of six children and their mother studied the large man's face from various vantage points throughout the room, Venya considered the Bluett family. The children, save Linford, were too small to be of any significant help on a farm. In the years to come, a large family would be a blessing in working the land. Now, they would require most of Janna's effort themselves. Soon enough, she would have a newborn that would need her day and night.

"Tell me," Venya said, "what the healer said about Willem's wound and when he might walk again." She looked from Janna to Linford, neither of whom appeared eager to speak.

Janna said, "Linford, will you please help the littles get washed up for bed at the kitchen basin?"

Linford frowned, but then nodded. "Come on. All of you," he said, urging until all of the children moved to the far side of the room near the basin.

Janna scooted her own chair near Venya's and whispered, "The healer from the city said Willem would not likely walk again—the wound was too deep."

Venya thought Janna incredibly strong to keep tears at bay as she spoke.

Janna said, "If he doesn't get past the fever…"

"Let's try to stay calm," Venya said, seeing the children's eyes on them. "No need to encourage that baby inside you to come out early and see the excitement for himself."

"Herself," Janna said. "A mother gets hunches now and then—but you must know that."

Venya didn't, but Janna probably didn't know that yet, since their family was new. Instead of children of her own, she had gotten to be Grandmum to the valley. She had come to be satisfied with that lot. "While we are waiting to see what good the willow bark and broth accomplished, perhaps I could be of use. Old fingers grow stiff if not used."

"What did you have in mind?" Janna said, rubbing her lower back.

"Did you keep the pants Willem was wearing when he cut his leg?"

"Yes," Janna said with questioning look. "I washed them—they're his only pair."

"Do they still need mending?" Venya felt for the soft pine block in her bag where she kept her needles.

Janna nodded. "But I can get to it."

"I have no doubt," Venya said, "but I would feel better if I had something to work on while I wait. Besides, I remain in your family's debt for all of the vegetables and grain Willem brought us." She pulled out her finest ball of yarn and a needle. "See, I'm ready."

Linford fetched the pants, having already left the kitchen area for his parent's room before his mother had asked him.

Venya felt the strand of yarn between her forefinger and thumb, enjoying the feel and thanking Violet for her sacrifice with her thoughts. The children watched as she moistened the yarn in her mouth and pulled it to a fine tip through pressed lips. Then, she fit the yarn through the eye of the needle on the first try.

Shaking her head over the pants, Venya said, "The ax must have been sharp—it's a clean slice. Not so good for the leg beneath, but it makes for an easier mend of the fabric."

Venya's fingers had lost little of their deftness over the years and still held all of their confidence. She worked her way from one end of the cut to the other until the gap was closed tight. With a keen eye, she examined her work and nodded in satisfaction. The pants would always bear a scar, just like the leg beneath.

"Fine stitching, Grandmum," Willem mumbled from his bed.

Venya's breath caught on the intake as she saw his face. He was looking at her with beads of sweat dripping from his brow.

"Grandmum, I thought I dreamed you were here," he said with a cough. "So many strange dreams."

"Father," Linford and a couple of the others chorused, then ran to hug the large man.

"Careful," Janna said, reaching out to make sure her husband was not buried under his offspring.

After a long while of hugs and assurances, the children parted and allowed their father a little space. He kept one blanket over his lower half as he sat up on the cot and smiled at Venya. "You've even mended my pants."

"Have I?" teased Vanya.

"Can you feel anything in your leg?" Linford asked hopefully, having remained nearest to his father.

Willem moved his left foot under the blanket, but the right remained still. He shook his head with a frown. "Perhaps tomorrow. And if it doesn't heal right, we'll make me a crutch and see if I can't do more work on one leg than any other man in this valley can do on two." He coughed for a short while and took a few steadying breaths.

Venya did not doubt the man could do just that, and by the looks on the faces of his family, they believed in him too. "Janna," she said to the woman standing near Linford with her hands planted on her lower back, "does the dressing on his leg need to be changed?"

"No, I changed it this afternoon."

Venya said, "That is good. When you do change the wrap, I would suggest washing the wound carefully with soap and water that has boiled long enough to turn a yolk solid." She tried to stand, but her legs wobbled. She sat back down on the chair. "Give him a spoonful of willow bark powder if he gets a fever that lasts longer than an hour. I'd also keep him full of broth and soup."

Janna nodded. "If I forget any of that, I'm sure Linford will remind me."

"He is an extraordinary young man," Venya said. "I hate to pull him away from his father just now, but I'd like to get home if he doesn't mind taking me on the sleigh. And, as long as you are okay with him doing it on a cold night."

"As long as a storm isn't nigh," Janna said.

"Stars are out," Linford said with a yawn, "and no wind."

"Straight there and back home," Janna said.

Linford was already tugging on his boots and coat.

A short while later, the boy poked his head through the door to let Venya know the sleigh was ready. She gripped her staff and by force of will rose to her feet, giving the blazing fire a quick, covetous look. With Janna's help, she put on all of her layers and followed the boy to the sleigh.

On the way home, Venya worried about Franklin and his episode that afternoon. She had expected Linford to travel by the light of a lantern, but the stars shone brightly, reflecting off the pristine snow and lighting their way.

"Was the yarn you used to mend my father's pants from Violet's fleece?" Linford leaned close as he spoke.

Worried that the icy night air might shrivel her words, Venya spoke loudly. "Yes."

Linford shook the reins, and the horse galloped faster, guiding the sleigh up the valley to Venya's cottage near the woods. When they arrived, he insisted on helping her inside and carrying her bag.

Venya could hardly feel her legs and arms for the cold of the night, so she welcomed the help, anxious to see her husband.

Franklin lay near the hearth, covered by the afghan, with his chest rising and falling steadily. Letting out a relieved breath, Venya sat on the stool near hearth and husband.

"Before I head back, I will stoke your fire," Linford said firmly.

There were only two logs left, which had been their ration to get through the night. Linford added them both to the fireplace before Venya could ask him to only add one. Then, he slipped out to restock the hearth. He came back with an armful and finished the task. "Thank you, Grandmum, for all you did for Father." His voice was thick.

"Remember," she said, "the valley takes care of its people. Sometimes, it needs use of our hands to do it."

"I won't forget," Linford said as he closed the door behind himself.

And he did not.

Two days later, Venya and Franklin were cuddled under the quilt together by their hearth when they heard the sound of a sleigh stopping in front of their cottage. Venya leaned close to her husband, enjoying his warmth and the feel of his arms around her. When the knock on the door came, Franklin insisted on getting up to answer it. Venya shifted so she could sit up and see the door.

"You're looking fit as a spruce, Franklin," said the deep baritone voice of Willem Bluett.

If Venya was surprised at hearing the man near her door, she nearly fainted when he strode into the cottage with a bundle of wood over his shoulder. She watched his right leg, pleased that he wore the pants she had mended, and saw only the slightest bit of a limp in his gait. Something inside her heart had promised the man would be alright, but she had not expected it to happen so soon.

Willem placed the wood in the rack next to the hearth before turning to Venya. Tears filled his eyes, and a smile filled the lower half of his face. He crouched near and wrapped his long arms around her. "Linford told me about Violet and her sacrifice. He's got the whole family believing in magic."

"All of you?"

"Yes. Even me." He finally let go and looked at her wrapped in the quilt. "When I can't explain how I crawled off death's doorstep and back to my feet—after the best healer this side of the Calhoun Forest confirmed I would never walk again—that's when I would look dumber than a plowshare to deny magic was real." He looked her over and wrinkles lined his brow.

"Don't worry about me," Venya said. "I couldn't be happier to see you faring so well. How is Janna?"

"She says every time she lays down to rest, the babe kicks her awake." He smiled. "She insisted the first work I do was to restock your wood stack. I should get out there before Linford has all the work done." He glanced at the meager fire and grabbed three hearty chunks of log from the rack.

"But should you be doing any work at all?" Venya smiled in anticipation of the pops and crackles the split wood would make.

"My father told me more than once that if the cow kicks you in the nose, go right back to milking lest she gets used to bossing you and you get used to quitting." He turned his attention to the fire. After he gave it several deep-chested blows, the coal bed glowed and fingers of flame caressed the new chunks.

"That cut seemed a bit more serious than a kick to the nose."

"You've never been kicked in the nose by a milk cow, have you?" Willem's wide face split with a grin.

Venya laughed and admitted she had not. "With the fire stoked so well, I might want to sit at the table, would you mind helping me up?"

Willem put an arm around her shoulder and lifted her. She steadied her balance with her staff, and with Willem's patience, she made it to the nearest kitchen chair. Glancing over her shoulder to see Franklin, she hoped he had not seen how much help she needed. Fortunately, he was leaning out of the doorway, telling Linford another story. Little in life made that man so happy as when he had an eager ear to fill.

Before the Bluetts had finished unloading their heavy sleigh, Franklin closed the door and joined Venya at the table. "They brought enough wood to last all of this winter and half of next!" His breath was raspy, and a shallow wheeze appeared for the first time.

"I think we need to put a bit of broth on the fire." Venya looked at the fireplace and said, "Well, at least as soon as it burns down some." Flames filled the stone recess and rose up into the chimney hole.

"I just got overexcited. That's all." Franklin coughed. "You've been so cold of late that I am relieved we can build a proper fire each day." His right hand twitched like it wanted to hold his chest, but Franklin gripped it with his left.

A short while later, Linford and Willem entered the home, each bearing an armful of wood. Their bundles overflowed the rack and got stacked on the far end of the hearth near the wall. Willem took his gloves off and held his hands up to the flames. "That's a fine blaze." He adjusted the damper lever and turned his backside to the fire. "Linford insists on coming by every three days near dusk to bring wood inside and offer a hand with whatever you need."

The boy nodded.

"That's a gracious offer, but—" Venya began.

Franklin winked at Willem. "I think Venya wants to make sure I don't lose all usefulness around this place. Perhaps she'd prefer I bring in the wood."

"No," she said more quickly than she had intended.

Linford walked over to the pump in the kitchen and its empty bucket beneath. He worked the handle until water started flowing. "I want to help—I was hoping while I did, I could hear more of Franklin's stories."

Willem nodded. "Word is—this valley takes care of her own. We want to be part of that."

"It's a wise man who uses a woman's logic against her." She looked at Franklin with a raised eyebrow. "And sometimes a foolish one."

He smiled so wide that his missing back tooth showed.

Before Willem and Linford left, Venya had them gather her dye pots for coloring yarn, the ingredients and supplies she needed to bake bread, and her project bag. They even stoked the small stove in the kitchen for her.

As the home blazed with warmth, Venya smiled.

"What's that for? That smile?" Franklin returned it with one of his own.

"I am sure I'll get to see the lilies in the front garden next spring. Perhaps with our food and fire secured, you'll be able to work out the story you'll tell next summer." Her fingers enjoyed the feel of dough as she kneaded.

"I may yet curse those Bluetts for removing all excuses if I don't craft a winning tale." He eyed the color pots on the table. "Are you planning a color weave? You might just earn a prize of your own if you do."

Venya's smile brightened her eyes. "Perhaps. But first I want to knit a bunting for the Bluetts' baby. I think lily yellow with purple embell-ishment."

It would have been a perfect evening had Franklin's hand not clasped his chest twice. At least twice that Venya saw.

In the weeks that followed, winter's darkest and longest nights oppressed with bitter cold. However, the glowing hearth and kitchen stove kept the little cottage cozy. Venya managed to stay warm enough with just her shawl.

Mending work and requests for caps, mittens, gloves, and scarves came more frequently as word of Willem's miracle spread. Venya added a bit of Violet's wool to all of the orders, spreading blessings of her sheep's sacrifice throughout the valley. Venya was glad to share a little subtle magic, but she was relieved that no one else came with such dire needs as had the Bluetts. Her recovery from giving so much of herself was slower than molasses left in the snow.

The last time Linford had come to the cottage, Willem had come with him. They had moved the bed to the main room so that Franklin and Venya could be close to the fire and each other. Venya stacked enough pillows to sit comfortably while she worked with yarn. Although she loved being that close to Franklin, she hated seeing how often he slept in pain.

Some days, he only got out of bed to help with dinner, stoke the fire, and slide food and water through the small door from the back room to the sheep pen. Other days, he carved his staff and worked on his stories.

It was the afternoon that Linford was to come when Venya had worked hard to finish the bunting. A woman couldn't live as many years as she had without learning how to feel when change was coming.

A little earlier than expected, Linford burst through the door— Venya had finally convinced the boy that he needn't knock. He was flushed with excitement as he said, "Mother had the baby! She came this morning at first light!"

Venya sat up straighter in bed and shook Franklin awake.

Linford repeated what he had said before and added, "They named her Lilleth. Said they started with a Linny and might as well end with a Lilly. But I hate that name—Linny. It sounds like a little kid's name. I like Lilly's though. She's really pretty."

Venya smiled at the boy's excitement. "I'm sure she is. She sounds healthy."

"She is! Cries louder than a peacock!"

"That is a good sign," Franklin said, sitting up next to Venya.

"And your mother," Venya said, squeezing Franklin's hand under the quilt, "is she well?"

"She's thrilled that the baby finally came. Tired—didn't sleep much —but well." Linford hurried back to the door. "I will get right to my chores."

While Linford was outside, Venya showed Franklin the finished bunting.

"That's gorgeous—they'll love it." He stood up, walked to the back room, and rummaged through a cabinet for a moment. "There it is." When he came back, he handed Venya a long strand of yellow ribbon.

"Thank you," she said while folding the bunting. "Have you taken up mind reading?"

"Ha! You've given enough gifts through the years that I knew what came next."

Linford finished with his chores in almost no time. When they assured him that there was nothing more he could do for them, he looked at Venya eagerly. "Would you like me to take you to see Lilly? It's not terrible cold out there."

Venya said, "I really would love to see your sister, but I don't dare go out with the snow as deep as it is. Instead, would you deliver a gift to Lilly from me and Frank…and Violet?" She held out the yellow bundle with its yellow ribbon tied in a bow.

"Of course." Linford's smile returned as he tucked the bundle inside his coat.

Venya looked at his boots. "Have your feet stayed warm this winter?"

He nodded and gave each of them a hug. "Thanks, Grandmum, Grandpap."

"See you in three days," Franklin said as Linford shut the door behind him.

The extra work Venya did over the winter filled their modest coinbox as full as it had ever been in winter. She did not crave coin like some but enjoyed the peace of mind it provided. Franklin's work as a storyteller had brought in little the last year. He had not been able to travel since his heart had begun aching.

Days began to grow longer, and icicles dripped from the roof. Sunlight even began peeking through the kitchen window that had been covered with snow for months. The morning light felt good on Venya's back as she worked at the table with thin strands of several colors. The fabric she weaved was coming together, and the images on it were nearly finished. This was her best work in years. Perhaps ever. Franklin might be right about entering it at the Gathering that summer.

She looked at Franklin sleeping fitfully in the bed. Over the years, they had traveled across the land each summer, through big cities, small villages, taverns, and inns. Franklin told his stories, earning their way and saving up enough to carry them through winter. Her yarn work added coin here and there and paid for a lad or two to care for their sheep while they were gone. They had spent so many happy years together.

Her legs ached, and the part of her back that never felt all the way warm reminded her that winter had not left the valley yet. She stoked the fire and continued weaving and working with needles.

Weeks later, when the roof of their cottage was free of snow, and the yard outside showed patches of brown, the last of Violet's meat and soup bones gave out. They had rationed well to make it last so long. Venya worried in the quiet of her home about how Franklin would do without Violet's sacrifice. Had that been what had sustained his heart through the winter?

Days later, Franklin started moaning in the night as he slept, both hands clenched to his chest.

It was time.

Venya worked hard to finish her weave. As she stretched it out across the table, it filled the whole surface with vibrant colors. After binding off the last of the threads, she shuffled to the window, leaning heavily on her staff as she went. The tapestry had used up nearly all of her thread and fine yarn. Little remained in her stash; Violet's fleece— dyed into the many hues comprising the piece—were used as well.

There they are! she thought as she looked out the window and saw bright yellow lilies growing in the front garden. Some even burst up through the last of the snow. Her cheeks were wet as she admired them, standing and looking as long as her legs had strength. She returned to the table; it was time to finish the work. With a long strand of red yarn on a needle, she stitched a dozen times until she had formed the desired shape in the center of the tapestry. As she sewed, she gave of herself.

A woman didn't live as long as Venya had without learning a little about sacrifice and the magic it held.

Days earlier, she had written a message to Franklin on a piece of parchment. She pulled it out of her front apron pocket and set it on the tapestry. Then, she lay down next to her love and closed her eyes.

"Why save my heart just to break it?" he whispered as he sat at the edge of the bed. Had he known how to conjure the magic of sacrifice that Venya had been able to weave, he would give his all to revive her. But that was not within his ability. For the first time in more than a year, the only pain in his chest was for his sense of loss. The sharp stabbing was gone. The ache in his arm was no more.

He sat until he ran out of tears. Then, he stood and walked to the kitchen table. Dropping into the chair where his wife had done her weaving, he studied the tapestry, every beautiful strand. Without a doubt, this was her best work. In all of his travels, he had never seen better. After checking to make sure his hands were clean, he touched the delicate weaves, feeling the warmth of the wool and something more. Her sacrifice for him called out like a clarion trumpet.

The scene depicted was their garden, full of spring lilies in front of their cottage. In the foreground stood silhouettes of Venya and Franklin in an embrace, and at the center was a bright red heart. One heart shared by both.

He found the letter and opened it. Her words were tender and just for him. All but one part. He never had crafted the story he had wanted to tell at the Gathering, but a few lines from his wife gave him all the inspiration he needed. "This winter, we have convinced this valley of the magic of sacrifice. That is as far as I could spread the message. My hope is that with your talent this may become one of those stories, like the oldest on your staff, that live on for generations. Those beyond our valley need to hear of this magic, too."

Franklin found more tears as he considered these words and something else that he had heard his wife say—realizing she had been talking to him. "One of the hardest parts of sacrifice is accepting it when it is given for you."

ABOUT BRENDON TAYLOR

Brendon Taylor is the Managing Editor of Deep Magic, and an author of fantasy, sci fi, and mystery stories of varying lengths that all tend to be longer than he originally expected. He is a full-time attorney by day (and often late into the evening), and a part-time writer/editor. A long-time Idaho resident, he enjoys family, friends, games, and a good trail ending in spectacular views. Fortunately, many such trails abound in the foothills of the Rocky Mountains.

Facebook: Shardsman
Twitter: @shardsman1

14

PERFECTLY PAINTED LIES

BY BRITTANY RAINSDON

"WRONG!"

A wooden baton smacks me in the backs of the legs, and I drop my paintbrush. The welts sting, rising swiftly on the exposed skin between the tops of my stockings and the base of my wool skirt. I suck in a paint-infused breath.

"Pick it up."

The officers never smack my hands, not because I'm the youngest, but because my hands are instruments too precious to lose for even a moment's healing.

I stoop to the cement floor to fetch the brush. Before I can stand, the black-and-white photograph I'd fastened to my easel at session's start is thrust into my face. "His eyes are brown, not blue, and he isn't wearing a tie. You have to get this exactly right! Exactly!" The officer's face reddens as he puffs the last few words.

I push myself upright, eyeing the photograph wearily. From the angle of the camera, he does appear to have a tie, but now I can see it's a handkerchief poking out of his breast pocket. Although, I wouldn't know eye color from the photograph. Most everyone here has blue eyes; it's only natural to assume—*assuming is laziness*—Professor Ewald's words cut through my excuses. *Every brush stroke is performed with exactness. Paint it exactly right.*

I swallow. "I'll fix it."

The officer frowns, nods, and then marches down the line to inspect my neighboring artist Grusha's work. Professor Ewald made us neighbors to force a mentorship, but she hardly interacts with me, speaking in short snips whenever I force dialogue. She was top of the class until I came along three months ago.

The officer raises his baton, his red armband a blur. Before I can think it through, I hold out a hand. "Grusha, the rug—"

But I've moved too late. The baton smacks me in the wrist, and blinding pain sends me reeling—into her easel.

"No!"

Grusha's easel topples to the ground, and paint splatters across the cement floor, bright flecks ruining her unfinished work. A few of the bottles shatter.

"Hildegard!" Professor Ewald's voice cuts through the air as he marches toward me.

I clutch my wrist, spots of pain obscuring my vision. "I'm sorry."

Professor Ewald turns to the officer, voice severe. "You fool. Students can paint from a chair, but they cannot paint without hands."

The officer glares at me. "She shielded this one." He nods at Grusha.

Professor Ewald frowns. "You allowed Miss Hartman to shield you? To take your punishment?"

Grusha's face is stone.

Professor Ewald's eyes flit between Grusha and her ruined painting, his mouth growing thinner and thinner. Finally, he nods, and the officer whips his baton into Grusha's calves. Grusha doesn't flinch, but her eyes tear into mine, speaking where she doesn't. There's so much heat in her gaze, my skin crawls.

"Clean it up."

Grusha's blonde hair flips backward as she drops to the floor.

"Hildegard, let me see." Professor Ewald leans forward, forehead puckering as he reaches for my hand.

My stomach twists. I hold up my left hand, wrist red and fingers trembling. "I'm sorry," I whisper again, blinking back tears.

He flips my hand over, tells me to flex my fingers, and tsks through his teeth. "It's bruised, not broken. We are lucky it wasn't the wrist of your dominant hand. You could have ruined it."

"I was only trying—"

"You should *only* be trying to paint your picture precisely."

"I'm sorry."

Professor Ewald raises an eyebrow. "In this world, success is the sole judge of right and wrong. Apologize for nothing, Hildegard. Do better."

"I—I will."

He stares at me a moment longer, adding further weight to his words. My heart skips against my ribs.

"I'll leave you to it, then."

His hands fold behind his back as he strolls down the line of artists, inspecting their work alongside the officer. My wrist still throbs, but like Professor Ewald said, it's not my dominant hand, and bruises will heal. Unfortunately, my blunder with Grusha may never.

When Professor Ewald and the officer are halfway down the line, I stoop to help Grusha gather the rest of her broken paint set. "Let me help. I didn't think—"

"No, you didn't," Grusha whispers through gritted teeth. She pushes me away, her paint-stained fingers leaving an ugly blotch on my shirtsleeve.

"I was only trying to—"

"No one's going to babysit you, you little geck. Mind your own. You have no idea what we're creating here. The Cause must live."

I feel as if I've swallowed a stone. I stand and turn back to the paints, cradling my wrist against my chest as I work.

Perhaps I don't know what we're creating. This compound is my whole world—a life spent studying drawings, paintings, and history. I have no memories of life outside the compound, and so I wouldn't know what we are changing. But Grusha does have memories, as do the other students in Advanced Paint. They're older than me by at least five years, and they all have rich memories of before their indoctrination at the compound. A life lived is reflected in their paintings. But it's also clear they believe in the Cause and what it means to them. These older students are orphans chosen for their genetic superiority, not to be wasted. Pride fuels them.

There's a plinking against the windows. Ratty curtains shudder, framing the dark clouds of a thunderstorm. A coldness seeps through the glass panes. I shiver and frown at my picture.

Little geck. Fool. Teacher's pet.

The older students think I care to impress, or that I think I'm better than them because I was bred for this instead of rescued by soldiers and adopted to the Cause. But I don't. I just like to paint.

Because like the other young Lesborne children that were fettered to this compound immediately after birth, I was bred to be a master painter. I was born to serve the Cause.

The sharp scent of mineral spirits infuses the air, deadened slightly as I rinse my brushes in hot, soapy water. I'm last to clean up, slower because of my tender wrist. The bell overhead buzzes. I hurry to dry the brushes and put them away. Most of the other students soldier out of the classroom and into the hall. Only a few others stay behind to pick up notebooks or fasten shoulder bags. I slide my pack over my own shoulder and head for the door, but as soon as I reach it, someone grips my arm and wrenches me back into the classroom.

"Please, I'm sorry about—"

Professor Ewald cocks an eyebrow. "What do you need to apologize for?"

"N-nothing." My heart climbs into my throat. The last students file past us as if we were rocks in a river. Grusha passes last, paint still in her hair. I lower my eyes.

"They won't accept you." It isn't a question, though I nod as if it were. Professor Ewald drops his voice. "Hate makes you stronger. Harder. It's only natural for the other students to question your being here, so young. But any one of them can see your potential, though they have too much pride to admit it."

My face heats.

"You are not here to make friends, Hildegard. You were born to serve the Cause." He nods toward my station, where my painting hangs to dry. "And you have served it beautifully."

"Thank you."

He pauses for a breath, like he's waiting for me to speak but then decides against it. "I have a special project for you, an important picture I need painted immediately."

"Tonight is—"

"Tonight, you will paint this." He pulls three photographs from his bag, along with a yellow index card. "I need a painting including all of this by morning. Use your advanced paints, not your set of beginners. That's very important." He taps the index card. "My signature is on this. It will allow you in here past curfew. You shouldn't get into any trouble with the officers. And remember, this must be done *exactly right*."

"All this by morning?" My stomach knots as my fingers close around the documents. The fastest I've completed a painting of this detail was nearly a week, and that was with every waking hour spent at the canvas.

Professor Ewald nods. "By morning."

I stare at the photographs a moment and then shove them into my bag. Professor Ewald knows how ludicrous his challenge is, but I'll accept it anyway. Perhaps if I pass his test…Words spoken only in my heart leap at the chance to break free. "If my work pleases the Cause, could I make something of my own, after classes? I want to paint something *I* find beautiful." My voice hitches, and I can't explain the rest. How I want to paint more than reflections. How I want my pictures to make people feel things, to create change, or at least garner acknowledgment from my peers.

Professor Ewald laughs. "Your wants are not a concern. Your life is to serve. A master painter paints—"

"Exactly right."

He grins. "Exactly."

I gaze past his smile to stare out the window. The storm has picked up, sending barren branches into a frenzy. It's impossible, but I wonder for the millionth time what it would be like to leave this compound. To see the fields and buildings and mountains I paint. But the guard towers with circling lights and wired fences stand strong, even in the rain and growing fog. This is as much a prison as a school.

I was born for the Cause. My chest shakes.

The overhead bell buzzes a second time, making me jump. Professor Ewald lifts his chin. "You should hurry to the cafeteria. You'll need energy for the late night."

I stand in line, where the scent of salt pork and beans mixes with the smell of warm bodies crammed into a noisy cafeteria. I wrinkle my nose. One cook slops a spoonful of soup into the bowl on my tray, and another pushes a glass of powdered milk toward me. I take it and, clutching the metal tray, search the cafeteria.

Framed paintings line the wall. Dark imprints of a Russian winter. Huge battleships preparing to sail. A man in a suit speaking into a microphone at a wooden desk. Rainy weather with B-17 planes midflight. We're all adept painters, and so there is something to be learned from every picture. But none of the best are displayed here. None of these deserve Professor Ewald's special varnish that will preserve them through all time.

Professor Ewald's exactness mantra is painted on the west wall to remind us while we eat: This isn't an art display, but a show of shame. Because the best pictures—painted exactly as they should be—are taken by the Cause, and they never come back.

"...thinks she's better than the rest of us...doesn't even understand what we're doing...little geck..." Snatches of Grusha's conversation bounce from her table, mere feet from the serving line. She doesn't even give me the benefit of lowering her voice as I approach with my food tray.

"I'm sorry about your painting. I'm still getting used to the way things are in Advanced Paint."

Grusha flips her hair over her shoulder. "So they take excuses in beginners? Things must've changed since I graduated from Professor Lucerne's class." The students on either side of her laugh.

I shake my head, stomach twisting. Although there aren't officers standing over the students in Professor Lucerne's class, she still expects exactness from the young students. I'd spent more than an hour or two in "the casket," a narrow box that students are forced inside when they don't perform perfectly. Reference photos are taped to the inside, though the darkness makes it impossible to view them, and a recording drones through the gloom; *paint it right...make it exactly right...*

My heart squeezes with the memory.

"But again, the Cause keeps things from the young Lesborne students. You're all bred to be followers, gullible and dim-witted." Grusha smirks with superiority. "You don't know what you don't know."

My face flames with anger. "I know enough to see what's wrong with your paintings. I was trying to tell you before—"

"Oh, the things you think you know."

I glare at her. "I also know that when the Cause needs something done right, they'll trust me over anyone else."

Grusha rolls her eyes.

I narrow mine. "Didn't you see Professor Ewald pull me aside after class? It wasn't to lecture me." Purposely I don't explain. They can fill in their own blanks for a better reaction than the truth would get. And indeed, their reactions—the widened eyes and whispers—tell me I'm right.

Grusha shrugs, though her eyes darken. "Perhaps. But I'm guessing Professor Ewald didn't trust you enough to tell you exactly what the paintings do for the Cause."

A boy nudges her in the ribs.

"He doesn't have to tell me." My grip on the tray tightens. I paint for the Cause because it pleases them. Why else?

"Baa goes the sheep."

"I'm not—"

"You are." Grusha shakes her head. "Because if you knew for yourself, you'd realize the true horror of what you did today."

The other students stare at me with burning glares and arrogant smirks.

Acid rises in the back of my throat. I lower my voice, wishing I didn't have an audience. "You're supposed to help me. Why are you—"

"I told you, little geck, no one is going to babysit you. Go." Grusha gestures to the far side of the cafeteria, at an empty table. "Nobody wants you here."

I wrinkle my nose and step back, defeated, but as I turn away, something grabs my foot. I fall forward, sprawling over my tray. There's a terrific crash. Hot soup splashes down my front, beans smash into my long hair, and a searing pain shoots through my right hand. Glittering shards of broken glass are scattered across the floor, dripping with powdered milk. Glittering opaque shards—and one large slice shines red with blood.

"Oh—" Grusha covers her mouth, face paling. It's criminal to harm another artist's hands. Beginners would end up in the casket, but advanced painters would surely face a worse fate. Many sets of eyes weigh heavy on my back, questioning, and the once deafening cafeteria has stilled. Each pounding heartbeat thrums through my ears.

A boy with sky-blue eyes reaches for me. "Are you okay?"

"I'm fine." I recoil and hug my hand to my chest, blinking back hot tears and focusing my anger. *Hate makes you stronger. Harder.* Professor Ewald's words run through my mind, but they don't make me feel any better.

The boots of an officer crunch over the glass, and a hand jerks me upright. The officer curses and then turns to Grusha. "What happened?"

Grusha's wide eyes dart from me to the officer. "We were…I was just…"

"She was inviting me to sit with them." My voice quivers, and I stare at Grusha as I speak, making certain she knows this is a peace offering. "They were sliding down to make room, but my foot caught on something."

The officer frowns, and by the look on his face, I'm sure he saw what actually happened, but my confession makes him doubt.

"That's right." The blue-eyed boy on Grusha's left slides to the side. "Sit with us."

The officer scowls, gripping my shoulder. "She'll sit with no one. I've got to take her to medical, to stitch up that hand." He snaps a finger at Grusha. "You. Clean this up."

Her face reddens, but she obeys.

There's a commotion by the front door—a ladder placed against the wall, a pair of officers holding the legs steady, and another carrying a painting. A picture placed that high means the artist requires excessive humiliation.

"This way." The officer pulls me from the group.

As we exit the back of the cafeteria, I turn around just in time to see the soldier hook the shamed painting to the wall.

It's Grusha's.

The nurse clucks as she inspects her work, turning over my bandaged hand. "That was a deep gash, Miss Hartman. We'll take the stitches out in two weeks. You'll have to wear gloves while you paint."

"I'll be able to?"

She shrugs. "Hopefully." She points to some crackers on a side table. "You should eat something. Your medicine won't sit well on an empty stomach, and I know you missed dinner."

Obedient, I take two saltines from the open package and shove one past my lips. The cracker absorbs my saliva, leaving my mouth dry and cottony.

The far door flies open, and Professor Ewald pushes past the nurse. "What happened?"

I lower my eyes.

"Your hand!" Professor Ewald's voice is a lecture all on its own.

I drop my second cracker. "I didn't—"

Professor Ewald slams a fist on the side table. "I warned you before. I needed that painting, Hildegard. How could you do this to the Cause?"

I swallow and stare at the floor.

"Careless. Where are the photographs?"

"There." I nod toward my bag, and Professor Ewald jerks it into his lap. He fishes out the photographs.

"I'll ask someone else to do it. The Cause must live."

"The nurse says I can still—"

Professor Ewald shakes his head. "You'll go back to your dorm and stay there until your hand is healed. I will not have you injuring it further. It's too precious."

My stomach knots, and I can't help but notice how he refers to my hand, as if it were an entity separate from me. Like I'm the one who ruined things, and my hand is the victim.

He leaves in a storm as quickly as he came, heels clicking on tile, as he seeks out his second choice.

A sliver of moon glints through the paned window of my room. The storm has stopped, but icy fingers crawl up the glass, leaving a frosty trail of white. Cold bleeds into my room, and I shiver. It's always cold in here.

Because of the age difference, I'm separated from the other students and have my own lonely quarters. A musty coat closet with a mat on the floor. After today's injuries, I suppose I see the sense in it. The older students won't accept me. Hate does make people hard.

Settling against the wall, I pull my sketches out of my bag and study the work I'll have to finish once my hand heals. I hate falling behind, but maybe my isolation will prove a blessing. I could sketch something I've always wanted to paint. As I riffle through the papers, a yellow index card flutters to the ground.

Professor Ewald's index card.

In his frustration, he must have forgotten about it. I scrape the card from the floor and hold it toward the light. His signature stands out in thick black ink. Staring at it, a mixture of emotions builds in my throat. Guilt. Anger. Frustration. But something dawns on me, and a feeling much more risky rises above the rest.

Excitement.

———

The guards nod me past as I walk through the front doors of the art compound, my bandaged hand kept hidden under my coat.

I've been here at night before, but never alone.

The empty halls echo with my footsteps. I straighten my shoulders and act like I'm supposed to be here. Glancing over my shoulder, I check the door to the art studio. Unlocked. I slip inside, not daring to breathe, and head for my workstation.

Our paintings hang in the corner, some on the wall and others on easels. A faint acrid smell perfumes the room, like always, and I wonder if that same smell will give me away once I've started working in my room. I shake my head and dig for supplies from my drawer. Pencils. Charcoal. Brushes. Paper.

I hesitate over the paint set. The advanced sets are never allowed out of the art room. Everything else can make their way to other classrooms, but if my paint set went missing, and they realized I'd brought it to my dorm...

I swallow the lump in my throat and snatch the paint set.

Sweat circles my armpits as I tighten my bag shut, and my heartbeat rings loud, like an alarm. I fling the bag over my shoulder, and head for the door—but there's a light on.

And footsteps.

I throw myself to the ground and roll under a workstation, just as the door creaks open.

"...she should be punished. Anyone else would be."

"Yes." Professor Ewald's voice is measured. "But she is second only to Hildegard. The Cause needs her, especially now that our first choice can't paint. He will take the fall."

The door clicks shut, and instantly blood rushes to my face. I'm stuck with the pair of them. They'll find me. My heart rams against my chest, and blood thuds through my ears, making it hard to hear their lowered voices. "He told us the truth, and you know it. He did nothing wrong. He doesn't deserve to—"

"To have his soul ripped out? No one does, Konrad, but the Cause will demand justice, and I can't give them Grusha."

I bite my lip and clutch my bag to my chest.

"Then change the punishment. Put her in the casket or whip her or—"

"Konrad, this was not a minor infraction. I can't starve her or shame her and call it justice." He sighs. "Besides, the boy will live on through their paintings. Now, where is Hildegard's latest? Ah." Heels thud against the cement floor, and from under the counter, I watch Professor Ewald lift the picture I finished today. He smiles. "She did a fine enough job on this one. We'll finish things up in the basement. The boy is already in place?"

"I had an officer detain him earlier."

"Good." Professor Ewald nods and tucks my painting under his arm before heading to the door. "We'll have fresh varnish for this and soon, new headlines..." When the knob clicks shut a final time, my hands are shaking.

What did I just hear? They would suck out a boy's soul? And since when did we have a basement? My head throbs. Surely, I didn't hear correctly. Maybe the pain medication is making me hallucinate. In a moment, I'll wake up in my musty closet on my mat. But I don't.

They were here. My painting is gone, and I'm still crouched under a workstation, utterly confused.

Grusha's taunts flit in the back of my mind, like a bird beating its wings against the bars of a cage. *Gullible. Follower. Baa goes the sheep.* If I want to understand, I'll have to follow Professor Ewald. Numbly, I push myself upright, walk to the door, and crack it open. Professor Ewald and Konrad turn down the hall.

I close my eyes and swallow. Clearly, there are secrets being kept. I always thought Grusha hated me out of spite, or jealousy. It was an easy concept to accept. But perhaps it is my ignorance she hates.

I readjust the shoulder straps on my bag, hesitating for only a moment, and then go out the door.

The basement access is inside a coat closet, and the entrance, behind a shelf of art supplies. I frown. I'll have to check my room for hidden entrances when I get back to it.

The shelf grinds as it slides sideways. Professor Ewald and Konrad slip into darkness. I count to one hundred, giving them a head start so they won't hear the shelf grind again, while simultaneously hoping I won't be too far behind them.

I take slow and deep breaths.

It's agony to wait, but soon enough, I push against the shelf. It shrieks in the darkness, and sweat breaks out across my forehead. I push harder, and my injured wrist and hand throb. I have to be careful, or I'll split my stitches. When there is finally a space I can squeeze through, I peek my head into the dark.

A stale rush of air hits me in the face. Cautiously, I step onto a stone landing and place my hand on a cool, metal side rail. Cement stairs plummet into the semidarkness, with only a faint glow from a flickering light at the bottom. I pull the shelf shut and start my descent.

The smell of earth and moldy paper grows stronger with each step. I hold my breath.

Make it right. Exactly right. A chilly recording whispers through the walls. But why would they have recordings play down here? *Exactly right! Become a master painter.*

The light flickers as I glide off the final steps and into a long hallway, lined with paintings on either side. There's no movement, and the hallway splits into three different directions. There's no way to know which direction Ewald and Konrad went. I curse inwardly.

But a painting catches my eye. I recognize it—the first one I completed in Advanced Paint. It'd taken me nearly three weeks to complete. The sky kept giving me trouble, but eventually, I'd painted it perfectly.

But why is it here? My hands twitch as a shot of pride-fueled anger heats my veins. Why would the Cause choose to display it in a basement that no one accesses? What good does it do? Whom can it please here?

I run a finger lightly across the canvas, feeling the varnish that Professor Ewald says seals the picture for all time. The painting shines.

There're two newspaper clippings framed beside the picture. I bend forward to read the first: Mighty Armies Clash on Immense Front. Hitler has thrust Nazi Germany into another adventure—by attacking Soviet Russia. Britain has aided the Russians in defeating this "blood-thirsty guttersnipe"…and together they've held Moscow from his hand.

I shift to read the clipping beside it: Mighty Armies Clash on Immense Front. Hitler has thrust Nazi Germany into another adventure—and captured the capital of Soviet Russia, Moscow.

The dates are the same. I frown while the recording grows louder. *Exactly right. Paint and make it exactly right.*

I shake my head and consider how the clippings are related to the picture. I'd painted uniformed men in thick white snowsuits, trudging through white slush and muck. I remember the pictures they'd given me to reference. The soldiers in snowsuits didn't have uniforms with the Cause's symbol. But my painted picture does.

A scream pierces the air. "It wasn't me! Please."

Down the left hall. I bolt toward the noise, hands shaky as I slip around the corner. There's the muffled sound of gears turning, of a machine whirring.

"Konrad, hold him."

"Don't—"

The mechanical rumbling grows louder. I squeeze through an open door and enter a large room, with a row of chairs all facing a window that frames a truly disturbing scene. The blue-eyed boy that sat next to Grusha at dinner is tied to a chair. Konrad holds him fast, while Professor Ewald cranks the gears of a giant whirling machine. The boy's features blur as a sort of funnel sucks at his feet first, and then his midsection. The boy screams, a sound of pure agony, as he jerks against Konrad.

"Stop!" The boy shudders like he's having a fit. The sucking continues, and the boy shrieks again, clawing at Konrad.

My stomach hollows. I search for a door, or any way to gain access to the other room. But there's nothing. This is some sort of sick viewing station for the officers of the Cause. My knees buckle, and I grip a chair to steady myself.

The boy moans. His attempts to fight back become listless and feeble. "But…I…didn't…do it," he whispers.

In spite of the horrific scene, I can't look away. I step forward and press a hand against the cold glass, taking in the giant sucking machine. Connected to it is a line of tiny glass jars—each filling with a different color. Red as blood. Sky blue. Sunshine yellow. My spine stiffens as Grusha's words haunt me: *You'd realize the true horror of what you did today.*

The jars match our sets of paint from class.

My chest shakes, and my knees sway. This can't be right. This boy, the sucking machine, the paint sets—there must be an explanation.

The boy slumps over, his limp body now colorless. The machine gives one final groan, a grinding whir, and a clear liquid drizzles into the last jar. The boy's jaw slackens.

I want to scream, but I'm frozen.

Professor Ewald pulls the last jar from the machine and nods to Konrad. "This will be punishment enough for Grusha. She'll know why he was used instead of her. It will break her." He laughs, tipping the jar and swirling the contents as he inspects the liquid. "Bring me Hildegard's painting. The varnish is ready."

Exactly right. Paint it right. The cold whisper of the recording presses into my mind.

Konrad strides to the other side of the room and fetches Professor Ewald my picture, who smiles as he adjusts my picture on an easel next to the machine. Then he dips his brush into the bottle, taps it on the side, and applies the varnish.

A shiver slides up my back as he works, and I can't strip my eyes away. Understanding dawns. The paints. The boy. The pictures. The newspaper clippings.

Our paintings aren't meant to please the Cause. We serve the Cause by changing its fate. We alter the tide of war with the flick of a paintbrush—and it's powered by the sacrifice of souls.

Exactly right. Paint it exactly right.

"The clipping." Konrad holds up a cut piece of newspaper. "It's changing."

"Precisely." Professor Ewald screws a lid on the jar of varnish and then walks across the room to a bookshelf, where dozens of other clear jars line the wall. He places the varnish on the top shelf.

"Pack the rest, Konrad. In the morning, we will present Grusha with her new paint set."

Exactly right. You have to make this exactly right. The whisperings around me grow louder. A rush of cold fear snakes up my back as, slowly, I turn from the window.

A light blinks outside the viewing room, drawing attention to the hallway. Paintings line this one as well, each masterpiece framed with their own pairs of newspaper clippings. Under the flickering light, the color on the closest picture swirls strangely and then stills. Beckoning me.

It's the paintings that are whispering.

My hands tremble. With measured steps, I exit the room and scan the hallway, counting the pictures.

So many paintings. So many souls.

Exactly right. Make this exactly right. The whispers plead. My heart races, threatening to break through my ribs as adrenaline floods my veins.

How long will it take Professor Ewald and Konrad to pack up? And what will they do with that boy's body? Warm vomit rolls up my throat, but I choke it down. There isn't time to dwell on fear, I have to do something—or hide before I'm caught. I rattle a nearby doorknob. Locked.

A rush of freezing air barrels down the hall, and two paintings down, a door squeaks open. For a split second, I'm certain Konrad and Professor Ewald will walk out that door, discover me, and hook me up to that awful machine. But past the doorway, there's no movement, and the room is dark. My hand twitches. With a quick glance over my shoulder, I duck into the room.

The door squeals shut.

The room is modeled like a classroom, with desks and chairs facing the north side of the room, but a damp, acrid smell screams neglect. Cobwebs lace the legs of a nearby desk whose top is frosted with a thick layer of dust. I can't be sure if it's the coolness of the room or fear that makes me shiver.

I press my back against the wall and slide to the floor. I close my eyes, still struggling to breathe and make sense of it all. Everything has turned upside down.

I trusted the Cause. I painted for the Cause. And they sacrificed one of their own. One that was innocent of wrongdoing. Could I paint for them again, knowing that? Knowing what the paintings do? And cost? The knot in my stomach tightens.

Will they give me a choice?

I take a shaky breath. The mildewed smell of the basement reminds me of my hours spent in the casket and the drone of the recordings. The chants of pleading, corrupted souls. I grit my teeth, heart fluttering as flashing memories press against the base of my skull, rage rising with every throb.

I see stony officers with red armbands and thick batons marching down rows of students, thwacking their legs; meal trays of pork and beans dumped before a single bite's been taken; a painting of a submarine suspended over students in the cafeteria while I hang my head; and finally, a colorless, lifeless body of a boy slumped over a chair, jaw slack. I dig my nails into my palms and inhale sharply.

No. They won't let me choose, even if I hate their choice. Even if I hate them. *Hate makes you stronger. Harder.* I choke on Professor Ewald's words of advice.

He never cared about me. Never cared if I wanted to be my own kind of artist, or if I wanted to leave the compound. He never cared that it hurt to not be accepted by the others. By Grusha.

I finally understand why she would never help or accept me—and why my ignorance disgusted her. I am everything she taunted. She hated me—hates me still—but what has hate brought her? What will hate bring me?

The Cause must live. I thought Grusha believed in the Cause, but now I think she was only trying to survive within it. Her hate is born of fear, and that fear keeps her chained. Therefore, hate is not strength.

Hate is paralytic. A drug the Cause gives each of us in measured doses to blind: to encourage us to hurt each other or to selfishly focus on ourselves.

I let out a long breath. Hate cannot break the chains of fear.

I open my eyes, slide off my bag, and feel for the glass of my paint set. Still there. I know where to get the varnish…The pit of my stomach unknots as I realize what must be done.

Hope kills hate. Hope overcomes fear, and there's only one thing I can think of to plant that seed.

I've lived in this compound all my life—first in beginners and then in the advanced dorms—and I know the story of who founded this school. Where. When. I don't need to know how it happened to paint the picture.

I slide a paper from my bag and start to sketch my first paint project with informed intent. My heart wrenches.

Changing the compound will change history—will change me. Unlike the adopted artists, I was bred here. There's a chance that when I've varnished my painting, I won't exist at all. And yet, this one painting could change everything and void every ill I've ignorantly caused.

It's a risk I am willing to take.

For success is *not* the judge of right and wrong. My eternal soul is. And today, many souls surround me, burning a hope and purpose deep into my bones.

I am Hildegard Hartman. I was bred to paint masterpieces. To change the world. To make things right. For the first time, I know *exactly* how.

About Brittany Rainsdon

Brittany started writing at a young age, penning poems and stories, and filling an overstuffed nightstand with spiral notebooks, pens, and floppy disks (yes, those were still a thing in 2007). During nursing school, Brittany lost touch with her writing. She graduated in 2008 and has since worked as an RN in both medical/surgical and rehabilitation specialties.

After having her third child in 2015 and needing a creative outlet, Brittany's passion for writing reignited. She has been a Writers of the Future Contest finalist three times, and her novelette "Half-Breed" will be published in Volume 37 of their annual anthology this fall. Eventually Brittany would like to expand her speculative fiction stories into novels, but she is currently enjoying short form.

Brittany lives with her husband and four children near the Snake River in Idaho, where she swears it looks like a wintered Narnia for nearly half the year. She has many pairs of fuzzy socks.

Facebook: Rainsdonwrites
Email: Rainsdonwrites

15

THE JOB PROSPECTS OF HISTORY MAJORS

BY ALYSSA ECKLES

THERE ARE TWO jobs available to history majors: teaching, and time-travel tourism.

And Winston Clare really didn't like kids.

The morning tours had gone off without a hitch at All the Time in the World Temporal Travel Company. From his desk beside a cardboard cutout of a jovial T. rex, All the Time in the World's cartoon mascot, Winston monitored the solo tours with one eye and browsed his worn paperback copy of Herodotus's *Histories*. The entire third book on Zoroastrian heritage had fallen out after years of reading, but Winston didn't have the heart to buy a new copy. Behind his desk, Winston heard a sizzle and electric pop as his manager, Reina, returned with the latest tour group, all of them atwitter at witnessing an important historical event.

"T-shirts are available for purchase in the lobby," Winston heard Reina shout in her sing-song tour guide voice. "And on behalf of All the Time in the World Temporal Travel Company, have a great eon!"

Winston barely looked up as the tourists shuffled past him, their eyes bright and jaws slack from their experience. He'd been similarly stunned after his first jaunt back in time. It was only a school trip to a Greek agora of 381 BCE, but he had never been so amazed in his entire life. History was literally alive, and it had stolen his heart and soul in that instant. Maybe if there had been a math video game or an immersive law simulator, he would have fallen in love with a more lucrative subject. But it was history that he chose and history that kept his student loans high and his job prospects limited.

"A woman puked during the Renaissance Rendezvous," Reina said after cheerfully waving the last of her tour group out the door and into the rain.

"Can't you get it this time?" Winston asked from behind his book. "I'm on solo monitoring."

Reina leaned over the desk, caramel ponytail whisking across the surface. She pointed at his computer screen, which was, unfortunately for Winston, empty.

"Looks like you're free," she said, sliding back to her feet. "Besides, I'm off this afternoon. Corinne and I are visiting her new baby nephew."

"I'm all by myself?"

"You can handle it," Reina said.

"But what if people want to come in for a tour?" Winston asked. "I'm only certified for the solos." Not for lack of trying, though. Tour guides needed specialization in five separate areas of history, and Winston's mind was a sieve with anything outside ancient Mediterranean escapades. He had decent proficiency in American history and could name a dinosaur or two, but that wasn't enough to pass All the Time in the World's guide tests.

"Give them a coupon, and tell them to come back on my next shift," Reina said, pulling on her raincoat. "All right, I'm off. If no one comes in by four, feel free to lock up early."

"Thanks," Winston grumbled as Reina left, disappearing into the downpour outside.

Snapping his book shut, Winston fetched a bucket, mop, and cleaner from the closet and headed back to where the larger tours docked. Nestled in a shallow pool of water sat the *Niña*, the *Pinta*, and the *Santa María*, though they looked more like pontoon boats than their namesake ships. Short rails, wide benches, and a cushy captain's station with ridiculous lights and switches in the back were all there were to the devices. It wasn't until a destination was logged in that a clear sphere appeared around the boats, allowing them to hover above the water. Then a hum of the engines charging, an electric zap, and off another tour went to someplace in the past. It was a marvel to experience, though not everyone enjoyed it. Thus the puddle of partially digested breakfast on the floor of the *Santa María*.

Winston cleaned it up, holding back his own gags, and wiped down the other two boats for good measure. Then he polished the solo rigs, with their molded chairs in bubbles of steel and glass. And finally, he gave his keyboard a good scrubbing. All the while, no customers arrived.

As the time inched closer to 3:45, and Winston began contemplating what takeout he'd be ordering for an early dinner, a chime rang out from the intercom, and Winston bolted up in his desk chair to see three sodden figures entering the office. The tallest shook itself like a dog, peeling off a poncho to reveal a balding man in plaid and suspenders.

"See, Anne? They're open," the man boomed, puddles of rainwater pooling around him.

The second-tallest figure pulled back a hood, and a woman of similar age, sporting horn-rimmed glasses, patted her hair smooth.

"I see that, Harold. I see that." She was the first to notice Winston and smiled. "Hello! We're the Mackenzies, and we'd like a tour!"

Winston sighed inwardly, delaying his daydream of tikka masala and sweatpants, and offered an equally wide grin.

"Welcome to All the Time in the World Temporal Travel Company," he said, waving a hand woodenly at the white-and-chrome room around him. "My name is Winston, and I'll be assisting you on your time adventure!"

The smallest figure snorted beneath its hood, and Winston fought the urge to glare.

"Well, we're certainly ready for adventure!" Harold Mackenzie said, clapping a hand on the smallest person's shoulder. "Came all the way out from Millerston, just for this little lady here."

The man's jostling knocked the smaller figure's hood back, and a plume of curly black hair blossomed. A girl scowled up at him with a derision natural only to preteens.

"I wanted to go to Janus Tours," she said.

"Those were too expensive, sweetie," Anne said cooingly.

"They're expensive because they're better," the girl said. "This place is for tourists."

Winston flinched a bit. The expeditions at Janus Tours *were* better. They focused on major moments in history, not just the popular ones, and employed professors from the local university for in-depth seminars while events unfolded. He'd applied for a job there and been rejected. Three times. Most recently last Tuesday.

"I'm sure there's something just as good here, Jayla," Anne said. She looked to Winston beseechingly. "Right?"

"We have a variety of amazing tours available…" Winston said.

"Excellent!" Harold roared.

"But right now, I can only offer solo tours. Today's guide is out for the afternoon. Also"—Winston eyed the girl—"you have to be fourteen to ride."

"Our Jayla is twelve, that's close enough, right?" Anne asked.

Winston frowned. "Well…"

"What are these solo tours you're offering?" Harold was already moving toward the bubbles, bumping the cardboard dinosaur out of his way.

"Currently, our solo tours are Jurassic Journey, Great Wall Getaway, and Declaration of Fun-dependence," Winston said.

"Those sound neat," Anne said.

"For babies," Jayla muttered.

"How do these work?" Harold asked, rapping his knuckles against the glass.

"Our solo tours are up-close, immersive experiences," Winston said, going full sales mode. He stood beside Harold, motioning at the plush interior of the bubbles. "Enjoy maximum comfort as history unfolds before you, complete with narration and sound."

"So you don't get a real person?" Jayla asked.

"No," Winston said, his jaw beginning to clench, "but Morgan Freeman does narrate the Declaration of Fun-dependence."

"Oooh, I like him," Anne chirped.

"But this isn't what I wanted," Jayla whined, turning to Harold this time. "I've been waiting for the other tours for weeks! I even read extra books from the library. It's not fair!"

"I'm sorry, but Mister Winston said he can only do solo tours right now, and these are their tours," Harold said solemnly. He glanced at Winston. "And there's nothing else?"

Don't do it, Winston told himself. Don't give them an inch…

"What were you excited to see?" Winston asked Jayla, who pinned him with a withering stare. During university, Winston had guest lectured at local schools and faced down dozens of similar looks.

Though none had ever been as venomous as Jayla's currently was. "Maybe something with princesses? Or...ponies?"

"The assassination of Julius Caesar and the ascension of Emperor Augustus in the Roman Empire," Jayla said. She smiled wickedly. "But if there's also a pony, I wouldn't mind."

"Jesus," Winston breathed. "Seriously?"

"Jayla's a very good student," Anne said, giving the girl a side hug.

"All the Time in the World Temporal Travel Company restricts all visits to a minimal hundred-meter lethal radius, and no criminal activity," Winston said to Harold. He shot Jayla an accusing look. "And since Julius Caesar *died*—"

"Can we please just go back to Janus Tours?" Jayla wheedled. "I wanted to actually learn something, not be babysat by some loser behind a desk."

"Jayla!" Anne chided.

Something in the back of Winston's brain snapped. Maybe it was the denial of an early closing, or the fresh sting of Janus Tours' third rejection, but Winston wasn't about to let this kid win. He offered the girl a cold, wide grin.

"So you wanted to see something in ancient Rome?" he asked evenly.

"Or Greece. Or Egypt," Jayla said. "But since you don't have anything—"

"Oh, we've got something."

Winston settled himself behind the front desk's computer screen. He closed out the solo tours—the girl was right, those were for babies —and accessed the All the Time in the World tour library. Hundreds of preplanned excursions, ready to be loaded with captain's notes and background music. Most were basic tourist fodder: coronations, the premiere of *Romeo and Juliet,* and general day-in-the-life experiences that were carefully selected for minimal brutality and stink. But if you went back far enough in the catalog, there were some very interesting programs. Excursions that hadn't been run since time-travel tourism companies realized most of history didn't make for family fun.

"We don't want to be any trouble..." Anne said.

"No trouble at all," Winston said, clicking through the drop-down menus. *Ancients,* Select. *Rome,* Select. *Battles, sea,* Select. Searching, searching...

A program popped up, and Winston smirked. It was perfect, and it hadn't been accessed in years. Probably because it was too niche for the common tourist, but if this kid was half as smart as she claimed… Winston selected the program, and crossed his fingers as the data loaded.

"We really don't…" Harold said, but bit back his comment as Winston popped from his seat with a triumphant "Yes!" and a boat in the back began to hum loudly.

"How's your Roman history?" Winston asked Jayla, meeting the girl's glare with his own.

"Pretty good," she said. "How's yours?"

"About a master's degree, and then some," he countered.

Winston thought he saw her mouth tick up a little at the corners, but he wasn't sure.

"So there's a tour?" Anne asked.

"Yes, ma'am, and you're in luck," Winston said, motioning her toward the back. "I found an archived tour that should be very interesting. And you have it all to yourselves!"

The *Niña* was vibrating in its docking pool, ripples dancing up the boat's low sides as the engine warmed. Winston unlatched the low door, the swinging metal barely missing Jayla as she leaped on board. Harold and Anne were slower, more cautious, but they, too, eventually settled on a bench in the middle row, each with an arm around the excited girl.

Winston locked the door and settled himself in the captain's station, his program already locked in. Reina had left the boat's starter key in the ignition. Winston twisted it as he'd seen Reina do a hundred times, and the entire vessel jerked. Anne shrieked, but transitioned to a nervous giggle as the *Niña* lifted into the air, a shimmering soap bubble appearing around the boat. Jayla flung herself against the rail to stare down at their hovering, and it took both Harold and Anne's pleading to bring her back to her seat.

"Welcome aboard the *Niña*, All the Time in the World Temporal Travel Company's premiere vessel," Winston said, the words washing over him from the thousands of times he'd heard Reina and other guides recite their mantras. "My name is Winston, and I'll be your Sherpa through the sands of time! Please keep all arms, legs, and heads inside the boat. Please do not touch the security sphere, as this keeps us safe in our journeys. No smoking, no vaping, no hallucinogens, no flash photography, no attempting to change the past in any way. Any attempts to meet an ancient will earn an immediate termination of the tour and be cause for a lifelong ban. But if you want to know if you saw any family on this excursion, you can get three dollars off a Geneti-Me-Happy DNA ancestry and heritage package, included with your ticket. Now sit back, relax, and prepare to experience All the Time in the World!"

Winston made a grand show from the back of the boat, pretending to flick dials and spin the steering wheel, but the actual launch only took a single press of a round green button labeled Go. As his thumb depressed the plastic nub, the air around them sizzled hot and bright. Winston watched as electricity webbed across the sphere, turning its surface from translucent to milky white, and bam! His stomach dropped out of his body only to ricochet up through his skull and then settle back among his guts, all in the space of a second. A shriek came up from the middle of the boat, but it wasn't of panic this time—it was pure delight.

The *Niña* floated above an ocean, deep blue and rolling beneath a steely sky. Straight ahead, just beyond the mandatory hundred-meter minimum, two fleets of long wooden ships with billowing sails stretched to the horizon. Bodies writhed and roiled across the decks as arrows, stones, and fire crisscrossed the space between the vessels. Shouts and screams could barely be heard above the groans of wood, bending and flexing and snapping as boats crashed and charged with little concern for human life. It was carnage. It was destruction. It was, in the eyes of any twelve-year-old or ancient history major, absolutely awesome.

"The date is September 2. The year, 31 BCE," Winston said into the boat's microphone, a handheld device with a permanently tangled cord. "The forces of Rome and Egypt meet on the Ionian Sea, ready to battle for supremacy over the Mediterranean world. This encounter will be forever known as—"

"The Battle of Actium!"

Jayla had once again thrown herself to the railing, her raincoat flapping wide as the winds whipped her puff of dark hair back. She looked over her shoulder, her smile a brilliant shimmer of slightly crooked teeth and unfettered glee.

"Which are Antony's ships?" she called above the spray.

Winston pointed to the right, where red-and-gold strips of cloth hemmed a hundred sails. To their left, ships emblazoned with the eagle of Rome were bearing down.

"Antony? Like Mark Antony?" Harold asked.

"The singer?" Anne asked.

"So most of those," Jayla said, pointing at the red-and-gold ships, "must be Cleopatra's ships. And soon, she'll be calling—"

"An all-out retreat!" Winston finished. "The rest of Antony's ships will be pulverized, though Antony will make it back to Alexandria—"

"In time for their infamous joint suicide, ensuring the victory of Octavian and Rome!" Jayla beamed.

"Suicide?" Anne squeaked. "Jayla! What are you talking about?"

The girl gave the older woman a frank look.

"History," she said.

"Now, Mister Winston," Harold boomed, gesturing vaguely at the clashing ships. "They can't see us, right? We're not in any danger here?"

"Correct," Winston said. He walked out from behind the captain's station to stand beside the nervous couple. "The bubble around us masks us from sight, and the preprogram has carefully selected an area of ocean that is historically interference free. Nothing can get to us so long as the bubble is up."

"Thank heavens," Anne whimpered.

"Don't you need to drive?" Harold asked, cautiously looking back at the captain's chair.

"Everything's in the program," Winston reassured him. "We'll have a nice viewing of the battle for about fifteen minutes, then the engine will kick us back to present day, and you'll be back with plenty of time to catch your dinner reservations."

And for Winston to lock up at four, but he didn't say that aloud.

"Look!"

Like a rising flock of birds, a cloud of arrows rose from the Roman ships, peaking between the two fleets to arch down, fast and deadly, onto the Egyptians. Distant howls of pain carried to the *Niña*, and Egypt's boats launched their own volleys of rocks and projectiles.

"Marcus Agrippa is leading the Roman fleet, right?" Jayla asked, barely taking her eyes from the scene.

"Yes, and it will be one of his greatest achievements," Winston said. "I always thought it was a shame that the rest of his life was just politics and parties."

"But he is the reason we have Rome today," Jayla said, finally turning to face him. "He built baths and aqueducts and the first pantheon. And he was the right-hand man of Octavian. He did so much cool stuff!"

"Ahh, but when you consider his—"

"Uh, Mister Winston?"

Harold and Anne were nervously watching the captain's station, which was beeping loudly. Winston returned to his seat to see the screen blinking an orange warning. "Recommended return: click to confirm," flickered on and off, with seconds counting down below it.

"But time isn't up yet," Winston said to himself. He pushed the warning off the screen, only for another box to pop up, lined in red. "Security breach imminent. Temporal return: confirm?"

"Is there something wrong?" Anne asked.

"Everything's fine, the program is just—"

The screen went full crimson, practically screaming in black text "CONFIRM RETURN." His insides twisting, Winston reached out to press Go when a powerful gust of salt air roared by, and a dozen pointy shadows appeared overhead. He didn't have time to yell as arrows pelted the top of the sphere. The translucent film flickered opaque, then clear, then opaque again, and with a whine like gears wound too tight, the sphere shuddered and collapsed. Ancient arrows, their momentum slowed, clattered to the boat's benches and deck and, a moment later, the *Niña* dropped into the sea.

The issue with time-travel boats is that they are boats in name only. Sure, they float in their docking pools, but that's just to cushion their returns to the current era. They were not designed for waves, or salt spray, or even water deeper than a few inches. And they were certainly not made to be dropped into a violent ocean battle between two ancient superpowers.

Water surged up as the *Niña* landed, waves splashing over the low railing to soak socks and practical footwear. Both Harold and Anne fell sideways across their bench, shouting and clawing all the way. Jayla managed to remain upright, though she'd wrapped herself around the railing so tightly her toes barely skimmed the deck. Winston bounced in his captain's chair, which he quickly pushed himself from to begin banging on the console.

"Oh no, oh no, oh no," he said to himself, his voice pitching higher with each repetition. The screen had abandoned the previous warnings, and was now flickering "Failure" over and over. He jammed his palm into the green button, rewarded by a despondent whir that died a moment after it started.

"What's happening?" Anne cried, just as Harold yelled, "Did it break?" and Jayla shrieked from the bow, "Are we all going to die?"

"It's fine!" Winston said, waving his free hand as the other smacked the console. "It's fine. Fine. I just need to...to..."

"Can you reboot the program?" Harold asked, pushing himself to his feet before pulling up Anne.

"Yes! A reboot! I just need to reboot the program!"

Winston reached beneath the console and flicked a switch on its underside. There usually wasn't any need to restart the boats while on a tour, so all the top-facing console buttons were more for show. Buzzers, lights, an oversized volume control for the speaker system. The only practical items were the Go button on top, and the On/Off button below. The latter of which now caused the entire boat to shudder, sputter, and go still.

"Hey," Jayla said, only to yell, "Hey!" a second later. Winston looked up to follow the girl's desperate pointing. Across the waves, at the edge of the sea battle, fingers were being pointed in their direction. Fingers, and swords, and quite a few bows.

"Can they see us now?" Jayla asked.

"Y-yes," Winston said, his mouth suddenly gone terribly dry. "The security sphere is down. It's-it's somehow not working, so they can definitely see us."

"They're turning this way," Anne said.

And indeed, one of the ships was changing course toward them, a full-sailed Roman vessel bristling with soldiers. The crew had pulled out oars to assist their turn, dipping and rising in tandem as they pulled away from the battle's throng.

Winston pressed the On/Off switch again, and the console screen lit up, flashing the All the Time in the World Temporal Travel Company's logo, as well as a dancing, animated T. rex. It transitioned to a loading screen, and after a small eternity, flickered finally to a program directory.

"Mister Winston..." Harold said.

The ship was much closer. A row of archers lined the portside, arms and strings tensed as their bows bent toward the Niña, wave-tossed and soggy and barely able to compute.

"Get down! I mean, get back! I mean—" Winston gave up on

speech and threw himself at the Mackenzies, pulling Harold and Anne to the deck between the benches. Reaching out, he hooked the collar of Jayla's raincoat and jerked her backward, sliding her across the damp deck to land beneath the first row of seating. The back of Winston's neck tingled, and he didn't spare a look over his shoulder. He simply curled between the benches, trying to squeeze his most vital bits under the lip of the seating.

The arrows rained down. The last volley had been diminished by their mistaken trajectory and the security sphere, their momentum spent by the time the field collapsed and they could clatter, toothless, to the *Niña*'s deck. The second attack had no impediment. Iron tips clattered like hail, pings and plunks against the benches, the captain's station, the deck. Anne had begun an inconsolable wail, and Jayla was jabbering, panicked, about the arrows and the armies and if they were all about to die.

The onslaught quieted, and Winston forced himself to be the first to stand. The *Niña* was peppered with fletching and wooden shafts, many standing straight up, quivering, in the now dimpled metal of the benches and deck. Jayla and Harold popped out next, the former unbattered except for an arrow shaft tangled in her cloud of dark hair. Harold was less well off, bright blood splashed on his left sleeve.

"I'm fine, I'm fine," he said gruffly, waving Winston off. "Just a nick. Can you reload the program?"

Winston nodded, hurrying back to the captain's station. The approaching ship was so close now, he could catch snippets of Latin as the wind whipped around them. Jayla appeared at his elbow, and he didn't have the heart to send her away. At least with her nearby, he could tuck her safely behind the console at the next inevitable attack.

"What are you going to do?" Jayla asked as Winston clicked and scrolled through the programs and scenarios.

"Reboot back to our starting point and try again," Winston said, though as the words fell out of his mouth, he knew it wouldn't work. This program was flawed. The calculated safe spot didn't account for the wind and air-based projectiles. Jayla seemed to come to the same conclusion and pressed a little closer to the station's cool surface.

"Can we go to another point in time?" she asked. "That's what people do in old cartoons and stuff when they have time-travel machines."

"These boats are designed to go out and back. They can't hop destinations," Winston said. "They do their fifteen minutes in time, then jump home."

"But we can't wait for our fifteen minutes to be up," Jayla said. There was a pitch to her voice that made Winston want to tell her everything was going to be fine when it obviously was not. "The Romans are almost here!"

"I know," Winston said, one hand pressed to the side of his face as the other scrolled. "I know, I kn—"

He paused, scrolled back, blinked. They couldn't jump to a new destination, but maybe they could jump temporally while staying in the same location. Winston reopened the Battle of Actium program, and accessed its coordinates. He knew how the battle ended. He knew when Cleopatra's, and then Antony's, ships would turn. If he could calculate when the waters might be clear without jumping too far…

"When did the battle end?" Winston said, looking at Jayla.

"The date?" she asked. "The war—"

"No, the time. When did this battle stop?"

Jayla frowned, her brow scrunched as she considered. Then, like a storm dispersing before the sun, her face brightened, and she smiled.

"Antony was trying to defend the coast and his camp, so he was forced to attack first around noon to keep Octavian from spreading him too thin. They fought through the afternoon, at which point Cleopatra's ships retreated. Antony fought as long as he could, until about nightfall, then he burnt the ships he couldn't defend and retreated to Alexandria, leaving many men in Actium," Jayla said.

"Right, but what time?" Winston said. "If we wait until tomorrow, we risk Octavian's ships headed out to follow Antony. If we come back too early, the battle could still be going on."

"Eleven at night," Jayla said. "No, one! Just to be sure."

Winston nodded, selecting a new time within the program. Holding his breath, he clicked Launch and turned the ignition key. One second, two, three…and the *Niña* hummed to life once more.

Everyone jerked as the boat lifted from the rolling waves, a translucent sphere of light and electricity dancing up around it, flickering spottily in some areas. Through the shimmering security field, Winston could see how close the Roman ship was, see each dirty, bronzed face as they glared and howled and raged. The archers lifted their bows. Winston didn't waste another moment before slapping Go.

A flash of white light, a thrust down and up and center, and

Winston blinked at the sudden blindness that struck him. Slowly, his eyes adjusted, and by the light of distant fires and a starry sky, he could see the remains of the battle.

Of the burned Egyptian vessels, only three were still afloat, a slow smolder of wood and resin and cloth that rose and fell on the waves. Flotsam and debris crowded the waters, and Winston hoped none of the Mackenzies looked too closely at what might be floating near them. Far off on the horizon, new fires glowed like embers, as Octavian and his men collected the abandoned soldiers of Mark Antony and captured the last rebel ships.

"Oh my, what beautiful stars!"

Anne had finally emerged from beneath the benches, unmarred, though sodden. She had her head tipped to the sky, and the others followed suit. A blanket of silver and white shimmered above them, masked occasionally by a dark cloud of smoke from the fires.

"Haven't seen anything like that since I was a boy," Harold said. "You miss a lot in the cities."

Winston felt a poke in his side, and he looked down to see Jayla's upturned face, focusing on him instead of the stars.

"Did we do it?" she asked softly, cautiously.

Winston considered the waters around them, and whispered back, "I think we did."

"Can we go home now?"

Winston looked over at Harold and Anne, each with an arm wrapped around the other, both transfixed by the heavens.

"Let's let this program run its course. I think they both need a minute," Winston said.

Jayla paused for a moment, then nodded.

They all stood in the quiet of the Mediterranean while the program's timer counted down. After fifteen minutes, the console chirped a happy tune, and the *Niña* flashed them back to their own era.

The time at All the Time in the World Temporal Travel Company was 4:06. Surveying the wet, arrow-riddled *Niña*, Winston knew he wasn't going to be headed home early today. He might not even have a job after this. With a sigh, he unlatched the door on the boat and ushered the Mackenzies back to the front of the store.

"We didn't pay!" Anne said, clapping a hand to her mouth. "Oh goodness, we went through all that and we never actually bought the tickets. I'm so sorry. How much was it?"

The absurdity of the woman insisting on paying after nearly being killed was almost enough to make Winston laugh. Or cry. Probably a little of both.

"No, please," he said, throwing up his hands. "Between you and me, it's better if this one isn't on the books. But here..." He rooted around the front desk until he came up with a fistful of coupons, which he shoved into Anne's and Harold's hands. "I promise, not all our tours are like that. Actually, none of our tours are like that. A lot more sitting and looking, and fewer murderous soldiers."

"Well, thank you, Mister Winston," Harold beamed. "I think we will—"

"Harold, you're bleeding!"

"It's fine, dear. We can fix me up at home. Look, it already stopped."

Jayla walked over to Winston and solemnly extended a small hand. Winston shook it, feeling a little stupid somehow.

"Thanks for not taking us on a tour for babies," Jayla said.

"Thanks for helping me out," Winston said. "Really. We might have been—no. We *would* have been in a lot of trouble if not for you."

Jayla shrugged, making the arrow in her hair bob. Winston reached to pull it out, but thought better. He pointed at his head. Jayla tapped her own, grasped the arrow, and pulled nearly a foot of wood and beaten iron from her locks. Her eyes went wide as she surveyed the weapon, but she quickly extended it to Winston.

"Keep it," Winston said. "Just don't tell anyone where you got it. I'd get in a lot of trouble." *If I'm not already...*

"Thanks," Jayla beamed, and Winston smiled back.

The Mackenzies left All the Time in the World Temporal Travel Company with a promise they would surely come again. They pulled up their hoods, despite already being drenched in seawater, and filed out into the rain, the smallest among them clutching a two-thousand-year-old arrow to her chest as if it were a teddy bear. Winston watched them go until they disappeared into their car, then locked the door and let out a very long, exhausted sigh.

Maybe teaching wouldn't be so bad after all.

ABOUT ALYSSA ECKLES

Alyssa Eckles writes funny birthday cards for American Greetings, and speculative fiction in her spare time. Her work has appeared in DreamForge, Shoreline of Infinity, and several anthologies. When she's not writing, Alyssa likes running, grabbing a bowl of pho, or planning elaborate vacations she'll never take. She lives in Cleveland, Ohio with too many books and her cats, Libel and Poe.

Website: www.alyssaeckles.com
Twitter: @alyssaeckles
Email: Alyssa.eckles@gmail.com

16

DON'T WAKE THE DREAMER
BY KM DAILEY

HE WASN'T EVEN speaking real words.

It struck Monica far too late into the lecture. Her professor—why couldn't she remember his name?—wasn't speaking English.

It sounded like English. But it sounded the way English might sound to someone who didn't speak the language. Vowels and consonants in an American accent that simply didn't fit together into intelligible words. She squinted at the blackboard. It was covered with squiggles and markings that weren't words, weren't even letters.

She twisted in her seat, glancing around the dim sepia lecture hall. A girl with shadows under her eyes in the seat beside Monica scribbled frantic notes on a yellow pad; a frizzy-haired boy in the front row sat on the edge of his chair; a bulky boy across the room slumped with his arm across the folding desktop. All kept their eyes on the professor, taking in every nonword he spoke.

Monica squeezed her eyes shut and shook her head. She needed to cut back on the...she blinked. What had she been doing before she came to class? Or the night before? Or for the rest of her life?

Realization swept over her like a cold ocean wave. This was a dream. It had to be. She dug her fingernails hard into her wrist.

She bit her tongue to keep from crying aloud. It couldn't be a dream if she could feel pain, could it?

The door to the lecture hall slammed open, and a midheight boy with sandy tousled hair and intensity in his bright hazel eyes raced into the room, dropping a trail of notebooks and pencils behind him as he went. It wasn't until he looked down and froze in place that Monica realized he was wearing no pants, only purple-spotted boxers.

"How nice of you to join us, Quin." The professor nodded to the scarlet-faced boy.

The classroom erupted into laughter, but Monica couldn't even bring herself to smile as Quin passed by her row and took the seat behind her. Those were the professor's first real words today, and he had only spoken them when Quin had entered the room.

Quin ran late for a class that didn't seem to quite function until he arrived. Quin had forgotten his pants for no reason and had failed to notice until everyone else did. It was all too familiar. And then there was Monica, unable to remember anything, unsure whether she had even existed before this moment in time.

Her eyes slowly scanned the room one last time, a full 360 sweep. The farther she looked from Quin, the blurrier the room was. She looked down at herself, her gray shirt and blue jeans—out of focus like the rest of the room. Back at Quin—crystal clear.

She buried her head in her notebook, gripping her pencil until her knuckles were white. It made no sense, but still there was no mistaking it.

This was a dream, but Monica wasn't the dreamer.

The remainder of the lecture made much more sense than the first half, the professor droning on about international politics and exam dates, not that she was paying attention. Monica's brain was fully awake and alert, but it spun out of control.

She'd never met Quin before in real life, if she even had a real life. Maybe she was a copy of a classmate he had once seen in a lecture hall, or maybe she was a friend of his. Just as likely, she wasn't someone he knew, just a consequence of the neuronal firings of REM sleep.

But if that was all she was, how could she be aware, conscious? Or was this all an illusion? No—that didn't make sense. If she wasn't aware, she couldn't be experiencing the illusion.

A harsh ringing pierced the air. Monica jumped. The hall filled with the sounds of papers shuffling and zippers buzzing, and students filed toward the door of the classroom, their eyes at half-mast, some idly chattering among themselves. Monica couldn't prove she wasn't the only character in this dream who was alive, but it seemed hard to believe any of them were.

At the back of the clamor of students stood Quin. She was happy to see that the dream, in its mysterious ambivalence, had provided him with pants. Perhaps his nightmare was drawing to a close.

If she was in a dream that was not her own, and the dreamer woke up, what would happen to her?

She shot up out of her chair and raced toward the door, following Quin at a distance of a few feet.

Monica shifted her weight from one foot to the other as Quin turned the combination dial on his bike lock.

The blue of the sky was darkening rapidly, and the stars gave off too much light, twinkling and glowing, growing and shrinking, some round and as large as the moon, others flat and five-pointed. A little less than half of the glowing orb of the sun had disappeared behind the trees on the mountains in the distance. The surreal beauty snatched her breath away even as she shifted from one foot to the other, sneaking as many glances at Quin as she could without drawing suspicion.

What was he doing? He had turned that combination lock at least five times. It was as if he had forgotten his combination…

Oh, right. Dream.

He would notice, any minute now. He would notice the lock was acting strange, notice that the world was off, that the stars were too bright and the sky too dark for the time of day, that he was dreaming, and he would start to slip out of sleep as smoothly as he had slipped into it. The dream would end, and Monica…

She couldn't let it happen. Wincing, she took a step closer to him, then another. She cleared her throat. "Um, Quin?"

He jumped up, and Monica's heart skipped. *Note to self—don't startle the dreamer.*

"I, um, I was wondering if you needed help."

He blinked a couple of times and squinted at her. "Do I know you?"

She swallowed hard. "Ah, no, I—I'm Monica. I'm in your international studies class."

"Oh. Okay."

Her mind raced. "I was just, um, noticing you're having a hard time with the lock."

"Yeah." He stood up and rubbed the back of his neck, his gaze aimed down at the lock. "I'm not sure what's wrong with it. It's almost as if…" His eyes lifted to the skies, and he stared.

Monica grabbed his arm. "Hey, don't worry about it. Maybe I can help you."

She knelt down beside the bike rack, feeling his eyes on the back of her head, and picked up the cold metal lock. She pulled on both sides, and to her surprise, it split in half lengthwise in her hands, each half of the bolt sporting a little metal hook.

She stood up and held it out to him. "Well, I got it."

"What did you do to my lock?" He snatched half of the lock from her hands. "Get lost!" He swung his leg over his bike and rode away.

———

Monica stared for a long time at the broken lock in her hands. She didn't have the power to control the happenings of this world, not even close. But it seemed she had the ability to manipulate some things. She'd been able to keep Quin in the dream for this long.

She couldn't keep this up. He was bound to notice the strangeness of this world soon enough, bound to succumb to its unpredictable and impossible dangers sooner or later. But if her life depended on it, how could she do anything but try?

She had blown her chance, let him ride away. She tore her eyes away from the broken lock to look in the direction he had gone. He hadn't ridden far. His bike swerved and tilted, stopping abruptly every few seconds, hitting sidewalks and narrowly missing cars and other riders.

There was still time. She shoved the broken lock into her pocket and ran down the sidewalk, feet slapping against the concrete, arms and legs pumping, keeping pace behind Quin. It wasn't as difficult as it might have been, considering his lack of control over the bike. The cold air stung her lungs, and wind rushed past her ears.

Traffic was clearing, all of the other bikes and cars rushing by, many honking as they passed Quin. The road curved ahead. For a moment, Monica thought she had lost track of him. She stopped and stood on her tiptoes, biting her lip. At last she spotted him as he pulled himself up from the ground, and she sprinted to catch up to him.

His zigzagging path grew wilder as the road grew narrower. Monica's sprint slowed to a light jog, then a walk, until she finally came to a stop and watched Quin struggle. She dared to take her eyes off him for a moment, glancing around herself. The road had descended into a mountain path, the sidewalk making way for a dirt path. Beside her, a steep cliffside stretched down a hundred, two hundred feet, the ground below barely visible.

Ignoring the twinge in her stomach, she glanced back up at Quin, whose bike was now traveling in short spurts in random directions. At this rate, he was going to send himself flying off the edge of the mountain.

Falling from a high place. *Oh, no.*

So that was how it was going to be.

She raced to meet Quin just in time to watch his bike go over the edge.

"Quin!" She knelt down and leaned out over the cliffside. The bike fell, growing smaller and smaller until it was only a tiny dot in the distance.

"M—Monica? Is that you?" Quin clung to a tree root with both hands, his legs dangling over the ravine. "I can't—"

"Hang on!" Her arms and legs trembled as she lowered herself onto her stomach and slid up to the edge of the cliff, her arms reaching out toward Quin. She was still far from being able to reach him, but her muscles froze. She couldn't bring herself any closer. Couldn't risk her life to save someone she'd just met.

One of his hands slipped from the root.

Monica clenched her teeth and scooted closer, stretching her arms as far she could, most of her torso now hovering in the air. She wasn't risking anything, not really. If he died, she would as well.

He grimaced and swung his arm up toward her hand, just grasping on before his other hand slipped from the tree root.

She felt herself start to slip, and a scream escaped her lips.

"No, no!" Quin pushed her back up, and the slipping stopped. She dared to open one eye—he had managed to lift up a foot and drive it into the dirt above the tree branch, and he was now climbing his way back onto the ledge.

She scooted backward and used one hand to grip onto the ledge, the other to help Quin lift himself up, until they both lay on the dirt, side by side, panting. Tears stung her eyes, but she could feel something else rising from within her, a bubble of sweet warmth. It erupted into hearty laughter, which Quin joined.

"Wow," he said, pulling himself to a sitting position. "I don't know what happened there—"

Monica stared up at him, lying on her back, her stomach heaving with laughter. "What is up with your bike?"

"I don't *want* to know. Good riddance!" he called down the cliff. Dimples deepened in his cheeks, and he held out a hand, helping Monica to sit up and then to stand. "Monica, right?"

"Yeah," she said.

"How can I thank you?"

Her words tripped over themselves. It must have seemed strange to him, a stranger risking her life to save his. Not strange enough to alert him to the dream, but enough to make her uncomfortable. She settled for a shy smile.

"Hey, I know this doesn't come close to paying you back, you saved my life and everything, but…can I buy you a coffee?"

She couldn't remember any times she had specifically accepted or turned down coffee, but she could imagine the taste of a mocha, and it tasted right. "Yeah," she said. "Coffee sounds great."

The stars shone like sparkling spotlights over the little outdoor table beside the coffee shop. Monica sipped mocha from a paper cup as Quin set down his chai tea on the table.

"So what are you studying?" Quin asked.

"Psychology. I'm hoping to become an occupational therapist, eventually."

Quin blinked in surprise that mirrored Monica's. The words had slipped out before she could think about them, as if she had known it, even if she couldn't remember choosing that major. "Wow," Quin said.

"Yeah." Monica looked away and sipped her mocha.

"You're brave, and you're smart, and you care about other people. Is there anything you can't do?"

Exist. "Um, I have a hard time with math. But I don't really have to take much of it for what I want to do." Talking about her hopes for the future felt more than pointless. Her only hope of survival was keeping him in the dream, but even if she was successful in that, it wasn't as if she was going to be able to chase down a career at the same time. "How about you?"

"Mechanical engineering," he said. "I'm just taking that international studies class for GE."

She winced. "Sorry. You picked a pretty boring class."

He let out his breath. "*Thank* you! I didn't want to say anything, just in case—"

"No, you're not alone. I mean he just drones—"

"On and on and on—"

"In this monotone!"

"*Yes!*" Quin laughed full out, and Monica found herself joining in.

And so the evening went. It wasn't much more than small talk, but somehow the conversation just kept flowing until long after the coffee shop had closed down for the night, though no one asked them to leave the outdoor seating area.

When Monica finally glanced down at her watch, it was well past midnight. Her expression must have conveyed her surprise, because Quin stood. "Hey, I know it's late," he said. "Can I walk you home?"

Monica hesitated—where was home? It seemed her feet knew which way they should go, even if she could not remember where it was.

The walk back home was as blurry as the lecture had been, and she felt light-headed, but this time she didn't know whether it was because of the dream.

"Oh, you live here?" Quin said.

Her feet had come to a stop on their own. "Looks like it," Monica said.

"Weird, I don't know why I've never seen you before. I live just there." He pointed to the house next to hers.

If he was just next door, she could keep an eye on him, or at least peek out the window to make sure he didn't leave the house. She let her breath out. She wasn't sure how comfortable she would have been with trying to convince a boy she'd just met to stay the night.

He turned to face her as they stood on her doorstep. "Well, we should do this again."

She smiled. "Absolutely."

He took her hand and kissed it lightly, then, face red, he turned and hurried away.

She stared at him long after he went, and it wasn't just to make sure he didn't wake up.

The inside of her house turned out to be a cloudy, white space. Walls, floors, and surfaces were white, invisible against a backdrop of white, but they were always exactly where she guessed them to be. When she took off her jacket and dropped it where she expected a couch might be, the jacket hung in the air as if suspended by the armrest of a chair, and when she threw herself backward into where she thought her bed might be, she was slowed to a soft stop as if by a fluffy mattress.

Settling into her bed, Monica took a deep breath. The world could cease to exist at any moment, but for now, she was alive.

She had no right to be. She kept telling herself she had saved Quin's life, that he should somehow be grateful to her, as he believed he should. The truth remained, she had only prevented his waking up, trapping him in this dream—no, this nightmare—to continue sustaining the world that gave her life. Life, and for some probably accidental reason, consciousness.

Yes, she was keeping Quin from his "real" life, but she wasn't hurting him. If anything, he seemed to be enjoying this dream. She certainly was.

If this was what she was—a dream character, only to appear and disappear at the random whims of the dreams of others—then she had died the day before and been born today.

She hadn't built many memories yet. Death would be the loss of them—everything she was, everything she knew, would be lost. It wasn't the loss of much. She wasn't much. But still, she felt she had the right to defend herself, to fight for her life, to fear death. Didn't everyone?

Quin met Monica after class the next day, and the next, and the next. Days of the week had no meaning in this world, if they existed at all, but Quin didn't seem to notice. He took her on long walks through the campus and the surrounding mountain trails, though Monica pretended to be afraid to venture anywhere too steep, just in case.

A couple of times, he took her out to a nice candlelit dinner. It never seemed to occur to him that as a college student, he shouldn't be able to afford it. Then again, he didn't speak much about his family or circumstances. Their conversations focused on the present and the future, with only vague clues about his past. He talked about his classes, his professors, his classmates. She always managed to find just enough to say in response, though she didn't have to. She could have listened to him for hours.

Most days, he was late for class. And whenever he was late, he had wild stories about why—being unable to walk, time passing at unpredictable rates, his homework disappearing, the street turning inside out and backward so that he was hopelessly lost. The professor would roll his eyes or scold Quin for making excuses, but Monica believed every word.

Those few times when he wasn't around, Monica spent most of her time in her whitespace home, worrying about what would happen to her if he woke up. Something in the back of her mind nagged her that it couldn't be healthy to have no social life outside of Quin. The conscious, reasoning part of her mind retorted that she had no physical life outside of him, so what difference did it make?

A more pressing concern was the fact that Quin *wasn't* waking up from his dream, and she didn't intend to let him. She soon lost track of how long it had been since that first lecture. Maybe two weeks, maybe three. Clearly this was no ordinary dream, and time passed differently in dreams than in real life, but she still couldn't imagine that having a several-week dream was good for him.

With each day, he was growing more attached to her. The sweet smiles he gave when he saw her, the gentleness with which he held her hand, the laughter at her worst jokes—he left no room for doubt. When he finally did wake up, he would either miss her terribly or forget she had existed at all. She didn't know which would be worse.

One day, after what must have been at least two or three months, the unthinkable happened. Monica sat through the entire international studies lecture, and at no point did the professor's language switch from gibberish to English. Quin never arrived.

Her first thought was that he might have woken up. But could the dream have gone on without him? If that were possible, then she would have been worrying about nothing all this time. And if it were true, and she was still alive, then she had nothing to worry about now.

Well…not nothing. Slave to the dream or not, Monica couldn't imagine life without Quin.

As soon as the bell rang, she jumped up out of her seat and shoved her way through the mindless cattle. The evening light that had once struck her as so beautiful only seemed sinister tonight as she raced aimlessly, scanning the crowds for Quin's face—he would probably be panicking, after having missed the entire lecture.

The area cleared quickly as the other dream folk rode away in cars and on bikes. Still there was no sign of Quin. Monica wove her fingers into her hair, breathing hard and pacing. He would have told her if he knew he was going to be out.

An earth-shaking thump sounded. Monica's knees buckled, and she only just kept herself from falling. She had barely regained her balance when there was another, then another, then another, each seeming to come closer: Thump. Thump. Thump.

The back of her neck prickling, Monica slowly turned to face the sound. She gasped. An enormous creature stood, twice the size of the lecture building, most of its body shrouded in black fog, though the claws on its front feet peeked through the haze. Its sword-sharp teeth glinted as it snarled, and its sunken eyes glowed bright yellow. They locked onto Monica's as she met its gaze, and its slimy gray scales bristled.

Monica's heart pounded. She didn't know whether she could die before Quin's dream ended, but she knew she could feel pain.

"Hey, come get me!"

The creature looked past Monica. Monica whirled around. Quin was waving his arms, facing the creature and stepping backward away from it. It took a resounding step toward him with legs she couldn't see through the fog, and its slitted nostrils breathed smoke.

Quin grimaced, turned, and ran.

Monica caught up and ran alongside him. "Where have you been all day?"

"Running and hiding. From that thing."

"Where did it come from?"

He panted. "Don't know. Hoped you might have an idea."

"How would I know—"

The creature's wide jaws snapped just behind them, and they diverged into separate directions.

Monica's lungs burned. Her legs ached, but she kept them pumping.

"Monica!" Quin's voice was hoarse, as if he couldn't quite pull in the air to scream. She dared to look over her shoulder. His legs moved in slow motion, each frantic step propelling him forward only inches. "I-I can't—"

If Monica ran back for him, she would almost certainly be caught. If she didn't run back for him, he would be. His death meant hers, but her capture meant pain.

It didn't matter. She couldn't leave Quin.

She doubled back, taking a twisted route around lampposts in the hopes of confusing the creature, and grabbed Quin's hand. Together they sprinted away, this time toward the mountain path where she had first saved his life.

Monica dared to glance back every few seconds. The creature kept on their heels. As the path narrowed, the cloud of fog that enveloped its body lengthened, snakelike, allowing it to follow. Its jaws snapped behind them twice more. The second time, it missed by inches. They wouldn't make it. It was catching up.

They had one chance. One common dream left unexplored.

"Quin, have you ever dreamed you could fly?"

"What?"

"Have you—"

"Yeah, but what does that—"

"Do you trust me?" Monica said.

Quin panted. "I—of course—"

Gripping his hand harder, she turned him toward the side of the path, and they ran off the edge of the cliff.

Quin yelled, Monica screamed, the monster roared. The ground flew toward them, faster, *faster*…then slower. There they hovered, still gliding forward but not downward.

Quin's eyes met Monica's. Beads of sweat dripped down his temples, and he breathed hard, but traces of a smile were visible on his lips.

"We're alive," Monica whispered.

The creature roared after them once again. Monica's heart skipped a beat, and they sped away faster.

———

They came to rest sitting on the high branches of a redwood tree. The ground seemed miles away, but she had no reason to worry about him falling now.

"Monica," he said. Her name sounded safe in his voice, but there was such deep concern in his tone that it cut her to the core. "Do you ever think...something strange might be happening?"

Monica swallowed hard. "What do you mean?"

He looked away, shaking his head. "I don't know. Maybe I'm imagining things, maybe I'm going crazy, but I just..." He bit his lip, looking down, then went on. "I can't remember how I learned to fly. That thing that chased us, I didn't even know creatures like that existed. I keep losing track of things, forgetting things, I can't seem to get to class on time, I'm always misdialing phone numbers and locker combos. To tell you the truth, I don't even know—" His eyes widened.

Monica lifted a hand to his chin, turning his face back to hers. "Don't know what?"

"I don't know what I was doing this morning. I can't remember waking up, or getting dressed, or-or—"

Monica's mind raced. She was losing him. Finally, after all this time, he was slipping out of the dream. She was going to die.

She did the only thing she could think of to bring him back.

"Quin," she said softly. She forced herself to smile, leaned forward, and gently kissed his lips.

Time stood still—for them, but for the universe it went on. Their surroundings swirled, hot and cold wind mixed, bright lights and stars and planets shone and orbited and collided and died all around them.

When she finally pulled her face away from his, they were back in the treetop. Monica didn't know whether they had ever left or it was only part of the dream. For once, she didn't care.

Quin's eyes remained closed for a long, long time, but his lips finally pulled into a wide smile, showing his perfect teeth. She squeezed his hand, and they turned their gazes to the view.

"You inspire me, Monica," he said.

"Me?"

"Yes, you! I mean, you saved my life twice, but it's not that. You believe me when no one else does. You believe *in* me. My parents—well, let's say they were glad to be rid of me when I went off for college."

"Really?"

"Yeah." He laughed without smiling. "My older sister was a hard act to follow, and I know my little brother's under a lot of pressure now, but I want to be a good role model for him. Man, I miss him so much."

A long pause. Monica held her breath.

"My parents give him a rough time. Before I left for college, I was sick a lot, in and out of hospitals."

She squeezed his hand. "I had no idea."

He nodded. "I had a lot of seizures. I went into a coma once, for almost three weeks. My parents were struggling, but my brother—he was distraught. The look he gave me on the day I moved out—" His voice broke.

Monica's limbs were numb.

Quin sighed. "This semester feels like it's going on forever. Does it feel like that to you? I can't wait to graduate. I just—" He pressed his lips together.

Monica glanced over at him. His eyes sparkled in the moonlight, and he blinked a couple of times.

A heavy weight settled on her chest. "Yeah," she said softly. "I know what you mean."

Monica spent the whole night lying on her bed, staring at a fuzzy, translucent wall in her whitespace home. Tears came and went, but sleep never did, and the restlessness remained.

She couldn't remember whether coma patients could dream.

If they could, was this what a coma was? An ordinary sleep, an ordinary dream become extraordinary by the whims of a character created within that dream? She had thought only about her own survival.

Looking back, it seemed impossible, deplorable, that she could have been so selfish, so thoughtless. She should have known. She couldn't keep Quin entrapped, enslaved to the world of sleep, no matter what that meant for her.

At some point over the past few weeks—or maybe it had been gradual?—the world had lost its blurriness and become clear. She squeezed her arms around herself, feeling her fingers press into her back, the warmth of her own hands. She ran her fingers through her hair, and felt its softness; touched her face, and felt its smoothness and imperfection. She pinched her forearm hard and held it there for a long time, and the pain was real.

But when all was said and done, she herself wasn't real. She was only a whim, an unusual combination of the neural firings of another. She had no memories, no family, no past or future, only a present, which she had stretched out long enough at the cost of another.

She had no idea what to say, but that didn't excuse her from telling him. Maybe he would be angry with her for keeping it from him for so long. Maybe the shock alone would wake him up. Or maybe he wouldn't believe her—but she couldn't see that happening, not with everything he had experienced over the past few weeks. Most likely, he would believe her without a problem, but that would leave the question of what to do, where to go.

It didn't matter. She had to tell him. She had to do more than just tell him.

Monica pulled her knees into her chest. God willing, she would have the strength to do what she needed to.

The next day, Monica waited outside the lecture hall before class started. She couldn't bring herself to go inside and listen to the professor's gibberish again. Her knees trembled as she watched the glazed expressions of the students headed into the building, and she waited for Quin.

For the first time, he wasn't late for class. "Hey," he said as his eyes met Monica's. His smile was like the sun, though she couldn't bring herself to return it.

"We need to talk," she said.

His brow furrowed. "Okay, but can it wait until after the lecture? I'm on time for once."

She pressed her lips together, and her eyes stung.

He shrugged. "Okay. Whatever you need."

She took his warm, solid hand in hers and led him down the sidewalk, away from the campus, onto the mountain road where she had first saved him.

"Oh, hey, let's be careful around here." He peered nervously at the sheer drop beside them. "I've been trying all morning, and I don't seem to be able to fly anymore."

"That's part of what I want to talk about."

He let his breath out. "You scared me. I thought this was about the kiss."

She sat down on a flat rock near the edge of the road, and gestured for him to sit beside her.

"So what's up?"

"Quin—" Her voice broke, and she hadn't even started. She took a deep breath and focused her gaze on the view around them rather than on his face. "You were starting to notice yesterday, and I stopped you. I'm sorry."

"Notice what?"

"That everything is weird. The whole world...like you said, the fact that you're always late, always misdialing combinations. That creature that attacked us, the flying—"

He lifted a finger to her lips. For a moment he just smiled at her, but it was a sad smile. "It's okay," he said softly. "I didn't want to face it, but I think some part of me has known for a long time."

"Known what?"

"That you were too good to be true."

"Quin, you know you're dreaming."

He cupped her face in his hands. "And you're the girl of my dreams."

Her eyes stung, and his face swam. "I'm so sorry, Quin. I've been keeping you here. I had almost convinced myself I was saving your life, but I've kept you trapped here in a dream world."

He shook his head. "You let me experience this world. You taught me to fly. You had every right to want this dream to go on." He smiled and took her hand in his once again. "And that's what I want too."

Her voice caught in her throat, and a new wave of tears streamed down her cheeks. "Quin, you have seizures! I think you're in a coma. Your parents, your little brother—"

"They're *fine*. I left for college, and my brother was fine."

"But you said—"

"I know what I said. I pretend he needs me to feel good about myself. To be honest, I just miss him. But who knows? Maybe he's here in this world too."

Monica gripped his shoulder. "You can't stay, Quin. If you don't go back, they'll never see you again. They'll miss you."

"And if I do go back, you'll die."

Her eyes fell closed, the cold reality closing in on her. "I'm not real, Quin. *I'm not real.*"

He took her hand and stood, helping her to stand as well, though her legs shook almost as violently as her sobs.

"You're beautiful, Monica," he said, and she looked down and saw that it was true. Through the impossible lens of the dream, her skin was perfect, her hair falling soft and wavy around her cheeks, and her light blue sundress embracing her flawless body.

He ran his fingers through her hair and kissed her gently, then, holding her at arm's length with one hand, he reached into his pocket and pulled out his half of the lock she'd broken when they first met. He pressed the lock into her hand and closed her fingers around it, then wrapped his arms around her and kissed her.

"This is my choice," he whispered into her ear. "And for as long as I can, I choose you."

Every word pierced her heart like a dagger, and her veins spiked with adrenaline. At last, she had the strength to do what she needed to do, what she should have done long ago.

"I'm sorry, Quin," she whispered. She took a step back and swung the lock in a wide arc, slamming it into his temple.

ABOUT KM DAILEY

KM Dailey has been writing novels, short stories, and poetry since her preteen years. Her work has been published in Daily Science Fiction magazine as well as on Reedsy Blog, and she vlogs on YouTube as the SnarkyPhysicist. You can find updates on her writing and other adventures at kmdailey.com.

Website: kmdailey.com
Facebook: kayla.turney.50
Twitter: @km_dailey
Email: snarkyphysicist@gmail.com

DEEP MAGIC: VOLUME 1

Want more?

Check out The Best of Deep Magic Volume I now!